/00

Peter Matthiessen

Naturalist, explorer and writer, was born in New York City in 1927. By the time he had graduated from Yale in 1950 he had already begun his writing career and the following year he co-founded the *Paris Review*. He is the author of five novels including *At Play in the Fields of the Lord* (recently made into a film directed by Hector Babenco and starring Kathy Bates, Tom Berenger, Daryl Hannah, John Lithgow, Aidan Quinn and Tom Waits) and of the story collection *On the River Styx*. Among his many celebrated non-fiction books are *The Snow Leopard* and its sequel *Nine-Headed Dragon River*, *The Tree where Man Was Born* (with Eliot Porter's photographs), *The Cloud Forest*, *Under the Mountain Wall*, *Indian Country* and *Men's Lives*. His latest book is *African Silences*, an account of a series of journeys made in search of endangered African species – including the mountain gorilla, the jungle peacock and the forest elephant.

From the reviews of *Killing Mister Watson:*

"Sometimes good writers find the one subject for which it seems their whole life has been a preparation. Matthiessen, ecologist, celebrator of common lives, angry patriot, has found in the legend of E. J. Watson the story he was born to tell"

FREDERICK LINDSAY, Scotsman

Further reviews overleaf

"Matthiessen superbly portrays the precariousness of the pioneers' existence and the strange fascination of their environment . . . One has a real sense, if not of tragic inevitability, then certainly of destiny which is rare now that there are so few frontiers left"
WILLIAM HOBSON, *Sunday Herald* (Melbourne)

"Peter Matthiessen, the master writer, has, in *Killing Mister Watson*, created a masterwork"
PETER I. ROSE, *Newsday*

"Matthiessen richly brings to life a legendary killer and the ragged clans who pioneered one of America's last true frontiers"
CARL HISASEN, *Chicago Tribune*

"A compelling visionary metaphor"
CARL MacDOUGALL, *Glasgow Herald*

"No one who reads Mr Matthiessen's book will ever be able to see the Florida Everglades again plain. His imagination has fixed another place in time for ever"
HERBERT MITGANG, *New York Times*

"A magnificent yarn"   MALCOLM JONES JNR, *Newsweek*

"In time, every killing on the islands is sheeted home to him, whether he could have done it or not. His legend builds like a sulphurous cloud. So too does the fear he generates. He seems more and more like a man superhuman in his force and dark power"
BILL WARNOCK, *The West Australian*

"A tour de force: a big book of complex characterizations, beautifully rendered regional voices, and . . . the lush background of the Everglades"
New York Times Magazine

"Aggressive and gregarious, without ethic or introspection, both hugely talented and dangerously addicted to untamed power, Edgar Watson finally seems to represent great potential gone awry, or America at its worst. Exploratory and exciting, handsomely researched and written, attuned to the necessary preservation of the heart and soul of the world, *Killing Mister Watson* represents Peter Matthiessen at his best"

RON HANSEN, *New York Times Book Review*

PETER MATTHIESSEN

Killing Mister Watson

Flamingo
An Imprint of HarperCollins*Publishers*

First published in Great Britain 1990
by Harvill
an imprint of HarperCollins Publishers

Special overseas edition 1991

This paperback edition first published in Great Britain 1991
by Flamingo
an imprint of HarperCollins Publishers
77–85 Fulham Palace Road
Hammersmith, London W6 8JP

9 8 7 6 5 4 3 2

BRITISH LIBRARY CATALOGUING IN PUBLICATION DATA

Matthiessen, Peter, *1927*–
Killing mister watson.
I. Title
813.54 [F]

ISBN 0–00–654455–X

Printed and bound in Great Britain by
HarperCollins Book Manufacturing, Glasgow

To The Pioneer Families of
Southwest Florida

In a six-year search, I have had great help from at least one member of almost every family mentioned, and am grateful to dozens of native Floridians for their time and courtesy and help, including a few who have not survived to see the finished book – the late Ruth Ellen* Watson, Rob Storter, Robert Smallwood, Sammie Hamilton, and Beatrice Bronson, three of whom offered childhood memories of Mister Watson.

Special gratitude is due to Larry (Watson) Owen, who made a great variety of contributions; also to Mary Ruth Hamilton Clark and Ernie House. My sincere thanks to Frank and Gladys (Wiggins) Daniels, Marguerite (Smallwood) and Fred Williams, Nancy (Smallwood) and A. C. (Boggess) Hancock, Bert (McKinney) and Julia (Thompson) Brown, Loren "Totch" Brown, Bill and Rosa (Thompson) Brown, Louise Bass, Paul Duke, Doris Gandees, Preston Sawyer, Buddy Roberts, Edith (Noble) Hamilton.

I am also indebted to the researches, writings, and good counsel of the historian Dr Charlton W. Tebeau, author of *Man in the Everglades; Collier County: Florida's Last Frontier; The Story of the Chokoloskee Bay Country;* and other excellent works on pioneer Florida.

None of these friends and informants are responsible for my interpretations of their accounts of the life and times of their own families and others, for all which I accept full responsibility.

* Not her real name.

AUTHOR'S NOTE

A man still known in his community as E. J. Watson has been reimagined from the few hard "facts" – census and marriage records, dates on gravestones, and the like. All the rest of the popular record is a mix of rumor, gossip, tale, and legend that has evolved over eight decades into myth.

This books reflects my own instincts and intuitions about Mister Watson. It is fiction, and the great majority of the episodes and accounts are my own creation. The book is in no way "historical", since almost nothing here is history. On the other hand, there is nothing that could *not* have happened – nothing inconsistent, that is, with the very little that is actually on record. It is my hope and strong belief that this reimagined life contains much more of the *truth* of Mister Watson than the lurid and popularly accepted "*facts*" of the Watson legend.

Marco

To Fort Myers

LEE COUNTY

Caxambas

FAKAHATCHEE KEY

Everglade

CAPE ROMANO

PANTHER KEY

Chokoloskee Bay

Chokoloskee

©A·Karl/J·Kemp,1990

TEN THOUSAND ISLANDS

Chokoloskee Pass

Rabbit Key Pass

RABBIT KEY

PAVILION KEY

Arcadia

Lake Okeechobee

Calusa Hatchee

Fort Myers

Immokalee

Punta Rasa

Survey (Bonito Springs)

BIG CYPRESS

Gulf

of

Mexico

Everglade

Lemon City

EVERGLADES

Area of Map

CAPE SABLE

Flamingo

Key West

Kms.
0   6

0   6

Miles

Kms.
0   40

0   40

Miles

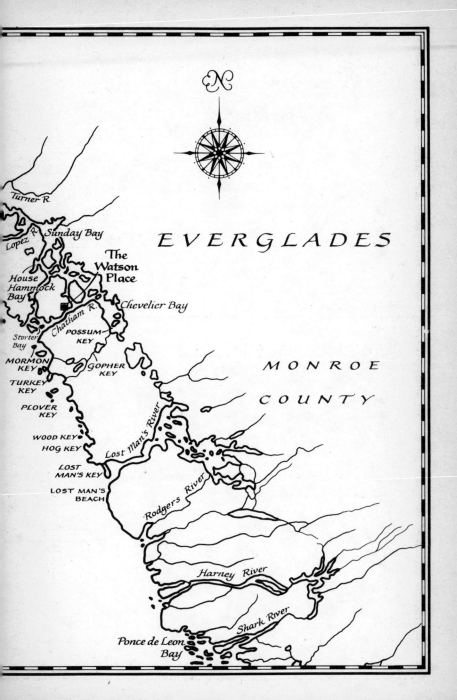

OCTOBER 24, 1910

Sea birds are aloft again, a tattered few. The white terns look dirtied in the somber light and they fly stiffly, feeling out an element they no longer trust. Unable to locate the storm-lost minnows, they wander the thick waters with sad muted cries, hunting signs and seamarks that might return them to the order of the world.

In the hurricane's wake, the labyrinthine coast where the Everglades deltas meet the Gulf of Mexico lies broken, stunned, flattened to mud by the wild tread of God. Day after day, a gray and brooding wind nags at the mangroves, hurrying the unruly tides that hunt through the broken islands and twist far back into the creeks, leaving behind brown spume and matted salt grass, driftwood. On the bay shores and down the coastal rivers, a far gray sun picks up dead glints from windrows of rotted mullet, heaped a foot high.

From the island settlement on the old Indian mound called Chokoloskee, a baleful and uneasy sky out toward the Gulf looks ragged as a ghost, unsettled, wandering. The sky is low, withholding rain, and vultures on black-fingered wings tilt back and forth over the broken trees. At the channel edge, where docks and pilings, stove-in boats, uprooted shacks litter the shore, odd pieces torn away from their old places have been strained from the flood by the limbs over the water. A clothesline flutters in the trees; thatched roofs are spun onto their poles like old straw brooms; frame buildings sag. In the dank air a sharp fish stink is infused with corruption of dead animals and black-ened vegetables, of excrement in overflowing pits from

1

which shack privies have been washed away. Pots, kettles, crockery, a butter churn, tin tubs, buckets, salt-slimed boots, soaked horsehair mattresses, and ravished dolls are strewn across the pale killed ground.

A lone gull picks disconsolate at the softening mullet along shore, a dog barks without heart at so much silence.

A figure in mud-fringed calico, calling a child, stoops to retrieve a Bible, then wipes wet grime from the Good Book with pale dulled fingers. She straightens, turning slowly, staring toward the south. From the wall of mangroves far off down the bay, the drum of the boat engine comes and goes, then comes again, a little louder.

"Oh, Lord," she whispers, half-aloud. "Oh no, please no, sweet Jesus."

Along toward low gray-yellow twilight, Postmaster Small-wood, on his knees beneath his store, is raking out the last of his drowned chickens. What the hurricane has left of Smallwood's dock – a few poor pilings – sticks out at angles off the end of the spoil bank where he'd dug his canal for Indian canoes. From there the pewter water spreads away to the black walls of mangrove on all sides.

He crouches in the putrid heat. Voices are whispering, as at a funeral. One pair of bare feet, then another, pass in silence on the way down to the landing. He knows his neighbors by their gait and britches. Over the whispering, over short breaths, comes the drumming of the motor, softened by distance, east through Rabbit Key Pass from the Gulf of Mexico. In a shift of wind, the *pot-pot-pot* comes hard as a pulse, as if he heard his heart for the first time.

Three days before, when that boat had headed south, all ten families on the island watched it go. Smallwood was the only man to wave, but he, too, prayed that this would be the end of it, that the broad figure at the helm, sinking into darkness at the far low line of trees, would disappear forever from their lives.

Said Old Man D. D. House, "He will be back."

The House clan lives one hundred yards away, east of the store. Ted Smallwood sees his father-in-law's black Sunday boots descend the Indian mound, with Bill House and Young Dan and Lloyd barefoot behind. Calling his sister, Bill climbs the porch and enters the store and post office, which has the Smallwood family rooms upstairs. Feet creak on the pine floor overhead.

In the steaming heat, in the onset of malaria, Smallwood feels so sickly weak that when his rump emerges and he tries to stand, blood thumps his temples and the trees go black. He is a big man and bangs heavily against the wall of his frame house, causing his wife, somewhere inside, to cry out in alarm. Slowly he straightens, arches his stiff back. He takes a deep and dreadful breath, gags, coughs, and shudders. He hawks the sweet taste of chicken rot from his mouth and nostrils.

"Look what come crawling out! Ain't that the post-master?"

The postmaster's spade, jammed at the black earth by way of answer, grates on old white oyster shells of the huge midden. Again he jams it, and it glances off a root. The House boys laugh.

"Keep that spade handy, boy. Might gone to need it."

Ted Smallwood says, "Got four rifles there, I see. Think that's enough?"

The old man stops to contemplate his son-in-law. Daniel David House has silver in his brows and his mustache juts into axhead sideburns. Though he wears no collar underneath his beard, he is dressed as if for Sunday, in white shirt, shiny black frock coat, wiped boots, and stiff black pants hauled high by galluses. He stands apart from the sandy, slow-eyed boys delivered him by the former Ida Borders.

"Where's his missus, then?" the old man says.

"She's right inside here with her young 'uns. With your daughter and granddaughters, Mr House." When the old

3

man grunts and turns away, Ted's voice goes higher. "Them women and children gone to have 'em a good view!"

Henry Short, expressionless, moves past, holding his rifle down along his leg.

"You, too?"

"Leave Henry be," says Bill House, coming out. Bill House is thirty, a strong florid man creased hard by sun.

Mamie Smallwood has followed Bill outside. When her brother turns to calm her, the plump young woman cries, "Let me alone!" She weeps. "Where is her little boy? He's only *three!*"

Old Man Dan shakes his big head and keeps on going, refusing to listen anymore. Young Dan and Lloyd follow him close, down toward the shore.

A young woman comes around the house. "Mr Smallwood? Please? Tell me what's happening?" When the postmaster stands mute, she cries, "Oh Lord!" and hurries off again. She is still calling her boy.

The island men are gathering, twenty or more. All have shotguns or rifles.

Charlie T. Boggess, who twisted his ankle in the hurricane, is limping. "All right, woman, all *right!*" he shouts, to his wife's calling. To the postmaster he says, "Why couldn't he keep right on going? To Key West!"

Ted says, "Don't hear Ethel hollering? You best hobble home, take care that ankle."

Isaac Yeomans, coming by, says, "Key West? Nosir! That feller ain't the kind likes to back up." Isaac is fiery with drink; he looks almost cheered up by what the others dread. "You recall Sam Lewis, Ted? At Lemon City?"

Smallwood nods. "They lynched Sam Lewis, too."

Bill House stops on the steps. "This ain't no mob!"

"Don't think so?" The postmaster pitches his voice toward Bill's father. "What if he's just coming back here to pick up his family and keep right on going?"

4

Bill House says, "Keep right on going, Ted, just like you say, and do the same thing somewheres else."

"Mr Smallwood? Have you seen little Addison?"

The men turn their backs to the young woman and stare away toward the south. The oncoming boat is a small dark burr in the pewter light of Chokoloskee Bay.

Henry Short leans his 30.30 Winchester into a fork of the big fish-fuddle that the hurricane has felled across the clearing. The gun is hidden when he leans against the tree, and his arms are folded as if in sign that none of this is any of his business.

Twilight gathers behind the coming boat. The armed men stand half-hidden in the undergrowth, too tense to slap at the mosquitoes. In the dusk of a dark day, in the tree shadow, the postmaster can no longer make out faces beneath the old and broken hats. His neighbors seem anonymous as outlaws.

Not slowing, the boat winds in among the oyster bars. The helmsman stands in silhouette, his broad hat forward on his head.

Isaac Yeomans breaks his shotgun and sights down the barrels, pops two shells in, sets his felt hat. "Seems like you ought to throw in with us, Ted." Isaac is gazing out over the water. "We're in friendship with him too. We don't care for this no more'n you do."

"He pays his bills, plays fair with me. I ain't got a single thing agin him." Smallwood speaks urgently to Yeomans and to Boggess, who have been his friends for fifteen years. "You boys never had no trouble with him, and you can't hit nothing anyway. Put them damn guns down."

Others hesitate beside the store, as if loath to go down to the landing. They have worn the same shirts for a week, they are scared and cranky, they are anxious to involve Ted Smallwood. At the very least, the postmaster's participation might make what must happen more respectable. If no one is innocent, who can be guilty?

5

Storm refugees from Lost Man's River stand back by the store porch, a hundred yards from the boat landing.

One calls, "Looks like y'all are fixing to gun him down." Henry Thompson is a tall and sunworn man, lank as a dog.

Another man nods urgently, clearing his throat. "Thought you fellers was aiming to get deputized! Thought you was aiming to *arrest* him!"

"Won't *let* hisself get arrested," Bill House says. "Men here found that out the other day."

"Best if nobody hangs back!" calls Old Dan House.

One man says, "I believe Ted knows what must be done as good as we do. He just don't want no part of it." Another cackles, "Why, hell, Ted, bushwhacking ain't nothing to be scared of! Not with his one against two dozen!"

"Maybe I ain't scared the way you think. Maybe *I'm* scared of killing in cold blood."

"*He* ain't scared of cold blood, Ted. Colder the better."

"Ain't nobody proved that in a court of law!"

"Ain't no law down here to prove it by."

Behind the men skulk ragged boys with slingshots and singleshot .22s. Shouted at, they slink into the trees and circle back, bright-eyed as coons.

In his old leaf-colored clothes, in the brown shadows at the wood edge, Henry Short has sifted in against the tree bark like a chuck-will's-widow shuffling soft wings. He seems intent on the white bow wave where the dark boat parts the gray chop of the channel, and the rifle-fire *pot-pot-pot*, loud and louder. The silhouette of the lone boatman rises slowly on the evening sky.

The women are calling from the wood. Old Man Dan shouts to his son-in-law, "If you're his friend, go find his little feller!"

He circles through the wind-stripped trees. The wood is hushed, the last birds mute, the dogs gone still. Only mosquitoes are abroad, keening in the twisted gumbo-limbos.

He calls and calls.

A razorback hog grunts abruptly, once, in the startled silence.

The young mother follows him back to the house and goes inside. In white aprons, behind the salt-dark screen, the women loom like ghosts. Neither weeps. Their little daughters tug softly at their skirts. The children's eyes stare toward the boat over sucked thumbs.

Smallwood pushes past, indoors, not sure where he is headed. His wife is gripping the hand of the boy's mother. "Ought to kept him home," he says. When he bangs his lantern, Mamie raises a finger to her lips, as if the man out in the boat might hear.

"Daddy's the one behind this, ain't he?" she whispers. "Bill and Dan, too!"

Smallwood slaps a mosquito, lifts his fingers, investigates the blood. "Light that smudge," he says. Little Thelma runs to the crumpled bucket of black mangrove charcoal damped with earth.

He gazes at his Mamie Ulala, ignoring the young woman, who appears entranced. He says, "They're all behind it. All but the men from Lost Man's."

This dark day has been coming down forever. Even the young woman, in her pale foreboding, seems to know this. The day is late, and a life runs swiftly to its end.

"They want an end to it," he mutters.

Little Thelma and her friend Ruth Ellen stand in the corner, guarding the toddlers from something scary. Ruth Ellen's mother clutches Baby Amy, born five months before down at Key West. "Ad," she whispers to the missing boy. "Oh, please."

The motor dies, in a long wash of silence. "Daddy," Thelma says, starting to whimper. When the postmaster takes her up into his arms, she sucks her thumb. Beside himself, he thrusts her at her mother and follows the young woman back outside. He cannot stop yawning.

Seen through the broken branches, in the onshore wind, the launch coasts down on Smallwood's landing, just west

7

of where the dock had been before the storm. Ted's heart pounds so that the boatman must surely feel it and take warning, must sense the islanders in the dark trees.

In the last light the postmaster sees little Addison hid in the sea-grape, spying on all those grown-up men with guns. Smallwood's voice breaks when he calls the boy, and goes unheard. Hurrying down the steps, he does not call again.

What had he feared? That his neighbors would denounce his call as a shout of warning?

Warned or not, the man would come in anyway.

Now Henry Short glides like a shadow from the trees, crossing behind the men, down to the shore. He wades without a splash into the water, just to the right of Bill House and Bill's father.

A suck and wash as the bow wave slaps ashore. Time stops, spun upward in a vortex. Smallwood's heart caroms, his hands rise to his ears.

The boat stem crunches old dead mollusks. Silence.

The earth turns. A quiet greeting, an exchange of voices. The men drift forward, spreading out along the water. Smallwood gasps for breath. With the day of reckoning unbearably deferred, the postmaster's relief is mixed, without elation.

Soon Mamie and her friend venture outside. They talk and smile to ease their nerves, starting down the little slope toward the water.

A twig snaps and the twilight stiffens. A hard shift, the whip crack of a shot, two shots together. There is time for an echo, time for a high shriek, before the last evening of the old days in the Islands flies apart in a volley of wild fire.

The young woman stands formally before his house, as for a picture, brown dress darkened by the dusk, face pale as salt.

Mamie runs to her, but it is she who takes the sobbing

8

Mamie to her bosom, strokes her hair, regards the postmaster over his wife's shoulder without the mercy of a single blink. She appears calm. It is Mamie who has shrieked; he can still hear it. He wanders toward them, feeling weak and shy.

Mamie twists away from him, mouth working. In a low and awful voice she says, *"I'm leaving! I am leaving this godforsaken place! I'm leaving!"* The children stare. He shoos the little girl inside, to the staccato of boys' hoots and scared dogs barking. When little Thelma whines, he shakes her hard. "Inside, I said!" At the fury of his voice, her face disintegrates, she runs into the house.

The young woman goes to her little boy, who has tripped and fallen in his wailing flight and has patches of hurricane mud daubed on his knees. She pulls him to her, as if away from the armed men, who are milling in the dark like one great animal. Some turn to stare.

In a moment, she will crawl under the house, dragging her brood into the chicken slime and darkness.

"No, Lord," she whispers, as the terror overtakes her.

"Oh, dear God," she moans.

"Oh Lord!" she cries. "They are killing Mister Watson!"

HENRY THOMPSON

We never had no trouble from Mister Watson, and from what we seen, he never caused none, not amongst his neighbors. All the trouble come to him from the outside.

Ed J. Watson turned up at Half Way Creek back in '92, worked on the produce farms awhile, worked in the cane. Hard worker, too, but it don't seem like he hoed cane for the money, it was more like he was getting the feel of our community, what was what and who was where. He was a strong, good-looking feller in his thirties, dark red hair, well made, thick through the shoulders but no fat on him, not in them days. Close to six foot and carried himself well, folks noticed him straight off, and no one fooled with him. First time you seen the man you wanted him to like you – he was that kind. Wore a broad black hat, wore denim coveralls over a frock coat with big pockets. Times we was cutting buttonwood with ax and hand saw, two–three cords a day – that's hard and humid work, case you ain't done it, and even them coveralls got sweated – Ed Watson never changed his outfit. Used to joke how he kept his coat on cause he expected some company any day now from up north.

Nobody knew where this man come from, and nobody asked him. You didn't ask a man hard questions, not in the Ten Thousand Islands, not in them days. Folks will tell you different today, but back then there wasn't too many in our section that wasn't kind of unpopular someplace else. With all of Florida to choose from, who else would come to these overflowed rain-rotted islands with not enough high ground to build a outhouse, and so many

10

skeeters plaguing you in the bad summers you thought you'd took the wrong turn straight to Hell.

Old Man William Brown was cutting cane, and he listened to them men opining how this stranger Ed J. Watson was so friendly. And when Old Man Williams never said a word, they was bound to ask him his opinion, and he took him a slow drink of water, give a sigh. "Never knew a real bad feller yet that wasn't nice and easy in his ways. Feller running his mouth all the time, I done this and I'm fixing to do that – no need to pay that feller no attention. But a feller just taking it easy, waiting you out – you better leave that man go his own way."

So Willie Brown, strong and lively little feller, thought a lot of Mister Watson all his life, Willie Brown said, "Well, now, Papa, are you telling us this man is a bad actor?" And his daddy said, "I just *feel* something, is all, same way I feel the damp." The men respected Old Man William, but there wasn't one out in the field that day that took him serious.

All the same, we noticed pretty quick, you couldn't draw too close to Mister Watson before he eased out sideways like a crab, gave himself more room. My half uncle Tant Jenkins claimed he once come up on Mister Watson letting his water, and Mister Watson come around on him so fast that poor Tant thought this feller aimed to piss on him. Well, it weren't his pecker he had in his hand. By the time Tant Jenkins seen that gun, it was halfway back into them denims, he wasn't so certain he seen it after all.

Tant was always brash and kind of comical. He says, "Well, now, Mister Watson! Specting some company from the north?" And Mister Watson says, "Any company that shows up unexpected will find me ready with a nice warm welcome." Very agreeable, y'know, very, very easy. But he never let nobody come up on him.

For many years Tant Jenkins and myself run his boats for Mister Watson. Especially when Tant was drinking, which was mostly all the time, he would tease poor Mister

11

Watson something pitiful. Told him that no friend of S. S. Jenkins had a single thing to fear from north *or* south, though sometimes east and west could give Tant trouble. Mister Watson got a real kick out of that. "Well, Tant," he'd say, "knowing *you* are on the job, I'll sleep much better."

Ed Watson had money in his pocket when he come to Half Way Creek, which ain't none of my business nor yours neither. In all the years that I knew Mister Watson, right up until them bad days near the end, he always come up with money when he had to. We didn't know till later he was on the dodge, and maybe even Half Way Creek – half way between Everglade and Turner River, on the east side of Chokoloskee Bay – was too close to the lawmen for his liking. Ain't nothing much out there today but a few old cisterns, but Half Way Creek had ten or a dozen families then, more than Everglade or Chokoloskee or anyplace else from Marco Island south to Cape Sable. Weren't hardly more'n a hundred souls in all that hundred miles of coast, counting the ones that perched awhile at the mouths of rivers.

Mister Watson weren't at Half Way Creek but a few days when he paid money down for William Brown's old seventy-foot schooner. Later he bought the old *Veatlis* off Ben Brown, and he always remained in friendship with that family. Used to stop over at Half Way Creek, talk farming with the Browns, every time he come up to the Bay. Ain't many men would buy a schooner that didn't know next to nothing about boats, but a man that is good at one thing most generally's good at another, and Ed Watson could put his hand to anything. Time he was done, he was one of the best boatmen on this coast.

I seen straight off that Mister Watson was a man who meant to go someplace, I seen my chance, so I signed on to guide him down around the Islands. I had already worked for a year down there, plume hunting and such for

Old Chevelier, before I turned that Frenchman over to Bill House. Me and Bill was just young fellers then, a scant fourteen, but a man got started early back in them days. Until some years into this century, there weren't no regular school on Chokoloskee, so you went to work. Nothing else to do when you come to think about it.

Folks ask, Would I have throwed in with Mister Watson if I knowed about him what I know today? Well, hell, I don't *know* what I know today, and they don't neither. With so many stories growed up around that feller, who is to say which ones are true? I was just a kid, though I never would admit it, and what I seen were a able-bodied man, quiet and easy in his ways, who acted according to our ideas of a gentleman. And that was all we had, ideas, cause we never seen one in this section, unless you would count Preacher Gatewood, who first brought the Lord to Everglade back in '88 and took Him away again when he departed.

Mister Watson and me cut buttonwood all around Bay Sunday and down Chatham River, run it over to Key West, three dollars a cord. Cepting Richard Hamilton, who run off down there back in the eighties and stayed on in the Islands fifty years, most of the Island pioneers was drifters. There was even a few old runaways from the War Between the States, never got the word that the war was finished. Never had nothing but thatch lean-tos and a skiff and pot and guns, and maybe a jug of *aguedente* for fighting off the skeeters in the evening. Plume hunters and moonshiners, the most of 'em. Put earth in a tub, made their fire in the skiff, had coffee going morning, noon, and night.

A man who called himself Will Raymond was the only settler down on Chatham River – more of a squatter, you might say, camped with his wife and daughter in a palmetta shack on that big forty-acre mound down on the Bend. Will Raymond was like most of 'em down in the Islands, getting away from it all, you know, living along on grits and mullet, taking some gator hides and egret plumes, selling a little moonshine to the Injuns. The Frenchman had the Bend before him, and Old Man Richard Hamilton before that. Biggest Injun mound south of Marco and Chokoloskee, which was why the Frenchman went there in the first place. The Injuns always called it Pavioni. But in them days Pavioni was all overgrowed cause Will Raymond weren't much of a farmer, and Mister Watson would cuss him out every time we went downriver, saying how pitiful it was to see so much good ground going to waste. And maybe he'd already reckoned that Chatham Bend was across the line, in Munroe County, with the closest law near a hundred miles away, down to Key West. But that never occurred to nobody, not at the time.

Oh yes, we seen plenty like Will Raymond in the Islands, thin piney-woods crackers with them knife-mouthed women, hollow-eyed under bent hats, lank black hair like horses, touchy, on the run. Go crazy every little while, get their old-time religion all mixed up with guns and whiskey, shoot some poor neighbor through the heart. I guess that's what Will done more'n once, he got the habit of it.

Will must have been wanted pretty bad – dead or alive, as you might say. Probably should have picked him a new name, got a fresh start, cause the law got wind of him some way and deputies come a-hunting him, out of Key West. Will said Nosir, he'd be damned if he'd go peaceable, and he whistled a bullet past their heads to prove it. But he was peaceable and then some by the time the smoke cleared, so they threw his carcass in the boat. The law asked the Widder Raymond would she and her daughter like a boat ride to Key West along with the deceased, and she said, Thankee, don't mind if we do.

Next thing you know, Ed Watson tracked the widder down and bought Will's claim, two hundred and fifty dollars. That was a lot of cash in them days, but there was forty acres of good soil and more across the river, the most high ground anywhere south of Chokoloskee, and Mister

14

Watson liked Pavioni from the start. Protected on three sides by mangrove tangle – you had to come at him straight on or not at all. And he admired the deep channel in that river, used to talk sometimes of dredging out the mouth, make a harbor and stopover place for coastal shipping.

Oh, he had big plans, all right, about the only feller down there ever did. Started right out by building a fine cabin, used buttonwood posts to frame it up, had wood shutters and canvas flaps on the front windows, brought in a wood stove and a kerosene lamp and a galvanized tub for anyone that cared to wash. We ate good, too, all the fish and meat you wanted, had a big iron skillet and made johnnycakes the whole size of that pan. Put a little oil to his good flour, cooked 'em up dry. I remembered them good johnnycakes all my whole life.

Mister Watson said Will Raymond's shack weren't fit for hogs, so he patched it up before he put our hogs in it. We had two cows, and chickens, too, but E. J. Watson had a old-time feel for hogs. I can take a hog or I can leave it, but that man loved hogs and hogs loved him, they followed him all over, I can hear him calling down them river evenings to this day. The hogs was brought in every night cause of the panthers, which was very common on the rivers, and he fed 'em garden trash and table slops and such so they wouldn't get no fishy taste from feeding on crabs and orsters at low tide like them old razorbacks of Richard Hamilton. Kept a old horse for breaking up the ground, and sometimes he'd saddle up of a fine evening and ride around his forty-acre farm like it was a spread of four thousand and forty.

Mister Watson worked us like niggers, and he worked like a nigger alongside us. Brought in a couple of regular niggers from Fort Myers for the dirty work, and *they* worked hard – that man knew how to get work from his help. The niggers was scared of him cause he was rough, but they kind of liked him when he wasn't drinking. Told 'em nigger jokes that had 'em giggling for hours, but I

15

never got them nigger jokes too good. Me and niggers just don't think the same.

The old-time Calusas was the ones built up that shell mound, same ones that killed Old Man Ponce de León maybe right in that same place four hundred years ago. And Calusas was still there, the Frenchman said, back in 1838, at the time of the Army expedition to the Islands. In his opinion, them Pavioni people was the last of them big fishing Injuns, said that big Pavioni mound must of been Calusa for two thousand years, same as the big mound at Chokoloskee. Them redskins set there shucking a good while, to fling a forty-acre shell pile over their shoulders. Somewhere not far from Pavioni, on a mound hid from the rivers, there had to be a sacred burial place, the Frenchman said. Used to talk sometimes about sacred rites and human sacrifice and such, like it was common knowledge, but I never really got the hang of it.

Old Man Chevelier spent most of his last years out hunting his lost mound, shooting plume birds and museum specimens just to get by. Most of my knowledge about Injuns come from him. Maybe he wasn't no American, and atheistical, to boot, but he was the most educated man ever turned up here. Seems funny it would take a foreigner to know more about Injuns than we did. Our own old fellers never cared one bit. Said, Shoot them pesky redskins first, ask questions later, cause they ain't one bit less ornery than your common Spaniard.

Old Man Richard Hamilton was mostly fishing when he had that place, and Chevelier and Will Raymond, who come after him, never farmed neither, not to speak of. Ed Watson was the first one since the Injuns to hack out all that thorn, dig out palmetta roots thick as your leg, scrape off enough of that old shell to make a farm. That's why it's called the Watson Place today. Grew all kinds of vegetables, and cane for syrup, and tomatoes and alligator pears that the old Clyde Mallory Line shipped straight out of

16

Key West for New York City. One time Mister Watson come back from Fort Myers with some seed potatoes! Them farmers at Half Way Creek and Chokoloskee liked to laugh behind his back, but Mister Watson shipped potatoes for three–four years before he reckoned potatoes didn't pay, and he always raised a few for our own table.

We got good money for our produce, but too much spoiled before it reached the auction room down to Key West. Coleman and Bartlum, General Commission Merchants – we're probably on the books down there today. And pretty soon, except for our own table, we give up on general vegetables. Long as he could scare him up some field hands, Mister Watson figured there was more future in sugarcane, cause cane don't spoil. After that he figured out that making syrup right on the plantation, instead of shipping all them heavy stalks, made a lot more sense in a out-of-the-way place like Chatham River, cause syrup could be stored till he got his price.

Meanwhile he worked out his own way of letting the cane tassel before cutting. Syrup from tasseled cane will boil down a lot stronger without sugaring. When he went over to our high-quality syrup is when Mister Watson made his first good money, and got him a bigger schooner from Key West, called her the *Gladiator*. Packed that syrup in one-gallon tin cans, six to the case, shipped it to Port Tampa and Key West. Our Island Pride syrup become famous. There was planters at Half Way Creek like Storters and Will Wiggins, and Old Man D. D. House up Turner River, they made plenty of good syrup, but Mister Watson had 'em beat right from the start.

Ed Watson was the only planter south of Chokoloskee that ever made more than a bare living in the rivers, he was the best farmer I ever saw. And all the while we done fishing, too, sold some salt fish, took turtle eggs in season, shot gators and egrets when they was handy. Up them inland creeks, Last Huston Bay, Alligator Bay, egrets was thick, pink curlew, too, and we never failed to take a deer or two for venison, sometimes a turkey. Trapped otters and coons and panthers for the hides, and every little while we'd kill a bear. I thought I was pretty handy with a shooting iron, but I'm telling you now, Mr Ed J. Watson was a deadeye shot. Only man I ever saw could shoot like that was Henry Short.

After D. D. House moved his farm from Turner River down to the hammocks back of Chatham River, Henry Short used to come over from House Hammock on a Sunday to see how young Bill was getting on with the Old Frenchman, who lived up the river, Possum Key. Henry and me got on all right, I never held a thing against him, but when he visited the Hamiltons, them people let that nigger eat right at the table. That ain't James Hamiltons I'm speaking about. This is Richard Hamiltons.

Only one besides me and Mister Watson hunting plume birds in them creeks was Old Chevelier. One afternoon Mister Watson seen the Frenchman's skiff coming out in back of Gopher Key. Sometimes Chevelier had Injuns with him, and this day I seen a log canoe slide back behind the green, soft as a gator. In the Glades Injuns use dugouts made from cypress logs, and they use push poles. Never seen Injuns paddle a canoe in my whole life.

In a dugout, the braves are standing, so they always seen you first, you were lucky to spot a Injun at all. But Injuns was watching you most all the time, that was something you got used to or you didn't. Watched us white men when we come into their country and watched us when we went away, the same way the wild critters did, the deer, the panther, stopping at the edge of cover and looking back over their shoulder. Give you a funny feeling to be watched like that, you begun to think the trees were watching, too. But a man wouldn't hear nothing but the moan of wasps, them creeks used to be full of wasp nests way back then.

If Mister Watson seen that dugout, he never paid it no attention. Chevelier lifts off his straw hat to mop his head,

18

and Mister Watson hikes his gun and shoots that hat out of his hand. That bullet clipped right past his ear, made him skedaddle like a duck into the mangroves.

You won't hear me deny it. I was shocked. There was a silence fell across that water for a mile away. Weren't nothing to be seen in them long mangrove tunnels but green air and brown stilt roots, and that hard sparkle where the sun come through the trees, but I could feel the black eyes in them stone faces right between the leaves.

Mister Watson hollers to them trees, "Sir, that hat can be replaced at Chatham Bend!" I knew the Frenchman would not see the joke of it. Scared that poor old man to death, I reckon, cause we never heard a whisper from the mangroves.

I told Mister Watson all about Chevelier, how he was a hermit collecting rare birds for museums, used three different-size guns so as not to spoil 'em, and paying his keep by selling plumes; how he had all kinds of books there in his cabin, knew all about Injuns and wild critters, spoke some Injun lingo and had wild Injuns visiting that would never go near to Chokoloskee Bay. Them wild ones traded hides and furs through Richard Hamilton, who claimed to be Choctaw or some such, though nobody never paid that much attention. The Frenchman was always close to that Hamilton bunch, and probably it was Old Man Richard who brought them Injuns to him in the first place.

I could not stop telling all about the Frenchman, because Mister Watson was watching me so hard I just got nervous. That feller would look right past your eyes and not show nothing, or look at you straight for a minute or more without a blink. Then he would blink just once, real slow, like a old turtle, keeping his eyes closed for a moment as if resting 'em up from such an awful sight.

It was that day, while he rested up his eyes, that I first took notice how fiery he looked, that chestnut hair the color of dried blood, and the ruddy skin and sun-burned whiskers. Them whiskers had a little gold to 'em, he looked

19

like he was glowing from inside. Then them blue eyes was watching me again, out of the shadow of that black felt hat he wore winter and summer. Only hat in the Ten Thousand Islands, I imagine, that had a label into it from Fort Smith, Arkansas.

Then he looks up, cuts me off in a hard voice. "What's that old man up to, back yonder?"

I told him about the clamshell midden that the old Calusas had built back in that hammock, and the clamshell canal that come all the way in there from the open water. The way I figured it, I said, Old Man Chevelier was hunting Calusa treasure back on Gopher Key.

His eyes flicked, but he made no comment, just waited politely for my talking to run out. Then he replied, meaning no offense, that he'd give a lot for some educated company like M'sieu Chevelier – Che-*vell*-yay, he called him, stead of Shev-uh-*leer*, the way we said it – and he reckoned he'd picked a piss-poor way to scrape acquaintance.

He was right. I knew that Frenchman, knew he had grit or he wouldn't have made it by himself out in the Islands, where the skeeter whine can get so loud you think some kind of a meteor is coming. Richard Hamilton was going to hear about that bullet, and this story was not over by a long shot. But from that day on, we had the egret rookeries to ourselves.

I worked for Mr Ed J. Watson for five years in the nineties, and run his boats in later years when he came and went. If he done all the things laid at his door, it seems to me I would have knowed something. S. S. Jenkins worked at Watson's a good while, and if you could take and dig Tant up, he'd say the same. A whole heap of people from Caxambas, Chokoloskee, Fakahatchee, including more'n one of my own kin, worked at Chatham Bend at one time or another, and a heap more had dealings with him here and there. E. J. Watson drove him a hard bargain when that mood was on him, cause he had a good head for business, but the only one would ever claim that Mister

Watson done him wrong was Adolphus Santini, who got cut in the neck in that drinking scrape down to Key West. There's men will tell you old Dolphus was drunk, too, and had it coming, but I don't want to say that, cause I wasn't there.

Sir –

The enclosed material relating to E. J. Watson is culled from interviews with pioneer Floridians made years ago for the History of Southwest Florida *which drew your attention to my modest researches in the first place. Though I placed no emphasis upon our subject, these interviews (arranged here in a rough chronology) contain a remarkable amount of comment on "Mister Watson." Decidedly they affirm his eminence in the imagination of his wilderness community, so isolated from the new century on these coastal islands.*

Also included are pertinent clippings from the American Eagle *and the Fort Myers* Press, *including excerpts from their local news columns. These contemporary accounts seem more dependable than the many magazine articles and books in which E. J. Watson's name has since appeared, which tend to contradict one another on small points as well as large, and fail to represent a picture consistent with the man remembered in these narratives by those who knew him best. Indeed, they raise as many questions as they answer concerning the enigmatic figure who looms behind the few hard facts of his dark history.*

The following sketch of Watson's life is submitted in the sincere conviction that is it truthful in its general statement as well as in significant particulars. It is largely based on two brief chronicles published in the 1950s, each of them considerably more accurate than any of the better-known accounts. One appeared in a letter submitted to a "Pioneer Florida" column in the Miami Herald *by the late Dr M. B. Herlong, "a pioneer physician in this state," who apparently knew the Watson family in his younger days, both in South Carolina and later in north Florida. The other, by*

22

the late Charles Sherod "Ted" Smallwood, who was raised not far from Mr Watson's district in north Florida and became his friend in the Ten Thousand Islands, turns up among Smallwood's reminiscences. The absence of contradictions in these two accounts (by firsthand sources entirely unacquainted with each other) seems to strengthen the reliability of both.

Edgar Watson was born on November 1, 1855, in Edgefield County, South Carolina, just across the northeast Georgia line. According to Dr Herlong, who was also born in Edgefield County, Edgar's father was Elijah Watson, a sometime state prison employee and celebrated brawler, known, from a knife scar that encircled his eye, as Ring-Eye Lige. The doctor says that Ring-Eye Lige so brutalized his family with his drinking and intemperate behavior that Mrs Watson felt obliged to flee with her two children to relatives in northern Florida.

The family traveled to the Fort White region of Columbia County rather early in our subject's life, since both Herlong and Smallwood state that he was raised there. Dr Herlong relates that Edgar and his sister, Minnie, "grew up and married in that section."

"One bright moonlight night," Dr Herlong continues, "I heard a wagon passing our place. It was bright enough to recognize Watson and his family in the wagon. The report was that they settled in Georgia, but it couldn't have been for long."

Probably Ted Smallwood was correct in saying that Mr Watson married three women from Columbia County, and one may assume that the people in the wagon included a son by the first marriage, Robert or "Rob" Watson; his second wife, Jane S. Watson; his daughter, Carrie, born in 1885; and an infant son, Edgar E., born in 1887. Another son, Lucius, would be born out West. Whatever its cause, Watson's flight occurred sometime before early 1888, when the Watsons are first reported in the Indian Territory.

Popular accounts of his career assert that before this departure from Columbia County, he had killed his brother-in-law, who was "cut to pieces." Another account specifies "two cousins." Smallwood mentions "a shooting" involving a brother-in-law but does not say that this shooting was fatal. Herlong mentions no killing in Columbia County in this period, but neither does he speculate on why Edgar Watson set out on his long journey in the dead of night.

Though the facts of this episode are probably lost, the many reports of his subsequent association with Belle Starr, "Queen of the Outlaws," in the Indian Territory, are unanimous in the claim that when Mr Watson departed for the West, he was wanted for murder in the State of Florida.

I am in correspondence with historians and librarians in Arkansas and Oklahoma in the hope that some details of Mr Watson's sojourn in Oklahoma can be salvaged from the great amount of myth and nonsense that has been written about Mrs Starr. Should this material be forthcoming, copies shall be sent along at once . . .

At the end of his stay in Oklahoma, Mr Watson apparently returned to Arkansas, where he was tried and imprisoned as a horse thief. Apparently he escaped from prison, at which time he returned to Florida, though some accounts speak of an intervening stay in Oregon. (There is also occasional mention of an earlier sojourn in Texas, for which no evidence whatever has come forward.) For several years after 1889, his movements are obscure, though it seems clear that he had parted with his family.

Mr Watson told Ted Smallwood that upon his return to Florida in the early 1890s, he visited Arcadia, at that time a wild cattle town on the Pease River (on some maps "Peace," after the treaty in 1842 that ended the Second Seminole War), where he slew a "bad actor" named Quinn Bass. "Watson said Bass had a fellow down whittling on him with a knife and Watson told Bass to stop, he had worked on the man enough, and Bass got loose and came toward him and he began putting .38 S&W bullets into Bass and shot him down." (Though Mr Watson is apparently the source of the Bass story – and presumably the Oregon reference, too – we must decide for ourselves if he told the truth.) According to Smallwood's chronology, this event took place not long before he appeared in southwest Florida "in 1892 or '93."

From Arcadia, Mr Watson proceeded to Everglade and Half Way Creek, two small farming communities on Chokoloskee Bay, in the northern part of the Ten Thousand Islands. These pioneer outposts on the swampy mainland, together with nearby Chokoloskee Island, were the last points of civilization on the southwest coast.

RICHARD HAMILTON

I done a lot, lived a long time, and seen more than I cared
to. I remember what I seen, and learned some from it, but
I was born on the run like a young deer and never had no
time for improvement. What little I come by I owed to
that Frenchified old feller who was Mister Watson's closest
neighbor next to me.

First time I met that mean old man I tried to run him
right off Chatham River. That was the winter of '88, two–
three years before the day Mr Ed Watson come around
the bend. We was living at Pavioni then, which is the
Watson Place today. There was forty acres on that Pavioni
mound, but we farmed just the one, for our own use. We
was making a fair living, salted fish, cut buttonwood, took
plumes in egret breeding season, took some gator hides,
some otter, done some trading with the Indins, and eased
on by.

That morning I felt something coming, though I never
heard a thing. Looking south across the field, I see my old
woman, Mary Weeks, and it is like looking at a stranger.
In a queer shift of wind and light off of the river, what I
see is not my Mary but a big dark cruel-mouthed woman
in long gingham, hard bare feet, bad scowl half-hid in the
shadow of her sunbonnet. She is out on the riverbank and
she is pointing, like she' seen a vision in that glaring sky
out toward the Gulf. Though I can't hear, she is hollering
into the wind, her mouth round as a hole.

Big Mary is the kind who don't come hunting you, just
hollers what she wants from where she's at. Sometimes I
play deaf, pay her no mind. But this day I had sign of

something, so I set down my hoe and come in from the sweet potatoes, telling my two older fellers to keep at it.

This skinny old man has rowed in from the Gulf, three miles or more against the current. He is wearing knickers, with a necktie and jacket laid across the seat, like he was out taking the air. Damndest thing I ever seen on Chatham River. I figured he had got loose off one them steam yachts that been showing up on the Gulf Coast in the winter, and I hollered at him to get the hell back down the river where he come from. He just waves me off, like I'm a fly. Picks up his spyglass and looks straight into the mangrove like he sees something in there besides mangrove, then keeps right on a-coming like he never heard me. Has to row hard cause the tide is falling, quick funny strokes, but he rowed very strong, I was surprised.

By the time he hits the bank, he's pale and peaked, but he's all excited. "How do you are!" he says, lifting his hat, then points downriver. "Cuckoo!" he says.

"Cuckoo yourself," I say, hitching the gun.

This little stranger has thick spectacles and wild round eyes. His black hair sticks up like a brush, and cheeks so bony that light glances off, and wet red lips and a thin mustache that runs all the way around his mouth, and pointy ears the Devil would been proud of. This time he says, kind of cranky, "*Mawn-grove* cuckoo!"

"Don't try nothin," I say.

"What to hell you doing here?" His voice is kind of sharp and cross, like it's me who don't belong on my own property. He's too bony to be sweated up, but he takes out a neckerchief and dabs his face, and then he reaches for a shotgun he's got leaning in the bows. Had a load of bird shot in it, and he's just moving it because it's pointing at my knees, but I never knowed that at the time, couldn't take no chances. I hoist my barrel so he's looking down the muzzle, to give him an idea just what was what.

"What to hell!" he says again, no particular reason. When

27

he shrugs and pulls his hand back from his gun, I see he ain't got all his fingers.

"Made that mistake before, I see."

"Do not self-excite, m'sieu," he says, dabbing some more.

I never had no experience with such a feller, and I'm getting riled. I pick his gun out of the boat and break it, toss the shell into the river. He flings his hands up, rolls his eyes to heaven. "What for you *waste!*" he yells. "What is matt-aire with this foking country!"

"You don't hear so good," is what I tell him, laying his gun back in the boat. "Git on back yonder where you come from."

"You are vair uppity, my good man," says he. And damn if he don't hop over the bow, push my gun barrel out of his way, and climb the bank. Hands on his hips, he looks around, like he's inspecting his new property.

Behind me I hear my woman snickering. Ol' Mary Weeks has a mean mouth and a mean snicker. I jab the barrels into his back, and damn if he don't whip around and wrench that gun out of my hands and back me up with it, and when he's got me backed up good, he breaks the gun, picks out the shells, and drops 'em like dead mice into the water.

I tell you, it scared me how quick and strong he was, and crazy. A man would try that when a stranger has the drop on him has got to be crazy or so fed up with life he'd rather get shot than take more shit off *any*body. Willie Brown now, he is small and very strong, but he is *built* strong, and he's young, while this man here is getting on, he looks plain puny. I know right then he has the Devil in him. Even Mary Weeks is spooked, cause she ain't snickering no more, and Mary Weeks don't overlook too many chances.

Around about then John Leon comes out of the shack dragging the rifle. Even at four, John Leon knew his business. Never says one word, just drags that gun across the

28

yard a little closer so's he can line that stranger up real good and don't waste powder when he hauls back on the trigger. His plan was to shoot this hombre quick, get the story later.

The stranger hands over my gun while Mary Weeks runs and gets ahold of our youngest boy. She don't care nothing for me no more, but John Leon is her hope and consolation.

The old man is rubbing his sore back, disgusted. "You shoot stran-jaire just for coming on the shore?" he asks, riled up at the whole bunch of us. "In this foking country even enfant are shooting pipples like I shooting birts!"

He brushes his jacket off and puts it on, never mind the heat. He has a pair of glasses on a string. Puts them on, too, then stands on tippy-toes in his laced boots to see who he is dealing with on this damned river. "Is Chatham Bend?" He looks around again, shaking his head. "*You* are squatt-aire. *You* have squatt-aire right?" This old feller has spotted my dusty hide, he has mistook me for some kind of help.

In them days there weren't but maybe ten souls altogether on this whole eighty mile of coast, south to Cape Sable, which is why this feller is so surprised to find us pioneers back up the river. He complains that the Bend was uninhabited when he passed by here plume hunting a few years ago. Why, only last week, folks at Everglade and Chokoloskee had told him he could move right in. "Many year my heart have settled on this place!" he yells, putting the fingertips of both hands on his heart. "For why nobody knows it you are here?"

"They know I'm here," I say.

At that he turns to look at me more careful. Then he looks at the woman in the doorway of the shack, and our little boy.

"You met John Weeks up there at Everglade? That there woman is his daughter, and that there little feller is my youngest boy." At them words, Mary looks away and goes inside. "Or supposed to be," I say. She bangs a pot.

29

I can tell from the stranger's face that he has heard some rumor on this matter. "Ah, je com-*prawng*!" he says. He weren't no Yankee, I knew that much.

Since our visitor was taking things so hard, I told him stay awhile, have a look around, and he shrugs some more like he is doing me a favor. We go down with the tide to detach his gear off a Key West schooner, Captain Carey, that was anchored at Pavilion Key. The captain hollers after him, "Sure you're all right? When shall I fetch you?" But the old man perched in the stern don't hardly wave at him, don't even turn around, and finally the captain drops his arm, shaking his head.

The Frenchman is so busy asking me questions that he don't hardly wait to get an answer. As days go by, I inform him how this once was Pavilion River, but these Indins around here don't know nothing, so they say Pavioni. Well, this dang French know-it-all tells *me* how Pavilion got its name! Says a pirate from the Spanish Main was camped here on a offshore key with a young girl off a Dutch merchantman. Girl said even though he had killed off all her family, she would gladly suffer the fate worse than death so long as he spared her own dear life. Well, his crew got sick of looking on while he lay down with her, they said it was her or him, and so he had no choice but to poison her. Before he left, on account he loved her, he built her a thatch shelter to keep the sun off while she died in agony. When an American man-o'-war caught up with him, the Spaniard described this kindness to the Dutch girl to prove how such a courtly feller did not deserve to hang. After they hung him, they went up there and found most of the girl under that shelter. Called it a pavilion, named that key for it, and we call it "Pavilion" to this day.

Chevelier said he'd found no "Chatham" in the old accounts. Said "Chatham River" might of come from the Indin name of Chitto Hatchee, or Snake River, as it was called on the old war maps around 1840. Fakahatchee, now, where John Leon was born, that is Fork River. The

Frenchman knew that Indin tongue like he was born with it.

This old French feller – I always think of him as an old feller cause of that stiffness in him, though he weren't so many seasons older'n me – he told us later that he come from France with a French "ornithologue" name of Charles Bonaparte. He was an ornithologue himself and never cared who knowed it, but he sold bird plumes, too, to make ends meet. Looked like some rare old bird hisself, damn if he didn't, quills sticking out all over his head, beady eyes and a stiff gait – the dry way a man will look who lives too long without a woman. Spent too much time with his feathered friends, looked like to me, cause when he got excited, his hair went up in back just like a bird crest, he looked all set to shit and no mistake, and he screeched as good as them Carolina parrots he was hunting for.

It was right there on Chatham Bend that Jean Chevelier shot the first short-tailed hawk was ever seen in North America, something like that. Weren't much of a claim cause it weren't much of a bird – tail too damn short, I guess. Why he thought this o' scraggy thing we couldn't eat would make him famous I don't know. He seen Carolina parrots, too, far away up inland, freshwater creeks. Bright green little things, size of a dove, all red and yeller on the head, but they was shy and he never did come up with one.

Them parrots used to be thick as fleas back in the hammocks. I told him I would eat a few when I went in there after deer and turkey. *"Eat it? Mange? Le perroquet?"* He squawked and slapped his brow. Well, that was a long time ago, I told him, and I ain't seen one since. I believe they told me not so long ago that them pretty birds has flewed away for good.

Christmas 1888, Captain Carey brought presents from Key West for all the kids, give each one an apple, candy cane, and Roman candle. That evening Old Man Chevelier says,

How would you like to help me collect birds? And he spells out all the kinds he wants, not a plume bird in the bunch. Wants wild eggs, too. I'm nodding away to show I get the drift, and when he says "swallow-tail hawk" I nod again and smile and say *"Tonsabe."*

At that he flies right at my face – "Where you get it that word?" I tell him that is Indin speech for swaller-tail hawk, and he asks, real sly, *"Which* Indin?" "Choctaw," I says. I call myself by my mother's tribe just to get on in life. Choctaws was *good* Indins, I tell him, helped Ol' Andy Jackson fight them Creeks, helped him steal most all of Georgia for the crackers. But when they made him president, Ol' Hickory packed the Choctaws up right along with the dang Creeks, sent the whole sad and sorry bunch off to Oklahoma. I told the Frenchman that Ol' Hickory kept a soft spot in his heart for Choctaws all the same.

That Frenchman weren't much interested in my historical lore. He asks what is this river in *my* language, and I tell him that the old words for this country have been lost. He nods quick, like he's sprung a trap. *"Tonsabe* is old word, is it not?" He grins. *"Tonsabe* is Calusa, is it not?"

He had took me by surprise and my faced showed it. That word ain't used by Mikasuki, nor Muskogee neither, that word come straight down from my granddaddy, Chief Chekaika.

Back in them days, Chekaika's name was a dirty word to white people, so I says, real coony, "Choctaw and Calusa must be pretty close." But he keeps staring right into my eyes, nodding his head like he can read my brain. Then he sets down on a crate, so we're knee to knee.

"Vair few Calusa words survive," he says, nodding and staring.

I decide to trust him just a little, cause it ain't often I find somebody who knows what I am talking about. Well, I say, my people was not Calusa, not exactly, they was what white men called the Spanish Indins.

Damn if that don't overjoy him so, he has to jump up

32

and sit down again. He tells me Spanish Indins was descended from Calusas that the Spaniards took over to Cuba. Being Spaniards, they snuck some Indins back in to this coast to stir up trouble when the Americans was grabbing off the State of Florida. "So! You are Calusa!" Gives me that skull smile of his when I do not answer. "You know all about where is Calusa burial!" I shrug again.

Chevelier told me he had studied up the maps and such, read the Spanish archives in Madrid, visited all of the big mounds in the Ten Thousand Islands before he decided that Chatham Bend was a main Calusa mound way back in Spanish times. Somewhere pretty close to here, the Calusa took eighteen canoes and attacked Juan Ponce de León, and maybe they withdrew into these hidden rivers to escape the Spanish poxes, cause poxes done a lot more damage than all them swords and blunderbusses put together. If his theory was right, then somewhere in these godforsook green islands was a burial mound, built up higher than the village mounds, using white sand, and one sign of it would be traces of canals out to open water, like some he had seen already, up the coast. Any temple would be gone by now, and the white sand overgrowed, but all the same there was a burial mound on one of these here islands, *had* to be! He was very excited, but gave up in disgust when I just shrug. "I ain't nothing but a dumb old Indin," I tell him.

"Indians say 'dumb Indin,' white pipples say 'dumb Injun' – why is that?"

"Maybe dumb Indins are too damn dumb to know how to say 'dumb Injuns,' what do you think?"

"Ay-coot," he says, "I am vair interest in Indiang pipples. These foking crack-aire are know-nothing, are grave robbaire! Are *des*-ecrating!" He talks this way to get on the good side of this dusty feller who might not care too much for his cracker neighbors.

He wanted to study a Calusa burial place, he says, blurting it out.

33

"Calusa treasure?" I smile him my best smile. He does not answer.

All the while the Frenchman talked about his mound, he was watching my eyes like a cardplayer to see if I might put him in the way of it. I knew him a little bit by now, and I believe he *did* want to study that mound, just like he wanted to study birds, cause he was a real scientist, he was born curious, he was the nosiest damn man I ever come across. But he would loot them graves first thing, because some way he was starved by life, and greedy, and here was maybe his last chance at fame and fortune. I was watching him as close as he watched me, and I seen his crippled hand twitch while he spoke.

"Well," say I, "one day I was out *des*-ecrating with my oldest boy, had ten–twelve pretty skulls lined up on a log, airing out, y'know. Chip the crown off for your ashtray, rig the head for your cigars. For a human humidor you just can't beat it." I hum a little, taking my time. "Them redskin skulls done up artistic for the tourist trade will bring you some nice spot cash down to Key West."

He is really staring. "Com*maung*?" he says. These Frenchmen say "Come on!" like it's a question – Com-*maung*?

"Yessir. One them skulls had a hole conched into it, and I give that one to my boy, and he stuck a buzzard feather in there, looked real pretty." I let him sit with that one for a minute.

He says in a funny voice, "Where this place *was*?" He couldn't take the chance I might be fooling.

"Nosir," I says, "I wouldn't let on to my worst enemy about that place!" and I drop my voice right down to a whisper and touch knees. "Cause when we lined them skulls up, put the feather in, why, all of a sudden, them trees went silent on us! That silence was so silent it was *ringing*!" I set there and nod at him awhile. "Yessir, we was plenty scared, and we got out of there, and we ain't never been back. Left them twelve skulls lined up on that log grinning good-bye. Cause that ringing silence, know what that was? That was the venging spirits of Calusa Indins!"

Then I show him my Indin face, refusing to answer any questions for his own damn good, and he had to accept that out of his great respect for the noble redskin. He went away, shaking his head over the idea that a Indin could desecrate Indin graves, and bound and determined to do some desecrating on his own. I knowed just the mound the Frenchman wanted, and after that day, until he died, one of my kids was generally his guide, to keep him headed off the scent, keep him away from there as best we could.

Every one of these small creeks and canals had some kind of small shell mound at the head of it, he could hack his way into a hundred and not hit the right one. But south and west of Possum Key, well hid from the world in all them miles of mangrove, was a big old clamshell mound called Gopher Key, had a Calusa-built canal we called Sim's Creek and led straight out to the Gulf of Mexico. Don't know too much about ol' Sim, might been one them misfits from the Civil War hid out back up there on that key, took plenty of gopher tortoise for his dinner. Gopher Key weren't the place Chevelier was after, but it give him enough shell to dig the whole rest of his life.

Anyway, we took him over there to keep him busy. He got excited when he seen how well hid it was, and that long and straight canal built out of shell was his sure sign that Gopher Key must be a sacred place. For some years, the poor furious little feller was back in there digging white shell every chance he got. Heat was terrible, and the skeeters bit him up so bad he didn't have no French blood left in his old carcass. My boy Walter – that's the dark one – Walter said, Time those skeeters finished with him, that Frenchman would of lost all that French blood, he'd talk American just as good as we did.

Speaking of blood, my grandfather was real pure-blood Spanish Indin, didn't want a thing to do with the Muskogee

35

and Mikasuki Creeks – the Seminoles – that was taking over his Calusa country. But finally he understood what Chief Tecumseh warned us, that if Indin people didn't put away our feuds and fight the whites all in a bunch, there wouldn't be no land left to fight over. Sure enough, the white men lied and broke all their agreements. Here in Florida, they aimed to pen up any Indin they hadn't killed, ship that redskin sonofabitch to Oklahoma.

So Chekaika took some Spanish Indins and Mikasukis and went up the Calusa Hatchee and licked Lieutenant Colonel William Harney and his soldiers that was setting up the trading posts in Indin territory. Yup, Chekaika run Old Harney off into the bushes in his underwear, which were not forgiven and were not forgot. Chief Billy Bowlegs was a young man then, he was in on that one. After that, Chekaika took seventeen dugouts down around Cape Sable and over to the Keys, went to the Port of Entry on Indin Key, killed Dr Henry Perrine, the famous botanist, and caused a uproar. People called it a massacre, but this Dr Perrine had been recommending a canal to drain Cape Sable, in Calusa territory, they leave out that part.

From Indin Key Chekaika went back to Pavioni, but he figured the Army knew about them gardens, and Pavioni'd be the first place they'd come looking, so he took his people and went up Shark River to a big hammock maybe forty miles from the east coast. Shark River in them days was called Chok-ti Hatchee, the Long River, cause it was the main river of the Everglades, flowed all the way south from the Big Water, Okee-chobee. Not knowing about "Chok-ti," the white people figured them dumb Indins was trying to say "Shark," and that was that.

One afternoon he showed my mam the beautiful swal-low-tail hawk, kiting back and forth across the trees. *Ton-sa-be*, he said, very slow and careful, so his little daughter would remember it forever, the sun and the bird and the shining water-grass west of the hammock. *Tonsabe*. That word come rumbling out of him like a voice out of the earth. He told her how, seen from above, that bird's wings reflected the sky blue, but only God could see it from above, so *tonsabe* was God's bird, sent to watch over us.

Some of them whiskey Seminoles took dirty money to scout out Chief Chekaika's camp, and the Army sent Harney in pursuit out of Fort Dallas, on the Miami River. Took him by surprise on his home hammock. My mam and some others run off into the reeds, but her father was shot, and they strung him up before he finished dying. His people crept back in under the moonlight a day later, seen him hanging in the shadows of that big madeira, turning and turning. They took him down and buried him Indin way.

Mikasukis call that hammock Hanging Place, and they claim Chekaika for a Mikasuki, although he were Calusa to the bone. Chekaika was the biggest man in the People's memory, them Mikasukis will say the same even today. Some Mikasukis claim Chief Osceola, too, though Osceola was half-breed Muskogee Creek. Them poor Indins are desperate, I imagine.

After Harney got revenge on Chief Chekaika, he went on west across the Glades, come out at what they now call Harney River. The white people said he was the first to cross the Glades; Indins don't count, of course, and never did. After that he went out West, killed a bunch of Sioux. Made ol' Harney a general for that one, but he never got to be president like Andy Jackson and Zach Taylor and the rest of them Indin-fighters we had down here, cause us red fellers whipped Bill Harney's ass from start to finish.

The spring after Chekaika's death, the few warriors left put out word at the Green Corn Dance that any Indin seen talking to a white man would be killed, and they kept on hiding for another twenty years, till the whites got sick of getting licked and went off to fight their civil war instead.

The Florida Wars was the only Indin wars the U.S. Army never won, had to trick and bribe and steal to get the job done, get one Indin fighting with another. Finally they got to Billy Bowlegs, who had started out with Chekaika on the Calusa Hatchee. Took Old Billy over there to Washington, D.C., give him the name Mr William B. Legs, snuck him into some upstanding hotel where no durn greasy redskins was allowed. A few years after that, they made him rich, and Billy took his people west, out to the Territory.

Before Harney lit out for the Wild West – Chevelier told me this – that sonofagun was recommending the drainage of the Everglades, same as Dr Perrine. Recommended the ruin of south Florida is what it was, though it took 'em up till the new century to get around to it.

My mam went west to Wewoka, Oklahoma, with Billy Bowlegs's people from Deep Lake, signed right up with the Catholic mission so's to get her kids a bite to eat. I was out there in the Indin Territory all through my younger-hood. Later I went for a soldier in the Union Army, whole cavalry regiment of breeds and nigras slapping leather and raping and carousing all over the Territory and beyond. Some of them men was half-red and half-black, come down from strong slaves that run off across the wilderness and were taken in by Indins who prized their bravery, and they was the biggest, strongest men I ever saw. Indins called us buffalo soldiers cause the darker ones was buffalo color, with the same dark woolly nap. Indin women who seen us coming would lay down quick and throw sand up inside theirselves to take the fight out of us boys, y'know unless we got a lasso onto 'em first. That was part of the game, and seems like they had as much fun as what we did. Most of 'em, anyways.

Today I might be a little ashamed that I took up arms against my own Indin people, but in soldiering days, I didn't see them western tribes as people. Them lonely plains wasn't our country, and anyway, your Kioways and Comanches and Pawnees and whatnot weren't nothing but bare-ass renegades, couldn't make out a single word we said.

It was only later I got talking to an old medicine man, a Creek, and he asks me where I was born and bred, and I tell him Florida, and he says, How come you ain't standing on the land? Took me a while to see what he meant, Indin way, and then I seen it, and I run off from the buffalo soldiers and started working my way back south and east to the Land of Florida. Last thing I heard, the Union was still after me, but that was a long time ago. I was what you might call a deserter, and I been deserting ever since, least when it comes to white men and their ways.

There were three good reasons I come home. The Indins here – wild Mikasukis hiding back there in the Cypress – were still real Indins that never surrendered to the missions, never mind the Union. Also, the Islands was a sacred place of the Calusa homeland. Also, Chekaika lived at Pavioni before he retreated back into Long River, so Pavioni was as close to home as I could get.

Long about 1875, I threw in with William Allen, who was the first pioneer down in the Islands. Settled on Haiti Potato Creek – Haiti potato, that's cassava, so the Frenchman taught me – and changed the name to Allen's River. Kept that name right up until the nineties, when the Storter family changed the name to Everglade. I was never a man to be scared off by hard work, and things went along real amiable with my feller pioneers until I got close to Mary Weeks, at Chokoloskee Island, down the Bay.

Chukko-liskee, way the Indins say it, means "old house" – old Calusa house, I reckon, because Cypress Indins wasn't there in early times. Nobody remembered no old house, but the Frenchman figured it must of been some kind of temple. That big mound is back in there where Turner River comes down from the Glades with good fresh water – Turner River was once Chukko-liskee Creek – and it's well sheltered by five miles of outer islands. The settlements at Everglade and Half Way Creek was only mud bank, had their feet in water, but Chokoloskee Island

39

is a shell mound of one hundred fifty acres, some of it twenty foot above the sea. Them Indins knew what they were up to, they'd never be washed off Old House Key, not by no hurricane.

My father-in-law, Old Man John Weeks, pioneered truck farming down at Cape Sable in the Civil War, moved up to Haiti Potato Creek, moved around the Islands. He come full circle, washed ashore at Cape Sable once again before he died. This stumpy feller was the first to settle Chokoloskee Island. Pretty soon he sold off half the island to the Santinis, and after that Old Man Ludis Jenkins – Tant Jenkins's daddy – come in there with his Daniels woman and her Daniels children. One of them Daniels girls was later spoken for by Nicholas Santini and the other one was Henry Thompson's mother.

Old Man John Weeks, he passed for white, he had his honor there to think about, but it took me a while to figure out white people's attitudes. If I was a Choctaw, like I said, then I was a "good Indin." And if I was mulatta, like they claimed, then I was a free man, a free citizen. But this was 1876, right at the end of the Reconstruction, when the Rebs got things turned back their way all over the South, and life got uglier than it was already for people wasn't pink enough to suit 'em. So these crackers decide to protect their womenfolk and run this dang Choctaw right out of the settlement, maybe tar and feather him while they was at it. You ever seen a man in tar and feathers?

Well, I left quick, but I took Mary Weeks right along with me. We headed south, down the Ten Thousand Islands, all the way to the Calusa mound at Pavioni.

Folks never bothered us in them first years. It was only after Watson come, and mounds got scarce, and the Bay men was drifting farther south to find good fishing, that they began to take a different attitude. They was even friendly when I went up there to do my trading, once they seen I wasn't showing off my woman. They had her figured for a tramp that run off with a brown boy, and just so long as I didn't brag on it by showing her off before God-fearing citizens, why then it was not the nigger's fault, is the way they said it. Cause when it comes to white women, they'd say, a nigger just can't help hisself. Being a animal at heart, the poor devil just goes all to pieces.

Now that don't hardly mean that dingy rascal won't get gelded, burned, and lynched, cause they's only so much of his deviltry that decent Christian folk is going to tolerate. But so long as he respects their religious feelings, the way I done, and takes his low-life slut – that's what they called her! – and lives with the runaways and desperados, way out to hell and gone in them dark Islands where only the Devil is witness to their sacrilege – well, then, by Jesus, live and let live, ain't that right, boys? Let the Blessed Lord Above take care of His own sinners, cast 'em straight down to perdition on the Day of Judgment.

Some of them gray summers in the Islands when that rain never stopped, and children crying, and nothing for days and days and days but mud and hunger and bad skeeters, in a hellish steam wet and thick enough to stifle a dang frog – them long gray summers in that heat made a man half wonder if Judgment Day wasn't arrived already.

Once we was down on Chatham River, that place was our own Hamilton territory. White was welcome at my table, but not no more than any other color. Might been the one place in the country I could get away with it, but that don't mean it was forgiven. Mary's sister Sally married Jim Daniels, and later on their daughter Blanche married Frank Hamilton, whose daddy, James, moved to Lost Man's River along about that time. James Hamilton weren't no kind of kin, I don't believe that were his lawful name, no more'n it was mine, but his boy married right into our family. So James Hamiltons was kin to us, and they was our neighbors down that way for many years, but they told people they was no relation.

Long ago I give up trying to explain. I look at my hand and know there's seasoning in my blood, can't get away

41

from it. But John Leon would be a white man anywhere, and Eugene, he has white skin, too, also Annie, the youngest. But Walter, he is pretty dark, good narrow features but his skin is shadowed, and my older girl is a pretty shade of coffee. That color could be my mother's side, from times when Indins and slaves was on the run together all across north Florida. But that old woman was Indin to the heart, she never thought nothing but Indin way.

As for Mary Weeks, *her* mother Elizabeth was full-blood Seminole, supposed to be, the granddaughter of Chief Osceola. They can call us mulattas all they want, but we are Indian. Why heck, if this Hamilton bunch ain't Indin, then they ain't no Indins left in the U.S.A.

That first year, 1888, the Frenchman bought my claim on Chatham Bend. Said kind of gruff that we was welcome to stay on, but I had sign that it was time to go. I never felt right at Pavioni, never liked the feel of it. Pavioni had some old bad history, back to early times. It was what Indins call a power place, but it was bad power, something dark.

Indin people go by sign, they don't need no excuse to leave someplace that don't feel right, they just pick up their hind end and move it elsewhere. In them early years, we owned no more than we could pack into one boat, we traveled light. Get up and go and throw up a lean-to when you get there, and lash together a thatch hut where you might rest a spell.

Where we went was Possum Key, which wasn't but a few miles up the river. Had seven–eight good acres there, a lot more garden than we ever needed. That spring I was plume hunting for the Frenchman, and Possum was close to the big rookeries up the Glades creeks back of Alligator Bay, and handy to the Mikasukis, too, trading plumes and otter. The last Mikasuki renegades was hid in the Big Cypress on them hammocks back in Lost Man's Slough, and they was about the last wild Indins left. They never signed no treaty with no Great White Father. One dugout that come in to trade at Everglade in the late eighties was the first Indins seen by white people in thirty years. But they was spying around Possum Key maybe two years before that, they brung us turkeys, venison, and such, and we took their furs and bird plumes in to Storter's, got 'em trade goods, ordered a few guns from Colonel Wall's hardware store up in Port Tampa, and gave 'em a little cane liquor, too, to keep things lively.

Chevelier slep bad at Pavioni, same as we did, but it took him a whole year to admit it, that's how scientifical he was, and how cranky about giving up so much good ground. That was the greed in him. When I told him Pavioni was no good to him if he didn't farm it and couldn't get no sleep there, he'd shout at me, waving his arms. My kids could imitate him pretty good: "What you tek me for to be? A soo-paire-stee-shee-us domb redda-skin?" Pretty quick most everybody on the coast was imitating Jean Chevelier, we could speak his lingo near as good as he did.

Jean Chevelier sold his rights to the very first hombre who showed up, man named Will Raymond. "Is only for I cannot farm this forty ay-caire, is only for is foking shame is going to waste!" So we took the Frenchman home to Possum Key, built him a house to shelter all them books and bird skins and keep his old skeeter-bit bones out of the rain, and never got so much as a thank-you. When we was done, he shooed us out, acted tickled pink to see the end of us.

Oh yes, we kept the Frenchman in our family, though he didn't know it. To the very end, he frowned and squabbled like a coon. For a while he had a young boy helping, Henry Thompson, and after Henry left, he had Bill House, but he never trusted neither of 'em, never let 'em in too close, for fear them boys might let on about the treasure that any day now he was sure to find on Gopher Key. He yanked them boys hard, by the ear, and kept them scared of him. He was just too strong for a man his age, which is why folks always said the Devil owned him.

43

The Frenchman come right out and said he didn't hold with no Father Who art in Heaven. "Man is made in God's ee-mage? Who say so? Black man? Red man? Which man you talk about? White man? Yellow man? God is all these color? Say tabsurde! *Homo sapiens*, he got to shit, same like any foking animal. You telling to me your God got to shit too?" And he would glare all around at the green walls, the white sky and the wet heat, the summer silence, nodding his head. "Well, maybe you got something, Reechard. Maybe this foking place is where He done it."

Or that old man might point quick at the sun, point at a silver ripple in the water, saying, "Look quick! See there? *That* is God! *That* is *le Grand Mees-taire!*" He meant "Big Mister," case you don't speak French.

Being a Catholic, Mary Weeks hated that French heathen talk worse than the blasphemy. Even a God who moved His bowels was better than one who popped up every time you turned around. "Is right? Birt shit on your head, *that* is God too!" To keep the peace, I just shook my head over his terrible French ways, but I knew the truth of what he said all the way back in my bones, about sun and silver ripples, yes, and bird shit, too. However, for my Mary's sake, I told him what he sounded like was a dumb Indin.

So Pavioni went over to Chevelier, then Will Raymond. For a while it was called the Raymond Place, like Will was some kind of upstanding citizen. Don't think he was. I ain't pointing fingers, so I will say that the Frenchman and Old Man Atwell, back up Rodgers River, they was damn close to the only ones down in the Islands in them last years of the century that wasn't wanted someplace else.

Probably Will Raymond should have picked him a new name, got a fresh start. His widow sold his claim off to a stranger, and that stranger stayed here in the rivers close to twenty years, give or take a few years in the middle. If that bad power at Pavioni bothered him one bit, I never heard about it. I got friendly with him and took some pains to keep it that way, cause them years Mister Watson was our closest neighbor, never much more than a rifle shot away.

Mister Watson was a real good neighbor, yes, he was. Good farmer, too, the first to make the most of that good soil. Went right to work on a palm-log house, built two big rooms. Had hogs and two cows and red chickens, brought in a bay mare for plowing, set up a syrup mill, run his schooner from Port Tampa to Key West, and done just fine. Later on he brung in carpenters and good pine lumber, built him a fine frame house painted white, built docks, built sheds. Only ones between Fort Myers and Key West had anything to stand up to the Watson Place was Bill Collier at Marco and George Storter there in Everglade, both of 'em outstanding men along this coast. Well, Ed Watson kept right up with 'em most of the way.

All the same, I kept my distance, and warned my gang they was to do the same. If Mister Watson needed help we would be neighborly, you know, the same was he was, but all the times we was up and down his river, we never stopped to pass the time of day.

The day come when we had enough of Possum Key. The skeeters plagued the younger children, and their mother couldn't hardly fight 'em off, not when she cooked meals outside and done her chores with nothing but a smudge pot. So I moved my family to an island off the river mouth, where that sea wind kept them skeeters back into the bushes. I always called that place Trout Key, cause of all the sea trout on the grass banks off the shore, but the crackers called it Mormon Key, on account of that no-account old Richard Hamilton had other children by a common-law wife who was still living up around Arcadia. And after a while that fool name stuck, we used it too.

Them Chokoloskee boys called me mulatta, and they got that put down in the 1880 census. Talked against me not

45

so much because my skin was dark, but because a dark man had him a white wife. Well, Mary Weeks, who was writ down as white, she was darker than I am and still is, but she was daughter to John Weeks, so nobody paid her color no attention. John Weeks was white, and Mary's mother was Seminole Indin, so that dark come from her mother's side, unless there's something Old Man John ain't telling. My Mary, she tells our kids I am Indin, but when we are drunk and get to scrapping, she likes to recall how her daddy swore I was mulatta, and got that writ for all to see right on the 1880 census. She rues the day, as she often says, that a "colored man" went and stole a white girl's heart.

Henry Short was one of 'em who heard her say that, and I seen that muscle twitch along his jaw. Later I challenged him, inquiring what that wince was all about, and finally Henry blurted out how he didn't intend no disrespect, but some might say that running off with Richard Hamilton made my wife the shiftless one, not me. I reckon there is different ways that I could take that.

Henry Short would come visiting Bill House, who worked with Chevelier a year or two, and later years he'd stop over with us at Mormon Key. Big fine-looking young feller, color of light wood, looked more like a Indin than I did. He was lighter than all of us except Gene and Leon, and his features weren't so heavy as what Gene's were, but the Bay people called him Nigger Henry, Nigger Short. Gene didn't like it that he ate with us, said if Hamiltons had a nigger at their table, folks was bound to say that we was niggers too. And his own dark brother Walter would just look at Gene until Gene looked away. "I guess I can eat with Henry Short," he'd say, "if Henry Short can eat with me."

Which don't mean that Gene was wrong about what folks would say. He wasn't.

According to Jean Chevelier's way of thinking, there ought to be a law where any man who don't marry a different color would get castrated. That way *Homo sapiens* would stop his misery and plain damn stupidhood about his races and go on back to the color of First Man, which in Chevelier's opinion would work out pretty close to Richard Hamilton. Said the Hamiltons was making a fine start cause we had almost every shade of color, all we needed was a whisker of Chinese.

If you live Indin way, then you are Indin, color don't matter. It's how you respect the earth, not where you came from. Mary Weeks, she's a kind of Catholic, and our kids is Catholic, and I go along with it somewhat, and read my Bible, because I was raised up in a Catholic mission back in Oklahoma. But in my heart I am still Indin, which is why I kept on drifting south to Lost Man's River, as far from those mean-mouthed cracker folks as I could get.

Crackers don't know nothing about Indins cepting to shoot at, and most of these Indins you see today don't know nothing neither. Back in the First Seminole War, the runaway slaves fought side by side with Seminoles, and lived as Indins, a lot of 'em. You take some of them ragtag Muskogee Seminoles up around Lake Okeechobee, a lot of 'em's got a big swipe of the tarbrush, but you'd never know it from the way they act toward colored people.

These Cypress Indins, who are Mikasuki Creeks, some of 'em still know a little about Indin way. They can't keep it going too much longer, and they know it, and maybe that's why they sometimes act so desperate. In the old days, if a Mikasuki woman trafficked with a black man, or a white man, either, her people might take and kill 'em both, and leave the child to die out in the cypress. Maybe that made 'em feel a little better, but it never made a spit of difference in the long run. People move around these days, get all mixed up. Don't matter what our color is, we all going to be brown boys when the smoke clears.

After Bill House left, Old Man Chevelier kind of adopted

47

Leon and young Liza and they visited with him and took care of him and kept an eye on him, and he stayed right there on Possum Key until he died.

*Until the second half of the nineteenth century, the south-
ern half of the Florida peninsula, and in particular its far
south-western region, was scarcely known. This rainy and
mosquito-ridden labyrinth of mangrove islands and dark
tidal rivers was all but uninhabited, despite the marvelous
abundance of its fish and game. "The Ten Thousand
Islands," as one naturalist has written, "is a region of
mystery and loneliness: gloomy, monotonous, weird, and
strange, yet possessing a decided fascination. To the casual
stranger each and every part of the region looks exactly
like the rest; each islet and water passage seems but the
counterpart of hundreds of others. Even those . . . familiar
with its tortuous channels often get lost . . . wandering
hopeless for days among its labyrinthine ways."*

*Of the thousands of islands, less than a hundred – mostly
in the north – rise more than one foot above sea level, and
on most of these, the high ground is too limited to build
upon: the more or less habitable barrier islands include
perhaps thirty on the Gulf with sand banks up to six feet
high and about forty "hammock" islands farther inland.
On these, as a precaution against hurricane, the Calusa
constructed substantial shell mounds – or, more properly,
hilly ridges – up to twenty feet in height, on which pockets
of soil suitable for farming had accumulated. There were
also extensive mainland mounds at Turner River that were
later farmed by Chokoloskee pioneers.*

*Chatham Bend, the largest shell mound between Choko-
loskee and Cape Sable, is first described in the journals of
Surgeon-General Thomas Lawson, who in February of
1838, during the First Seminole War, led a U.S. Army
expedition against "the Spanish Indians" – people of
Calusa ancestry returned from Cuba to Florida by the*

Spanish – to discourage smuggling of guns and ammunition from Cuba to the Seminoles.

> We anchored opposite the mouth of Pavilion River, near which we saw a smoke, and on the banks of which, six or eight miles up, the Pilot stated positively that we would find twenty families of Indians, and perhaps others from the interior of the country. . . . Here again we were doomed to meet with disappointment, for the town was tenanted by no living thing, man or beast. . . . The site of this village is very beautiful . . . and the ground on both sides of the river more valuable than any I have seen in this section of the country. The only objection to it is, that there is no fresh water on it, or in its vicinity. . . .

A later Army expedition found a village of twelve palm-thatch houses and a large forty-acre garden, but which Indians these were was not determined; they may have been the last wild band of Mikasuki under Arpeika, called Sam Jones, or perhaps a remnant of the "Spanish Indians." In the late eighties Pavioni, as the Indians called it, was occupied briefly by Richard Hamilton, who sold his claim to a Frenchman, M. A. LeChevallier, who sold it in turn to a fugitive, Will Raymond.

Richard Hamilton and Mr. Chevallier, who settled nearby islands, were Mr Watson's closest neighbors for many years. Hamilton was rumored to be a grandson of the great Spanish Indian war chief Chekaika, who perpetrated the massacre of Dr Perrine and others at Indian Key in 1840 and who was subsequently shot, then hung, by Lieutenant Colonel Harney's expedition of pursuit from the Miami River into the Everglades.

> Our tent was pitched within a short distance of the tree on which Chakika was suspended. The night was

beautiful, and the bright rising moon displayed to my
view as I lay on my bed the gigantic proportions of this
once great and much dreaded warrior. He is said to
have been the largest Indian in Florida, and the sound
of his very name to have been a terror to his Tribe.

The expedition continued south and west, emerging at last
at what is now called Harney River – the first white men
ever to traverse the peninsula of southern Florida.

On the Coast and Geodetic Survey charts for 1889,
Chatham Bend is identified as "the Raymond Place," but
Will Raymond gave up Chatham Bend a few years later,
having been killed by sheriff's deputies from Key West.
Why Richard Hamilton, then Chevelier, abandoned that
large mound so speedily is more mysterious. But Pavioni
had a malevolent reputation, and E. J. Watson, who
acquired the rights from the Widow Raymond, was the
only white man ever to remain more than a year or two;
he farmed the Bend for nearly twenty years.

Monsieur LeChevallier, known familiarly along that
coast as "Jean Chevelier" (pronounced "Shovel-leer") or
simply "the old Frenchman," was a significant figure in
Mr Watson's early years in southwest Florida. Monsieur
Chevelier (as we may as well call him, since "Chevelier
Bay" commemorates this spelling in the Ten Thousand
Islands) was probably the first large-scale commercial
hunter in that region of egret and other species killed for
their decorative plumes. In 1879, he established a bird
plume operation at Tampa Bay which apparently occupied
him for about five years. In 1885, he hired the sloop Bonton
to conduct his party from the new settlement on the Miami
River around the Keys to the Ten Thousand Islands. The
party included Louis and Guy Bradley, young plume hunters of the region. (Guy Bradley later became the first
Monroe County game warden, with salary paid by the
Audubon Society. He was murdered by a former associate

51

in 1905 — one of the several local killings popularly attributed to Mr Watson, who by that time had become notorious.) Charles Pierce kept a lively journal of the voyage, which took place in the spring and summer of that year.

I had heard a great deal about an old Frenchman, M. LeChevelier, a taxidermist, collector of bird skins and plumes, who was living up the Miami river.... Mr Chevelier is French and cannot talk good English.... Pelican skins are the main object of the trip, plumes next, also cormorant skins, in fact all kinds of birds. Mr Chevelier has a market for all of them in Paris. He gets fifty cents for the pelican skins, twenty-five cents for least tern, $10 for great white heron and $25 for flamingo. Great white herons are scarce and flamingos more so. If it was not for that we would soon make the old man rich.

Despite a right hand crippled by his own gun, Chevelier blazed away with his young associates. The Bonton *log is a catalogue of destroyed birds, relieved here and there by lively accounts of storm and wayfarers, mosquitoes, and old Key West, where the party was welcomed and assisted by Chevelier's associate, "Capt Cary." Presumably this is Elijah Carey (see House and Hamilton interviews), who would later join Chevelier in his plume-birding operations.*

In the Ten Thousand Islands, the Bonton *anchored off Shark River and also "inside of Pavilion Key," in pursuit of roseate spoonbills, egrets, boobies and white pelicans. Farther up the coast, "we came to an island that had a palmetto shack on it where lived an old Portuguese named Gomez with his cracker wife. Mr Chevelier had known Gomez some years before." This was Gomez or Panther Key, from which Gomez guided them on a hunt for roseate spoonbills (or "pink curlew") the next morning.*

Juan Gomez, like Mr Watson, was a local legend in the

Islands, still celebrated for the claim that in his youth he had been addressed kindly by the emperor Napoleon in Madrid, Spain, and had later sailed with a buccaneer named Gasparilla. By his own calculation, Gomez was 108 years old at the time of the Bonton's *visit, and he was still there in 1900, when a visitor described this region as "that maze of intricate channels . . . a place that was once the refuge of pirates, and even now retains the flavor of blood-thirsty tales."*

Although harshly criticized a few years later by W. E. D. Scott (in the Audubon Society publication called The Auk) *for "wanton destruction" at Tampa Bay in 1879, M. Chevelier was a dedicated naturalist. Doubtless the plume-bird shooting financed his scientific investigations, since he was collecting in Labrador and donating bird skins to the Smithsonian as early as 1869. Since Scott's day, three "LeChevellier" bird skins have turned up at the Smithsonian and at the American Museum of Natural History in New York. Scott himself listed seven rare bird specimens credited to "A. Lechevallier," including two short-tailed hawks collected at "Chatham Bay" in 1888 and early 1889.*

Jean Chevelier was drawn fatally to this wild coast, where he would spend the remainder of his life. In his first year he lived on the great Calusa mound on Chatham Bend, having purchased quitclaim rights from Richard Hamilton (see interviews); the Hamilton clan, which remained close to him, was also closely associated with Mr Watson.

BILL HOUSE

I worked for the Frenchman for some years, guiding, plume hunting, and bird collecting, nests and eggs. Chevelier claimed he never shot uncommon birds except as a collector, and he liked to tell how he'd trained boys like Louis and Guy Bradley, also Henry Thompson and myself, not to shoot into no flocks but single out the birds we was really after. I guess that was mostly true, most of the time.

Plume hunters never shot cept in the breeding season when egret plumes are coming out real good. When them nestlings get pretty well pinfeathered, and squawking loud cause they are always hungry, them parent birds lose the little sense God give 'em, they are going to come in to tend their young no matter what, and a man using one of them Flobert rifles that don't snap no louder than a twig can stand there under the trees in a big rookery and pick them birds off fast as he can reload.

A broke-up rookery, that ain't a picture you want to think about too much. The pile of carcasses left behind when you strip the plumes and move on to the next place is just pitiful, and it's a piss-poor way to harvest, cause there ain't no adults left to feed them starving young 'uns and protect 'em from the sun and rain, let alone the crows and buzzards that come sailing and flopping in, tear 'em to pieces. A real big rookery like that offshore island the Frenchman worked, up Tampa Bay, four–five hundred acre of black mangrove, maybe ten nests to a tree – hell, might take you three–four years to clean it out, but after that, them birds is gone for good.

It's the dead silence after all the shooting that comes

back today, though I never stuck around to hear it; I kind of remember it when I am dreaming. Them ghostly white trees and dead white ground, the sun and silence and the dry stink of guano, the squawking and shrieking and flopping of dark wings, and varmints hurrying without no sound – coons, rats, and possums, biting and biting, and the ants flowing up all them pale trees in dark snaky ribbons to bite at them raw scrawny things that's backed up to the edge of the nest, gullet pulsing and mouth open wide for the food and water that ain't never going to come. Luckiest ones will perish before something finds 'em, cause they's so many young that the carrion birds just can't keep up. Damn buzzards gets so stuffed they can't hardly fly, just set hunched up on them dead limbs like them queer growths on the pond cypress limbs in the bare winter.

The Frenchman looked like some kind of raccoon – regular coon mask! Bright black eyes and sharp brows, kind of a humpy walk, little thin, wet legs, all set to bite. Maybe his heart was in the right place, maybe not.

Chevelier never did approve of humankind, and he purely hated the rich Yankees off them yachts who come whooping up our rivers in the winters, blazing away at anything that moved, purely hated fellers like Ed Watson, who shot up the best rookeries in spring. I told the Frenchman that to live here in the Islands, a man had to take everything in its own season, but that old fella would just cuss me out in French, waving that shot-up hand of his to shoo me off. Pretty quick, he would start in to yelling about Watson's big ideas about developing this coast, draining the whole Everglades while he was at it. L'Empereur! Chevelier called him. L'Empereur! That drainage talk went all the way back to General Harney, who come out on the wrong coast through Harney River, but it never got cranked up, y'know, till Watson's time. Well, they built them big canals and dikes, crisscrossed the eastern Glades, but this west part is more lonesome that it ever was, cause the big animals and birds are mostly gone. Used to call this place God's country, and we still do, cause nobody but God would want no part of it.

It's true, we had no use for no invaders, and fast as the federal government put in channel markers for them yachts, we'd haul 'em out. Home people didn't need no markers, and we didn't want none. From what we heard, there wasn't a river in north Florida but was all shot out, not by us plume hunters but by Yankee tourists on the river steamers. Real hunters don't waste powder and shot on what can't be eaten or sold, but these sports shot at everything that flew. They crippled up a lot more than they killed and kept on going, just let them dead birds float away downriver.

We never had no time for sport, we was too busy living along, fighting the skeeters. In the Islands we worked from dawn till dark, just to get by. Didn't hardly know what sport might be till we all got hired out as sport-fish guides and hunters. This was some years later, after the fish and game was gone for good.

That Old Frenchman was fighting mad at some Yankee ornithologue named Scut who claimed right in a magazine that Jean Chevelier shot more birds than anybody on the Gulf Coast. "This foking Scut," the Frenchman said, "come here on his vacation to look at his fine feathered foking friends. Visit one big rookery at Pinellas, defam LeChevallier for the worse butch-aire in west Florida! Well, who it is buy my birt specimen? Who it is write that ivoire-beel wooda-pecker ver' rare, then go and shoot ivoire-beel wooda-pecker from the only nest he evaire find? Who it is? This foking Scut! Sham me among my colleague, attack-a me in *Au-du-bon* Society! All of the same, he buy from my Punta Rassa colleague this short-tailed hawk LeChevallier collect at Chatham Bend! And after I am died, you are going to see it! Damn foking Scut collect first short-tailed hawk in North Amerique! Wait to see it what I am telling it to you!"

56

Sometimes his old plume-hunting partners Louis and Guy Bradley would come north from Flamingo, prospecting for new rookeries along our coast. We were glad to have the company, but we never passed along no information. Guy never said much but he looked at you so straight that you felt shifty just on general principles. He was the first hunter I heard say that plume hunting was winding down in southwest Florida. Guy Bradley said, "Plain disagrees with me to shoot them things no more. Ain't got my heart into it." I never did admit to Guy how I was collecting bird eggs for the Frenchman. Swaller-tail kite got up to fifteen dollars for a egg, depending on how bright that egg was marked. People all over America and Europe wanted them wild bird eggs, no telling why.

One night the old man came home from Gopher Key, and I laid out a nice swallow-tail clutch next to his plate, and all he done was grunt out something cantankerous about halfwit foking crackers setting out kite eggs where they was most likely to get broke. When he didn't hardly stop to look 'em over, I knowed I was in for it. Henry Thompson told me when I signed on with the Frenchman that the old frog croaked at everyone to hide how lonesome his life was out in the swamp, but this one night I wasn't so dang sure. I put on my best Sunday smile and sing out bright and cheery from the stove, "Come and get it, Mister Chevelier!" He didn't need no more'n that to huff up like a tom turkey and start gobbling.

"Only in this sacre Amerique could 'Monsieur le Baron Anton de LeChevallier' become 'Mis-ter Jeen Shovel-leer'! These am-bay-seel damn crackaire call me Shovel-*leer*! For *why*? I ask you it – for *why*?"

He stabbed at the venison and grits on his tin plate, then jabbd his fork like he aimed to punch my eyes out.

"What is this craziness of *guns* in this con-try barbare? First time I go to Chatham Bend, Richard Hamilton stick his rifle in my face like I stick this fork to you! Then his blond angel, John Leon, *he* come running out, prepare to shoot! A little boy! *He* wish to shoot me! Nex t'ing, Will Raymond, they shoot *him*! For why? Because Will Raymond shoot some *other* crazy crackaire! And who come next? This foking Wat-son! Foking crazy man! Satan foo! Try to shoot my head off of me! For why? For the plaiseer! I hear him *laughing*! Satan *foo*!"

Henry Thompson allowed as how his Mister Watson was an expert shot, that he never missed except on purpose, so I advised the Frenchman how maybe it was some kind of joke.

"*Choke?* You are crazy, too?" Chevelier held up thumb and forefinger to show how close that bullet clipped his ear. "A man who choke with bullets . . . ? That is *choke*?"

Next day Chevelier ordered me to row him down to Mormon Key because he wanted to consult with Richard Hamilton. We had to go by the Watson Place, and I had an eye out for the owner, just shipped my oars and drifted past so's Mister Watson couldn't hear them thole pins creak against the current.

That was before the big white house was built, there was just Will Raymond's old palmetta shack that Watson was using for his hogs and a small thatched cabin for humankind. I didn't see no sign of Henry Thompson, but I seen Watson out in his high cane, and I edged the skiff in closer to the bank so's he wouldn't see us.

Well, damn if that man don't stiffen like a cat caught in the open, turn his head real slow, and look straight at us. He was already half into a crouch, and when he saw us, he dropped quick to one knee and reached into his shirt. That quickness, and the way he knowed that we was there, give me a chill.

How come he carried a gun into the field? And why did he go for it so fast?

I find out quick. That old French fool is standing up and ricketing around, and I turn to see he has raised his shooting iron and drawed a bead on Watson! I yell *Sit down!*

and I row that boat right out from under him. He sits down in the stern sheets hard, nearly goes overboard. I row all-out and get in under the bank and down around the Bend before Ed Watson can run up to the water's edge and pick us off. The news was just out about what he done to Dolphus Santini at Key West, and when we was safe away downriver, I tell the Frenchman, Please, sir, don't go pointing guns at Ed J. Watson, not while young Bill House is in the boat!

While Mr Chevelier was away down at Key West, I was to work my keep out at the Hamiltons'. I weren't so easy in their company, though they was kind to me. Mrs Mary Hamilton passed for white, but Hamiltons didn't have much use for white people, which was probably why they lived way off down in the Islands. That Hamilton gang was kind of outcasts, didn't fit with niggers and whites wouldn't have 'em, so them and that Frenchman naturally got friendly. Old Man Richard called himself Choctaw, and he had Injun features, that's for sure, but one look at his boy Walter told you that Choctaw wasn't the whole story.

Of that whole bunch, only Eugene ever made good friends at Chokoloskee, and he was very friendly to me from the start. But some way I could not warm up to Gene, and never did, the whole rest of my life. Right from a boy – back there in 1895, he was just twelve – Gene had something to prove, he weren't never just take-me-or-don't like his brother Leon.

Henry Short used to visit with the Hamiltons, used to eat at their table, and he held a high opinion of that family. The Hamiltons acted white as anybody, but I don't believe that Henry thought so or he wouldn't have made himself so much to home.

Henry said he come down there to see me, and maybe he believed that one himself, cause we were raised together, but the one he really come to visit was young Liza. I believe it was love at first sight, on his side anyway. She weren't even a woman yet, but she was a golden coffee color, and I would have give up my right arm, or left arm anyway, to see her spread out in the sun without no clothes on. It thickened up my blood merely to think about it. Henry was in the same fix I was, one look at each other and we'd start to laugh, that's how jittery and fired-up young Liza made us.

Henry Short, who was raised up by my daddy, was only half a nigger, maybe less, had very light skin and narrow features, but him and Old Man Richard had bad hair. One time me and Henry was visiting the Hamiltons, and Old Man Richard was carrying on about Injun ancestry, and how Henry Short looked like a Choctaw, too. And Henry kept looking across at me, got more agitated than I ever seen him, cause Henry Short was a born stickler for truth. Finally he whispered, "Heck, I ain't Choctaw, Mr Richard, I am chock full o' nigger, that's what *I* am." The old man looks around, see where his wife was, and after that he said, "Well, don't go telling my Mary," and he laughed. Didn't care none, long as his old woman didn't hear about it.

Those were Jim Crow days for nigras in this country, and Old Man Richard probably knew that Henry might of said that just to show me that eating at the Hamilton table didn't give him no funny ideas about his place. Or maybe all of 'em was teasing me, come to think about it. I just don't know. Hell, we don't know those people, we just think we do. Funny feeling, being the outsider – ever try that? I didn't care for it, I'll tell you. Made me think too much.

Back in Chokoloskee, I told the men what Henry Short had said to Richard Hamilton, and pretty soon that got twisted around, cause folks was always looking for to laugh at Old Man Richard. Way they said it, it was Nigger Henry telling that goldurn mulatter, *Hell, no, you ain't Choctaw! What you are is chock full o' nigger, just like me!* No, no, I told 'em, that ain't the way it was! But I laughed, too, and I paid for that laugh all my life. Cause they're *still*

60

telling that old tale down there about chock full o' nigger, don't care one bit about the truth, and I flinch every time I have to hear it.

Anyway, young Eugene Hamilton didn't care none for what Henry said. Gene jumps up so fast he spills his plate. "Well, we ain't niggers, boy, at least *I* ain't, but it sure looks like we're nigger-lovers around here, letting you set at our table!" Gene is looking more at me than Henry, and I got the idea this was a message that Bill House was supposed to take on back to Chokoloskee, that Gene Hamilton didn't care to eat with niggers even if the rest of 'em put up with it. "It ain't my table," Gene is sayng to Henry, glaring at his daddy, "so I can't run you off, but I don't have to eat at it, neither!" And he grabs his plate and marches out onto the stoop.

Richard Hamilton never liked commotion, and he ain't figured out yet how to handle this. But the older boy, Walter, he's a lot darker than Henry Short, he looks at Gene marching out and laughs. "Go to hell!" Gene yells out. Hearing that language, his mother comes a-running from the cookhouse and whaps his head with her wood ladle.

I catch Walter's eye and wish I hadn't. He had winked at me when Gene stomped out the door, but sitting there in his dark skin, he was shamed bad. I snuck a good look at him after that, probably first time I ever did. Next to young Liza, dark Walter Hamilton was the handsomest of all that handsome family.

The Hamiltons flagged down the *Bertie Lee*, Cap'n R. B. Storter, who took the Frenchman over to Key West. Two weeks later that old man was back with Elijah Carey, who aimed to go partners with us in the plume trade. There was bigger rookeries down around Cape Sable, which the Bradleys was working with the Roberts boys, but the Cape was just too far from Gopher Key. With Watson around, Mr Chevelier wanted some company, and to make sure he got it, he told Carey his high hopes about Calusa treasure. He was getting too old to dig all day in hot white shell, and didn't want to let me help him for fear I might let on at Chokoloskee.

Captain Lige Carey stayed awhile, built him his own house on Possum Key. One night Lige told what had took place at George Bartlum's produce auction room down at Cayo Hueso, or Bone Key – that was the real name for Key West, Lige informed us – how Watson come in there good and drunk and announced to Dolphus Santini of Chokoloskee that he needed help with a land claim in the Islands.

Adolphus Santini was amongst the oldest settlers on Chokoloskee, our leading landowner and farmer right up until the time he left, in '99. John Weeks come first in '74, if you don't count whoever planted them large lime trees, and he give half the island to Santinis to keep him company, and that family got the other half after Weeks moved to Flamingo. The Santinis built their first real house above the drift line of the '73 hurricane, and later on they built a chapel – they was Catholics.

Dolphus's brother Nicholas, called him Tino, was a fisherman, took turtle eggs for about four months in the spring season. He used to say the Santinis was Corsicans like Napoleon, but he never said why they left South Carolina, and nobody asked; that was a question that was never asked down in the Islands. Old Man James Hamilton, down Lost Man's River, it come out on his deathbed that he was known in other parts as Hopkins, but nobody asked why he got tired of that name, and he never said.

Along about 1877, Santinis filed a claim to "160 acres more or less on Chokoloskee Island among the Ten Thousand Islands of Florida." That's mostly less, cause there ain't one hundred fifty acres on the whole island. Old Injun War scout named Dick Turner, same feller who guided the U.S. Army on a raid to smoke out the last of Billy Bowlegs's warriors and got his captain killed up around Deep Lake

– Dick Turner filed a claim back in '78 for eighty acres of Calusa mounds that he was farming up on Turner's River. Later he sold 'em to a Key West man, who sold 'em to my dad, Daniel David House, for two thousand dollars. Far as I know, Santini and Turner was the only claims except Storters in Everglade that was down on paper at that time, and even them ones wasn't validated until 1902. All anybody had was quitclaim rights, Watson included. Pay me to get the heck off, that's all it was.

Watson knew about them paper claims, he was always asking questions. What he wanted to do, we figured later, was tie up as much high land as he could from Chatham Bend to Lost Man's River, maybe all the way south to Harney River, then file a claim the way Santini done. Santini knew his way around the law, and Watson went to him for help. But rumors about E. J. Watson had commenced to wander, and maybe Ed figured he needed an upstanding citizen to back him up.

Well, I wasn't there so I don't know what happened, but Elijah Carey said he seen it. Dick Sawyer always claimed that he was there, Dick never missed much, and he told me pretty good about it, too.

Santini was our leading citizen, and he was also the outstanding farmer, nobody near him, mostly cause he owned all the good land. Chokoloskee is just one big mound that them old Calusas started up from scratch. Tomatoes did fine high on the mounds, sugarcane down on the flats, with any vegetable you wanted in between. By 1884 Dolphus Santini had over two hundred alligator pear trees, and he also had Jamaica apples, sour and sweet oranges, bananas, guavas – biggest farm in that part of the country. Most all our Chokoloskee produce went south to Key West, cause Key West could claim eighteen thousand head if you was to count Yankees and nigras. In them days, Fort Myers, the biggest city in Lee Country, never had but seven hundred. On the coast between, not counting Injuns, I don't believe there was two hundred people, and half of 'em lived on Chokoloskee Bay.

Dolphus had been hearing a sight more than he cared to about this feller Watson down on Chatham Bend, how Watson raised up bigger hogs than anyone around, how Watson could grow tomatoes on an orster bar, could grow him damn near anything and a lot of it. He had also heard rumors that Watson was a wanted man. Dolphus was a drinker, too, and that night he was drunk. According to Captain Elijah Carey, who was in the thick of it, Santini advised Mister Watson that the State of Florida would not give preemption papers to any citizen who had not paid his debts to society, said Watson better look out for his own business.

Watson didn't show a thing, just kind of nodded, like what Dolphus said made pretty good sense. Then he put his hand into his pocket and moved up alongside Dolphus, never spoke, and the whole crowd skittered to the side like baby ducklings, that's how fast they made that man some room. And this was before they knew what they know now about Ed Watson.

It was the look on Watson's face that scared 'em worst, or that's what Lige said. Watson could cuss him a blue streak when he got aggravated, but the worse he cussed, the easier you felt, cause he'd end up saying something so outrageous that the whole outburst would collapse, he'd bust out laughing. When he was truly angry he went cold. That ruddy face went stiff and dead, it turned to wood. What Elijah Carey noticed was, them stone eyes never blinked but once – that's how come he noticed it – and that blink was very, very slow.

Though Watson hadn't touched Santini, he stood much too close, he had ol' Dolphus backed against a table. Then he whispered how he hadn't heard too good, but it sure sounded like some dirty guinea slander. Would Dolphus care to make his meaning plain? Watson spoke to him very soft, and that soft voice should of been a warning, but

Dolphus was too puffed up to hear, he probably thought he had this feller buffaloed.

The whole auction room fell still, but Dolphus was too full of his own noise to hear that quiet. He cleared his throat and smiled at all the men, winking one eye, and then he says, "Our state of Florida don't welcome desperados on the run from somewheres else."

Watson's bowie knife was at his throat before he finished. Watson drew a thin red line, then told Santini to beg his pardon or have his throat cut. Santini was too scared to talk, so Watson went ahead and cut his throat, near took his head off, spattered blood across three bushel of cucumbers. Would have finished the job, too, if they hadn't stopped him. Captain Lige claimed he was one of the men who got that knife away.

When Watson drew that knife under Santini's jaw, in the split second before the blood jumped out, he looked as careful as a man slitting a melon. That, Lige said, is what scared folks the most. But when they grabbed his arm, he about went crazy, hollered out that nobody weren't going to lynch Ed Watson, took four or five of 'em to rassle him down to the floor. By the time they got that knife away, he had started laughing. "I'm ticklish," that's what he said, and laughed some more.

Somebody run quick and fetched a doctor, and it was known that Dolphus had survived it by the time the news got back to Chokoloskee, though he carried a thick purple scar for life.

At the hearing Watson raised up his right hand, swore on the Bible that he never meant to kill Mr Santini. If he'd meant that, why it stands to reason that he would have done it. He said this looking real sincere, and everybody laughed, and he grinned too, grinned right at Dolphus, who looked like he was strangling in all them bandages.

Dolphus's boy Lawrence told me once that Watson struck his father without warning, just reached around him from behind and cut his throat. That may be true but it ain't the way Lige Carey told it.

At that time there was no law down here, men settled their differences amongst themselves, and a killing was not what you might call uncommon, though the Islands never was so bad as outsiders make out. But Key West had some law, so Ed paid Dolphus nine hundred dollars in hard cash not to take the case to court, and that was that. We never thought too much about it.

But Key West was getting tired of Ed Watson, and Sheriff Frank Knight liked to use his telegraph machine, so he sent around to see if Ed had any record, got word this man was on the dodge, just like Dolphus said. Telegraph said a Edgar A. Watson was the only one was ever charged with the murder of Belle Starr, Queen of the Outlaws, out in Indian Territory back in '89. There was a prison escape from Arkansas, and a killing in north Florida some years back, and another in Arcadia on his way here.

Watson explained all that away. Said Edgar A. Watson was a well-known polecat, he had knew him personal, but Edgar J. Watson was a solid citizen and a fine feller. By the time the word come to arrest him, ship him back to Arkansas, Edgar J. was way back in the rivers.

The man killed in Arcadia was named Quinn Bass. Our family homesteaded in Arcadia awhile before we drifted south to Turner River, and my pap knowed the dead man as a boy, and he thought Quinn Bass was better off deceased than not. Sheriff O. H. Dishong up there must of thought so too, cause they let Ed Watson pay his way out of that scrape, same as they done in Key West with Santini. Only difference was, Quinn Bass never sat up to count his money.

So word got out that in Arkansas, maybe north Florida, too, Ed Watson was still a wanted man, which was why he come down here in the first place. Well, naturally, folks begun to worry. They was used to drifters and backcountry

66

killers, not well-dressed famous desperadoes who was wanted all over the Wild West.

But nobody put no questions to this feller. If lawmen was hunting him across four states, it was not our business. That was his own responsibility, and he took it. If any man could of used a change of name, it was Ed Watson, but Ed was always who he was, come hell or high water, and you had to like that. Cepting Mr Chevelier, we *all* liked the man, that's the God's truth. We seen from the first that he was a good farmer and a generous neighbor, and for many years we done our best to forget the rest.

"Key West" (from the Spanish "Cayo Hueso") was made a Navy base in the 1830s to deal with the rampant smugglers and pirates. An account of 1885 provides the flavor of Key West as E. J. Watson must have known it in his first years in the Islands.

Moonlight beautiful over the harbor. Find anchorage near the wharf. See many boats and lights about us. All quiet except chickens and dogs.

Wind from south, very warm and sultry. . . . Engage a carriage for a view around the town. The island is seven by three miles in extent, prettily built in places with frame houses, with green blinds, surrounded by thick luxuriant growths of tropical trees and flowers. Streets narrow; rather hard roads on the bed of natural limestone rock . . . a great many pools of stagnant water in the streets. Many Spanish faces and voices; strange hotels with strange fruits and customs. The tropical coconut palm is all prevalent and very striking; some house yards have numbers of them. The laurel tree . . . almond trees, tamarinds full of their bean-like fruit. Many varieties of the acacia family. Sappadillo, lime trees, date palms, sugar apples, Pride of India, banyans, and many others. Drove over to the empty fort commanding the harbor, and down the beach, on which were washed up a good many cup sponges. Past the sponge-drying yards, and back to the boat for supper. Beautiful evening; all sat on deck until late, enjoying the warmth, the setting sun glow, and the moonlight.

HENRY THOMPSON

Mister Watson told me he had family someplace, but he never said too much about it, not in front of Henrietta Daniels. Henrietta – he called my mother Netta – come to keep house for Mister Watson and brought Tant with her. Tant Jenkins was her young half brother, not much older than me.

That day Mister Watson come back from Everglade so darn excited, Tant was plume hunting back in the rivers. He snuck off every time Mister Watson went away, left the work to me. Henrietta is setting there on the front stoop with Minnie hitched up to her bosom, and Mister Watson ain't hardly tied up before he hollers all the way from the boat landing, "Netta honey, you better start thinking about packing up, I have my people coming!" He shows me a letter from a Mrs Jane D. Watson of north Florida, and in it was a brown picture of three kids in Sunday best. Young Eddie and little Lucius wore white high collars and black knicker suits, and Miss Carrie in her prim white frock with a big ribbon bow and buckle shoes was the prettiest little thing I ever saw. On the back was written, "Rob was shy, he would not sit for his picture!"

"Rob's not shy," Mister Watson said, "Rob is so sore at his daddy that his tail's sizzling like a rattler!" I don't know why that struck him funny but it did, and he laughed some more when he seen that I weren't laughing. "Well," he sighed, "I don't believe that Mrs Watson would have got in touch with us if her husband was such a terrible bad feller, what do you think, Henry?" And he chuckled some more, that's how tickled he was by the way his life was working out. Before leaving Everglade, he said, he tele-graphed money for their tickets, and expected to meet 'em at Punta Gorda toward the end of the month.

Mister Watson was so overjoyed he clean forgot about our feelings. So there I am at the landing helping with the boat, and I don't know where to look, that's how ashamed I am, for me and my mother both. I got on good with Mister Watson, and after two years, his place was my home. This was the first real family I ever knew, cause Mister Watson was kind of a dad to me, and let me think so, that's how good he treated me. Now I'd have to head out, too, with no idea where to go and start all over.

When my mother first come to Chatham Bend, I been out on my own for a few years, and she seemed more like some noisy older sister. I never known my father, never laid eyes on him, he was a English sailor at Key West that came and went. I got borned there back in 1879. Had a younger brother, Joe, called him Thompson, too, but Henrietta left Joe behind with our uncle John Henry Dani-els at Fakahatchee, hardly seen him one year to the next.

Well, Henrietta was good-hearted, never mind her loose bosom and loud ways, and with her and Tant there, we made a family at the table, I got to feeling I belonged someplace. So I hated the reckless way that Mister Watson was fixing to toss her out like nigger help, and his own infant, Minnie, along with her. I was feeling all thick and funny in my heart and chest, ready to fight somebody. When he swung that crate of stores to me off of the boat deck, I banged it on the dock so hard that a slat busted.

That bang was somewhat louder than I wanted, and the sharp noise caught him by surprise, cause he crouched and dropped the next crate to the deck, that's how fast his hand shot for his pocket. Then he straightened slow, picked up the crate, carried it across himself and set it carefully on that dock longside the other.

"You look like you swallowed a frog, boy. Spit it out."

He was hot, but I was hotter, and I set my hat forward

on my head and spit, not too close and not too far from them Western boots he always wore when he went up to town. I was scared to talk for fear my voice was pinched or all gummed up, so I just give him a sideways look like a mean dog and put my hands on the next crate, to let him know I'm here to do my work, never mind no questions.

But he keeps on gazing, stone eyes, no expression. Put me in mind of a big ol' bear I seen with Tant one early autumn evening up back of Deer Island, raring up out of the salt prairie to stare. It's like Tant says, a bear's face is stiff, never moves no matter what he's thinking. He don't look mean or riled, not till his ears go back, he just looks *bear* down to the bone, that's how intent he is on his bear business. It's up to you how much you want some trouble, he will wait you out while you make up your mind. Mister Watson had that bear-faced way of letting you know he had said his piece and weren't going to repeat it and weren't going to take no silence for no answer. I couldn't look him in the eye.

"Well, heck, ain't you the daddy of that baby girl? Ain't *we* your people, too?" Sure enough, my voice come out all garbled and too high, and I spat hard again to cover that up, and show who didn't give a damn one way or the other. Mister Watson looks down beside his boot, nodding his head, like inspecting another feller's spit was common decency, and then he's looking me over again. All this time he's never blinked, not even once.

"You want me to tote this crate or what?" I says, trying some sass on him.

He's still waiting. He aims to ream this thing right out of me. That makes me madder still, but damn if I don't come blurting out again with something stupid. "You want to run me off this place along with her, ain't that right? Ain't it?"

He turns his gaze away like he can't stand the sight, same way that bear done, giving a *woof* and dropping back down to all fours. He steps back over to the deck and swings me another crate, too hard. "No," he says. "Rob will be with 'em, and I mean to train him in your job. With all these orders for our syrup, we're going to need a full-time schooner crew, so you and Tant can run this boat if we ever get Tant in out of the Glades."

Well dammit if tears don't jump into my eyes, and he seen that before I turned away. Know what he done? Mister Watson stepped over to the dock and took me by the shoulders, turned me around, looked me straight into the eye. He seen right through me. "Henry," he says, "you are not my son but you are my partner and you are my friend. And the Good Lord knows poor old Ed Watson needs every last friend he can find."

Then he roughed my hair and went off whistling "Bonnie Blue Flag," to make his peace with Henrietta Daniels. I picked up a crate but set it down again. Looking over my new ship give me something to do while I pulled my nerve together, in case they was laughing at me from the house. At sixteen years of age, at least in them days, a man was a man and could not be seen to cry.

For a long time I stood there, thumbs looped into my belt, shaking my head over the boat like I was planning out the captain's work. Knowing Tant, I knew who would be captain – Tant was twenty and already a fine hunter, but he didn't care none for responsibility.

That afternoon, to work off his high spirits, or maybe just to get away from Henrietta, Mister Watson come out with a hoe into the corn patch. Me and the niggers hoeing weeds was stunned by the weight of that white sky that sank so low over the mangrove in the summer, but Mister Watson was singing his old songs. *Hoo-rah! Hoo-rah! For Southern rights, Hoo-rah!* He was the only man I ever saw who could outwork everybody and sing at the same time: *Hoo-rah for the bonnie blue flag that flies the single star!* He straightened long enough to do the bugle part: *Boopet-*

72

te-boopet-te-too, / *Te-boopet-te-boopet-te-boopet-te-poo,*
marching around us, hoe over his shoulder.

That man never took his shirt off, not even when it stuck
to them big shoulders. One time he told me, "A gentleman
don't strip his shirt when he works with niggers. It's all
right for them but not for us."

There was another reason, too. He usually wore a striped
shirt with no collar that Henrietta sewed him from rough
heavy mattress ticking, but it weren't thick enough to hide
the shoulder holster that would show up underneath when
he got sweated. Even out there in the cane, he had that
gun where he could lay his hand on it. The niggers seen
it, too, and he didn't mind that, he just grunted when they
went to hoeing harder.

Another time he said, "I learned to keep my shirt on,
Henry. It's good manners. You never know when you might
have a visitor."

That day Tant spoke up kind of smart to Mister Watson,
"A visitor from the north?" Mister Watson turned and
looked at Tant, and I did too, first time I *ever* took a look
at Tant, I was so used to him. Tant were skinny as a fish
pole, black curly hair and a big smile stuck to the top. He
done his best to hold that smile but couldn't do it. Then
Mister Watson said, "Boy, don't outsmart yourself." That
hard way with Tant were most uncommon and it kept the
smile off of Tant's face almost till supper.

Tant weren't out there that bad day when Mister
Watson, chopping a tough root, swung back hard and
caught me good longside the head. Next thing, I was laying
on the ground half-blind with blood, and them scared niggers backing off like I'd been murdered. Mister Watson
went right ahead, finished off that root with one fierce chop
– "*That* got her!" he says – and then he stepped over and
set me on my feet. There was blood all over, and my head
was burning. "Got to give a man more room, Henry," he
told me. Never said he was sorry, just told me to run up

to the house, get Henrietta to stick on a plaster, he'd be along there in a little while.

Henrietta was plenty upset already, she was raging and caterwauling in the kitchen. "I bore his *child*!" she howled, jouncing poor Minnie and kicking hens and banging a tin pot of sweet potatoes. The way I look at it today, my mother was in love with Mister Watson, but back then I thought they must be sick and crazy to get into same bed with the other.

When my mother seen my bloody face, she gasped straight off, "He done that a-purpose!" That fiery devil was out to murder her poor boy, that's what she said once the news come out that Mister Watson had killed in other parts. She was taking me right back to Caxambas, that was that. "In the meanwhile," she yelled as he come up on the back porch, "don't you *never* turn your back again on that bloody scoundrel!" I have heard it said that Netta Daniels was short on sense as well as morals, but no one ever said she lacked for spirit.

Mister Watson paid no mind, just washed his head at our hand pump from the cistern. That was the only pump down in the Islands at that time, we was pretty proud about it. When he straightened up to mop his face, he was kind of studying Henrietta. Them blue eyes under them thick ginger brows was sparkling like flints over that towel, and they seen my eye go right to where his sweat marked out his gun. He held the towel there a half minute, until Henrietta stopped her sputtering and whimpered. Then he snapped it down, looking real gleeful cause he'd scared her. He got out his jug of our cane liquor and sat down to it at a table in the other room, his back into the corner, way he always done.

For once, Henrietta didn't jump on him for tilting chairs back, weakening the legs, which was her way of trying to show what good care she was taking of his home. Home was where the heart was at, that's what was wrote on the needlework sign she hung on our parlor wall to make things cozy, and prove what a good wife she would make a man with sense enough to appreciate her fine points. But this day, knowing what he had overheard, she was scared to speak.

He knew that, too. He took him a long pull and sighed, like that poor old manatee out in the river the time we shot her young 'un for fresh sea pork. Finally he whispered, "Better watch out for that loose mouth, Netta. Even a murdering scoundrel like me can get hurt feelings." And he asked if she was packed, ready to go.

She pulled me out onto the porch. "I ain't leaving you here, Henry! You can't never tell what that man will do next!" She was whispering, too, but loud so he could hear, and he made a funny bear growl for his answer. "You're coming home with me, young man, and that is *that*!" said Henrietta.

"Home," I said, rolling my eyes. "Where's home at? Where the heart is?"

"That nice needlework come down in our family," Henrietta said, kind of reproachful.

"*What* family?" I said, feeling meaner'n piss.

"*Our* family! Your own grandma married Mr Ludis Jenkins that was first settler on Chokoloskee twenty years ago, Jenkinses and Weekses and Santinis!"

Nobody never counted Old Man Ludis, cause he come to nothing, he got enough of it and shot himself. I didn't remind her about that. I said, "Tant's daddy weren't no kind of kin at all."

Tears come to my young mother's eyes, made me feel wishful. But this was the first time Henrietta ever said she aimed to take me with her, and it kind of confused me. She was a young girl when she had me, and I left by the back door. She never brought me here, it was me brought her. I got her work with Mister Watson, and Tant, too. She didn't have no home no more'n I did.

I whispered I weren't going to go. And she said, Don't

75

you backtalk me, you are my child! And I said, Since when? That hurt her feelings, too.

Anyway, said I – I am still whispering – I am the new captain of that schooner, I ain't no kid no more! Since when? she said, rubbing the blood off my head much too rough. Look out! I yell, I ain't no sweet potato! Since *when*? Netta said again, and we broke out giggling like little kids, I don't know why. She hugged me then and started in to cry, cause she didn't have no idea at all where her and Little Min was going to go.

I go all soft and lonesome then, and hug her back. I missed someone bad but didn't rightly know who it could be. I ain't so sure I found out to this day, not even when the deacons told me it was Jesus.

"Called her Minnie after his rotten old sister," Henrietta blubbered, "and I hate that name, and Min will hate it, too!"

That talk about his sister made me nervous. Mister Watson is doing some drinking now and his silence is coming through the wall. I hush her quick. From the gumbo-limbo by the cistern comes the voice of a small greeny-yellow bird that sings even in summer, *wip*-dee-chee! and pretty soon the same again, over and over.

Mister Watson calls in a hard voice, Get in here, Captain, there is business to discuss!

Henrietta tugs my sleeve, her big eyes round. How had that man heard my whispering, heard all my bragging? But as Tant used to say, Mister E. J. Watson could hear a frog fart in a hurricane. That don't come so much from hunting, Tant said, as from being hunted.

CARRIE WATSON

THIS DIARY BELONGS TO MISS C. WATSON

September 15, 1895 The train south from Arcadia stayed overnight at Punta Gorda before heading on back north, and the kind conducters let us sleep on the red-fuzz seats after brushing off the goober shells and what not. Papa had wired his instructions that we were to put up in the new hotel as soon as we arrived, to get some rest, but Mama said she has learned her lesson not to count on rest in life or anything else. We should not spend good money on hotels in case something went wrong as it usely did and Mister E. J. Watson failed to appear. Anyways, this might be the wrong man, cause her husband was Mister E. A. Watson when she knew him. Mama was in a funny mood and no mistake.

Last night I was so tuckered out I was sleeping and sleeping. Had a nightmare about crocadiles but did not wake up. At daybrake they helped us off the train and left us in a little pile here on the sand. The train gave a great whistle and hard clank and pulled away, getting smaller and smaller, it went right down to a black smudge where the rail shine made a bright steel point against the sunrise. We waved and waved and waved then the train was gone and not even an echo, just two thin rails like silver fire piercing away north to where we came from.

The depo is locked until next week and not one sole to be seen. Buzards tilt back and forth across the sky. This sky in southern Florida is white with heat as if ash was falling from the sun. In the hot breeze, the spiky little

77

palms stick up like clusters of black knives, and the fire ball coming up out of the palms sharpens their edges. With the sun up, the wind dies and the redbirds and mockers fall dead quiet, and a parched heat settles in for the long day, just dry dry dry.

Mama tries to cheer us up, she gives that funny little smile. She says Well, well, here we are at the end of the line in farthest southern Florida! as if this dead silence and this scary white sun, all this hot sand and dry thorn, was what we'd pined for all of our hole lives.

And still no sign of Mister Watson and no word.

I call him "Mister Watson" just like Mama, who is very very strict about our maners, and sometimes says when she is blue that maners is about all that we have left. But in my heart I think of him as "Papa" because that was what I called him back in Arkansas. Oh, I remember him, I really do! He was most always so much fun that he made up for our dear Mama when she was sereous and sad. He brought toy soldiers from Fort Smith, and sat right down with us on the cabin floor to play. (Rob was too old, of corse, he was out slopping the hogs, he'd scoot as soon as he heard Papa coming.)

I gave Eddie the "dam-Yankee" bluecoats, him being too young to know the difference. Lucius was only a baby then, he can't remember Papa hardly, just pretends. But Eddie and me – Eddie and I? – have never forgot our dear dear Mister Watson, and surly our Rob never forgot him either.

Plenty of time for you, Dear Diary, because Rob is serly, Mama is thinking, and I am dog tired of trying to soshalize with little brothers. It was Papa who gave me the idea of my dear diary so long ago when I was a little girl. I found him out under the trees, writing away in a leather book. I asked him what that was, and he took me in his lap and said, Well, Carrie honey, it's a kind of jernal. I'm calling it Footnotes to my Life. He smiled in the shy way he does sometimes when he doesn't think he has amused you. Said his spelling was no good because as a boy back there in Carolina in the War Between the States, taking care of his mother and sister with his father gone, he had very little chance to go to school. But he kept up his jernal from his youth because that was a tradition in our Watson family.

Papa's jernal had a lock on it, and he swore he would never show it to a sole, even when I powted and looked saucy. I asked him, Never? Perhaps one day, Papa said. I knew Mama was terified to pick it up let alone read it the few times she laid eyes on it, but I thought I was diferent. He warned me that any diary that is not completely privet is no longer a diary, no longer quite honest, and therefore no longer "a trusted friend." So I keep mine secret from the hole hole world, and also Mama.

Rob was near twelve when Papa rode away. That was back in Crawford County, Arkansas, when Lucius was just a very tiny baby. Rob stood right up to those rough men that came galoping in. He told 'em they was trespissing on Papa's propity and they'd better look out or get shot between the eyes. And one of the men said to another, "In the back, more likely," and Rob went after him before Mama could shriek. It was just terifying, that pale dark boy socking so fureous on that man's knee, which was as high as he could reach. Got his hand cut bad by spurs and got knocked sprawling.

Mama told us that Papa had to leave on business, gone to Oregon. We was all alone quite a few years before we left Arkansas and went on back to Columbia County Florida and stayed a year with Granny Ellen Watson and Aunt Minnie Collins and our cousins.

Rob acted mean about coming to see Papa. He made Mama admit she had wrote to Papa, and that Papa never sent for us until she did that even though he was doing fine on his new farm. Probably has another woman now is what Rob told her. Rob is rude about poor Papa, rude to Mama, reminding her every two minutes that she's not his mother and how he doesn't have to mind her less he feels

79

like it. And Mama says calmly, I may not be your mother, Rob, but I'm all you've got. Just goes calmly on about her business, leaving Rob staring after her. Those times he looks all twisted up and funny like he'd fell off a horse onto his head. Once he caught me looking at him when he felt twisted up that way and he came over and he hit me hard but never said one word.

Rob passes for handsome with that straight black hair and fierce black brows and fair white skin that must have come down from his poor dead mother. The only thing he shows of Papa are the round red dots high on his cheekbone and those blue blue eyes from the highest heaven where blue comes from. Blue eyes with black hair are kind of scary. Those dots jump out like spots of blood, that's how fair his skin is, where Papa is so weather-browned and ruddy that the dots don't hardly show only when he's angry. Then they glow like fire, Mama says. Us kids can't wait to see our Papa glow like fire.

I don't look like Papa nor like Mama. I feel like some strange little thing people call Carrie but they don't know where she came from. Papa is heart-faced while Mama's face is long, and mine is somewhere in between, not fat-faced and not thin-faced but high cheek bones with full kind of lips, "bee-stung lips," as Mr Browning wrote in Mama's poem book. I have brunet hair, Lucius and Mama sort of ashy blond, while Papa's is dark reddish chestnut, with gold hairs in summer.

Eddie takes after Papa more, he'll be big and broad and strong like that, with reddish coloring, though his hair is corse and skin more fair. His hole manner and expression, Mama says, is very different, as if Papa's fire had died down or had no heat in it. (I am most like Papa, Mama says, I have his "prominent and penetrating eyes," what Granny Ellen calls "those crazy Watson eyes.")

Lucius has Mama's narrow feetures and that crooked little twitch that so seldom breaks out in a real smile. His eyes are dark and deep, look kind of shadowed. He'll be the tall one. (I am quite tall, too, there'll be quite a lot of Carrie, Mama teases.) Lucius is gentle, very sensitive. All the same our little boy is not so sereous as Rob and Eddie, he has got more fun in him. I'm light-hearted, too. Mama says what I am is light-minded, can't stick to my studies, I want to jump up and run outside and *see*. What should a person do who is plain cureous?

I was first to see the sail, white as a seabird's wing, way down toward the mouth of the Peace River. I knew it was Papa, no one else. I'd never seen a sail before, and I wanted to run right over to the landing, wave and wave. But Mama went pale, said, We don't *know* it's Mister Watson, we shall wait right here.

Pretty soon the sail was so close we could hear it ticking in the breeze, and Mama said, In case that's Mister Watson, we'd best stand up so's he can see us, not make him go over there to that hotel for nothing. So we all stood up in a line outside the depo, all but Rob, who was slowched off to one side. Rob wouldn't put on his Sunday suit, he wanted to make it plain as plain that he had no part in this hole dumb plan of the family taking Papa's charity down in south Florida.

It was pretty close to noon, there was no shade, and we stood in the hot wind watching the shore. In the glare they looked like two black creeturs, a thick one and a thin one, kind of shimmering. I thought the sun had made me dizzy. I cried, Mama, let me run to meet them! But she shook her head, and so we stood there, stiff as sticks.

A big man in black Western hat with a tall thin boy behind came walking across the white sand flat between the landing and the depo. Here came our long-lost Papa, and not one person smiling! I felt sorry for him! But our line never broke, and finally he stopped a few yards away and took off his broad hat and made a little bow, and nobody came up with a single word. He still had his gold watch on a chain, and took a look at it. "I'm sorry we are late," he said. "Rough weather." His voice was deep and pleasant, kind of gruff, as if he had no claim on us, not yet. He came no closer.

Mister Watson was dressed in a linen suit and black string tie, boots glissening and mustash waxed, and kept his hat off. He looked real glad to see this gloomy bunch, saying My O My with a big smile for us four frights all in a line that dared to call our selves his family.

I could see Mama yerning to smile back but she just couldn't. The lovely new rose bonnet she had scrimped for, saying over and over how buying it was a plain disgraseful waste cause who knows she might never wear this thing again – that pesky hat had gone all lopsided like it was melting and she never even noticed, that's how wore out the poor thing was from no sleep and bad nerves. Her red hands she was so ashamed of were clenched white at her waist and her long elegant face looked pale and peaked. Seeing her this way, I felt heart-broken, because our Mama has been sad and poorly. I wonder if that is why she wrote to Papa.

Papa said, "Well, Mrs Watson, that's a fine-looking family you have there!"

Mam nodded, too upset to speak. The best she could do was give a smile to the strange boy to make him welcome, cause he looked just as shy and scared as all the rest of us. He was skinny and real brown-skinned with sun-whitened hair, and very long legs in his outgrown pants, the kind that other boys called High-pockets in school because his pants hung so high above his dusty ankles. Cepting his long bare brown feet, he was dressed like Rob, rough shirt with no collar and a pair of gallises yanking his pants up, maybe underwear, too – what Rob calls Injun underwear cause it creeps up on you. Except I don't hardly imagine this boy wore any underwear which I admit is none of my fool bizness. I will say he looked cleaned and didn't smell much.

I gave him a big sudden smile and turned it off again real quick, just scarred the daylights out of him. That boy went tomato red, frowned something terible, he looked straight up at the sky serching for birds, and when he came down again, he was faced away from us, trying to whissle.

Papa, too sudden, stepped across the space toward Mama, holding out both hands for her to take, and I watched her red hands give each other a last clutch as if for courage. The poor fingers started up, then quit and grasped each other, and Mister Watson let his own hands fall. His hands was opening and closing, just a little. The four hands at a loss were just so sad!

I couldn't stand one bit more suspense, someone had to *do* something or dumb little Carrie would bust into tears! I let out a yip and darted forward, threw my arms around our Papa and hung on for dear life, hoping for the best. I knew he was looking at his wife over the top of my red ribbon bow. Then I felt it, he let out a breath, and something eased in his hard chest, and his arms hugged me.

Sure enough, when I turned around, Mama was smiling. And darn it all if that silly little Carrie didn't start to blubering, and Mama, too, but she was smiling all the same, like sun in rain. It was a beautiful smile, kind of unwilling, crooked, full of hope, I never saw such a dear expresion on that lonesome face, it made my temples tingle.

Her smile was like a signal to the boys to run and jump onto their father, not because they loved him the way I did, they were much too young, but just the way that boys will do, for the old heck of it. Mama was covering her tears up pretty well by scolding those boys for wrinkling Mister Watson's linen suit, but Papa Bear was woofing and rolling around just like he used to, thretening to run off into the woods with a hole arm lode of kids that he would eat up later in his cave. Eddie was screeching to ease his nerves, pretending to be frightened, but little Lucius, only six, let himself be bounced and tossed without a sound, turning his head so's to watch Mama over his Dad's shoulder, just to make sure she didn't go away.

All this time that poor fool Rob never budged an inch from where he was, just rocked on his heals, hands stuck in his hip pockets, and gave that serly stare to Mister Watson. So finely everyone was forced to look at his bad maners and his old curled lip, the way he wanted. But Rob could not meet his father's eye, so he jerked his chin at the strange boy as if to say, What's it to *you*? You better keep your durn eyes to yourself or I'll punch your nose off!

Mama warned him, just a murmur – "Rob?"

Papa put the small ones down, then straightened his coat up, kind of slow and formal. "Well, boy," he said, and stepped forward to shake hands. Oh how it scared me to see that, knowing Rob was going to refuse. That hand was out there for so long I could see the wind twitch the gold hairs on it.

I'd surly pull back a lonesome hand that someone else won't shake, but not our Papa! He had guessed what Rob would do and he was ready, keeping that hand right out there in mid-air, minute after minute, while that fool's face went a dark red and that serly stare fell all apart, and he shot a desperite look over at Mama.

Then Rob came out with a ugly voice I hadn't heard since a few years back in Crawford County, when he had that sad little mustash and all those hickeys. "How come you run off and never left us word, and never sent for us? Never *would* of, neither, if *she* hadn't come crawling – !" Well, right there that durn fool stopped short because Papa's fist flew up and back, cocked like a gun hammer.

Mama cried, "O Edgar please, he's just upset, he doesn't mean it!" Those were her first words to her husband in five hard long years.

He brought his arm down, and he spoke to Rob real quiet. "I have some explaining to do, that's right, boy. I mean to do it when I'm ready. And next time you talk that disrespectful way, you better be mighty careful I don't hear you."

"Or you'll shoot me? In the back?"

Those were Rob's very words! And a bad sneer! We could not believe it! But this time he had scared himself, and he backed up a little, set to run.

Papa took a great big breath, turned back to Mama.

"Mandy," he said, "this young feller here is Henry Thompson. He's been my partner for some years, and he's going to make me a fine schooner captain. Henry, I have the honor to present my wife, Mrs Jane Watson. She is a school teacher, and I hope she will see to your education, and mine, too, because we need it. This beautiful young lady is Miss Carrie, and these fine young fellows are Eddie and Lucius."

Lucius is six, but Papa picked him up like he was two and held him straight out in mid-air for a good look. "I have not seen Lucius since he was in diapers and he's turned out fine," he said.

Lucius gave a shy sad look at Mama to see if she thought he'd turned out fine like Papa said.

The tall thin boy shook our hands all around. His hand was very hard and callised, and I hung on to it just an extra second, wouldn't let it go, to get him serching in the sky for birds again, but I let go quick when I saw Papa was watching. Without taking his eyes off Rob, he said, "And this is my oldest son, Master Robert Watson" And he took out that gold watch again, as if Rob was running out of time.

Henry Thompson put his hand out, and Rob made him wait a breath before he took it. But when Rob yanked the boy off balance, just for devilment, Henry did not fall. He would not let go of Rob's hand, and he looked at Papa, and Papa just put his arms behind his back and looked straight up at the blue sky and commensed to whissle.

The boy yanked Rob's arm around behind, twisted it up hard until Rob squeaked. When Rob gritted his teeth, we knew he would never squeak again, not even if his arm got twisted off like some old chicken wing. But the boy did not know that yet about our Rob, and Mama said gently, "Mister Thompson? Please." Henry Thompson gave Mama a shy look and let Rob go.

Rob jammed his hands right back in his hip pockets. He looked from Henry Thompson towards our father and then back again, nodding his head. I knew what he was thinking: if Papa had taken him along when he left Arkansas, the way he should of, Rob Watson would be his schooner captain, not some beanpole cracker.

HENRY THOMPSON

Sailing north to Punta Gorda, Mister Watson and me hit some rough seas in the Gulf, right up until San Carlos Bay, and the train was gone away when we put in there. I felt real sorrowful, I'll tell you, cause that train was the first I ever would of saw. I never had no chance again for twenty years, that's how far my life took me away, down in the Islands.

Mister Watson and me walked over to the depot. First depot I ever seen, let alone rails. Until a few years after the turn of the century, Punta Gorda was the end of the west coast extension of the South Florida Railroad, laid down our way from Arcadia ten years before. Fort Myers passengers went south from there by horse and hack, five hours on old cattle trails to the Alva ferry. Ted Smallwood, now, he lived awhile up near Arcadia, and he run that hack during his youngerhood. It weren't until 1904, I guess, that a railroad bridge was put across the Calusa Hatchee and the Florida Southern steamed into Fort Myers. The man who got the credit for that was the same man who married Carrie Watson.

Miss Carrie was just as pretty as her picture and put me in a haze soon's I laid eyes on her. Mrs Watson was very kind to me, everyone was kind except young Rob, who was a year older than me and plain unruly. Rob didn't look the least bit like them others, he looked skinny and black-haired and pale – not so much pale and peaked as just pale, like the sun couldn't figure no way to get at him.

We stayed the night at the Henry Plant hotel, ordered up our grub right in the restaurant. Early next morning we set sail, bound for the Islands, and put in for the night at Panther Key. Juan Gomez called it Panther Key cause once a panther swum across and ate his goats, and that place is still Panther Key today.

Johnny Gomez, as us locals called him, boiled our newcomers their first Florida lobster. Never stopped talking and never once took that broke-stemmed old clay pipe he called his nose-warmer from between his teeth. Mister Watson had planned this feast with him on the way north, so's his kids could listen to the old man's tales, how Old Nap Bonaparte bid Juan godspeed in Madrid, Spain, and how he run off for a pirate and sailed the bounding main with Gasparilla. Mister Watson got some liquor into Johnny, got him so het up about them grand old days that he got his centuries confused, that's what Mrs Watson whispered in my ear. She done her best not to smile at how he carried on. She was a schoolteacher, you see, she had some culture to her, and she advised me to take Old Johnny with a grain of salt.

One thing there ain't much doubt about, that man were old. Claimed he fought under Zach Taylor at Okeechobee, 1837, way back in the First Injun War. And that could be, cause one day there at Marco, I heard Captain Bill Collier's old daddy tell the men how he knew that rascal Johnny Gomez up to Cedar Key before the War Between the States, said Johnny was a danged old liar even then.

Juan Gomez ranted on into the night, and Mister Watson drank right along with him, slapping his leg and shaking his head over them old stories like he'd waited for years to get this kind of education. He was watching the faces of his children, winking at me every once in a while to get me going, I never seen him so happy in my life. And the children were happy, too, all but young Rob, who never smiled, and never took his eyes off me or else his daddy. From his lip I seen he didn't think too much of neither one of us.

Mister Watson were a stately man, for sure, setting there

88

in the bosom of his family in the crackling firelight under the stars over the Gulf with his children all around him, and Miss Carrie's eyes just ashine with worship. And I already knew that if that girl would ever look at me like that, my heart would stop and I would go happy as a lamb to meet my Maker.

I couldn't take my eyes off of her, and Mister Watson teased me some when we went to piss. Standing there shoulder to shoulder outside the firelight, he warned me man to man but friendly not to try nothing stupid that I might regret. I'd been asking some coony questions about Carrie, but I guess they weren't as coony as I thought. He advised me she weren't but eleven years of age, and here I thought she must be going on fourteen, which is mostly when girls married in the Islands. I like to perished then and there of pure embarrassment, and put my pecker back into my pants as quick as possible.

To cover and change the subject, I told Mister Watson that if I were him, I'd take Old Juan the Pirate with a grain of salt, and he just grinned. "Well, Henry Thompson, you're *not* me and never will be, so you better go easy on that salt. You take this life with too much salt already."

Sailing down the coast next day in a fair breeze, and the spray flying, Mister Watson's people all got seasick, and I had to hold Miss Carrie by the belt to keep the poor thing from going overboard. Miss Carrie got slapped across the face by a wash of foam rolled up along the hull, but when she come up for air, that girl was laughing, never mind them flecks of spit-up in her hair. She had a fine free spirit on that day, and far as I can tell, she never lost it. Some way my heart went out to Carrie Watson, and all these years later, I ain't so sure that I ever rightly got it back.

Eddie was eight and Lucius six, but them green-faced little brothers had some grit. I rigged 'em bait lines. Pasty and puke-stained as they was, they trolled for kingfish and Spanish mackerel like their lives depended on it, and

Carrie, too. We was flapping them big silver fish onto the deck until their little sunburnt arms wore out, they couldn't pull no more. Even Mrs Watson looked contented, calling her children to see the dolphins that slipped across the bow, and the gray-green waves sliding ashore onto bright beaches, and the green walls of mangrove with no sign of human kind, and the towers of white clouds over the Glades. Hearing her fine words, I stared wherever she pointed, same as they did, like I was seeing the whole coast for the first time.

Rob Watson never hollered when he seen the dolphins, but he didn't miss nothing, and after a while, he lent a hand dragging in fish, which we was going to salt and smoke for our supplies. I knew my job and Rob could see that, he was watching careful how I done things, he learned quick. I hardly noticed him, I was so busy showing off for that sweet dark-eyed girl. That day on the schooner sailing south was the happiest I ever knew, I ain't never forgot it.

All the way down along the coast, Mister Watson went on about his plans for developing the Islands. Watching him pound his fist and wave his arms, Mrs Watson smiled and shook her head, looking kind of peaked.

She caught me noticing. "I'm just remembering," she said, "how Mister Watson always waved his arms that way." She kept her voice low in case he would get contrary, but he heard her all the same. "No, Mandy," he said, "I only wave my arms when I am happy." He spoke more softly than he ever spoke to Henrietta, reaching over from the helm to touch her tenderly, and for a minute she looked wishful, like something was coming she was going to regret.

Henrietta had not left the Bend like she was told, hadn't hardly swept or done the dishes. She got drunk instead, and there she stood in the front door of the house with her ginger-haired baby, waving Little Min's fat arm at the nice visitors. Her bright black Daniels eyes dared Mister Watson, who hauled out his watch. She was planning to stay till she had the house all cleaned up nice, she said, then go to Tant's sister Josie at Caxambas.

Mister Watson said nothing at all. He put back his watch. He had that stiff look at the cheekbones, ears laid back close to his head. Seeing that, she begun to dither, said she'd sent word to her brother Jim but he never come. I knew she never. Jim Daniels lived down at Lost Man's Beach, near old James Hamilton. Henrietta had stayed on out of pure vexation, knowing Mister Watson would not harm her, not in front of his own children.

Mister Watson went up close, put his hand on her shoulder near her neck, never said a word. The rest of us couldn't see his face, but hers went white. She whined, "Tant never come for me, I told you!" forgetting that Jim Daniels and not Tant was supposed to fetch her.

When Mister Watson turned around, his face had settled, but his eyes stayed cold. He introduced my mother as the housekeeper. His family was staring at Min's hair, turned by the sun to the dark fire color of his own. And seeing his wife's face, and Rob's, Mister Watson gathered himself up, and coughed, and come right out with it. "This is your baby sister, Rob. Her name is Minnie, after your Aunt Minnie." He made a small regretful bow to Mrs Watson.

Mrs Watson seemed not to expect no better, and knowing her as I come to do, I believe she was relieved he had not lied. She took out a lace handkerchief and dabbed her lips, then smiled at Henrietta. I was grateful. When Henrietta went inside, she turned to her husband and said quietly, "Pity the place wasn't swept out before we got here."

I run my mother to Caxambas the next morning.

When Mister Watson learned that his family would come join him, he had the pine boards for a big new house shipped down from Tampa, and carpenters, too, and all the people on the place turned out to help. Used Dade County pine, which is workable when green but cures so hard you'd be better off trying to drive a nail into a railroad track – best wood in Florida. When his house was finished, he painted her white, and he kept her painted, and that big white house stood high in them dark rivers for the next half century. Except Storters at Everglade, there was nothing between Fort Myers and Key West come close to it, not even the old Santini house on Chokoloskee.

The few families squatting in the Islands had nothing like that house on Chatham Bend. What other people called a house was nothing more than old gray storm boards flung together. Most of 'em settled for dirt floor and palmetta thatch, grew a few coconuts and vegetables, maybe some cane, got by mostly on white curlews and mullet. Mister Watson was experimenting with all kinds of vegetables, tobacco, had his horse and cart, beside two cows, and hogs and chickens. Only victuals we traded for was salt and coffee. Bought the green beans, wrapped 'em tight in burlap sacking, hammered 'em up with a marlin spike. We smoked our meat, made our own grits and sugar and some spirits, too. Seasons when vegetables was short, we'd pole up the Glades creeks to the pine ridges, gather coontie root for starch and flour, cut cabbage-palm tops in the hammocks and some Injun greens.

Miss Jane was poorly when she got to Chatham Bend, and he took care of her. Even when she could still walk a little, he liked to carry her around the place, set her chair in shade where the breeze come fresh upriver from the Gulf, under them blood-red poincianas planted years before by the old Frenchman. Passing by where she sat so still against the heat, in her dress of pale blue like the Gulf sky, I always wondered what sweet kind of thoughts was going through her head. Miss Jane watched the mullet jump and the tarpon roll, and the silent herons flying up and down the river, and the huge old gator like a cypress log on the far bank. Every year it come down out of the

Glades with the summer rains, and our kids called it the giant crocodile.

One day she beckoned me in close and said, "Since little Min is your half sister, Henry, we're some kind of kinfolk, isn't that true?" And when I nodded, she said, "Then please don't call me Mrs Watson. What would you think about 'Aunt Jane'?" And she seen the tears come to my eyes, and took me in her arms real quick so both of us could pretend she never saw them.

Wasn't too long after she come that Mister Watson decided he would pack up Mrs Watson and go to pay a social call on the Frenchman, "let bygones be bygones with that old-fangled sonofabitch whether he likes it or not" is what he told me. His idea was that educated company would per-suade his wife that life in the Islands might not be so dreadful as she thought. He were somewhat drunk but quiet, feeling friendly, and he took his jug along. Took his guns, too, "in case M'sieu didn't take kindly to a social call. I won't put up with his rough language," Mister Watson added, "not in front of Mandy."

Aunt Jane wasn't feeling well, but this day he didn't pay that no attention, just bundled her down to the dock. A world of good would come from a little turn along the river, is what he told her. When they come back late that evening – it was summer, there was still a little light – he told me they wasn't so welcome at the start but things smoothed out like cream as they went along. By the end, he said, "M'sieu Chevalier was all that might be wished for as a host." Hearing them words, Aunt Jane just smiled that thin and crooked smile, too tired to talk. All the same, that visit perked her up. She had liked the Frenchman more'n he did, and made a plan to exchange books with him, but never did.

Aunt Jane always kept her books beside her, but after a while she never looked at them. Mister Watson read to

93

her from the Good Book every day because she needed that, and he read to the rest of us on Sundays, "whether we needed it or not." He never got sick of that old joke long as I knew him. *Pour out the vials of the wrath of God upon the earth!* – that man would keep us on our knees for an hour at a time, burning in his message of hellfire and damnation. *And the sea became as the blood of a dead man, and every living soul died in the sea!* He'd work himself up into such a wrath, looming over us so fierce, booming and spitting, that you might think he was Jehovah Himself – either that or he was laughing at Lord God Almighty, that's the way Rob seen it. And I think today, maybe Rob was right, maybe he was. But any young person who didn't praise the Lord would feel his razor strop; he beat that poor Rob something pitiful near every Sunday. As for Tant, he weren't so scared as he pretended, but would carry on in a way somewhat more holy than was wanted, rolling his eyes up to the Lord and warbling the hymns until Mister Watson had to frown to keep his face straight.

Tant had a sassy way with Mister Watson, having learned real quick that he ran no risk at all. He got took up by Mister Watson in a way I never would be, for all my loyalty and longing. And the thing of it was – this ate my heart – Tant never cared a hoot about what I would have given my right eye for, all he seen was ways to have some fun and smooth his road.

Sometimes in the evenings Mister Watson read from Rob's book, *Two Years Before the Mast.* Captain Thompson is flogging this poor sailor, who shrieks, *Oh Jesus Christ, oh Jesus Christ!* And the captain hollers, *Call on Captain Thompson, he's the man! He can help you! Jesus Christ can't help you now!*

We was all shocked when that part was read out, not the words so much as the way he read it, he was just delighted. He'd tease me, call me Captain Thompson, because that captain's name was Thompson, too. "You could learn a thing or two from a man like that," he said. Aunt Jane told me right in front of him to pay him no attention. To him, she said in a low voice, "You do them harm."

One time I asked, Mister Watson, sir, do you believe in God? And he said, Believing in Him doesn't mean I trust Him.

Sometimes he would tease Aunt Jane by telling us how all the greatest hymns was wrote by slavers, cause slavers was so religiously inclined. And his wife might smile but she would whisper, "I pray you make your peace with God before you die." We didn't know what either of 'em was trying to say, and wasn't meant to. And he would whisper back, "I have, I have," and lift his fine voice toward Heaven like an offering.

> . . . how sweet the sound,
> That saved a wretch like me!
> I once was lost but now am found,
> Was blind but now I see.
>
> Through many dangers, toils, and snares
> I have already come.
> Tis grace has brought me safe thus far,
> And grace will lead me home.

Before his family come, Mister Watson never had no interest in religion, not one bit, and he never had none after they was gone. I didn't neither. Time he was done with me, all I believed was what I saw in front of my own face, day in, day out. Later in life, there was a few held my Godless ways against me, but I couldn't help it. I didn't know who God was, or Him me.

One morning not long after Aunt Jane and the children arrived, I heard men's voices shouting off the river, and I knew his visitors from the north had come for Mister Watson. I run downstairs as he jumped to get his gun. Mrs

95

Watson went all trembly, saying, "Oh, please, Edgar!" She didn't want no trouble and I don't guess he did neither, not with little children in the house. So what he done, he took a bead and skinned half the handlebar mustache off of the ringleader, who had stood up in the boat and was hollering about how E. J. Watson was under arrest. Mister Watson shut him up and run that posse off his river with one bullet.

Later Bill House come along and told me how it started, and I told him how it all panned out. Bill thought it was funnier'n I did, but he was excited all the same, and had all kinds of questions about Mister Watson. Bill House was in that Chokoloskee crowd on that black Monday in October 1910, and he talked about Mister Watson all his life.

BILL HOUSE

Not long after Elijah Carey fixed up Richard Hamilton's old house, along come a well-knowed plume hunter and common moonshiner from Lemon City way, south of New River. Crossed the Glades and paddled up to Possum Key from Harney River, brought quite a smell of the east coast into our cabin. Kept his old straw hat on even in the house, leather galluses, shirt buttoned to the collar, wore a lot of beard and grime to head off miskeeters. Big chaw of Brown Mule stuck into his face, and spat all over our nice clean dirt floor. What Ed Brewer liked the best, folks said, was to spike a barrel of his shine with some Red Devil lye, then head out into the Glades, pep up his heathen clientele so's they couldn't think straight, let alone chase him, then trade the dregs of what them redskins called *wy-omee* for every otter pelt and gator flat he could lay his hands on. Rotgut sold by fellers like Ed Brewer killed more Injuns than the soldiery ever done, and give us honest traders a bad name. He had a squaw with him that day, couldn't been more than twelve years old, and so dead drunk he laid her out under the eaves and just forgot about her. Later her band would throw her out for sleeping with a white man, and this was the one who come to a bad end, down Chatham River.

Ed Brewer were a watchful and slow-spoken man, thickset and sluggish as a cottonmouth till that quick moment when he lets you have it. Passed for white but more likely a breed, with bead-black Injun eyes and straight black hair. His hands set quiet but them black eyes flickered in a funny way, like he was listening to voices in his head that

97

had more interesting business with Ed Brewer than what was happening around our table. Sheriffs was after this poor feller on both coasts for peddling *wy-omee* to the Mikasukis, so he was looking for a place to settle, get some peace of mind.

When he finally spoke, he cut off Captain Lige like he wasn't there. "Way I heard," Ed Brewer said, handing around his deluxe jug without no lye in it, "that big old Injun mound at Chatham Bend might be just the place for an enterprising citizen such as myself."

Captain Carey, a big red-faced feller with soft and easy ways, took him a snort of Brewer's hospitality that made his eyes pop. He shook it off, banged down the jug, and give a sigh like some old doleful porpoise in the channel.

"Whoa!" he says, and puts a big soft hand up. "Feller already *on* there, Ed."

"So I heard," Ed Brewer said. Them other two looked at him like they expected him to explain hisself. He didn't.

While he was pondering, the Frenchman poured himself a little lightning, eyebrows way up higher than usual and his bony nose just a-twitching with disgust, as if to say, This shit sure ain't what your quality likes to drink back in the *Old* World! But Captain Lige grabbed the jug again and hoisted in onto his elbow, American-style, just to be sociable, and helped himself to another slug of our guest's hootch. Next time he surfaced, he coughed out a Key West rumor: The one who cleared the way on Chatham Bend, letting on to the sheriff where he could find the late Will Raymond, was none other than a feller named Ed Watson.

"Heard that one clear across to Lemon City," Brewer said, pushing his jug at Lige again, "Any sonofabitch would do that to another human bein ain't got *nothin* comin, if I take your meanin."

"In a manner of speaking, yes and no," Captain Lige told him, raising his pink palm to advise caution. "Paid off the widow for the claim, so he has rights. According to the law," Captain Lige added.

"Law!" the Frenchman scoffed, disgusted. "In la belle France, we cut off foking head!" We done our best to work around him, but he went off on one of his tirades, quoting Detockveel and Laffyett and some other old Frog fellers that could tell us boys a thing or two about America.

"*Foking!*" Ed Brewer said, trying that word out. I can't explain why Ed spoke in French, lest he wanted to befuddle up the Frenchman. Then Brewer told us that the news was out in Lemon City how this skunk Watson were a wanted man in two–three states. Here was our chance, says Ed, to do our duty as good citizens and a good turn to ourselves while we was at it.

So all us citizens sat forward, put our heads together, while Brewer laid his cards upon the table, at least some of 'em. Them three able-bodied men – him and Carey and the Frenchman – was going to get the drop on Watson, claim they had a warrant, hogtie that sonofabitch, Ed Brewer said, and take him in. Even if there weren't no reward, Watson was sure to get sent back to Arkansas, serve out his term, and while he was paying his debt to society, us honest citizens would have the plume trade to ourselves.

Here's where Brewer got the lowdown on Ed Watson. Over there in Lemon City, Brewer's friend Sam Lewis worked as bartender in Pap Worth's Pool Room, and Sam Lewis introduced him to two hombres on the dodge from Dallas, Texas. They was old friends of the late Maybelle Shirley Starr, and they was asking questions about Watson. Well, they sat down at the bar and told Ed Brewer how they come east to Arcadia to take work in the range wars for a while. A gunslinger from Oklahoma, one Jack Watson, had put some bullets in a Quinn Bass while in town, and they got the idea from the description that this Watson was none other than the polecat that shot poor Maybelle clean out of the saddle on her own birthday, February '89. So Ed Brewer told them Texans, Boys, a feller of that selfsame description sliced the daylights out of somebody down to Key West.

"*Jack* Watson?" I said.

"E. Jack Watson," said Ed Brewer, waving me off. "Selfsame sorry sonofabitch as we are talking about right here tonight."

That was the first and last I ever heard about Watson traveling under the name Jack – I had my doubts. But the Frenchman hissed at me, "Wheep-aire snap-aire!" so I hushed up.

Well, one of these Texans, name of Ed Highsmith, vowed he would go gunning for Jack Watson soon as he sobered up enough to figure out where Jack Watson was at. "Yessir," Ed Highsmith declared, "when I ain't snot-flyin drunk, this E. Jack Watson goin to be my hobby."

Well, I knew Ed Highsmith weren't made-up, cause I recognized his name, Sam Lewis, too, from Ted Smallwood's story of the year before when him and Isaac Yeomans were clearing citrus land around Lemon City.

Lemon City, north of the Miami River, was a few groves and maybe two hundred people counting all of the outlying homesteads. The east coast railroad coming through brought chain-gang workers to lay track, had foremen out there with black whips to keep them criminals on the job, and ones that died was dumped in the limestone sinkholes by the right-of-way. After that come saloons and a whorehouse, there was a lot of scrapes, a lot of shooting.

Way Ted told it, these two Texans, Ed Highsmith and George Davis, come in and got drunk every Saturday, picked fights with anyone they wanted. Only feller they never fought with was a moonshiner, Ed Brewer, who kept 'em in liquor and told 'em he'd put 'em on the track of E. Jack Watson soon as they put two sober days together.

One day Ted and Isaac run into these fellers, and Davis had a lot of teeth knocked out and bleeding. According to Smallwood, Davis said, "We are old boys from Texas, slightly disfigured but still in the ring." A couple of days

later they caused a uproar at Pap Worth's Pool Room &
Bar, got to winging billiard balls at the barkeep's head
cause he wouldn't leave off telling 'em to behave.

This barkeep, Sam Lewis, was known to be a hothead
and a deadeye shot with his Marlin .44, could shoot a man's
bung hole out so clean he'd wonder if he might of cut a
fart. So when Sam grabbed his rifle off the wall, them two
decided it was time to take their leave. As they went out,
Sam's bullet split the doorframe maybe a possum's-pecker-
length over Highsmith's head, and only that much because
somebody had sense enough to knock his arm up. Highsmith and Davis were so irked on top of being drunk that
they hollered at Lewis through the window they would be
back to settle their account first thing next morning. Might
have had a second thought when they woke up, but having
said that, why, they had to do it. In them days there was
still some honor, and a man was careful not to say nothing
he wouldn't stand by. Otherwise nobody took him serious,
they walked all over him.

Ted and Isaac was eating up their grits in Doddy and
Rob's Restaurant when them two Texans come along the
street, and Sam Lewis stepped out with his Marlin .44 and
got the drop on them. He told Highsmith if he did not get
down on his knees in that there mud and apologize for
braying like a goddamn Texas jackass, he would have to
shoot him. So Highsmith said, Well, shoot then or shut up,
you sonofabitch! Never thought to ask his partner whether
Davis thought them words was wise or not. So Lewis put
a bullet through Ed Highsmith, and Highsmith went in by
the back door of the restaurant so's not to bother nobody
and lay down on the floor to think it over.

George Davis spun sideways to give Lewis a hard target,
and Sam Lewis shot him through the heart, dropped Davis
dead there in the road. They dragged him in and laid him
out beside his partner, and Highsmith opened his eyes up,
took a look, and closed his eyes again. "Slightly disfigured,"
he sighed, "and all my fault."

Ted and Isaac went in with the crowd to hear High-smith's last words. "Tell the Freemasons," he said, " that Ed Highsmith is gone. Tell 'em I brought damnation down without no help from nobody at all."

Might seem to some that Lewis done what was meet and proper to keep them highfalutin boys in line. But Sam Lewis come from other parts and was not popular, and poor George Davis left behind a little family, so they called Sam Lewis a bloodthirsty killer that would shoot a family man as quick as look at him, and being family men them-selves, they all took cover. Not one would come out, help dig the grave, for fear Sam Lewis might take it in his head to send a few more family men to meet their maker.

The two pretty Douthit girls was looking on, so Isaac and Ted stepped forward. They dug the one grave big enough for both, and them two fellers went to hell together. Bob Douthit and some other fellers formed a posse – Ed Brewer claimed he was on that posse, wanted to try the other side, I guess – but Sam Lewis hid out and got away, went on across to the Bahamas.

The people knew Sam Lewis was dead stubborn. They expected him back to get his gear cause he'd said out plain he had not done one thing wrong, so the whole settlement was armed and laying for him. And out of his honor he come back, knocked on a door after dark and asked for food, and when the woman asked Who's there?, damn if he didn't come right out with it – Sam Lewis!

A homesteader guarding that house shot Sam Lewis, broke his leg. He took Sam's Marlin .44, then bent and lit a match, and the woman hollers, If that there is Sam Lewis, shoot again!

There was a young boy on guard, too, and that boy was raring to do his duty and put a bullet in the culprit. Sam Lewis pulled a pistol and put a bullet in the homesteader and sent another singing past that boy. After that he crawl-ed into a shed. He told the lynch mob through the door he would go peaceable if he could go to trial, otherwise he aimed to take as many straight to hell with him as the law allowed.

They rode Sam Lewis to the jail at Juno, Florida. When the homesteader died a few days later – this was July of 1895 – the men went to Juno and took Sam Lewis out and lynched him, and shot the nigger jailkeeper while they was at it. Made what you might call a nice clean job.

Anyways Ed Brewer figured that bringing in the famous E. Jack Watson would improve his reputation with the sheriff on top of earning the reward. But Chevelier warned him there was no way of coming up on Watson by surprise. The small stretch that overlooked the Bend was the only break in them green walls, cause the place was surrounded on three sides and more by a mangrove tangle a greased Injun couldn't slip through. Besides that, everybody knowed how that high ground, in storm, drew every critter on these rivers, it was one of the worst places for rattlers, let alone cottonmouths, in all the Islands. Them vipers piled up on Chatham Bend, time of high water, and they never left.

"We'll come down the river in the dark," Ed Brewer said, "surround the house, and take him when he comes out in the morning."

Lige Carey's chuckle didn't sound too good. "Mister Watson never goes unarmed, and he is a dead shot," Lige says. I catch the tightness in his voice and so does Brewer, who says, "That so, Cap'n?" He takes up his rifle and steps out the door and shoots the head clean off a snake bird that's craning down from the top of a dead snag over the creek. He let that bird slap on the water and spin a little upside down, legs kicking. Then he comes back in, sets his gun back by the door, and says, "I reckon three can handle one, we put our mind to it."

I ain't spoke up for a while so I says, "Better make it four!" I ain't got one thing in the world against Ed Watson but I don't want to miss out, and I shoot pretty fair, too, if I do say so. (Also I want to make damn sure that none of these drunks goes over there and shoots poor Henry Thompson, who is somber enough already without getting shot.) Them men just scoff cause the way they see it, I am still a boy. So I missed my chance to join a Watson posse, had to wait another fifteen years.

In Captain Lige's opinion, which me and the Frenchmen got to hear a lot, we gentlemen was sick and tired of violence in south Florida. Why, taking the law in your own hands was worse in Florida, yells Lige, then out in the Far West, where men was men, what with so many desperadoes and bad actors hiding out down here in our trackless swamps like dregs in the bottom of a jug of moonshine. Ol' Lige come right out and shouted the word *moonshine!* as a hint to our guest to do his bounden duty, he give me a big wink when he done it, and Ed Brewer sloshed some shine in my tin cup, *glug-glug, glug-glug,* to get the whippersnapper liquored up long with the rest.

"Now you take this Watson fellow!" Lige was shouting. Down in Key West, most people said that Dolphus Santini was smart to take that money – well, Elijah P. Carey disagreed and didn't care who knew it, he slapped his hand down on the table, spilling drinks. "Watson had that sum right in his pocket! Nine hundred dollars! And every red cent of it ill-gotten, you may rest assured!"

What happened to a leading citizen should not go unpunished, Captain Carey said. Well, nine hundred dollars were pretty good punishment back then, was my opinion; that's what Smallwoods would pay for Santini's whole damn claim on Chokoloskee. Lige Carey never knew Santini, never knew how he got to be leading citizen in the first place. You show Dolphus nine hundred dollars, his eyes would glaze right over like a rattler. He was a rich man by our standards, and he earned every penny, and I guess you could say he earned it this time, too.

Anyway, he took Ed Watson's money. Maybe Dolphus was worried about lawyers' fees, or maybe he thought the federal attorney, who was one of Watson's drinking partners, might bring a poor attitude to the case. This weren't unlikely, cause of ol' Ed was just as popular as not around Key West. And maybe Watson had him scared so bad that he didn't want to rile him any further. He had no choice about the scar, so he decided he would take the money. This way, next time they met, there'd be no hard feelings. Watson could say, How's that ol' scar doing, Dolphus? And Dolphus could holler, Why just fine, E J.! Coming along fine!

Elijah Carey was still shouting. "How could Santini accept a bribe after such an experience, instead of putting that villain behind bars where he belonged? Gentlemen," he yells, "I am astonished!"

"*Astonish!*" sniffs the Frenchman, inching a little more lightning into his glass like it was medicine. "I am astonish from first foking day I sets foots in America. What is require is *la guillotine*, in ever foking vee-lage in this foking con-trie."

Might seem sassy for a boy to interrupt, but being from Chokoloskee Bay, I was the only one acquainted personal with D. Santini, and the time had come to tell my partners what was what. "Nothing astonishing about it, gentlemen!" pipes up young House.

The other citizens all stared at me, kind of impatient, and I had to get my say in quick before Chevelier could shoo me off. "Old Man Dolphus likes money, that's why he's got so much. For nine hundred dollars he can buy what little farm land he don't already own on Chokoloskee."

There was no law in the Islands, I reminded 'em, a man took care of his own business, and a killing was not what you might call scarce – though the Islands was kind of like them Hamiltons, as Tant Jenkins used to say, they never was as black as they was painted. However, Key West was trying out some law after a long spell without none, so Watson paid Dolphus in hard cash not to take the case to court, let bygones be bygones. That was that. Nobody at home thought much about it.

"It's the *principle* of the thing!" Ol' Lige cries out. "The principle!" And the Frenchman wags a finger – "*Le pranseep!*"

Them two gentlemen are frowning at me kind of outrageous, but I seen from his wink that Ed Brewer thought the same way I did, being a common swamp rat, same as me.

To make a long story somewhat shorter, this Brewer could shoot him a blue streak, and he was a man without no fear of man nor beast, or so he advised us by the time we had his liquor polished off. Chevelier and Carey could shoot pretty good, too, and it sure looked like this deadly bunch had Watson's number. But Cap'n Lige from start to finish had no heart for the job. Maybe he seen that one of his partners was a drunk outlaw with his eye on Watson's property, and the other a loco old Frenchman so fed up with life he couldn't see straight, let alone shoot.

Every few minutes Ol' Lige described Ed Watson cutting loose down in Key West, shooting out light bulbs in the saloons, never known to miss. If he said it once he said a hundred times that drunk or sober, E. J. Watson was no man to fool with, but his partners was just too liquored up to listen. First light, they fell into the skiff and pushed off for Chatham Bend, figuring to float downriver with the tide. Cap'n Lige never had the grit not to go with 'em.

Come Sunday, I snuck off to Chatham Bend. Henry Thompson and me tied up to a mangrove and baited us some snappers while we compared our lowdown on that posse. I told Henry how them three deputies was up all night getting their courage up, and he told me what happened the next morning. Maybe they was bad hung over and their nerves wobbly, he said, because what they done was stand off on the river and holler out, "E. Jack Watson, come out with your hands up! You are under arrest!" That river is pretty broad there on the Bend, and they was way

106

over on the farther side, so they had to shout with might and main just to be heard.

Watson got up out of bed and poked his shooting iron through the window. He knowed Ed Brewer from saloons down to Key West, so Henry said, knowed him for a moonshiner and durn east coaster, and he also knowed that the Key West sheriff weren't likely to appoint no wanted man to be his deputy. So when Brewer reared up in the boat and hollered, Watson let a bullet fly that clipped that feller's handlebar on the left side. When that bullet sang and Brewer yelped, Cap'n Carey and the Frenchman near fell out of the skiff, that's how hard they put their backs into them oars.

What he *should* of done, Watson told Henry, was give them varmints a bullet at the waterline, sink the old skiff and let 'em swim for it, cause there weren't nowhere but the Watson Place for them to swim to. When he cooled off some and got to laughing, he let on how he had skinned Brewer a-purpose, and Henry Thompson testified for the rest of his long life that Watson never aimed to kill Ed Brewer or he would have done it. Course Ed Brewer claimed that E. Jack Watson tried to blow his head off. After Watson died, he liked to tell about his shoot-out with the most fearful desperado as ever took a life around south Florida.

When them men slunk back to Possum Key, Ed Brewer shaved off what was left of his mustache, bellering when the razor bit on his burned lip. Although they was feeling weak and poorly, he cussed his partners up and down, he wouldn't talk a civil word to nobody. Before noon he was headed east for the Miami River.

At Lemon City, Brewer accused E. J. Watson of attempted murder, which made Watson's reputation even worse. Lige Carey took the story to Key West, where Watson got the game the Barber. That was the first nickname they give him. A few years later they were calling him the Emperor – the Frenchman said it first – because of his big ambitions for the Islands. It was only after he was safe under the ground that anyone dared to call him Bloody Watson.

Ed Brewer's posse weren't the last that went into them rivers after Watson. After all his scrapes down at Key West, the law had enough of him and called for a volunteer to bring him in. Only deputy spoke up said, Well, now, Sheriff, if I go to all that trouble, I might's well run for your job when I come home. Guts was all that poor feller had going for him, because Watson got the drop on him soon as he got there, took away his hardware, and put him to work out in the cane. Got two weeks hard work out of the long arm of the law before he give him back his gun and told him he were lucky to be alive. That deputy must have thought so too, cause he went away with no hard feelings, told everybody in Key West how the Watson Place was the only so-called plantation in the Islands that amounted to more'n a small squirt of sawfish shit. Why, by God, he would say, he was proud to have worked for such a man as Ed J. Watson! Watson were chortling over that till the day he died.

In one way, Henry Thompson said, Watson was riled by being blamed for killings that he didn't do, but he also encouraged them bad stories – not encouraged, exactly, but he never quite denied them, neither. His reputation as a fast gun and willing to use it kept deputies and other nuisances off Chatham Bend and helped him lay claim to abandoned plantations, which was pretty common on the rivers by the time he finished.

Only thing was, he never knowed when somebody like Highsmith or Ed Brewer might come gunning for him. He told Henry Thompson he had enemies, and he kept his eye out, and ears, too. Like I said, there was no way to come at him by land, through all that mangrove, and when he built his house, he built her high enough so he could see the peak of any sail out on the Gulf, through a west window up under the eaves, so nothing moved along the river that he didn't know about.

After Brewer and that deputy, nobody went up in there after Ed Watson. If he shot some renegades in there, or they shot him, it was good riddance. So long as he stayed in that lonesome river, he would be all right. All the same, he remained watchful, and when he sailed up to Fort Myers, he went quick and he went armed. Got there after nightfall and laid low. Lee County sheriff, ol' Tom Langford, didn't want no part of him, and as for Frank Tippins, who come in as sheriff round the turn of the century, he didn't know just *what* he wanted, unless it was Ed Watson's handsome daughter.

For the next few years, after his family come, Mister Watson settled down, stayed out of trouble. He run a fine plantation and successful syrup business and helped his neighbors anywheres he could.

Sometimes of a Sunday them young Hamiltons would sail up Chatham River on the tide, visit the Frenchman, and drop back down to Mormon Key when the tide turned. Mary Elizabeth and John Leon was just youngsters at the time, but Liza was as pretty put together as anything I ever saw, made me ache to look at her, and Leon was a fine big strapping boy. He stuttered a little, but he learned early how to grin at life and never lost that.

Maybe them two was brother and sister but they looked like vanilla and chocolate in the boat. Henry Thompson used to tell that Leon's daddy was a white man, Captain Joe Williams, who got into the pen when Richard Hamilton lived at Fakahatchee, he heard that from the Daniels clan up there. A lot of Island people had it in for Old Man Richard, so I don't know if that story's true or not – can't even figure how folks knew it unless Joe Williams had made a claim on Leon, which he didn't. But the truth don't count for much after all these years, cause folks hang on to what it suits 'em to believe and won't let go of it.

Leon and Liza grew pretty close to that old Frenchman after I left there, right up until the time he died. Nobody knows too much about that. One day he was snapping like a mean old turtle and the next day he was gone for good. This happened when Watson's fame in other parts was catching up with him, so naturally the Frenchman's death was laid on Watson, who was known to have his eye on Possum Key.

Henry Thompson don't believe that. Henry said that Watson took a liking to the Frenchman, took his wife to meet him. Watson called Chevelier the Small Frog in the Big Pond, Henry didn't know why. Henry never was much help when it comes to jokes. Anyway, that poor heartbroke old foreigner was dying pretty good without no help.

Ted Smallwood knowed Mr E. J. Watson from their first days at Half Way Creek, they was always friendly. Families both come from Columbia County, up in the Suwannee River country of north Florida. Ted come down this way from Fort Ogden, near Arcadia, and he worked for us on Turner River for a while. He married our Mamie back in '97, bought a small place from the Santinis when he came over to Chokoloskee that same year. About the only settlers on the islands then was McKinneys, Wigginses, Santinis, Browns, and Yeomans. There was still a half dozen families at Half Way Creek, another half dozen at Everglade, and a few more perched here and there down through the Islands.

McKinneys started out the same as we did, farming back in Turner River, set up a sawmill. Wonderful soil there the first year, but once it was cleared, and the sun burned down and killed that land, C. G. McKinney couldn't make a living. So he cleared another mound downriver, made a bumper crop, and the next year it wouldn't grow an onion. Old C.G. had comical names for everything, called that place Needhelp.

McKinney come on to Chokoloskee, built a house and

110

store, got in his supplies from Storters' trading post in Everglade. His billhead said, "No Banking, nor Mortgaging, no Insurance, no Borrowing, no Loaning. I Must Have Cash to Buy More Hash." Made no bones about what he sold; called his bread "wasp nest." Had him a gristmill, started the post office, done some doctoring when old Doc Green left Half Way Creek.

C. G. McKinney was a educated man according to our local estimation, and Mr McKinney didn't hold with plume hunting. Jean Chevelier used to rant and rave at everybody except himself that hunted plumes, but he also hollered "*Eepo-creet! Eepo-creet!*" about McKinney, who went on just one egret hunt before he give it up for good. C.G. seen all them abandoned nestlings and the crows picking on 'em and figured what he was doing there was not God's will.

Ted Smallwood felt the same way as McKinney when it come to plume hunting, but I guess he had a blank spot in his heart when it come to gators. The year after he married our Mamie was the great drought year of '98, when every gator in the Glades was piled up into the last holes, and a man could take a ox cart across country. Tom Roberts out plume hunting come on a whole heap of gators near the head of Turner River; he went up to Fort Myers for wagons and a load of salt, then got a gang together and went after 'em. There was Tom and me and Ted and a couple of others, we took forty-five hundred in three weeks from them three holes that make up one lake in the rains. That's Roberts Lake, and that's how it got that name. Didn't waste bullets on 'em, we used axes. Skinned off the bellies, what we call the flats. Don't reckon them buzzards got it cleaned up yet today. Floated 'em down Turner River to George Storter's trading post at Everglade, we got in early and we got good money. That year R. B. Storter's schooner carried ten thousand gator hides up to Fort Myers out of Roberts Lake alone.

After that, it was war against the gators, the hides was

111

coming from all over, otter pelts, too. Bill Brown from the Boat Landing trading post east of Immokalee, he brung in one hundred eighty otter on one trip, got a thousand dollars for 'em, and he brought gator skins by the ox-wagon load. One trip he hauled twelve hundred seventy into Forty Myers, might been the record, that was in 19 and 05, and he'd brought eight hundred not three weeks before. Even gators can't stand up to that kind of massacre.

Yessir, a lot of God's creation was left laying dead out there, it give me a very funny feeling even then. Bill Brown said all them water creatures was going to die off anyway soon as Governor Broward got going on his drainage schemes, said he hated waste so he aimed to take every last gator in the Glades. Three years later, that was 1908, the gator trade was pretty close to finished. And the Injuns was close to finished, too, cause they didn't have good guns or traps, they only took enough to go and trade with. They never killed them critters out, not the way we did.

Ted never said if killing all them gators was in God's service or not, but he sure had some nice cash set aside. Two years later, him and his father bought the whole Santini claim on Chokoloskee. Them Santinis and the son-in-law Santana, they was Catholics, but they was one of our pioneer families, and folks was surprised to see 'em pull up stakes. Nicholas – that's Tino – his wife was Mary Ann Daniels, sister to Aunt Netta, who kept house for Watson, and maybe that led to something ugly Dolphus said to Watson that he wished he hadn't. Tino moved up to Fort Myers, and as for Dolphus, he lit out for the east coast, about as far from E. J. Watson as he could get.

According to Ted Smallwood's reminiscences, E. J. Watson had not been in the Islands long before he assaulted "one of our best citizens," Adolphus Santini of Chokoloskee Island, at Key West. (See the excerpts from the Bill House interviews, which describe the Santini episode in detail.)

In her memoirs, Mary Douthit Conrad corroborates Smallwood's version of the Highsmith/Davis killing, which strengthens one's confidence in the accuracy of his "Ed Watson Story," cited above. She also provides additional details from the perspective of the fair sex. "After all this excitement the Village Improvement Association of Lemon City [now subsumed by Greater Miami] put on a box supper and ice cream social at the church to raise enough money to send Mrs Davis and her two boys back home to Texas."

In the last year of his life, Jean Chevelier made an ill-advised attempt to arrest Mr Watson, assisted by his aforementioned associate Elijah Carey, and a plume hunter and moonshiner named Ed Brewer. The arrest attempt was entirely unsuccessful, and the posse fled.

Due to the paucity of Key West records, there is little to be learned about Captain Carey, but Brewer turns up in Florida frontier literature as early as 1892, in an account of a journey up the Calusa Hatchee from Ft. Myers that voyaged across Lake Okeechobee and emerged at the Miami River: "At the hotel [the Hendry House in Fort Myers] we talked with several men who had been in the employ of the Disston Drainage Co. and who claimed to be familiar with the border of the Everglades. They said no man other than an Indian had ever been through the 'Glades except one 'Brewer' who had been arrested for selling whiskey to the Indians and released on bond, when

113

the Indians in order to effect his escape had carried him across to Miami."

Brewer later served as guide to a Navy lieutenant Hugh L. Willoughby, who crossed the Everglades in 1896. Willoughby recorded this high opinion of the man, despite warnings about his desperate reputation:

Ed Brewer . . . had always made a living by hunting and trapping. He would sometimes be in the woods, and partly in the Everglades, for six months at a stretch without seeing a soul except an occasional Indian. He was a man of medium height, heavily built without being fat, black hair, black eyes, inured to hardship, and able to make himself comfortable in his long tramps, with a canoe, a tin pot, a blanket, a deer-skin, a mosquito-bar, and a rifle, with perhaps a plug or two of tobacco as a luxury. My experience in hunting with him the year previous had shown that he was just the man to face with me whatever dangers there might be in store in my attempt to cross the Everglades. Although warned by some of my friends that he was a dangerous character, I preferred to rely upon my own judgement of human nature rather than unproved stories about him. In our solitary companionship, far from the reach of any law but that of our own making, I always found him brave and industrious, constantly denying himself, deceiving me as to his appetite when our supplies ran low that I might be the more comfortable, and many a night did he stay up an extra hour while I was finishing my notes and plotting work, that he might tuck me in my cheese-cloth from the outside.

Ed Brewer is treated with less reverence in a useful book about the south Florida backcountry of that period, which belittles Willoughby's accomplishment (pointing out that the Glades had already been conquered several times, dating back to the Harney crossing in 1842). And he has *been remembered elsewhere, usually in reference to the Willoughby journey or his chronic troubles with the law. Whatever his merits, Ed Brewer was someone to be reckoned with, despite his humiliation at the hands of Watson.*

RICHARD HAMILTON

What took the fight out of my old friend the Frenchman was some news that come from Marco Key back in the spring of '95. Bill Collier was digging garden muck for his tomatoes from a little mangrove swamp between shell ridges, just down the Caxambas trail from his Marco property, when his spade come up with some Indin war clubs, cordage, and a conch-shell dipper, and some peculiar kind of old wood carving. Cap'n Bill always made a profit out of everything he touched, and it might seem he just had the luck to stumble on what Old Jean searched for all his life. But Bill Collier was also the one man on this coast with enough ambition to report it, and if you was Indin, you would not doubt that he was guided by Calusa spirits on account it was time them old things was brought to light.

For saying such heathen things to her innocent children, Mary cussed me for a idle worshipper, cussed her poor old husband black and blue. Mary lost her Indin heritage before she found it – her daddy John Weeks seen to that – but in her heart she knew that what I said was true.

Captain Bill Collier showed this stuff to some tarpon-fishing Yankee, and this one told another, and next thing you know, them sports was in there shovelling for fun. They take what they don't break back North for souvenirs, and some scientists up that way heard about it, and a famous desecrator named Frank H. Cushing came down to Caxambas right away. Mr Cushing visited Cap'n Bill's diggings that same spring and come back again, winter of '96, took out a whole pile of carved objects, religious stuff, that the Old Calusas had whittled out of wood and shell.

There was bone jewelry and shell cups, ladles, a deer head, a carved fish with bits of turtle shell stuck into it, and some terrible wood masks worn by the shamans. Mr Cushing lugged all these treasures back to Pennsylvania, and Hamilton Disston of Philadelphia, man made such a mess of dredging the Calusa Hatchee, paid for everything.

Them Yankees had gone and stole the Frenchman's glory. I sure hoped nobody would be fool enough to tell him that, least not before I took him out and showed him what he was hunting for close to ten years. He might as well have a look at it before he died. But by that time he was old and poorly, rotting in his bed, with John Leon and Liza trying to tend him. When I told him it was time to show him a Calusa burial, he stared at me like I was crazy, same way he used to. "Throw tar," he said sadly, something like that.

What really twisted up the Frenchman was a wood carving of a cat kneeled like a man. A drawing of that cat was in the papers, and when Lige Carey took them papers up to Possum Key, Chevelier give it one hard look, then sat back hard. After staring out the door a little while, he whispered the one word "Egyptian!" and begun to weep. He was like a man shot through the spine, didn't move for days.

Finally he said to Captain Carey, "I know right away what I am looking, from vair first time I see big foking mounds! But I am looking in wrong foking place!" He never went back to Gopher Key again, he just give up on life. Didn't have no fight left in him, didn't last the year.

"I am . . . homesick?" he would tell my children, to explain his tears. "That is how you say it? Sick of home?"

When the kids visited, they would set him outside like a doll while they cleaned the cabin, but he never noticed nothing, in or out, just set there on his little stoop staring at the sun till he couldn't see no more. Struck his self blind. Might let out a yelp once in a while, but that's about all. Wouldn't let them bathe him, just waved 'em off, that's

117

how furious he talked inside his head. Showed no interest in his feed, just wasted away. Jean Chevelier died of his own spleen, he choked on life.

Young Bill House had been gone a while from Possum Key, and Elijah P. Carey only came and went. Toward the end, as lonely as he was, the old man got tired of Cap'n Carey. "I am alone," he said one day, "no matter he is here or isn't. Silence is better."

Cap'n Carey weren't such a bad feller, but he told himself too many lies. He was a man needed to *talk*, couldn't stand no silence very long, and when that old man paid him no more mind, didn't hardly notice he was there, the poor man took to giving speeches to the wild things that watched from the green walls that was closing in. He was getting so crazy back in there with that silent old man glaring at the sun that he could hear the sun roar and the trees groan in the night, that's what he told us. Had to listen to God's silence, and what he heard put a bad scare in him, is what it come to. He weren't cut out for solitude, and anyway he was always scared his neighbor Mister Watson might recall him from Ed Brewer's posse, maybe take a mind to put a stop to him for good. As for Indins, he was sure them devils was spying on him night and day.

The captain clean forgot how much he despised redskins, that's how lonesome he got when he seen they would not make friends. He was always a big cozy feller, arm around your shoulder, but Indins didn't feel so friendly, not in them days. They was up to something, in the captain's estimation. He'd *feel* their eyes on him and whip around and see 'em standing there. He'd laugh, you know, like they had played a joke to fool him, but they never blinked. The Indins took what he had in trade for plumes and pelts and hides, then went away again, as deaf as ghosts, paying no attention to his holler.

When he got desperate, the captain would pay us a call, and get all upset and red in the face over how mean and ungrateful that old man was who wouldn't even *talk* to

118

him! We didn't have nothing to say to that, and anyways, our family never spoke much cept on Saturdays. Nobody spoke much in the Islands cepting our gabby Liza. That river silence closed over our words like wet mud filling a fresh coon print. Still and all, we'd set with him a little, simmer him down some with good coffee, fish, and grits, and more and more he would not leave, he'd want to stay the night. He wasn't easy in our company, and as my dark boy, Walter, said, you had to feel sorry for a man would take the charity of mixed-breed people. All his life our Walter spoke real quiet, and I never did learn how to read his smile.

One morning that big white man heaved up from our table and kept right on going, headed south. He left some money but not much to take care of his old partner till he come back, he almost threw his arm out waving good-bye. That is how afeared he was we might think poorly of him, which I guess we did, cause we knew that was the last we'd see of Elijah Carey. That big cabin we built for him on Possum Key is up there yet, all thorn-growed and blind windows, and the varmints slinking in and out, and flowers growing through the chinks where wind and rot clear space for the sun and air.

Not long after the captain left, E. J. Watson and his missus paid a call on the Old Frenchman and engaged in a fine educated conversation. When Chevelier told me that, I though he must of had him a French nightmare, but years later, Watson told me the same thing. Neither one cared to speak about it much. But Old Jean told John Leon later he had satisfied himself our neighbor was a murderer, and crazy, too. He begged us to shoot Watson like a dog, first chance we got.

I guess I liked that cantankerous old devil. He spoke plain, he knew some things, and he give me a education, right from the day he came to Chatham Bend. This was four–five years before Watson came there. Jean Chevelier

119

was first to see that Mister Watson would mean trouble, and that he would change our life there in the Islands.

John Leon and Liza tended the old man on his deathbed. He called 'em his godchildren and kind of let on he would leave 'em his property to repay their kindness cause he had no kin. And Leon was very happy about that, cause he had took a liking to Possum Key the time we lived there, and had his heart set on a life down in the Islands.

One day John Leon took Gene to Possum Key because that day his sister could not go. John Leon was twelve–thirteen at the time, Gene two years older. Going upriver with the tide, the two boys passed the Watson Place and never seen a soul, but when they got to Possum Key, they found Ed Watson standing on the shore watching 'em come, and when they waved at him, the man did not wave back. Gene was all for turning tail and heading home but his young brother said Nosir, not till we give Mr Jean his fish and vegetables. Watson watched them till they had that skiff tied up, they was sidewinding to walk on past him when he cleared his throat and said, Good morning, boys. When he asked what they wanted, John Leon tells him they have brought some vittles for the Frenchman.

Mister Watson says, "He has died off of old age." He points to a fresh mound of earth where he has buried him, and the three of 'em stood a little while, thinking that over.

After a while John Leon says, "Never said nothing about me and Liza?" Watson shakes his head. Says he has bought the quitclaim to the place, he is the owner, and that is all he knows. Leon is upset. He says, "Mr Jean looked pretty good, day before yest'day!" And Watson says, "He don't look good today."

Seeing that man smile a little, Gene give a moan and lit out for the boat, John Leon close behind. The boys never knowed nothing bad about Ed Watson – I never told 'em nothing, cause I didn't want to scare 'em – but that day they got wind of something dark, and they headed for home as fast as they could row.

The way John Leon told it puzzled me awhile, cause he admitted Mister Watson never said a single thing to fright 'em. And there was no doubt Jean Chevelier was going to his reward that week if he had one coming. He didn't need no help from E. J. Watson, never mind what Eugene would say later. So maybe those kids was just upset by the shock of hearing the old man had died.

Only mystery was why my old friend changed his mind about his will. Lige Carey always did complain that Jean Chevelier was born ungrateful, and I guess he was.

Next time I seen Mister Watson was in McKinney's little trading post at Chokoloskee, but I never asked that man a single question. Never asked how a dying man planned to spend the money that he got from Watson for the quitclaim, nor what become of that quitclaim money after Old Jean died. So far as I know, ain't nobody asked them questions, then or later, and I'll tell you why.

Folks told themselves they didn't know Chevelier, never liked him any, he was a outsider, ain't that right? Hobnobbed with the Devil and never cared who knowed it, so maybe it was the Devil who come got him. Anyways, it wasn't nobody's damn business what that cranky old foreign feller done with his money. Maybe them mulattas done him in, maybe Carey run off with his silver dollars, who's to say? Never *could* trust them Key West pirates – that's the way it went. Nobody blamed Ed Watson, even behind his back, that's how scared they was that he might hear about it, cause after Santini, the fear of E. J. Watson had grown up thick as weeds in a June garden. Watson knew that and enjoyed the stir in every place he would walk into, and later this was held against him, too, along with being better educated than most everybody else, not to mention smarter, and a better farmer, and a better trader.

But I was in friendship with that Frenchman, we was

121

both outsiders, and I couldn't come up with a good excuse to turn my back on it. Watson knew what my kids must have told me about Jean Chevelier's fresh-dug grave on Possum Key, and maybe he knew I could not let it pass. He never missed much. I seen as quick as I come into the store that he knew I was on the island, he expected me. It was very hard to take that feller by surprise.

I told John Leon, Stay outside. I don't mind saying I was feeling gloomy.

Ed Watson and me got on all right, and it was natural to say good morning. He had on that frock coat he always wore when he come up to Chokoloskee Bay on business, and he shifted as I come forward, cocking his head with that little smile of his, and put the lard tin he was buying back down on the counter with a small sharp click. That freed his hands and give me fair warning, both.

Facing him down made Watson dangerous, you could feel him coiling. I had heard how quick he struck Santini, how quick Dolphus went from a big mouth to a slit throat. Watson's smile had no give to it at all, he was just waiting on me, ready to let go whatever I seen building up behind them eyes.

"Why, howdy, Ed," is what I said.

"Howdy," he says, dead flat. Didn't use my name. His voice advised me there was no way to question him about Chevelier without hinting that he knew more than he should of, and it also advised me to back off while there was time.

I did. I ain't proud about it, but that is what I done. If his knife come out, never mind his gun, there wasn't a man in Chokoloskee would jump in on the side of Richard Hamilton, cause no damn redskin, let alone no damn mulatta, asked hard questions of a white man. The only one who would jump in was John Leon, and I couldn't risk him even if I felt like going up against Ed Watson, which I didn't.

When Watson seen I was aiming to be sensible, he sticks

his hand out, and I shake it. Only hand was offered me all day.

"What's the news," he asks me, "from the Choctaw Nation?"

I was raised not far from where Watson used to live, out in the Nations, Oklahoma territory, so this was just to pass the time of day. But some of my wife's Daniels kin, they heard us, and took his words as a joke on Richard Hamilton. They laughed real loud to flatter their friend Ed, and I grinned, too. I told myself long, long ago to live and let live, not react to the mangy ways of white people, and I never regretted it. I said, "Indins ain't never got no news, Ed, you know that."

My second boy was the one who spread that story about how he caught Ed Watson red-handed at Possum Key, and how it sure looked like Watson killed the Frenchman. Gene was scared to death of Watson, claimed he hated him, but the rest of us had growed accustomed and were not afraid. Ed Watson was always bountiful with my family, never failed to help us out when times were hard. John Leon got real friendly with him in later years, and his sweet wife, Sarah, even more so. They knew what kind of man he was and liked him anyway. Yessir, they was proud to know that feller.

My opinion, Watson never killed my friend Chevelier, and he never bought nor paid for Possum Key. He went over there to talk about it, found Jean Chevelier dead, and he just took it. Being it was only that mean Frenchman, folks was content to let him get away with it.

Even when Mister Watson disappeared, not long after the turn of the century, no one squatted on Possum Key for a long time. Not until a few years later, when it looked like he was never coming back, did people here start in to saying that he done away with that old foreigner to get his money and the claim on Possum Key. And I reckon that's what Mister Watson wanted people to believe, so long as

123

he knowed we wouldn't do a thing about it. It was less trouble to scare squatters off the mounds than it was to shoot 'em.

There's another part to this Chevelier story I don't tell too much. Some way them Mikasukis in the Cypress, they learned about what was dug up at Marco, and they didn't like it. Those old things should been left where they belonged. An Indin burial place had been disturbed, the earth was bleeding from the massacre of birds and gators, and the Mikasukis was afeared that bad spirits of their old enemies might be set loose.

To give fair warning to the white people, the chief medicine man, Doctor Tommie, went to Fort Myers with the trader from Fort Shackleford, east of Immokalee. That trader brought in a covered wagon with three yoke of oxen, an eighteen-day round-trip of seventy miles, all loaded down with gator flats for Henderson's store. Doctor Tommie set quiet on them flats until they got there, then stood up on that wagon to protest all the ruination of his country. That old Indin give warning to the white people, especially Bill Collier and Cushing, and also Mr Disston, who had paid, that something bad was bound to happen if them sacred masks and ceremony cups and such were not give back to the mother earth where they belonged.

This was early 1898, the *Maine* had just been sunk in Havana Harbor and the Spanish-American War was cranking up, and nobody had time to listen to no loco savage in queer headgear and long skirt. Straight off Doctor Tommie seen that the white people did not care to hear his warning, and so he wouldn't speak no more but walked back out into the Cypress before they decided to ship him off to Oklahoma.

Weren't two weeks later, Bill Collier's schooner *Speedwell* capsized in a squall in the Marquesas, down here about eighteen miles off of Key West. Two of his young sons drowned in the cabin along with a whole family of passengers, and Captain Bill, who scarcely got away with his own life, seen their little hands scratching on the port-hole glass as that boat slid down. Meanwhile, Disston killed himself from not knowing what to do with all his money, and pretty soon Frank Cushing died, not fifty years of age, never knew fame nor fortune from his great discovery. Cushing's house burned down after his death, and most everything he looted from sacred Indin ground went back into the earth by way of fire.

You will say that all of this is funny coincidence, but if you was Indin, you would understand it. Indins don't know about coincidence, that is just white-man talk.

SARAH HAMILTON

Richard Hamilton asked the Frenchman to be godfather when Leon and Mary Elizabeth, called Liza, got baptized by a traveling priest. Seemed peculiar that Daddy Richard chose the Frenchman in spite of the way Chevelier ranted on against the Church, and even more peculiar that a man in cahoots with the Devil would agree to it. But both those old fellers were mischievous to start with, and Daddy Richard, once in a long while, liked to stick a pin in that big wife of his to hear her scream. As for the Frenchman, he esteemed Richard Hamilton without ever admitting how much he depended on his kindness. Them two was a couple of old misfits, sure enough, but Daddy Richard stayed real calm, never tangled with nobody, while the Frenchman was thorny as old cat-claw, raked everyone who come across his path except Liza and Leon.

Richard Hamilton was dead honest, and there ain't too many who can handle that. Never said what he did not know to be a fact, he'd tell you no less than the truth but not one word more. He was very cut and dried, never added and he never took away. When Leon's fool brother got all lathered up, yelling what he would do to this one, say to that one, and working himself into a uproar, his father would just set there looking innocent, like he was listening to a bird or something. "That so, Gene?" he'd say. He believed in live and let live, and if Eugene wanted to holler, let him do it. But if you asked him straight if there was anything to what Gene said, he'd shake his head. "No, there sure ain't," he'd say, and spit, case you missed the point.

Right to his end, and he lived close to a hundred, Leon's pap was a no-nonsensical old man. He wore a white mustache and beard on skin smooth as mahogany, wore a round straw hat and galluses, and he went barefoot. Pap walked away from his last pair of shoes back in '98 and his feet still thanked him every day, is what he said. His boys took after him. Up until the day we left the rivers, 1947, there weren't one self-respecting pair of shoes in the whole family.

The way Mother Mary always told it, Richard Hamilton's mother was a Choctaw princess who got wooed out of her doeskins by an English gentleman, a gun dealer, back in Oklahoma. "Booze peddler and his squaw woman is more like it," Pap said. All the same, Pap had narrow English features to go with his mother's skin, which you might call dusty. He was reared up around a Catholic mission, and he read the Catholic Bible and lived by it, too, till the day he died, and called himself a Oklahoma Indin.

My mother-in-law, she was Seminole on her mother's side, but because her daddy was old John Weeks, the pioneer settler at Chokoloskee, she seen herself as white as a nun's buttocks. She always acted like she done her man a favor to run off with him, though to my mind just the opposite was true. My husband, John Leon, was her baby boy and her favorite among her children, and mine, too. That was about the only thing I ever did agree upon with that gruesome female, and even on that one, our reasons were not the same.

I loved that big strong boy because he stuttered when he got excited, and had him a generous heart under all that roughness. But his mama liked him mostly for his looks, and his fair skin especially. However, I will say for that woman, she was loyal to all her children, even Gene. To hear her tell it, they were the only children in southwest Florida that was worth their keep. She'd say, Folks is always carrying on about how lonely it must be for womenfolk in them awful islands, rain and mud and nothing but skeeters and sand flies to keep you company. And I just say, Heck no, it ain't lonely! Don't *need* no company when you got children like mine!

John Leon was born the year the Hamiltons give up farming Chatham Bend and went fishing for a year on Fakahatchee. The next year they came back to Chatham Bend, but they were fishermen from that time on. Walter, Gene, and Liza was all born on Chatham Bend in the 1880s, then Ann E. on Possum Key about the time Mister Watson first showed up. Walter was oldest, Eugene in the middle, and then John Leon – they were all two years apart. Gene was fair-haired, and as fair-skinned as Leon, but his nose and lips was kind of thick, you know, and his hair had a kind of little wave to it.

Them long-tongues up in Chokoloskee called Leon Hamilton a white man, but that was just their way to swipe at Daddy Richard, who started the fracas by going off with John Week's daughter. The one reason Leon was white, they said, was because a white man got into the pen when the family spent that year at Fakahatchee.

Mother Mary always said, "John Leon is a Weeks,." She didn't want her baby boy called Hamilton, and that was because she was a cruel and stupid woman, and didn't care if she humbled her own husband, broke his heart. Daddy Richard would have gone along according to his peaceable philosophy, but John Leon said Heck no, he was Leon Hamilton, even though being a Weeks might have made his road in life a whole lot smoother. But she made Eugene ashamed of his own father, and for a while there, as a boy, he tried to call himself Gene Weeks, but nobody took that very serious except his mother. It was his own Weeks cousins had to beat it out of him.

Loving mother though she was, Mary Weeks cared less for her darker ones – for Liza, who was coffee-color, and for Walter, her firstborn, whose skin drank every drop that wasn't white in both his parents. Walter had his daddy's narrow features – he was handsome! – but that poor feller could of passed for colored anywhere he wanted. Walter Hamilton was a loner, came and went in silence, and later in life he moved back out of sight, up Lost Man's River.

Walter Hamilton kept so quiet, and he *moved* so quiet, that it was easy for Gene to pretend he wasn't there. Gene spoke in his rough way whether his own brother heard or not, and sometimes I think that's the way both of 'em wanted it. In a boat, Walter was always in the bow, and never looked around if he could help it. Had his own world in his head to keep him company, poor Walter did.

Leon always loved his brother Walter, and when they were boys, Gene and Leon were good brothers, too, but as life went on, they grew to hate each other, and the seed of the trouble, Leon told me, was Gene's bad attitude toward Walter, which came from a bad attitude about himself. Once in a while one of his Weeks or Daniels cousins would get drunk and tease Eugene – Your brother Leon, now, he looks almost like a white man, don't he, Gene? – and all Gene's rage would get roiled up, he'd fight to prove that he was white till he was black-and-blue, and in the end, it was Walter got the blame. In later years, when Walter stayed off by himself, Leon held that against Gene, he came right out with it. Said, "Gene, if your own brother ain't good enough for you, then you ain't good enough for me." Just wouldn't tolerate it. We moved across to Plover Key till Leon cooled a little.

Cruel Mary Weeks claimed to be color-blind, pointing at her husband as her proof, but in her heart it was her own color she despised. Dark blood was nor the poison that was passed down in the family, it was that despising.

These Cypress Indins, or Mikasukis, were Creeks same as the Seminoles, Daddy Richard said, only their language was Hitchiti, not Muskogee, they were more hunters than farmers, kept no cattle. They stayed apart from white people, and was real strict. Back in the old days they used to put half-white babies to death, and the parents, too. Today most Indins want to be whites, and seeing that whites look down on blacks, they have got so they think they are somewhat better than what blacks are. Don't matter what color their own skin is, they have that poison. Mary Weeks come down from that poisoned kind, in my opinion.

So she said her husband was descended from a Choctaw princess, and her own Seminole mother was a princess, too. Come right down from Chief Osceola, straight as an arrow. She was no kind of kin at all to any real flesh-and-blood Indins that you could point at, she would not admit to a single redskin relative that ever peed a drop on Florida soil.

This whole darn foolishness of blood will be the ruin of this country. As Old Chevelier told Daddy Richard, human beings was all one shade when they first appeared on earth, and only turned into different-colored races when they scattered out across the continents. The way they breed around these days, the Frenchman said, they were sure to wind up all one color again, and the sooner the better, too, he'd say, because life was terrible enough without this useless misery of color.

We had all colors in the Hamilton clan, and that's for sure. Jean Chevelier called Hamilton "the true New World family," because Richard Hamilton never thought about your color. If you came along and you were hungry, why he fed you, and he made Old Mary go along with that, and Eugene, too. Otherwise he would not bother his head, he let his wife make the decisions. Leon and me, we felt the same way as his daddy, we shared our table with all kinds and creeds. For that we was called nigger-lovers by the ones that didn't come right out and call us niggers. Course folks with manners, they might say mulattas.

My mother was a Holland, Irish Catholic, and my daddy Henry Gilbert Johnson was no kin at all to the Charley Johnson bunch at Chokoloskee nor that Christ Johnson from Mound Key whose bad son Hubert run off later on with Liza, nor Johnny Johnson who was one of Josie Jenkin's seven husbands. Chokoloskee people called my dad a conch from the Bahamas, but he come from the Channel Isles of England to trade some furs and feathers off the Indins. I showed up in '89, same year as Lucius Watson. Later in life, me'n Lucius was always just a little bit in love, but not so's anyone would notice, even him.

Gilbert Johnson used to camp at Lost Man's before the Hamiltons came on south from Chatham River. I recall the day we found the Hamiltons at this Wood Key camp. I was just thirteen, Leon a few years older, and we took one look and my heart was throbbing and everything else too. My sister Rebecca felt the same for Eugene, so my dad got us out of there, but after a year, those two boys came and took us.

Mother Mary said, All right, but we had to marry – being the white person, she naturally made all the decisions in the family – so Gene and Leon married us nice and proper in the old Ocean Chapel in Key West. I never regretted it, I married a good man. But Becca's man was sly and ornery, and by the end of it, his own daddy wouldn't have one thing to do with him.

I guess Daddy Richard missed old Jean Chevelier, cause after he moved down to Wood Key, he got the same kind of scrappy friendship going with my daddy. Even when Dad come to roost alongside Hamiltons on Wood Key, spent his old age fooling with fish and boats, he'd look at Richard and just shake his head. "How I rue the day," he'd sigh, "that I ever fell afoul of these bloody Hamiltons!" I been saying that to Leon all my life!

A critical asset in E. J. Watson's tumultuous career was his strong connection with the powerful cattlemen and bankers of the west coast city of Fort Myers, Florida, commissioned as Fort Harvie during the Third Seminole War, then reactivated during the Civil War as a base for Union raiders harassing the cattle trains that were still supplying beef to the Confederacy. Should you care to inspect it, the following material from my History of Southwest Florida *may give some indication of why the marriage of Mr Watson's daughter to W. G. Langford had such profound reverberations on Watson's life.*

Fort Myer's first cattleman, Jake Summerlin, had worked cattle from the age of seven, bartering the twenty slaves in his inheritance for his first herd of six thousand head in the 1840s. He was a veteran of the Seminole Wars and a pioneer cattleman on the Alachus Prairie, moving huge herds with his cowboys and a grub wagon all the way from the St. Johns River southwest across Florida to the Calusa Hatchee. In the Civil War, Jake Summerlin sold cattle on the hoof to the Confederacy and smuggled cattle through the Union blockade to sell in Cuba. In the last year of the War he sold herds to the Union, which paid better.

After the War, Fort Myers was abandoned, but by 1869, Summerlin and his partners were moving their herds south once more and swimming them across the Calusa Hatchee and down to the pens and docks at Punta Rassa, where Summerlin took over the old Army barracks. Leasing pens and docks from the International Ocean and Telegraph Company, he made a fortune, shipping ten thousand head of his wild range cattle to Cuba every year. The Spaniards came up the Calusa

Hatchee to buy his longhorns at Cattle Dock Point, paying Old Jake in gold doubloons, which he left about in sacks, old wool socks, and cigar boxes.

Already the homesteaders were descending on south Florida, creaking through the woods in covered wagons hauled through the hot sand by two or three yokes of mules or oxen. The pistol shot of their cracked whips, echoing across the hot dry landscape, could be heard a country mile away. At the Calusa River these Baptist "crackers" found good river-bottom land and built thatch houses, grew good crops, experimented with pineapples and coconuts, sugar cane and cabbage, and citrus plantations. But with the Key West market so far to the south, perishable produce could not survive the slow hot schooner voyage, and the pioneer farmers subsisted on hunting and fishing, living off the land. One day, the railroad would surely arrive, erupting with Yankee tourists and investors waving new green bills, and these trains would carry the bountiful winter produce to the northern markets. The Calusa Hatchee would be dredged and the Everglades drained, and Fort Myers would take a leading place in the new century.

These were the intoxicated years when Hamilton Disston, tycoon of Philadelphia, contracted with the State of Florida to acquire four million acres of the Glades for one million dollars, on the condition that his Atlantic and Gulf Coast Canal and Okeechobee Land Company drain the Kissimmee-Okeechobee region by way of the Calusa Hatchee to bring this natural wonder under man's dominion. Already Disston's mighty dredge was far upriver, past the Calusa mounds of clear white sand, past the ancient canals that joined the mounds to the clear and tranquil flow of the silent river. Churning out clouds of smoke and noise that drifted for miles across the shining waters, the dredge had shifted and resettled the vast muds of the Everglades in a mighty paroxysm of misdirected progress. By 1888, the dredge project

133

had foundered, but not before the fragile water system had been broken, and the whole Okeechobee drainage opened to settlement, driving the remnant Indians farther southward into the Big Cypress. Through raw canals, the detritus and overflow of Okeechobee poured away westward, down the old Calusa River, which only a few years before had run black and clear over shimmering white sands of ancient shell.

Soon that white sand was covered over in dead mud and slime. The only one who seemed to care was the proprietor of the Punta Rassa Hotel, renamed the Tarpon House after a New York sportsman caught the first "silver king" on rod and reel in '85. Ever since, rich Yankees had flocked here in winter migration, pursuing the tarpon, Spanish mackerel, and kingfish, the snook and redfish that flashed through the emerald passes of the barrier islands. The millionaires paid handsomely to "rough it" at the Tarpon House, with its manly fare and rude bare floors, tin washbowls, china slop jars, and frontier spittoons. But now the Okeechobee muds, clouding the river, were turning the flow of silver fishes farther and farther off short into the Gulf.

A newcomer, Jim Cole, was pleased by this evidence of human progress. Cole was soon in business with Captain Francis Hendry and son James in Cole & Hendry's general store, which in those days specialized in lumber. He called himself a cattleman, though from the start, this man seems to have been a dealer, less interested in cattle than quick sales. Cole also called himself a "boomer," since he aimed to make a boomtown of Fort Myers. His was the first place of business to install a kerosene street lamp and a sidewalk of white shell, barged from the gouged Indian mounds upriver. The year after his arrival, he pushed through the incorporation of the town, and within two years, his name — by now synonymous with the town's progress — was chronically cited in the Fort Myers Press for bold and

134

exemplary civic deeds. He soon sold his share of Cole &
Hendry to another cattleman, Dr T. E. Langford, and
the year after that he bought a Langford & Hendry
cattle schooner, the old Lily White, *after which he*
dubbed himself "Captain Cole," though never a soldier
or ship's captain in his life.

With the Democratic victory in 1886, Cole organized
the cattlemen in a crusade to create a brave new country
named in honor of the Confederate general Robert E.
Lee. Frustrated by lack of roads and rail, by the with-
holding of Monroe County funds for a bridge to the
north bank of the river, and by the lack of interest
shown by Monroe County officials in faraway Key West,
the cattlemen sought to separate the north part of
Monroe as Lee County, with Fort Myers as the county
seat. The "county fathers," Captains F. A. Hendry and
Jim Cole, were made county commissioners,and it was
Cole who rammed through Doc Langford's cousin as
first county sheriff, a job "ol' T. W." performed without
risk or distinction until a young cowhand named Frank
B. Tippins swept him out of office twelve years later.

In 1887, a west coast railroad terminus was finally,
established, not at Fort Myers but at Punta Gorda,
thirty miles off to the north. As cattleman-trader Francis
Hendry would observe, "America is moving, and Fort
Myers has been left behind." With no bridge across the
Calusa Hatchee and no roads, the town on the broad
tranquil river remained cut off from the rest of the
country except by sea, and commerce was limited to
nonperishable export products – otter and raccoon pelts,
deer and alligator hides, bird plumes, taxidermy speci-
mens, sugar and molasses, and beef cattle. The cattle
trade to Cuba was worth far more than all the other
businesses combined.

In the year of the financial panic, 1893 (when E. J.
Watson arrived in the region), the cattle industry on
which the town depended suffered badly, and so did the

growing trade in wild animal parts. But the following year, big freezes farther north in Florida drove many citrus growers south to the Calusa River. A rise in land values, a first rush of investment, was consolidated a few years later by new cattle profits from the Spanish-American War.

Without a railroad or a road bridge to link it to the outside world, Fort Myers remained a muddy cow town, or a dusty one, depending on the season. The cattle docks at Punta Rassa that T. E. "Doc" Langford and James Hendry had bought in the eighties from Jake Summerlin were still the foundation of the Fort Myers economy, as the cattlemen-traders extended their concerns to land development, rail commerce, and banking.

Under the circumstances, you will understand how significant it was that within five years of his arrival in the region, Mr Watson's daughter Carrie married T. E. Langford's son.

Meanwhile, Mr Watson's bouts of violent carousing were restricted to the seaports of Key West and Tampa. There is no report of intemperate behavior in Everglade or Chokoloskee, where his friends and neighbors had most chance to observe him, nor in Fort Myers, where his genteel family came to live. His son-in-law, Walter G. Langford, was a friend of Sheriff Frank B. Tippins from their cowboy days, which doubtless encouraged a certain lenience towards Langford's father-in-law. In addition, Mr Watson was protected by Langford's powerful friends, including the aforementioned Jim Cole.

CARRIE WATSON

March 3, 1898 What a momentous year, and scarcely started.

On January 1st, electric light came on for the first time at the new Fort Myers Hotel, and also in several business establishments, Langford & Hendry, for one. (Of course, our "fair city" has had electric light since 1887, when Mr Edison lit up his Seminole Lodge. That glorious blaze was the first electric lighting in the land, claims Captain Cole, but he warns us not to pester Mr Edison on that point. He's scared we might find out it isn't so!)

On February 16, our international telegraph station at Punta Rassa got the very first word in all America about the explosion of the great battleship *Maine* while lying peacefully at anchor in Havana Harbor! 260 young Americans, killed in their sleep! The "dastardly Spaniards," as our paper calls them, claim it was the ship's own magazines, but no one who wants the Spanish "off our doorstep" is going to believe that for a minute.

And here is the third historic piece of news! On 8 July, Miss Carrie Watson will marry Mr Walter G. Langford of this city!

In the evening Walter walks me down to the new hotel to see the new electric lights and the beautiful royal palms, and attend the weekly concerts of the Fort Myers Brass band at the new bandstand. The whole town turns out to hear patriotic airs in honor of "our brave boys" in Cuba, who have brought so much prosperity to our town. Afterwards, if there is room, he "courts" me – whatever can that mean? – on the old wood bench beneath the banyan tree just opposite the Baptist church, from where our good shepherd, Mr Whidden, can spy on us young "lovers" through his narrow windows.

Who would have thought "the Union banner" would ever be cheered here in Fort Myers? Well, Stars and Stripes are everwhere! What must it be like at Key West Harbor! And now we're after the "d — Spaniards" in the Philippines!

Remember the Maine! our cowboys yell, galloping through the streets, raising such dust! We're shipping our cattle to Cuba again, not for those cruel Spaniards this time but for Teddy Roosevelt's Rough Riders. The Hendrys and Summerlins, Captain Jim Cole and the Langfords are feeling very patriotic these days. Captain Cole says it right out, "War is the best damned business that there is!" (To which Papa retorts, "These civic leaders use up too much air!")

Mama deplores the cattlemen's tin patriotism, all this misty-eyed flag-waving and fine speechifying. Our brave young men, who have no say about it, are sent off to be killed so that thick-bodied old businessmen can wave the flag and prosper off our "splendid little war," as some politician dared call it. (How "splendid" is it for those scared homesick boys who do the dying? Mama asks.)

Papa, too, is fiercely patriotic (although the words "brave Yankee boys" still set his teeth on edge), but seeing the Langfords and Mr Cole make so much money off this "Yankee War" has made him cynical. The Watsons were planters in South Carolina when these people were still "ridge-runners," as he calls them, and he'll be d – d, says he, if he'll let himself be patronized by this "redneck gentry."

Walter calls Jim Cole a "man's man," while admitting he is a "rough diamond." I can't find any diamond in the man, a hard dull glint is all I see. Dear Walter has his weaknesses, like whiskey, but he is kind, that's why folks like

138

him. Captain Cole has no give to him, Mama observes, and knowing this, he takes Walter along to "grease" his business dealings – this is Papa talking.

Walter would like to "go bag him a Spaniard," but he cannot abandon his mother when his father is so ill, so he'll stay home and learn his father's business. Dr Langford is an excellent doctor, he takes good care of Mama, but in recent years – Papa again – his keen interest in finance makes him pay more mind to cattle than to people. "Doc" Langford and Mr Cole are grazing stock at Raulerson Prairie at Cape Sable, but Papa says the horseflies and mosquitoes will show them what damn fools they are if the poor coast grass doesn't starve their cattle first. If Papa didn't rest his cows in a screened shed between sunset and sunup, they would run out of blood, he says, let alone milk.

Papa met José Martí in Key West, and admired his Cuban Revolutionary Party, but he says we should not fool ourselves about our interests. He hates the Spaniards as sincerely as the next man, but says the U.S. picked this fight in Cuba, *Maine* or no *Maine*, it's just an excuse to clean Spain out of our hemisphere once and for all, and grab the Philippines and Puerto Rico while we're at it. The War with Spain isn't one bit different than what he still calls "the War of Yankee Aggression": the Old South, says he, was the first conquest of the Yankee Empire.

Dear Papa will not salute the Stars and Stripes. "An Edgefield man would die first," Papa says. Yet he doesn't like it when Mama quotes Mark Twain, who has recently written that Old Glory should be changed to a pirate flag, with black stripes and each star a skull and crossbones. As long as this great land of ours is fighting, the men aren't fussy about *who* they fight – this is Mama talking with her small bent smile. Papa smiles, too, but he is wary. Mama's needles fly as she quotes from an editorial read at the library. ' "The taste of Empire is in the mouth of the people, even as the taste of blood – " '

"Kindly let me read my own paper in peace!" Papa snaps his paper.

"This is God Almighty's war, we are only His agents' – do *you* believe that, dear?"

"For God's sake, Jane! Be still!"

'In God We Trust' – we inscribe God on our coins! So even when we torment and burn the poor freed darkies" – Mama speaks more and more softly, intent on her knitting – "we always know that God is on our side."

Mama hums a little to soothe Papa and ease her own frayed nerves. I see her bosom rise and fall. She explains to her children that the dreadful poverty and famine after the War Between the States had shaken our men's confidence that they could provide for their own families on the kind of wages being paid to new black citizens. Perhaps this was why so many of our men feared and punished darkies, who were desperate for a living, too, and were wandering the roads throughout the South.

Papa says nothing. He's no longer reading. I think, *Please* Mama! but she says, The men say they punish darkies to protect their women, isn't that it, dear?

Papa stared at her in dreadful warning, but she raised those innocent eyebrows and went on knitting. "A brave woman" – she pretends to address me, as if only females could make sense of the ways of men – "has recently petitioned President McKinley about the lynching of ten thousand Negroes, almost all of them innocent of any crime, and this in the past twenty years alone." And she points her needle at Papa's newspaper, which is lifted high to screen her from his sight. I am terrified by Mama's scary courage.

Papa slaps his paper down. I'll be back, he says, and leaves the room. Mama lets the air cool off a little.

I am startled by Mama's "radical" ideas, but Lucius and Eddie, who are now nine and eleven, want to run to Ireland's Dock and get their papa to buy them candy at Dancy's Stand before he sails off on the *Gladiator*. The two boys twist like eels upon their chairs, and Lucius pretends he is suffering a call of nature, but Mama doesn't let them off so easily. She tells them poor papa was Lucius's age at the start of the Civil War, and "not much more than Eddie's age," when it was finished. Grandfather Elijah had gone off as a soldier, and Papa had Granny Ellen and Aunt Minnie to take care of, and here he was, still only a young boy! Papa had never once complained, but she'd learned from Granny Ellen that his childhood had been very hard indeed. The family never had enough to eat, and he was deprived of formal education, while "you spoiled boys," Mama said, "have to be begged to do your lessons! And here is poor Papa, in his forties, still trying to learn something about Ancient Greece!" She pointed at Papa's poor old schoolbook, *History of Greece*, which resided on the table by his chair. She had brought it all the way from Oklahoma.

When Papa is not in the house, our Mama makes no bones about her strong opinions. She is still upset by the Supreme Court, which was upheld segregation on the railroads. "What can more certainly arouse race hate," she reads to us, quoting the dissenting Justice Harlan, "than state enactments which in fact proceed on the ground that colored citizens are so inferior and degraded that they cannot be allowed to sit in public coaches occupied by white citizens?"

Mama says that Indians would also suffer these new "Jim Crow laws" if we hadn't wiped most Indians out with our bullets and diseases. They sure don't count for much in Florida, there's so few left. Papa describes how they come in now to Everglade and Marco with dugouts full of hides and pelts and feathers. They trade for axes, knives, and kettles, candy, coffee, bacon, sewing needles, and even sewing machines. The women make up calico in yellow, red, and black – coral snake colors, Papa noticed. He thinks the coral snake must have secret significance.

It seems the Indians are still scared that the few families

141

left in the Big Cypress will be captured and removed to Oklahoma. They call themselves Mikasuki and not Seminole, but nobody listens to them, least of all Captain Cole, who declares in his clangorous way that he would gladly round up the whole bunch and ship 'em as far as New Orleans in his cattle schooner "at no charge to the government, just to be rid of 'em, because they ain't no different from wolves nor panthers or any other kind of skulking varmint, and sooner or later they are going to be in the way."

Papa says this was the first d – d thing he ever heard Cole say that he agreed with, and also the first that sounded sincere, all except the part about not charging.

May 6, 1898 Captain Jim Cole, acting too serious, has brought Mama a book. In a hushed voice, he asked her to read a brief marked section, saying he would return for it a little later. That was the one time, Mama told me, she ever heard Captain Cole speak quietly, as if he imagined one of us had died. That man was always first with the news, she said, turning the book over, bad news especially.

"Hell on the Border!" she exclaimed. "My goodness!" She held it on her lap for a long time before she opened it.

The marked pages told all about Belle Starr, the Outlaw Queen, and her "life of reckless daring" and how that life had ended on her birthday, February 3rd of 1889. Mama sniffed, saying her birthday was actually the day before. She closed the book again. I demanded it, and read aloud: "About fourteen months earlier, a neighbor, one Edgar Watson, had removed from Florida. Mrs Watson was a woman of unlimited education, highly cultured and possessed of a natural refinement. Set down in the wilderness, surrounded by uneducated people, she was attracted to Belle, as unlike the others, and the two women soon became fast friends. In a moment of confidence she had

142

entrusted Belle with her husband's secret, he had fled from Florida to avoid arrest for murder . . ."

After Belle was murdered, the book said, "suspicion could point to none other than Watson," who was released for want of evidence but was later imprisoned in Arkansas for horse stealing and killed while attempting to escape from an Arkansas prison.

"Well, there you are! I cried. "That last part proves that this know-it-all has the wrong Watson entirely."

Mama had resumed her knitting, but now her needles stopped. "No, Carrie, honey." She put her work down and took me in her arms.

My heart leapt so I had to press it with my fingertips. At last Mama whispered that the Florida death I was worrying about supposedly involved Rob's uncle. He was a most unpleasant man who had blamed Papa for Rob's mother's death. He lived some way off, in Suwannee County, and she had no idea what happened, the family never spoke about it. One day Papa came home to the farm and told her to pack everything into the wagon, they were going away. He said a shooting had occurred which would be blamed on him, said they'd be coming for him. He never said another word about it.

She held me so tight I could not see her face, I could feel a stiffness in her. Then she let me go and we sat quiet. My heart was pounding, so I knew it wasn't broken.

Even before the war, she said, a man's whole honor might depend on his willingness to fight a duel over almost *anything*. I knew she was thinking about Papa, our strange dear fierce Scots Highlands hothead, who sometimes drinks too much and gets in trouble, all the more when he imagines that his Edgefield County honor has been slighted. Grandfather Elijah, whom Papa rarely mentions, was also very quick to take offense, and so were many men from Edgefield County, well-born or otherwise, Mama said. When I asked if Papa was well-born, she said, Your Granny Ellen and Great-Aunt Tabitha in Columbia County

143

are educated people, and your father was taught manners, though his education was pitifully neglected.

I asked Mama if she had known Belle Starr, and she said she had. She said that Belle was a generous woman in some ways, not at all stupid, only foolish in her hankering after a romantic Wild West that never was. The Oklahoma Territory was a primitive and violent place where life was rough and cheap, and where whites, Indians, and Negroes – the worst elements of all three races – were mixed up together in an accursed country of mud, loneliness, and terrible tornadoes. Negroes were there early as Indian slaves, and after the war, a lot more blacks had drifted into the Indian Nations where civilization had been left behind. The inhabitants of this wild border country were mostly half-breeds. There was no law and no education, no chivalry, culture, morals, nor good manners, Mama said, and nothing the slightest bit uplifting about any of it. But Belle Starr's father had been a judge back in Missouri, and Belle had a little education, she played the piano fair to middling, and she wanted above all to be a lady. She rented some good bottom land to Papa and asked Mama to tutor her, for her own betterment was the real basis of their friendship.

"Mama," I said after a while, "did Papa kill Belle Starr or did he not?"

Mama muttered, as if quoting, "The case was dismissed because sufficient evidence was never brought against him." Again, she was holding on to me for dear life, murmuring into my ear. "Mister Watson never went to trial," Mama said. I couldn't see her eyes.

It is one thing to hear rumors about Papa's dangerous past and quite another to see it written in a book! Captain Cole asserts that *Hell on the Border* will cause a public scandal. I heard him exclaim to Walter on the veranda, "They's people snooping through this thing that couldn't read their own damn name, last time I seen 'em!' Right away he

144

hollered, "Begging your pardon, miss!" He knew I could hear him, he was looking around the way he does to see who he might be amusing. Mama says a man like this is always on the lookout for an audience, he never talks just to the person he is talking to. But sometimes he is sort of amusing, and when Mama is around, Walter has to frown real hard to keep from grinning.

Since that famous article was written a few years ago about our refined and cultured life here in Fort Myers, all our gentry try hard to live up to it, and dime adventure novels from New York about the Wild West and the Outlaw Queen are a popular diversion among our *literati* – an Italian term, our paper tells us, for "people who can read." Everyone in America today knows everything there is to know about Belle Starr, who is already immortalized in a book about notable American females. The women are on the march! Mama says, waving her knitting needle like a baton. She winks at me when Papa clears his throat. Being indoors in ladies' company, he stomps outside to hawk and spit and does not come back. That other time, he went all the way to Chatham Bend just to cool off!

Though Walter has said not a single word, Captain Cole assures us that the Langfords know about *Hell on the Border* (Who do you suppose showed them the book? sniffed Mama) and are "much perturbed." (It is a sign of ignorant pretension, Mama fumes, to use a long word or fancy phrase when a short and simple one will do.) Captain Cole told Mama it might be best if Papa remains in the Ten Thousand Islands at the time of the wedding. Mama assured him that our family would not require his advice on suitable behaviour, and bade him a very cool good day. I have never heard dear Mama take such a haughty tone.

"That man has the manners of a piney-woods rooter!" she exclaimed, banging the door behind him, but she had already come around to his old hoggish point of view about the wedding. I had, too, and alone upstairs, I cried and cried and cried. How very often I'd imagined the beautiful

145

church service and my dear Papa giving me away, knowing how handsome and elegant he would look there at the altar in his black frock coat and silk shirt and cravat, how much more genteel than these "upper-crust crackers," as Mama calls the cattlemen.

But but but – O dear and patient diary, most of my upset has been caused by my great shame, my *eternal shame*, for giving in to everybody's wishes! I was terrified Papa might drink too much, insult our guests, or provoke some violent quarrel (as he does regularly in Port Tampa and Key West, hints Captain Cole, and Walter knows about it, too). Heaven knows what might happen after that! Walter might withdraw from our marriage – *or be withdrawn*, poor dear, for nobody is quite sure, and his child bride least of all, how much our Walter was responsible for his own betrothal! Papa suspects that Captain Cole, who cannot keep those thick hands out of anything, was behind this fateful match from the very start.

Well, I love Walter, yes, I do, but no one can say any thought of this marriage was mine! I was simply told how lucky I was to make such a catch "under the circumstances" (Papa's bad name), and not to be silly about it, either, because grown-ups know best. I am frightened, truly, and sure to be found wanting.

God bless dear Mama! Being educated by our local standards, I can cook and sew. I have taken care of baby brothers since the age of five, I can run a household (with guidance from dear Mama!). But is that enough? The poor little bride, if truth be known, is scared to death.

I am scarcely thirteen – can that be old enough to marry? Oh, *everything* is so embarrassing, I can scarcely look one person in the face! This body of mine in an awful awful way gives sign that it is ready, or ready for child-bearing is what I mean, but it is a child's body all the same. A grown man will claim possession of it, humiliating the poor child trapped inside!

I am a child, a child! It *must* be a child's heart that wakes

146

me in the night, and starts to pound even in daylight hours. Is the heart part of the body? Or the mind? Are heart and soul the same?

Mr Whidden has pimples and upsetting breath and no good answers to such questions. (The Good Book says, the Good Book says, the Good Book says . . . !) He dares say I am much too young to "bother my pretty head about such metaphysical dilemmas," he dares say "things will work out in the end." What *I* don't "dare say," and least of all to him, is that what truly bothers me is this low creature of flesh, blood, and ugly body hair which imprisons the pure and spiritual ME! But since I can't mention my earthly form to Mr Whidden, we simply ignore this coarse female vessel that fidgets and perspires in his face, pretending the poor girl's sweet virginal inquiries come from some higher and more holy source.

Why won't they understand? I am still a little girl, an overgrown child. I go to Sunday School, I work hard at my lessons, and Mama tutors me and my squirming little brothers. In the evenings after school these days we read "Romeo and Juliet" together. Juliet was just my age when Romeo "came to her," as Mama reminds me when the boys are absent. She is trying to teach me something about life while there is time, but the poor thing goes rose red in the face at her own words, and as for me, I want to hide, I screech Oh *Mama!* and burst into tears out of pure embarrassment.

Juliet lived long ago, it is only a story, but here in my budding heart it is all too real. A grown man twenty-five years old, nearly twice her age, will sleep in the same bed with Miss Carrie Watson! Mama says he is a decent young man – what's decent about lying down on top of a young girl and doing ugly things without his clothes on! She says, Well Papa will talk to him – what can Papa say? Don't touch a hair on my daughter's head – let alone her you-know-what – or I will kill you?

No, it's not funny in the least, I can't think why I laugh,

the whole town must be snickering already! Oh, it's so scary, and so *awful*! How can Mama let this happen? I'm not ready, I'm just *not*!

Sometimes I cry myself to sleep.

And sometimes, riding my horse along the river, there comes a tingling that seems very far from religious yearning. Am I a sinner for seeking out these shiverings? A sinner for my curiosity – no, worse – about being kissed? A sinner for imagining that "the fate worse than death" might not be so dreadful after all?

With my sinful attitude, can marriage itself be a sin? Please God forgive me, please God don't let *anyone* find this diary, or I shall run and throw myself into the river.

One day out riding we saw a stallion covering a mare in a corral, and I was horrified (I hope), and Walter got all flustered in the face and seized the reins and turned me right around. I wanted to look back, isn't that awful? It is this darn old body following me around that wants to know so much!

Walter is very shy and gentle, he tries to tell me that he will be good to me, and will not hurt me, but he cannot find a way to say this without embarrassing both of us half to death. He supposes I have no idea what he is getting at, and for my part, I can scarcely hint I understand lest he think me wanton, and so we both nod and smile like ninnies, all pink and sweaty with confusion and distress.

These are the times I trust him most and love him best. He is so boyish, for all his "hell and high water" reputation! He is truly ashamed over that cowboy's death, he blames his drinking for the accident, and for how terrible poor Dr Winkler must feel. Walter makes no excuses for himself, he comes right out with it, says nothing would have happened if he and his cowboys had not tormented that poor old darkie. He vows his intention to make something of himself in his new job at Langford & Hendry, not just "punch cows," as he puts it, and waste his hard-earned dollars in pure devilment.

Dr Langford hasn't long to live (we just hope he will be strong enough to join the wedding) and Walter wonders if Mr Hendry will give him a fair chance in the business after his father's death or just ignore him as a young ne'er-do-well. If that should happen, he will quit the partnership and start out on his own. Since that terrible freeze in '95. Walter has had his eye out for good land farther south. He went down to Caxambas with Fred Ludlow to look at the Ludlow pineapple plantation, and now Mr Roach, the Chicago railroad man who has taken such a liking to him, is very interested in what Walter tells him about possibilities for citrus farming out at Deep Lake Hammock, where Billy Bowlegs had his gardens in the Indian Wars.

It was our own Papa who told Walter about that. Papa knows about these things, he always has these sure-fire ideas that he can't act on. There are still Indians out there today, but Papa declares that Indians will be no problem, there aren't enough of them to stand in the way of planters who mean business. Walter rode that wild country a lot in his cow hunter days, and says that the Indians' grown-over plantations have the richest soil anywhere south of the Calusa Hatchee.

The main problem will be getting the produce to market. From Deep Lake it is a terrible distance across the Cypress to Fort Myers but only thirteen miles south to the Storter docks at Everglade, and Mr Roach feels that a Deep Lake–Everglade rail line might be just the answer. (And to whom does John Roach credit *this* idea? – to our dear Papa!)

Papa has earned a fine reputation as a planter, his "Island Pride" syrup, which he sells wholesale in Tampa, is already famous in these parts. One day Mr Roach chanced to tell Walter what a pity it was that E. J. Watson was confined to forty acres in the Islands, considering what such an inspired farmer could do with those two hundred black loam acres at Deep Lake. But when I asked if there might not be some way that he could join their business, Walter

149

shook his head. "It may be best if your daddy stays in Monroe County" – that was all he said.

The first time Walter met Papa was on Capt Bill Collier's schooner going down to Marco, that time he visited the pineapple plantation. Papa had been in Fort Myers on business. That was in 1895, the year we came from Arkansas to Columbia County, and stayed with Granny Ellen near Fort White. The Langfords and Papa used to get along just fine, that's how T. E. Langford became Mama's doctor. But these days Walter has withdrawn from Papa. Everyone seems to know something that I do not.

Friday last, Papa stopped over at Fort Myers with a cargo of his "Island Pride," consigned for Tampa. He took Mama along, and they went to a concert by Minnie Maddern Fiske at the Tampa Theater! Mama did not really wish to go, she is feeling poorly these days and looking very old for thirty-six. No one seems to know whether poor spirits or poor health gives that scary yellow-gray cast to her skin. But she took advantage of some episode in Tampa – some drunken sally yelled across the street – to warn poor Papa that his presence at the wedding might cause difficulties.

"He refuses to be banished from his daughter's wedding," Mama sighed when she came home. "He refuses to bow to these provincial people." She was very tense, and so was I, all the more so now that Papa knew and was so angry. For such a self-confident, strong man, Mama says, our Papa's feelings are hurt easily, though he is too proud to wince, he only squints. For all his jollity, he keeps his feelings private.

Before heading south, Papa took me for a walk, nodding in his courtly way to everyone we met. He is such a strong vigorous mettlesome man with his snapping blue eyes and bristling beard, stepping our smartly down Riverside Avenue with his adoring daughter on his arm, as handsomely tailored and well-groomed as any man in town. If Papa has anything to be ashamed about, he doesn't show

150

it. He looks the world right in the eye with that kindly crinkle and ironic smile, knowing what our busybodies must be thinking!

I finally asked if he knew about *Hell on the Border*. The muscles in his forearm twitched as if he had been spurred, and after a little pause he nodded, and I felt ashamed. We walked along a little ways before he said, That author imagines Mister Watson is dead, and will therefore take these insults lying down.

At first I didn't see he'd made a joke, and then my laugh came like a shriek because his strange and still expression had unnerved me. When he makes such jokes, there's a bareness in his eyes, one has no idea at all what he is thinking. He watched me laugh until, desperate to stop, I got the hiccups. Not until I'd finished did he smile just a little as we walked along – not amused by his own joke, not really, but by something else. We didn't speak about the book again.

Papa confessed that, at the start, he'd been dead set against the wedding, not because he disapproved of Walter (he likes Walter well enough, everyone does), but because he disliked any meddling in our life by Captain Cole, who has appointed himself spokesman for the Langfords now that Walter's father is so ill. This damnable Jim Cole, he said, seemed to regard Ed Watson's daughter as a piece of negotiable property – "like some nigger slave wench!" Papa exclaimed. (Mama tries to persuade him to say "darkie" but he just ignores her.)

Out of breath with sudden anger, he stopped on the sidewalk. Is my lovely little Carrie to be led to the altar like some sacrificial virgin just to restore respectability to the Watson family? Because this family is already a damn sight more respectable than some damned cracker clan from Suwannee County! And he set off on one of his tirades about how his forebears had been landed gentry, about how Rob's namesake, Colonel Robert Briggs Watson, was a decorated hero, wounded at Gettysburg – all those old

151

honors that obsess poor Papa – while I glanced nervously up and down, alarmed because some passerby might over-hear.

Papa calmed down then and apologized for all his cuss-ing. It was too long, said he, since his knees had suffered the chastisement of a hard church floor. All the same, the very mention of Jim Cole and his insinuations – he made me laugh with a deadly imitation of that mud-thick drawl – got him furious. I'll grab that gut-sprung cracker by the seat of his pants and march him down the street and horsewhip him, growled Papa, right in front of this whole mealy-mouthed town!

Not long before, a cattle rustler out in Hendry County had stung up Mr Cole with a few shotgun pellets. Too bad that hombre didn't know his business, Papa said, with a very hard expression.

We walked along toward Whiskey Creek in silence. Papa knew what I was thinking, always had and always would. Soon he said in a cold formal voice that he had consented to this marriage because it was beneficial to our family. He stopped short, took my arm from his, and faced me. "I gave in, Carrie, I accepted their conditions. I am not in a pos-ition, not today, to dictate my own terms. But one day I shall be, you may count on it. I intend to protect my family *to my utmost ability* from the mistakes I have committed in this life."

I told him I was not quite clear about who "they" were, and he brooded a moment, then he growled, "This mar-riage is best for you, too, daughter, take my word for it." His expression stopped me when I tried to speak – "Please let me finish!" He squinted and muttered a little longer before taking my hands in his with great formality. "Don't ask your own father to stay away, you hear? I *agree* to stay away." He took a deep breath. "It is *best* I stay away. Please inform your mother."

"Don't blame Mama," I said. "It's my weakness, too – !"

"Your Mama is *not* weak," he said sharply. "She is merely

frail. A weak woman would not have faced me as she did. No, she is *strong*!"

I was sobbing, I was so ashamed, and still I tried hard to pretend that what I wept over was his decision to stay away. His hope had risen once again, yes, I saw it, for he waited a moment, eyes wide as a child's. When I did not try to change his mind, he nodded as if everything had come out for the best, which made me sob anew and all the harder.

"And Rob?" I sniffed. "Will Rob come?"

"No, he will not."

This curtness was all the punishment he ever gave me. He was not reproachful, but he peered into my eyes, squeezing my fingers urgently in his hard brown hands. "I shall always be very careful in Fort Myers, Carrie," he said. "Please tell your mother that, as well." He squeezed my hands hard as he spoke, until he hurt me. *"His family has nothing to fear from Mister Watson."*

He released my hands, and we walked back to the boat without a word. I thought of my tomboy days at Chatham Bend, and Henry Thompson's wandering eyes, and how Papa would growl that he'd tie net weights to my skirts if I climbed trees!

A darkness descended on my heart, but I would not let it in. After the *Gladiator* slipped her mooring, I ran along with her, waving desperately to Rob as the old schooner drifted downriver with the tide. Poor Rob and Papa were going home alone to that new house Papa had built to welcome his long-lost family to Chatham Bend – oh, how his pain twisted my heart!

I was jumping on the riverbank like some distracted thing, waving both arms to summon enough love to banish so much bewilderment and hurt. Seeing me, poor scowling Rob straightened and stared. When Papa bellowed from the helm, he lifted his hand a little and went on back to coiling up the lines.

HENRY THOMPSON

Aunt Jane Watson looked too old for a woman not so far into her thirties. Had a shine to her pale skin, like a rabbit pelt been scraped too thin, so the shadow of the sun come right on through. Soon after the old Frenchman died, she got so sickly that Mister Watson took her to Fort Myers, but she never abandoned him out of her own woe. She made up her mind to go that very day her husband shot the mustache off Ed Brewer. She didn't want her children in a place where strange men might come gunning for her husband – I heard her tell him that myself, and when she did, he took out that big watch and looked at it, which is as close as Mister Watson come to a nervous habit, though it made other folks a heap more nervous than him. There weren't too much that he could say. Also, George Storter in Everglade was sending his kids up to Fort Myers to go to high school, and Mister Watson already had the idea he would do the same.

When Mister Watson took Aunt Jane to see Doc T. E. Langford, Mrs Langford said, That island life is too darn rough for someone gently reared, you're coming to stay with us until you're better! Miss Carrie stayed on, too, helping take care of her, and Eddie and Lucius was lodged someplace, and went to school. Mister Watson told 'em all good-bye and come on back to farming his plantation.

That fine white house, so proud on Chatham Bend, was built for Mrs Jane Watson and her children, and when the family went away, it seemed to mope like a old dog off its feed, a mite dirty, y'know, and kind of smelly. We was like strangers come in off the river, camping there and messing them nice rooms. Mister Watson had lost interest in his house. He was real somber for a year, he set inside a lot, and more and more he took to heavy drinking. I missed them children, especially Miss Carrie, and her father missed her even more than I did. Him and Rob hardly spoke a word from one week to the next.

When I asked Rob why he had not gone with his family, he snarled, "Because that's not *my* family, any more than she is *your* Aunt Jane!" He was feeling sarcastical, I guess, and made me feel awful. "Reckon you miss your natural mother pretty bad," I said. And Rob said, "Wrong as usual. I never knew her."

Me and Rob was close to the same age, and I was willing to be friends but he just wasn't. All the same, we was never far apart, cause even enemies could pass the time better than nobody. After Bill House went away, after the Frenchman died and the Hamiltons left to spend a year down to Flamingo, we never saw another boat along our river.

Miss Carrie was soon spoken for by Walter Langford, who was kin to Sheriff Tom W. Langford, so Mister Watson knew he'd get no trouble in Lee County that he didn't ask for. Mister Watson's rowdy ways got him throwed in jail in Tampa and Key West, but he went out of his way to avoid trouble in Fort Myers, and so far as I have ever heard, he never had none.

After the family left, around '97, we traded mostly in Fort Myers so's he could visit with his people. Sail up the Calusa Hatchee in the evening, passing Punta Rassa after dark. In Fort Myers, Mister Watson dressed real nice and talked real quiet, never wore a gun like them drunk cow hunters, at least not on his belt where you could see it. But he always had a weapon on him somewhere, and he kept his eye peeled. We never went to no saloons and never stayed long, just tended to business first thing in the morning and went back downriver.

One time when Walter Langford's friend Jim Cole come

up behind him at the Hendry House, slapped him on the shoulder, Mister Watson told him, "Better not come up on me so sudden, friend." When he called a man friend, that was a warning, you could not mistake it. And Jim Cole, big talker though he was, backed off so fast he stumbled off the boardwalk, splattered mud on his new trousers, got himself whistled at by some drunk cowboys. Mister Watson turned and said, "I made another enemy" – not sorry, you know, but more like it was Cole who better watch his step from that day on. Didn't say it to no one in particular, not even me.

Round about '98, maybe '99, Mister Watson found Miss Jane a nice house on Anderson Avenue, which wasn't for colored like it is today, and Rob went away one season to Fort Myers school. He was older than any kid in class, and done poor cause he didn't try. He got in trouble, give his stepmother all kind of fits. Rob declared he would never be a bona fide member of her family, said he belonged at Chatham Bend if he belonged anywhere, said it so often that finally she agreed. His father brought him back to make a boatman of him, and it seemed right that he would take my place. Rob were Mister Watson's rightful son, and I never forgot it.

Not long after she moved to her new house, Miss Jane begun to waste away. That cheered her up, her husband claimed, being as how she was tired of life and knew her death was not so far away. I looked real close to see if he were teasing about death, the way he often did, and he said, No, Henry, I am serious. She makes a joke of it. The other day I said to her, You're not afraid of death, I see. And Mandy said, I guess I had it coming.

Telling me this, he had to smile, though I never knew if he was smiling at her joke or smiling because she could joke about such a thing or smiling because he seen I didn't get it. That is the trouble with no education – I guess I still don't get it. It was just some little joke between theirselves.

Mister Watson got lonely sometimes, too. We'd go to visit Henrietta and her Minnie, who was living these days at George Roe's boardinghouse there at Caxambas, and he got to know Tant's sister Josie Jenkins, who was kind of what you might call hanging fire. One day he brought Josie home to stay, but not before asking Henrietta if she minded, cause Josie were Henrietta's young half sister. Netta aimed to marry Mr Roe, and later did so, but this night she had drunk some spirits and was feeling sassy. She said, "Mister Ed, I don't mind a single bit, just so long's you keep that durn thing in the family." They all laughed to beat the band, and I did, too, that's how good we felt, being members of our family.

Aunt Josie Jenkins was a spry young woman, small and flirty as a bird, always winking with some secret she might tell you if you coaxed her right, and tossing her big nest of black curls. Aunt Josie said she had come to Chatham Bend to make sure that Tant and me and "that poor Rob" was being treated good by that old repper bait, but I believe she was really there to look after the old repper bait under the covers. Aunt Josie would flirt her eyes and wings, dance away when he reached out for her, but them two didn't waste no time getting together. Aunt Josie said, "This place ain't built for secrets!' and us boys was told to sleep down in the shed.

Mister Watson were in his forties then, still vigorous, God knows, and his wife had been a invalid for years. I don't blame him for bedding down Aunt Josie, cause she was a lively little thing, had a lot of spirit. Sometimes we was visited by her daughter Jennie. Can't recall who Jennie's daddy was, and I ain't so certain Josie would know, neither. Might could been the one they called Jennie Everybody, because she wasn't so particular, but she was a beautiful young woman, next to Miss Carrie the most beautiful I ever saw.

Aunt Josie had a baby while she lived on Chatham Bend, called her Pearl Watson. So what with Rob and Tant and

Jennie, and all our kin at Caxambas and Fort Myers, Mister Watson and me had us a family once again.

Tant was only a young feller then, not much older than me. He was Ludis Jenkins's son with his last wife, who was my grandmother Mary Anne Daniels. When Old Man Ludis got sick of life and killed himself, Grandma and her children went to live with her son John Henry Daniels on Fakahatchee. Uncle John Daniels's wife was part some kind of Injun, and a lot of it, cause wasn't one of them Daniels boys but was black-haired and black-eyed, Injun in appearance. There was bunches of Danielses and bushels of their kin, and they all kept moving from one island to another, so there was plenty of rundown Daniels cabins Tant could choose from. By the time they got done – well, they ain't done yet! – there weren't hardly a soul on the southwest coast that didn't have some Daniels in the family.

Tant was more Irish in his looks, black hair but curly, had a little mustache and Josie's small sharp nose. Tant was a sprightly kind of man, made people feel good. I never quite could get the hang of how he done that. Tant played hell with the deer and coons and gators, and he brought his venison and jokes and fleas from one Daniels hearth to the next one, all his life.

Tant never farmed nor fished if he could help it, called that donkey work. Even in his youngerhood he came and went in his little boat, you never knew where Tant would be from one day to the next. He was always a loner, never married, never lived a day under his own roof. Soon as Mister Watson went away, he was off hunting, and when he was at Chatham Bend, he fooled around making moonshine from the cane. I'm living off the land, said Tant, and drinking off it, too.

Tant were mostly drunk even when working. Sometimes he would lean way over to whisper in Mister Watson's ear, Ain't none of my damn business, Planter Watson, no sir, it sure ain't, but it looks to me like that damn worthless

Tant is drinking up all your profits. How Mister Watson could grin at that I just don't know.

We hardly seen hide nor hair of Tant come time for cane cutting, late fall and winter. He persuaded Mister Watson how he'd save him money supplying victuals for the harvest workers, venison and ducks and turkey, or gator tail, or gophers, sometimes a bear. A great hunter like him would be plumb wasted in the cane field, is what he said. That's right, boy, Mister Watson would agree, kind of exasperated. Because you are bone lazy to start with and too weak for a day's work on account of drink! And Tant would moan real doleful, saying, Oh, Sweet Jesus, ain't it the God's truth! And Mister Watson cursed and laughed and let him go.

Now Tant was strong and wiry as well as lazy, but he purely hated being stooped over all day amongst the bugs and snakes, arms wore out, and brains half-cooked, and the earth whirling – you was seeing things, that's how frazzled out you was with weariness and thirst and common boredom, whacking away in the wet heat at the sharp cane that could poke your eye out if you were not careful. On top of half killing you, the work was risky, cause them big damn cane knives sharp as any razor could glance off any whichway when a man was tired. One bad swing from the man next to you could take your ear off, or your knife might glance off last year's stalks and slash your own leg artery or sinew.

Most of our cutters was just drinkers or drifters, or wanted men, or hard-luck niggers, maybe young folks like them Tuckers from Key West, trying to get a start. Mister Watson scraped 'em off the docks at Port Tampa and Key West, sometimes Fort Myers, brought 'em back and lodged 'em in a dormitory we built back of the boat shed. Told 'em the roof and corn-shuck mattresses was theirs to enjoy to their heart's content but half their day's pay would be deducted for their grub. Made you sad to see them wornout people working them hard fields in their old broken shoes, never had straw hats nor gloves nor canvas leggings like what we had less they rented 'em from Mister Watson. Anyplace else, they was here today and gone tomorrow, but they was stuck on Chatham Bend, couldn't get off. Kept 'em scared of running off with all his talk of Injuns and cottonmouths and giant gators, and anyways, there was nowhere to run to, nothing but mangrove and deep-water rivers, miles from anywhere. Knowing how hard it was to find trained help, Mister Watson made sure they was always owing, never let 'em back aboard his schooner until they was too sick or lunatic to work. By that time they was begging to swap any back pay they had coming for a boat ride to most anywhere, having come around to Mister Watson's view that they was a lot more trouble than they was worth.

Sometimes his wife might protest, saying. Do unto others, Mister Watson, as you would have them do unto you. And he would say, They would do the same unto Mister Watson first chance they got – that's human nature. You're a hard-hearted man, she would say, shaking her head. And he would answer, I am not hard-hearted, Mandy, but I am hardheaded, as a man must be who aims to run a prosperous business and support his family.

Only man who stood up to him was a young feller name of Tucker who needed his back pay before we got the harvest finished in the autumn. Mister Watson got so irate that he run him off without no pay at all. But Tucker was mad, too, and hollered out, This business ain't finished by a long shot! And Mister Watson yelled, Might be finished by a *short* shot, I ever catch you on this place again.

The only feller who ever come back for more was a drifter and drinker, Old Man Waller, who had the same way with hogs as Mister Watson did. When Waller was sober, them two could talk hogs day and night. So Old Man Waller got put in charge of livestock, and snuck out of a fair amount of field work. One evening when Mister Watson was away he got drunk with Tant and went to the hog pen, give the hogs a speech and their freedom, too, and the hogs went straight to the damned syrup mash, got drunk right along with Old Man Waller. One full sow that went to sleep it off got half et by a panther, piglets and all. I told Old Waller it wasn't funny, but he didn't agree.

Waller decided to leave Chatham Bend with Tant early next morning, but a year later he showed up again with a fine hog, said he had seen the error of his ways and made amends. Mister Watson explained that Old Man Waller had replaced the hog but was wanted for hog theft at Fort Myers. But Waller said, Nosir, what it was – begging your pardon, Mister Watson – island life has been prescribed for me by my physician.

As time went on, something changed there at the Bend. I never was around too much of it, I was off running the boat most of the time, but everybody got to drinking up Tant's *aguedente*, they got the idea that they could let things go. Mister Watson would shout, "This place ain't fit for niggers!" and they'd jump up, rattle things around, go right back drinking. Tant might even holler out, Did I hear "*niggers*"? How about *white* trash? How about *outlaws*? Then Tant'd pretend he'd scared himself half to death, and apologize for calling Mister Watson a outlaw when he weren't nothing but a common desperader. Mister Watson might grunt a warning, but pretty soon he'd say, To hell with it, and pour more liquor. He grew heavy.

Finally our boss went on a rampage, just took and cleared that whole bunch out of there after the harvest, including some no-account niggers he brung in to cut the cane. Told 'em they had drank up all their pay, and his profits, too. He picked a day when Tant were gone, cause he hated to blame a single thing on Tant, who drank more than the rest of 'em put together.

That day I had come in from Key West, and I hardly had the boat tied up when them females and young come quacking down the path like a line of ducks, with Mister Watson right behind kicking their bundles – should of been kicking their fat *bee*-hinds, he said later. Hollered at me to get 'em the hell out of there before he lined 'em up and blowed their brains out, if they had any. Told me to take 'em out into the Gulf and throw 'em to the sharks, for all he cared.

I don't guess he meant that but they thought he did. Nosir, they weren't sassing him *that* afternoon! Them women was dead sober, they looked scared. They finally knowed that they had played with fire. It was only after we dropped down out of the river and was safe at sea that they started in complaining they had not been paid. If I had not come back there when I did, Cousin Jennie blubbered, that ginger-haired monster would have murdered the women and children, never thought twice about it.

In years to come, when them kinfolks who kept house with Mister Watson was living at Pavilion and Caxambas, they would repeat Cousin Jennie's words when they was drinking – not spiteful, you know, they done it to get attention to theirselves, get some excitement out of life, cause they was all of 'em sweet on Mister Watson, always would be. I never paid none of 'em much mind, and don't today.

All the same, it was them Daniels women got that story started how Mr E. J. Watson always killed his help on payday, and of course our competition in the syrup business was glad to hear an explanation of how come Mister Watson done so much better raising cane than they did.

That puts me in mind of his old joke down in Key West. Feller would ask him, What you up to these days, E.J.? And he'd wave his bottle and yell out, *Raising Cain!*

Heck, even I got *that* one! I would laugh my head off every time I heard it, and told it every time I had the chance, till folks begun to ask me to hush up about it. Well, I'd tell'm, it just goes to show you it ain't true that Henry Thompson got no sense of humor, way some say! Heck, I'd say, I like a joke good as the next man! They'd laugh along with those words, too, though some way I felt kind of left out.

Anyway, I never knowed him to be nothing but fair in his dealings with his help, he was hard but fair, and Hiram Newell, S. S. Jenkins, and all them other ones that worked for him would say the same. As for niggers, I never heard a nigger speak a word against him.

I took them women on back to Caxambas and stopped over for supper to George Roe's place, where Miss Gertrude Hamilton from Lost Man's River, age fourteen, was a new boarder. By that time Henrietta had hitched up with Old Man Roe, and a few years later, must been 19 and 03, some Yankees started the Caxambas clam factory, so our whole gang went down to Pavilion Key for the clam fishery. Uncle Jim Daniels was the crew boss, and Mr and Mrs Roe had the store and post office, and Aunt Josie was there, too, with her latest husband. Josie took seven by the time the smoke cleared, counting the one that she took twice, and she saw every last one of them fellers into his grave.

Speaking of funerals, old Johnny Gomez drowned in 1900, tangled his cast net on his ankle, looked like, and the weights pulled him off balance, tugged him overboard. He was still tangled when some men from Marco, stopping by on their way north from Key West, found him hooked by his trousers in the mangrove at low tide, with his nose-warmer washed up alongside him. Had a funeral at Ever-glade, and Mister Watson's good friend R. B. Storter – Mister Watson always called him Bembery – took the Widow Gomez home to Panther Key. She was still on the young side so didn't stay long. In later years, running the *Gladiator* for Mister Watson, I used Johnny Gomez's thatch shack for my camp when I stopped off at Panther Key to get my water and moon a little about Carrie, and when Hiram Newell took over my job, he used it, too. Matter of fact, it was Hiram found Old Johnny's body, him and his brother-in-law Dick Sawyer. Dick was another friend of Mister Watson, least he claimed to be. Claimed he was in the bunch that seen Santini's throat slit, and helped to get the knife away from Mister Watson.

One afternoon of autumn, 1901, I seen the towering black smoke of burning canefield from way out in the Gulf off Pavilion Key, and the fire was still going strong all the way upriver, the growing roar like storm, and the hard crackle, and that sweet odor in the air like roasting corn. As I come nearer, I could see the woods just shimmering in that heat, and the dark hawks and buzzards and the white egrets that will come from as far as they can see that oily smoke to feed on the small critters killed or flushed from cover in a burn.

I believe that Mister E. J. Watson might been the first planter in south Florida to try burning his field before the harvest, figuring work would go much faster with less labor once the leaves and cane tops was all burned away. Nothing but clean stalks to deal with, not much sugar lost, and a smaller payroll. Only thing was, cane sugar don't extract good from the stalks even a few days after a fire, and this here was a field of thirty acres, and he hadn't brought no cutters in for the fall season. There was only him and me and Rob, and maybe Tant if we were very lucky. He must of gone crazy is the way I figured, he was firing a canefield we would never harvest.

When I come into the Bend, first thing I seen was Mister Watson all alone out in his field, still setting fires, on the half run like he'd heard a shout from Hell. I didn't see no sign of Rob, let alone Tant. Mister Watson was the only man on the plantation, drifting over that black ground like a huge cinder swirled up by the wind, in a ring of fire. Had his shotgun with him, and that made no sense neither, cause the birds had no plumes in this season, and he hadn't lit fires on three sides the way we done sometimes when we wanted a shot at whatever run before the flames. In a unholy light where sun rays come piercing down through the smoke's shadow, something was hanging in that hellish air and whatever it was kept me from calling. I wouldn't go nowheres near a man who looked like he had set himself afire. I didn't go near the house even, just waited for him by the river. Toward nightfall, when the flames died down, and he come in, his face was fire-coloured, eyes darting everywhere. He was coughing hard, fighting for breath. "Who you hiding on that boat?" – that's his first words. He went on past, down toward the dock, and halfway down, he swings that gun around quick as a viper, like he means to throw down on me and fire.

I yell out, "Hold on, Mister Ed! I come along!" Cause orders was, if ever I come into the Bend with someone hid aboard, I would lay off there on the river, give him time to get in close behind the poinciana, get the drop on any man who tried to come ashore.

He don't lower the muzzle of his double-barrel. I face the holes. Ever try that? Makes you feel like you might fall in pieces even before you're blown apart. Then he swings back around and keeps on going. He don't like having his back to me but he minded his back turned to the schooner even more. And damned if he don't poke that shotgun into every cranny on that boat, from stem to stern.

Coming out, he mutters, That's right, boy, no harvest. He don't explain that but I understood it later. With all that cane unharvested, and no fire, he was afraid that next year's crop would be choked out.

I don't know where Rob is, and I don't dare ask.

Rob was very dark in spirit along about that time. One day, setting on the stoop, he picks up his dad's old double-barrel that is leaning up against the house. First he puts the muzzle in his mouth and turns so I can see. Then he points the gun at Rex, who is laying there in the poinciana roots having a nightmare. I am close by but inside, keeping away from him, I can hear him muttering at the skeeters through the screen. Says, "Rex, if I get bit once more, I am going to pull these triggers. And if this here gun is loaded, boy, then this is your last day as a dog, cause both barrels is aimed to blow your head off."

Well, that's exactly what he done, and after he done it he ran wild, ran around the house, round and round, and let out a shriek every time he passed the carcass. Mister Watson took that poor dog by the tail and flung him in the river, and still Rob shrieked each time he turned the corner. Must of run around the house nine times before we could catch hold of him and talk him down.

All me and Mister Watson ate for supper was Tant's cold venison, left on the hearth. No bread baked and didn't fix no greens. The meat weren't smoked through proper because Tant got drunk and let the fire die, it had a purply look and old rank smell to it. "Might be nigger meat," Mister Watson growls when he seen me gag on it, and he snorts like he's going to laugh but the laugh don't come, not once, not that whole evening.

I still had fears from seeing him on fire in that field, and I prayed to God he would not start in to drinking. All you could hear besides the skeeter whine was us men chewing meat. I thought I'd never get that meat down, that's how dry my mouth was, and I never cared for venison that day to this.

He gets the bottle out, but he don't drink. He just sits there with his shotgun, panting, staring toward the river. "Sometimes it gets me," he muttered once, but he don't explain it.

That evening I got to thinking about moving on. It was time for me to start out on my own. I was near to twenty and I had my eye on young Gert Hamilton, whose brother Lewis was to marry Cousin Jennie. Mister Watson had taught me good all about farming. I could shoot and trap, hang mullet nets and skin off egret with the best of 'em, and anyways it weren't hard to tell that our good old days at Chatham Bend was near their end.

After I done the dishes, he coughs and hacks, says, I am sorry for the way I acted. You are my partner, are you not? I am, say I, and proud to be so. He nods his head for a long time. Then he begun talking, slow at first, relating all about his life, and why it was he come down to the Islands.

Mister Watson confessed he were a wanted man in Arkansas and also in Columbia County, in north Florida. As a young feller in Columbia, he had a good farm under lease, and made him a fine crop, but after he sold his crop off, he hurt his knees in a bad fall at O'Brien, Florida, was bedridden a good while and his plantation went all to hell, and he had to borrow money from his brother-in-law. This was after he lost his first young wife in childbirth – that was Rob's mother.

In a few years he found him a pretty schoolteacher, Miss Jane S. Dyal of Deland, Florida, but that brother-in-law kept after him about the money, kept hounding him and sneering, "right up until the day that feller died," Mister Watson said. He smiled just a little when he said those words, and I give him a quick smile back. "It come down to a matter of honor," Mister Watson said, and he watched me again. Mister Watson never said he killed that man, and I never asked him, but some way the man's friends must of found fault with him.

Along about then, he decided it was time to go out West. "No sense getting lynched," he said, "before getting to tell my own side of the story." He packed up his family in the same old covered wagon his mother had brung south from Carolina, and him and his boy Rob and new wife, Jane, with little Carrie and Baby Ed, left by night and lit out northward for the Georgia border.

The following spring – this was 1887 – they sharecropped a farm in Franklin Country, Arkansas. Got his crop in and kept right on going, all the way to Injun Territory, maybe seventy miles west of Fort Smith, what he called the Nations. Injun Country was the first place he felt safe, because there was next to no law in the Nations. Injun police never messed too much with white men so long as they left Injuns alone; Injuns figured that any white in trouble with other whites couldn't be all bad, Mister Watson said.

That whole region was a hideout for outlaws and renegades from Missouri west to Texas, because the only law was the same law we had here, eye for an eye and a man's honor, so better shoot first and get the details later. Frank and Jesse James and the Younger boys who rode with Quantrill in the Border Wars and fought in his guerrilla troop for the Confederacy naturally went on to a life of outlawry, and most of them men hid out and drank and roamed anywhere they wanted in the Nations.

There was plenty of renegade Injuns, too, and the worst of 'em Mister Watson said, was Old Tom Starr, whose father was head of a wild Cherokee clan on a stretch of the South Canadian River where the Creek, Choctaw, and Cherokee Nations come together. Tom Starr was huge, and kept himself busy wiping out another clan who had a mind to bump off Tom Starr's father.

"Killed too many, got a taste for it, know what I mean?" Mister Watson said. I thought he give me a funny look, but he probably never. "Sure do," I said.

Tom Starr and his boys set fire to a cabin in this feud, and a little boy five years old run out, and Tom Starr picked him up and tossed him back into the flames, that's how bad the feud was.

"I don't think I could do a thing like that, could you, Henry?" Mister Watson said – he was frowning, you know, like he'd thought hard on it before deciding.

"Nosir," I said.

Old Man Tom Starr asked another Cherokee if he thought God would ever forgive him for that deed he done, and his friend said, No, I don't reckon He would.

"I wouldn't care to give that answer to a black-hearted fellow like Tom Starr, what do you think, Henry?"

168

"Nosir," I said.

"Nosir," Mister Watson said.

Mister Watson wasn't there a year when somebody put a load of buckshot into a woman named Myra Maybelle Shirley, who lived with a dang Injun, Tom Starr's son. Shot her out of the saddle on a dead cold day of February '89, and give her another charge of turkey shot in the face and neck right where she was laying in the muddy road. At the funeral at Youngers' Bend, Mister Watson was accused by Starr of murdering his dearly beloved wife.

"They tied my hands and they rode me over to Fort Smith, Arkansas, and Jim Starr signed a murder warrant in the federal court. Some of my neighbors gave depositions, mentioned the quarrel, said I lived pretty close by the scene of the killing. But I had a good reputation with the merchants, quiet church-going man who paid his bills, and so the local papers took my side.

"Here's the lesson I learned, Henry, and I learned it well, and it's stood me in good stead all my life: No decent American is going to believe that a man who pays his bills is a common criminal, no matter what!" Mister Watson's laugh come right up from his boots, as if the whole world weren't nothing but plain foolishness, and him right with it. I laughed along with him, never knew why, I heard my own laugh clatter in my ears.

Mister Watson fetched out a cigar box, showed me a yeller clipping from the Fort Smith *Elevator*. Had to read me it, of course; never had no school back then in Chokoloskee. The reporter told all about how Mister Watson had stood up to that pesky Injun and denied the charge, how the defendant Watson "was the very opposite of a man who would be supposed to commit such a crime."

Reading this out, Mister Watson stopped grinning and watched my face. "By God, Henry, you never let me down! That's the one thing in my life that I can count on – Henry Thompson won't die laughing! I'll have to do the laughing for us both!"

Mister Watson sighed, took his first drink. He was feeling good again.

"The commissioner gave Jim Starr two weeks to come up with some witnesses, some sort of evidence, but he never produced a goddamned thing that would stand up in court. The case was dismissed – I never went to trial."

By that time, the newspapers had taken up Belle Starr, made her famous all over the country. Mister Watson fished out a old book with a lady on the cover packing two pistols: "*Bella Starr*," he read in a disgusted voice, "*The Bandit Queen, or The Female Jesse James*. This book of lies was cooked up in New York in 1889, not six months after she died, and they'll be making up lies about her from now on, to go with the whoppers she told about herself. Remember that time you told me, boy, to take Old Man Johnny Gomez with a grain of salt? You'd need a keg of it for Maybelle Shirley!"

Mister Watson left the Indian Territory in early March of 1889, right after the murder hearing in federal court. He wanted to head farther west but needed money, so he joined the land rush in the Oklahoma Territory, April 1889, when most of the Creek and Seminole land was throwed wide open to the whites under the homestead laws. Unlike most of 'em he knew that country. He rode out on a borrowed horse on the dead run, made a fine claim on some good bottom land he'd had his eye on. Said it almost broke his heart to let it go, cause he could have made a good crop there that very season, but his wife said the claim weren't far enough from Tom Starr's country.

Lots of settlers left behind in that first land rush was willing to pay out ready money, and he sold his claim, went back to Arkansas, leased a good farm. Next thing he knew he was jailed as a horse thief – framed by Belle Starr's horse-thief friends, the way he figured it. He escaped from jail, swum across a river with bullets kicking up the water right around his ears. Got two good horses and a grubstake, headed for Oregon. Leased a farm in the Willamette Valley

170

and done pretty good for a year to two until one night someone who had took a disliking to him fired a shotgun through the window, giving him no choice but to fire back. Didn't wait till daybreak to head east again, for Edgefield Country, South Carolina, where he come from.

"I'd been gone from home a good number of years, and I reckoned my father would be dead, and all my boyhood trouble died away. But that old man was living still, and he was unwilling to forget, let alone forgive. I headed for Columbia County, Florida, to see my mother and my sister, see if I could fit my life there back together, but they warned me the warrant was still out, so I kept on moving.

"There was nothing to do but start my life all over. Some Columbia County folks had sent back word they were doing fine down around the Everglades, and people were saying that south Florida was the last place left where a man could farm in peace and quiet, and no questions asked.

"Only thing was, I stopped off in Arcadia, and a bad actor named Quinn Bass came after me with a knife in a saloon, so I had to stop him." Mister Watson shrugged, then cocked his head as if to see how I was taking it. "Had to pay good money to get out of that one. But some of that Bass clan was dissatisfied by the transaction, and someone will come after me, sooner or later."

He nodded his head, like revenge was a philosophy he could approve of. "I'll know him when he comes, and he'll find me ready," Mister Watson said. He was always ready, come to think of it, cause any stranger might turn out to be the man he waited for.

Mister Watson seemed pretty honest in his story, and I felt honored he had told me, it was just I could not get the details straight. I couldn't make out from the way he told it if he did or did not kill his brother-in-law, if he did or did not kill Belle Starr. He growled low every time I looked like I might pester him with questions, but them blue eyes seemed to dare me all the same. After a while, when I just kept whittling, his hand shot over quick and nabbed my

171

wrist, and his eyes fixed me. He don't say a word but those eyes want something.

I say, kind of conversational, "I was just pondering if this Quinn Bass feller died."

"That's what the coronor claimed," Mister Watson said.

He kind of tossed my wrist away, like he couldn't understand such a stupid question. It *was* pretty stupid, I guess. I'd seen him shoot many's the time, and when Ed Watson shot something, it *stayed* shot.

That evening Mister Watson never talked no more. The man just sat there for a long, long while, hands on his legs, like he aimed to jump up quick and leave but couldn't remember where he had to go. And of course there *weren't* no place to go, not in the Islands. At night there was only cold, cold stars, so high beyond us, and the awful tangle of black limbs, owl hoot and heron squawk, the slap of a mullet faraway down that lonesome river.

Later days, when he was drinking, Mister Watson would brag around Key West how he took care of Belle Starr and her foreman when they come gunning for him in a narrow neck of woods. Hinted as how he'd took care of a few in his wild and woolly days out West, but claimed he'd never killed nobody less they meant him harm.

Bill House had already advised me that Mister Watson weren't the law-abiding citizen I took him for, him being wanted in three states for murder. Give me something to think about all that long evening when I and Mister Watson were setting there alone by lamplight, yeller shadows flickering, with that old black river licking through them empty mangroves, pouring away into the Gulf of Mexico.

That night I went outside, feeling small and lost. It was like I had woke in some night country on the dark side of the earth that all of us have to go to all alone. First thing I seen, the schooner was gone, just drifted away, like Henry Thompson had forgot to tie her up. My heart begun to race too hard, I was so scared I wanted to cry out and run, but there was nowhere but them blackened fields that I could run to. The earth was ringing in a silver light, the stars gone wild. It was like the whole continent of America, with all us white people and Injuns and niggers, me included, lay sprawled like poor Miss Maybelle Shirley, with her end nearing, blacking out the stars. That poor soul had stared at Heaven like I was staring now, the whole universe grieving, and these night rivers bleeding her to death.

What happened was, Rob left where he was hid and run off with the schooner, just slipped her lines and let her drift with the current. Took her as far as Key West by himself, that's how desperate he was to get away. When word come back, Mister Watson went and got her, but pretty quick he left for other parts, leaving word for Tant and me to keep an eye on his plantation.

When Tant heard how Tucker died at Lost Man's Key, he swore he would never work again for Mister Watson. I never knew Tant any way except lighthearted, I never knew he had such upset in him. Over and over I told Tant, "It ain't proved it was Mister Watson," but he never listened.

After Tant left, I stayed on awhile, waiting for Mister Watson. When he never come, I padlocked our white house and went back to Caxambas. That was 1901, when Gertrude Hamilton from Lost Man's River was lodging at Roe's Boarding House along with us. That's James Hamiltons, not Richard – them people was another bunch entirely. Gert didn't last long in Caxambas School on account I married her and took her back to Lost Man's River.

I was borned in Key West back in '79 and lived on Chokoloskee in my later life, but I guess you could say them rivers was my home.

Lately I have come across another pioneer memoir that makes special reference to Mr Watson. The author, Marie Martin St. John, was a child of Jim Martin, former sheriff of Manatee County, who in the fall of 1899 moved his family from Palmetto, Florida (on Tampa Bay), to the old shack used by Jean Chevelier on Gopher Key, "to give them a taste" of the Florida wilderness in which he had grown up. Martin subsequently erected a new dwelling on Possum Key. The author was only five when she went to the Islands, and though her memoir is alive with savored reminiscence, it may be shaded by events and rumor of a later period.

We made port at Marco, a landing pier and little else . . . then sailed south for Everglades City [sic] and Chucoluskee [sic], one a landing pier, the other a mud bank. Finally we came to Edgar Watson's place, a sugar plantation on the Chatham River.

Watson was an infamous outlaw. Every lawman in south Florida was acquainted with his treachery and cunning . . . From time to time he was halfheartedly sought for trial, though few crimes seemed to lead directly to his door. The legend persisted, however. The native whites feared him as you would a rattlesnake, but the Indians and black people were susceptible to his manipulations. Frequently hungry, they would go to work for him, cutting cane. He rarely paid the money agreed upon, and if a worker rebelled, Watson was said to execute him on the spot. I heard that countless human skeletons were left bare in the bayou when a hurricane blew the water out. The bayou filled the next day, and it was business as usual.

This merciless man had an invalid wife whom he

adored. He kept fifty cats for her to pet. Of course I was intrigued with him the day we docked at the sugar plantation. I remember Mr Watson taking me on his knee and telling me to pick one out for my own. He seemed the kindest of men.

Not without trepidation, Papa made arrangements with Watson to bring lumber, roofing and other materials needed from Fort Myers to build our house, which we would do with our own hands and the help of friends. Like other people in this lost place, we were dependent on Watson's big boat, which made regular runs to and fro. We felt this dependency even more after we settled and commenced to farm. There was no other way to get our produce to market on a steady basis. The stranglehold Watson had over this section of Florida was not dissimilar to the unscrupulous activities of certain lawmen, other legal crooks, and even governors that our state was to suffer through its history.

It was sundown when we arrived at Gopher Key, where we would stay until the big house was built on a neighboring island. There was the little shack, not the most gracious of living quarters, and there was a murderer for our nearest and only neighbor, about thirty miles [sic] away. [Perhaps this was the year the Hamiltons spent near John Weeks at Flamingo.]

Our new two-story house [on Possum Key] was finished that spring. Papa had built it on an old homesite known as the Chevalier Place. The Frenchman . . . had planted guava and avocado pears, and they were now huge trees . . . What with Papa's fields of tomatoes, we soon had produce to send to market. We shipped, as contracted, with Edgar Watson. Immediately trouble arose. A messenger came from the sugar plantation bringing Papa a ridiculously small, sum of money. For his part Papa told this man to go back and tell Watson how much was still owed, and that he, Papa, would be coming for it. The poor messenger was terrified and begged Papa to let the matter drop. "He'll just shoot you, Mr Martin. That's the way he settles an account. No one argues with Edgar Watson and lives to talk about it."

The next day Papa went to see Watson. Hal and Bubba accompanied him. When they drew up to the dock in their boat, Papa told the boys to sit tight while he went in the house. Watson's whole living room could be seen through a wide screen. It was an armory: the walls were lined with guns. Papa did not carry a gun.

In the argument that followed the boys could see everything. Perhaps they thought of the skeletons under their boat as Watson became more and more strident. Then came a moment when Watson started backing toward his wall of guns. Papa was unrelenting; he demanded his money, and Watson's arm rose toward a pistol. At the height of this tense moment, a smile broke on Watson's face. From where he stood he could see the two boys in the boat fifty feet away, each with a rifle held in small, capable hands and a bead drawn on the man who threatened their father.

"Look," Watson told Papa, but Papa thought it was a trick to make him turn around. Watson understood and moved away from the guns and pointed to the boat. Papa grinned at his sons and even smiled at Edgar Watson.

"Do you suppose they thought I'd shoot you, Jim?" Watson asked.

"Do you suppose you'd have had the chance?" Papa sent back.

This man who never paid his debts paid my father and walked with him to the landing to get a closer look. All he saw were two nonchalant little boys sitting with their guns beside them, slapping mosquitoes.

Despite its clear affinity with later myth-making, including the heightened drama inherent in an oft-told narrative of

176

family courage, the many well-remembered details else-where in the account suggest that there is something to her story, including the growing atmosphere of terror that by the turn of the century was beginning to gather around E. J. Watson. While "the man who never paid his debts" seems at odds with Watson's reputation for impeccable dealings with Ted Smallwood and others, it may also be true that he dodged small debts with creditors who could be bullied.

The St. John account ends on Possum Key at the turn of the century, not long before the notorious Tucker episode took place. Perhaps it was the fear that swept the region in the wake of the Tucker deaths which persuaded Jim Martin to abandon his new house and uproot his wife and four small children. Apparently he remained in the Everglades region, since he appears in the local census of 1910.

SARAH HAMILTON

After our marriage, times was hard, and in early years, the man that helped to pull us through was Mister Watson. Coming north and south on his way to Key West, he liked to stop over and eat with us, and he always spared us extra grub, extra supplies just when we needed it. He done the same for the whole Hamilton clan, Gene and Becca, too, and they took his help, even though Gene would bad-mouth Mister Watson before his boat was over the horizon.

Leon never asked for help, not even once. Mister Watson could guess what us poor squatters needed and would bring old clothes from his own children, some spare food, maybe give us the lend of his good tools and equipment. We tried as best we could to pay him back, brought him fish sometimes, turtle and manatee for stew, palm bud, guava syrup. We did this and that, and I guess he knew we was ready to help out any way we could.

Course Gene told Leon that Mister Watson was just paying in advance for having the Hamiltons and their guns to back him if it come to trouble. I hated Gene for saying that but couldn't be so sure it wasn't true. Leon told me I was too suspicious, same way Gene was, but Gene's idea begun to eat at my poor man, and finally Leon give the order we was not to take no more from Mister Watson. We was getting more beholden to another man than he could live with.

Mister Watson was a generous man, and a real gentle-man, I never knew him not to tip that broad black hat. Many's the time he ate at our table, and we was always glad to see him, he was lots of fun. Leon says that Mister

Watson loved his children. But after his family moved up to Fort Myers, and them Daniels females came and went at Chatham Bend, Mister Watson went back to his hard drinking, he got mean and he got heavy, and didn't waste no time at all getting in trouble.

Not that Mister Watson killed as many as folks says he did. He never killed nobody in his whole life, he told us, except when saving his own skin, though of course it was him – this was his joke – who got to decide when his own skin needed saving. He allowed as how he always lived on one American frontier after another, and that to survive on the frontier you had to show yourself ready to defend your honor. If you backed down even once, showed the whites of your eyes, you would have to slink off with your tail between your legs, you would have to start all over someplace else.

After that story got out about Belle Starr, every violent death in southwest Florida got blamed on Mister Watson. One time he was eating at Daddy Richard's table, Mormon Key, when a man was killed down to Key West. Next thing you know, there was a sheriff's deputy up this way hunting E. J. Watson, figured he'd claim the reward all by himself. This was the man Mister Watson got the drop on and put to work out in his field, that's how fired up he was about injustice. Sent word back to Key West with that deputy that the next one might not be so lucky, and I guess they remembered that message at Key West, because them ones that come hunting him after the Tuckers died were not so cocky.

It weren't Tucker and his nephew, the way Chokoloskee people say, it was Walter Tucker and his young wife, little Bet. She and her husband come back from Key West with Mister Watson, they was fine young people, and she called him Wally. Wanted to get some experience farming and fishing, put a grubstake together with their wages, try it on their own, so they took work on the Watson Place at

Chatham Bend. Being kindhearted, Mister Watson built these newlyweds that little shack down the bank a ways from the main house, far side of the boat shed and the workshop. Like all young people, they just thought the world of him.

When their time was up, Mister Watson was still in need of help to finish up his harvest, which went from autumn right into the winter. So he told 'em they had never give him notice, said they was ungrateful after all he taught 'em, said he wouldn't pay 'em off till after harvest – that's the story he told us when he come back to the Islands a few years later. But he admitted he had been in a bad drinking spell, and he got so hot he run the Tuckers off the Bend without no pay. They headed for Lost Man's, stopping over to see us at Wood Key about a gill net and some grub and seed to get them started. This was the year of 1901, same year the Hamilton boys got started on Wood Key and was shipping sixteen–twenty barrels of salt fish a week to Key West and Cuba.

Now the Atwells had a longtime claim on Lost Man's Key, but they let the Tuckers knock that jungle down, set up a cabin. There was plenty of game and fish down along there, and a patch of good ground with a freshwater spring across the river mouth, not far from the north end of Lost Man's Beach. Wally figured they knew enough by now to live alone. Bet was expecting, and Richard Hamilton was nearby, he delivered all the babies in the Islands. The Tuckers aimed to buy the quitclaim from the Atwells as soon as they could save a little money.

Both gangs of Hamiltons and the Atwells back in Rodgers River, all had big clans for company and help. Without that, only peculiar people could stand up to the lonesomeness and heat and insects in them rivers, and that mangrove silence that lay over everything, like mold in rainy season. Being stuck too long in muddy camps with toilsome chores, half bit to death, nothing to look at, and nothing but scuffed-up kids and dogs to talk to, it was mostly women who

180

went crazy in the Islands. The men drank moonshine and got violent, to work them silences out of their system.

With the Tuckers it was just the opposite. We thought it was Wally might not have the grit to make a go of it on Lost Man's Key, but Bet had all the spirit in the world. Without his Bet, that sweet young feller would have howled his heart out in them swamps within the year.

Leon Hamilton

In '99 we sold our claim on Mormon Key to E. J. Watson and moved another ten miles south to Lost Man's River, halfway from Chokoloskee to Cape Sable, and as far away to hell and gone as a man could get. Moved between Hog Key and Wood Key, hugging the Gulf breeze to keep off the skeeters. We dried and salted fish for the Havana trade.

Folks might tell you that Hamiltons moved away from Chatham River because we was scared of Mister Watson, like them others. Well, I was the youngest boy, at seventeen, and all three, Walter, Gene, and me, could shoot good as our daddy, and our mama could handle a shooting iron, too. We was friendly with Ed Watson, but even if we weren't, the Hamilton clan was there to stay and Watson knew it. The Hamiltons wasn't going to be scared off.

Richard Hamilton moved because he had no taste for company, said his family was as much society as he could handle. Once Jean Chevelier up and died, there wasn't much to keep us around Chatham River. Squatters was roosted on every bump between Marco and Everglade, and some was already drifted south of Chokoloskee Bay. Gregorio Lopez and his boys was in north Huston River, that stretch that is called Lopez River today, and the House clan was farming a bird hammock off Last Huston Bay, and new people named Martins built on Possum Key. But in all them miles south of Chatham River, the only settlers besides ourselves was the James Hamiltons on Lost Man's Beach and Atwells up in Rodgers River.

Along in these years the news come out how it was wrote

right in a book that Edgar Watson killed Belle Starr, Queen of the Outlaws. Justice George Storter seen that book when he went to put his kids in school up in Fort Myers. Justice Storter could read good, and he read that news with his own eyes and brought it back to Chokoloskee Bay.

Not long after that, I went with Watson far as Chokoloskee, and Isaac Yeomans seen us going in McKinney's store. Isaac was always pretty brash, and once he's got a few there with him, he sings out, says he wants to know was there any truth in that there story about a feller name of Watson and the Outlaw Queen.

Mister Watson was paying off Old Man McKinney, and I seen his hand stop on the counter. That hand just set there for a minute, tapped a silver dollar. Then he turned slow and looked at Isaac until Isaac spooked and started in to grinning like he'd made a joke, and then Watson turned back the same weary way and went right on paying out his money. When he was done, he turned again and leaned back on the counter, looking the men over, cause by that time they was crowded in the door.

"That same book says that this man Watson got killed breaking out of prison." He pulled out his big watch and looked at it while everybody thought that one over, and then he said, turning to Isaac, "Nobody asking nosy questions about Watson should put much stock into that *last* part."

Isaac give a wild scared yip, trying to be comical the way Tant used to do, and them others done their best to laugh, and Watson smiled. But them stone-blue eyes of his weren't smiling, nosir, never even blinked, and pretty quick he let that grin fade out, just stood there gazing at them jackasses while they stopped braying one by one and tried to put their faces back together. Then he looks at me and winks, and we walk out.

Life wasn't the same down in the Islands once all them stories started up. His neighbors liked Ed Watson, sure, some called him "E. J." and was proud to let on to strangers what good friends they was with the man who killed Belle Starr. Well, their women never thought in that same way. To most of 'em, Ed Watson was a killer and a desperader who didn't draw the line at killing women, and them quiet, winning ways of his that women liked – that feller drew women like flies all the time we knew him – only made him the more dangerous to deal with. It was a long way to the next neighbor, too far to hear a rifle shot, let alone a cry for help. The men knew this but would not admit it. They liked ol' Ed – you couldn't *help* but like him! – but in their hearts, they was all deathly afraid.

By the turn of the century, the wild things was so scarce and wary that a lot of the trappers went over to fishing. Some guided Yankees in the winter, then come back mullet-seining in the summer, shot all our curlews off Duck Island, set their trout nets right there on the grass northwest of Mormon Key. They wanted our key for their own camp, they'd shout ashore at night – You damn mulattas ain't got no damn claim to it! They took to crowding us so much we was fixing to shoot one, give the rest something to think about. And it got so they *wanted* us to shoot, give 'em their excuse to put an end to us once and for all.

Already the fish was getting few because every creek down in the Islands was crawling with plume hunters and gator skinners, never mind the sports off them big yachts in winter and gill netters all summer and moonshiners the whole damn year round. You'd see some stranger once a month where you'd never seen a man every other year, and you'd be leery of that stranger, too, never wave or nothing, just watch him out of sight and go your way.

So Daddy sold Mormon Key to E. J. Watson, and nobody pestered a man like that about no claim. We bought Tino Santini's Lost Man's claim when Tino moved north to Fort Myers, but before settling, we went on south to Flamingo for a year so's Mama could be with granddaddy John Weeks before he died. When we come back, we settled on Wood

Key, raised good board houses, put in gardens. Dried salt fish until 1905, when run boats started coming in with ice, took our fresh fish away.

It was 1901, same year we got well started in the fisheries, that E. J. Watson followed us down south, bought the claim to Lost Man's Key from Shelton Atwell. That island lies in the mouth of Lost Man's River, seven–eight acres, enough high ground for a garden, with good charcoal timber, black mangrove and buttonwood, and one of the few springs along that coast. Has a little cove on the east side we called Home Creek where the old Frenchman's maps showed buried treasure.

Atwells was first real settlers in that section, come up from Key West back in the seventies, and they was first ones had a claim on Lost Man's Key. But when they was pioneering, Shelton said, they seen the damage up and down the coast from the hurricane of '73, and they was cautious. Up Rodgers River they located some good hammock ground with protection from the wind and common tides. Later on, when some years passed without no hurricane, Shelton's two boys got to thinking about Lost Man's Key, out on the Gulf, a lot less skeeters with that sea wind and very handy to fresh water, but some way they never got around to it. Said the move might be too much for the old woman, so they best leave well enough alone. Meanwhile they let squatters come and go, to keep the key cleared off. Ones that was on there in 1901 was young Wally Tucker from Key West and his wife, Bet, who had worked the year before for E. J. Watson.

Now Hamiltons had their eye on Lost Man's Key, but Ed Watson wanted it much worst and made sure we knew it. What he aimed to do was salvage that old Everglades dredge that the Disston Company abandoned up the Calusa Hatchee, ship it on a barge to Lost Man's River, deepen the channel, dig out a good harbor, set up a trading post like Old Joe Wiggins had at Sand Fly Key, give work to everybody. Stead of shipping our produce to Key West and losing half of it to spoilage, we would sell direct to E. J. Watson. He aimed to supply fresh vegetables and syrup, meat and fish, fresh water, dry goods, fish hooks, bullets, to hunters and fishermen and the Yankee yacht trade, make Lost Man's Key the most famous place on the southwest coast. If his friends farmed the few pieces of high ground, he would control the whole Ten Thousand Islands. Ideas like this one got him that name Emperor Watson, and they weren't crazy, cause on the east coast Everglades development was well started.

Watson's plan depended on that key in the mouth of Lost Man's River, and the Emperor told everybody who would stand still that he aimed to nail down Lost Man's Key just as soon as Old Man Atwell saw the light. The Atwells never rightly knowed just what he meant by that, and they weren't so anxious to find out. Not wanting to be unneighborly to Mister Watson, they passed the word they was thinking the deal over, and after that, they just set tight back up in Rodgers River, never went anywheres near to Chatham Bend.

It weren't that the Atwells didn't like Ed Watson, they sure did. One time when their cane got salt-watered by storm tide, Shelton and his older boy, one we called Winky, went to Watson for some seed cane for replanting, and Watson treated 'em like kings. Put 'em up for four days at the Bend and sent 'em home with hams and venison, anything they wanted. Atwells never did stop talking about how kind Mister Watson was when Winky and his dad went up to Pavioni. Well, everybody in our Hamilton clan had the same experience. Come to old-fashioned hospitality, you could not find a better neighbor in south Florida.

Them Atwells was twenty-five years in the Islands, longer'n anyone before our time. They had two plantations and a lot of fruit trees, grew cabbages, onions, pumpkins, melons, sweet potatoes, and Irish potatoes, too. They got them Irish potatoes off Ed Watson. All the same, and before that year was out, they moved back to Key West.

Old Mrs Atwell upped and said that twenty-five years in the mangrove was enough, she was going back where she was born and die in peace. Said she didn't mind getting bled to death by the dang skeeters, but she'd be darned if she would end her days having her throat slit or her head shot off by some darn bushwhacker from the Wild West. Anybody who wanted to tag along was surely welcome, but she was leaving home sweet home whether the rest of 'em went along or not. Turns out the whole bunch was raring to go, but nobody had wanted to come right out and say so.

They needed a grubstake for their new life, so the first thing Winky and his brother done was go up to the Bend and sell the claim on Lost Man's Key to E. J. Watson. Then they come to say good-bye to us before they left. How come you never offered it to us? we said. Cause we didn't want to cross him, they admitted. They didn't let on they was leaving the Islands, being scared that Mister Watson would take advantage. But taking advantage was not E. J. Watson's style, he was not a small man in that way. He was so excited to get hold of Lost Man's Key, and happy that his Island plan was working out without no trouble, that he just nodded at their asking price, he never blinked.

Yes, Mister Watson was very excited – *too* excited, Winky said. Not till he'd pocketed the cash did Winky tell him that the Atwells was leaving the Islands for good. Swamp angels finally got the best of us, ol' Winky said – that was Old Man McKinney's name for the damn skeeters – and Watson told 'em in a jolly way how grateful he was that "sharpshooters" and not him had run 'em off.

That day the Atwells paid their call at Chatham Bend, Mister Watson was the perfect gentleman, he went so far as to put on his frock coat before offering 'em a toast of his best whiskey. Yessir, said he, he seen Lost Man's Key as the heart of his whole scheme for this wild coast. Surveys was needed, he explained, because most all of southwest

Florida was "swamp and overflowed" land turned over to the state back in 1850, and the state gave most of it to the railroad companies for laying rails into north Florida. The Everglades and the Ten Thousand Islands were still wilderness, and nobody knowed what was where nor who owned what. But he was in close touch with his friend Joe Shands, Lee County surveyor at Fort Myers, and Shands had told him this, that, and the other . . . and so on and so forth, waving his arms like our old Frenchman used to do when he got his wind up.

Course Storters in Everglade and Smallwoods at Chokoloskee, they knew how to work them land claims, and them families are well-to-do today. But in the Islands, E. J. Watson was the only feller ever wanted paperwork. The rest of us went down there to avoid it. Didn't *want* no surveys nor preemption, didn't want to know what preemption *was*. Never got it through our heads that if we didn't file a claim we'd wind up handing it over to outsiders who had paid off politicians to make it legal to steal it out from under us. Some feller would show up waving a paper that proved he owned the land we'd done the work on – damn rock-hard mound we had cleared and hacked and hoed all them long years before that city feller ever heard of southwest Florida – and a couple of sheriff's deputies right beside him to make sure them squatters got off his land quick, didn't try no mulatta tricks on this here city sonofabitch that called himself the rightful owner.

All we knew was, no good would come from getting surveyors nowheres near to Lost Man's River. All filing land claims meant to us was paying good money that we never had for our own land that we cleared off when it was wilderness. First thing you know, we'd be paying taxes with nothing to show for it – no schools, no law, no nothing.

See, it wasn't only just the payment we was dodging but the whole damn government, county, state, or federal, didn't make one goddamn bit of difference. A man would live in a lonesome place like the Ten Thousand Islands is

188

a man that don't like any kind of interference. Ain't got much use for humankind, you come right down to it, including some that I won't name in his own family. Or maybe his neighbors don't like *him* – don't matter. Them kind I'm talking about don't want no part of them damn paper-wavers from the cities, trying to tell a man where he could take a shit.

Ed Watson didn't see it like the rest of us down in the Islands who never cared if the whole world passed us by. He told them Atwells all about Free Enterprise and Progress, that's what made this country great, is what he said. The Philippines! Hawaii! Puerto Rico! America was bringing light to the benighted, yessirree, expanding our commerce all over the world, same way them Europeans done in Darkest Africa! Asked did we ever stop to think about all them Chinamen? The millions of customers just ready and waiting once them Philippines was ours? Talk about "swamp and overflowed," Ed was just overflowing with good spirits, Winky told me, and hard spirits, too.

Mister Watson's oldest boy was there, never said one word. Rob Watson stayed a little ways off to the side, went back to the field soon as his father started in to drinking. Tant Jenkins's sister was there too, down from Caxambas, served up a fine ol' feed of ham and peas. Ol' Ed got a bit boisterous and hugged his Josie around her bottom as she passed his chair, she had to rap his knuckles with her ladle. She was a pretty little thing with lots of spirit, had her a brand-new baby, Little Pearl. At that time Mrs Watson hadn't died yet at Fort Myers, so Josie said, "The less said about our Pearl, the better!"

Ed gave them Atwell boys plenty of drink, told stories about comical nigras that his family owned back there in Edgefield County, South Carolina. "You doan want to 'rest me foh no Miz Demeanor, Shurf! Ain' nevuh touched *no* lady by dat name!"

He had cracked that joke at the Hamilton table, too. When we didn't laugh much, he opined, "Well, I guess

Choctaws don't care too much for nigger jokes." We knew he was baiting us, and we didn't like it, but Daddy never seemed to mind. Said something easy like, "Is that so, Ed?" and him and his guest would set there nodding and grinning at each other like they knowed a thing or two about this life, which I guess they did.

Anyways, Ed got to boasting, and he let on to them Atwells in no uncertain terms that he didn't need no goddamn Corsican or whatever to hell kind of Spaniard Dolphus Santini called himself to show Ed Watson one damn thing about land surveys, nosir, he didn't, not no more! His daughter Carrie had married one of them cattle kings, and them cattle kings would make damn sure that nobody messed with E. J. Watson. As for getting deeds and titles, his son-in-law's good friends had connections all the way up to the capitol in Tallahassee, so E. J. Watson was on his way! Can't hold a good man down, that's what he told 'em.

So they drank to his success, and he drank to their safe journey and happy days down at Key West, and after that, he come out into the sun with that black hat on and spread his boots and stuck his thumbs in that big belt of his and stood in front of his fine house, to see 'em off. Yessir, says Ed, I'll be down that way tomorrow, have a look at my new property.

Casting off the lines, Winky decided he'd better advise the new owner about Wally Tucker farming Lost Man's Key. Seeing Mister Watson so excited, he had not got around to that, but he felt bolder with the whiskey, so he did.

Mister Watson took the news calm as you please. He come down to the water, not hurrying or nothing, and set his boot onto the stern line as it was slipping off the dock. The current had already caught the bow of their little sloop, and she swung downstream till she was snubbed, then warped back hard against the pilings. Watson had his whiskey in his hand, still looking amiable, but he never took his boot off of that line. Never said a word while the Atwells tried to figure what them blue eyes warned 'em had better be coming next, and damn quick, too.

Knowing Winky, I reckon he was winking, along with taking desperate care, he said, not to stare at Watson's boot, which was about on the same level with his face. Ed Watson had the smallest foot of any man his size you ever seen, it was one of the very first things that you noticed, and after that it was hard to take your eye off, even worse than another man's blind eye.

Finally Winky started talking, and his words come out all in a ball. He told Ed Watson that Wally Tucker never had no kind of claim on Lost Man's Key, nosir, no claim at all, it was just he had been on there for a while–

"I *know* how long that sonofabitch been on there–"

"–and being as how Atwells never used it, we never had the heart to run him off."

Watson nodded and kept right on nodding, with the Atwells setting in the boat trying to show how much they agreed with him without saying nothing that might turn him ugly. They was nodding right along with him like a pair of doves.

"I'll tell you what you people do," Ed Watson said after a while. He cleared his throat and spat clear across their boat, and the Atwells looked politely at his big ol' phlegm floating away on the black water. "What you do, you notify that conch sonofabitch on your way home that the claim is sold to E. J. Watson, and you tell him to get his hind end off of there as soon as he can dump his drag-ass female and all the rest of his conch shit into his boat and haul up that old chunk of worm rock that he calls an anchor and get to hell back to Key West, where he belongs. Now how is that?"

The Atwell family being Bahamians, Winky didn't care much for that "conch" talk, but what he said was "That's just fine, Ed, not one thing wrong with it."

Watson's fury was so raw that Winky got him a bad scare,

knowing there was a shooting iron under that coat. Must been winking like a baby rabbit. He had clean forgot Watson's quarrel with the Tuckers, if he ever knowed about it. But what with all the whiskey he had drunk, he got his courage up and tried again. Thing was, he said, young Tucker had built him a nice thatch house and a good dock, and cleared off a good piece of land, and had his crops in, and his wife was about to bust with her first baby. Atwells knowed from their own firsthand experience how generous a man Ed Watson was – they let that sink in, Winky said – and maybe he could see his way clear to letting them young folks finish out their season.

Ed Watson didn't care one bit for that idea. Why should he ride herd on them damned people, with Lost Man's Key so far off down the coast? The Atwells had let Tucker on there, and it was up to them to get Tucker off there, right? And Winky said that sure was right, Ed, not one thing wrong about it.

"Something's eating you," Ed said, after a moment, and took out his watch.

And Winky said, No, no, *no*, Ed! It was only that Tucker was a proud kind of young feller, and might not take to being told flat out to get his wife, who was in a family way, off of that Key with not a scrap laid by to eat, no place to go, and not a cent to show for his hard work.

Watson was looking down at his own boot where it trod the rope, and in that silence, Atwells said, they felt like screeching. There was no sound at all in that slow heat but the river sucking at the mangroves. Finally Watson said, "I sure do hate to hear a white man talk that way. Where I come from, a damn squatter can be proud till he's blue in the face, that don't give him the right to go up against a feller that has bought and paid for legal title. Where I come from, the law's the law."

Well, Winky didn't argue none with *that*. He just couldn't believe that a man so kind to all his neighbors could turn so cold-hearted so quick. Winky weren't by no means a bad feller, and he seen Atwells was in the wrong. They should of damn well got it straight with Tucker in the first place.

He decided to give Watson back his money. Kind of sudden-like – he was nervous and upset – he stuck his hand into his pocket, and the next thing he knowed, he was looking straight down the black hole of a Smith & Wesson .38. From that close up, it put him in mind of a cannon he seen once, down at Key West.

Very slow, young Mr Atwell come up with that envelope and stuck it out, and very slow Ed Watson put that gun away under his coat.

Watson paid no attention to the money. He was angry he had showed that gun, and being drunk, he was red-eyed and wheezing heavy, staring away like he was thinking hard about something else. Winky murmured how he sure was sorry for giving Mister Watson such a turn, and when Watson just grunted, looking past him down the river, as if planning what he aimed to do with these boys' bodies, Winky's nerve broke and his voice broke, too. What he meant was, Winky squeaked – he got nervous all over again, just describing it – what he *meant* was, Atwells would be happy to return the money until they got this Tucker business straightened out. But Watson only shook his head and finally Winky's arm got tired and he put the money back into his pocket.

By now, all the Atwells wanted was to get to any other place as quick as possible. But Watson stood there, his boot on the rope, and all Winky could think about was trying to look away from that little boot. Finally Ed blinked, kind of surprised, as if he had just woke up from a long dream – them's Winky's words – and found these strangers setting at his dock.

"You people can return that money," he says in a thick voice, "or you can give the money to that fucking Tucker, or you can stick it up your skinny damn conch ass. But no matter *what* you do with it, E. J. Watson bought that claim

193

on Lost Man's Key, and he wants them people off of it by Monday next.'

Talk as rough as that kind of took the fun out of the visit. So Winky said, All right, then, Ed, why don't you just write out a paper saying what you want, and we'll take that paper down to Wally Tucker.

Watson reared back and throwed his whiskey glass as far as he could throw it, way out halfway across the Chatham River. And he stomped inside and scratched out a quick note and brought it back to them. He wasn't wearing his coat no more, and he didn't wave at 'em, nor watch 'em go. Drifting downstream toward the Bend, they seen him heading back into his field. Said young Rob just turned away and kept on working.

Wally Tucker was a fair-haired feller of a common size. Took the sun too hard, went around with a boiled face. Slowly, he read Watson's words, then looked up at the Atwell boys, who couldn't read.

So Winky said, Well, what's it say, then? And Wally read it off:

> The quitclaim to Lost Man's Key has been sold lawfully to the undersigned on present date. All squatters and trespassers and their kind are strongly advised to remove themselves and all their trash human and otherwise immediately upon receipt of this notice or face severe penalty. (signed) E. J. Watson.

Reading them words out loud like that made Tucker so plain furious he flung the note away, but Winky picked it up before he left, we seen it later. He turned around and looked back at his new house, where his young wife stood watching from the door. Told 'em Watson once grabbed at Bet's backside and she had slapped him, that's why he insulted her. "She never told me what he done till yesterday. Bet's going to have her baby any day now," he said, kind of dazed. "She don't need this kind of aggravation."

Then him and the Atwells hunkered down and looked out over the water for a while, getting their breath. "You people have sold our home right out from under us,' he told them, making angry X marks in the sand, "and you sold what you never even owned, what you never had no right to, by the law. This is state land, swamp and over-flowed, think I don't know that? Atwells ain't got quitclaim rights, cause you never squatted here, and you never made no improvements." He tossed his head toward his house and dock. "If any man was paid, it should been me."

Winky glanced over at his brother Edward, and then he took out Watson's envelope. "That ain't the way we figure it down in the Islands," he warned Tucker, "but we aim to be fair, and we will split it with you." For the second time that day the money was held out, and for the second time nobody took it. Then Tucker snatched it and peeled off sixty dollars before handing it back.

"Tell him I never took his dirty money," Tucker said, "only what he owes us in back pay." For a moment he looked frightened but then set his jaw again. "I ain't getting off of here," he whispered. "I ain't going to pull up stakes."

Tucker's grit surprised them, they was quite alarmed, they warned him about Mister Watson's temper. He gave Winky a funny look and said, "I already rubbed up against Ed Watson, and he ain't scared me yet. Long as I don't turn my back to him, I'll be all right."

Tucker wrote out his own note then, and the Atwells took it back to Watson the next day. Winky never knew what might be in it, because Watson never told 'em, just read it quick and tossed it on the table. He went away into the field. He wouldn't talk to them and he wouldn't listen. They called after him, said they'd sure be happy to return his money, but he never even turned around.

Starting south, the Atwells was uneasy, that's when they came in to Wood Key to say good-bye. They begged us to go reason with Wally, and we said we'd get over there in a day or two. So that's how the Atwells set sail for Key West, left it all behind 'em.

A fisherman, Mac Sweeney, showed up that same evening at Wood Key. Mac was a drifter, lived on a old boat with a thatch shelter and a earth bed built up in the bilges for his cooking fire. Didn't belong nowhere and took his living where he found it. He was looking for a easy feed, as usual. Says he went by Lost Man's Key at daybreak, seen Tucker's little sloop in there, but after he left the river, he heard shooting.

"Shooting varmints, most likely," said my brother Gene. Gene wouldn't look at me.

The day Mac Sweeney came was not long after us Hamilton brothers moved on to Wood Key to start our fishing ranch. Gilbert Johnson was already on there, and me and Gene had our eye on his two daughters.

My Sarah was a slim and handsome girl without no secrets, ran like a deer and laughed and jumped and said most anything she wanted. Sitting on the sand one day, her arms around her knees, something struck her so sudden and so funny that she rolled straight back and kicked them hard brown feet up in the air in the pure joy of it. Kept her skirt wrapped tight, of course, but I seen her bottom like a heart, a beautiful valentine heart turned upside down. I mean, I loved her for the joy in her, and that sparkly laughter, but I was drawn hard to her, too. It wasn't only wanting her, it was like she was a lost part of me that I had to have back or I'd never get my breath. Later on we lived at Lost Man's Key.

The one time I was ever snake-bit I was out with Sarah running coon traps, went ashore in a swampy place, walked up a log and jumped to cross a piece of water, landed barefoot right on top of a big cottonmouth. He got me, too, he couldn't help it, two foot of him was free to come around on me. I made a good clean jump away but I could feel it.

I leaned back against a tree, too weak to kill him, just watched that deathly white mouth waving in the dusk, felt worse each minute.

Sarah hollers, "What's the matter?"

"Think I'm snake-bit!"

"*Think?* Are you bit or ain't you?"

So she comes across the swamp, hikes up my britches to have a look, and there ain't a sign of nothing, not a mark.

"Well," I said. "I think I'm feeling a mite better."

"Don't think so much," says Sarah, plumb disgusted. She pokes that snake so it raises up its head and whacks it dead with one cut of her stick.

Sarah and Rebecca knew Bet Tucker well. Said it was her had the real pioneer spirit to make do with the hardship and the loneliness, said that her husband was a nice enough young feller but lacked the ambition and the grit to hack him out a livelihood there in the Islands.

Young Tucker had a lot more grit than Sarah and Rebecca give him credit for. He aimed to stand up to Ed Watson, which not many did. Ed could shoot, and Ed *would* shoot, that was the rumor. Lot of us could shoot real good, but we wouldn't trade shots with E. J. Watson less we had to, and by the time we knew we had to, we'd be dead.

Sarah Johnson weren't but twelve that year, we married two years later, but she was already the bossy kind that gets into the thick of the men's business. She said Bet was like an older sister so she wanted to go look, but I said no, cause night would fall before we got there. The men would go down there first thing in the morning, and Miss Sarah Johnson would stay home.

For once Sarah didn't argue, maybe because she loved me so darn much. "If Bet loses that baby, it's all Wally's fault" is all she said. And Gene busts out, "If that baby's all she loses, she'll be lucky!" We all knew that, of course. There was no call for Gene to upset my brave young girl.

This fine and frisky female had a way with E. J. Watson, knew how to smooth him down. He thought a lot of Sarah, he respected her, and later on it would surprise me how kind of shy this hard man seemed around her, almost like he needed her approval. Oh, she was blunt, she would come right out and want to know the truth about his life. He seemed grateful that someone cared to hear his side of the story, and it got so he confided in her, he told her things he would never say to no one else. Maybe some of 'em was true, maybe they wasn't. But Sarah couldn't believe that Mister Watson would "ever, ever harm such a sweet young person."

We was just figuring what we should do when Henry Short come in looking for Liza. Not that he ever said as much. He couldn't. He never mentioned that girl once, though he could hear her singing by the cook shack. Poor feller knew we liked him pretty good and he was welcome, but he also knew how our mama might feel about a brown boy paying court, never mind that Liza was browner'n he was.

In them days, all around the country, they was lynching black men left and right for lusting after our white virgins. Most of the settlers in these parts had come south to get away from Reconstruction, so they brought their hate of nigras to our section, wouldn't tolerate 'em. Earlier this same year I'm telling about, it come in the papers about a nigra in New Orleans who was desperate enough to resist arrest when they come to lynch him. This man turned out to be a deadeye shot, which nigras ain't supposed to be, and he killed a whole covey of police before they finished him. So these days Chokoloskee folks was talking about how Henry Short was a crack shot, too, and who the hell taught a nigger to shoot like that, don't people know no better? – stuff like that. So Henry Short spent a lot of time back in the rivers. He stuck close to the House clan, didn't make no extra commotion.

Well, Henry hunted around for an excuse for rowing the twelve miles down here from House Hammock, said he forgot his pocket knife last time or some fool thing, and we helped him off his hook as best we could, all except Gene, who was full of himself and full of piss and finding trouble every place he looked. Gene said, "Your dang knife ain't around here, boy, Liza ain't neither."

To smooth this over, we asked Henry if he noticed anything at Watson's on his way down Chatham River from House Hammock, and he nodded. "Funny thing," he said, "I always notice everything at Mister Watson's." Said there was no boat at Watson's dock, no sign of anyone. Nobody hailed him, and there was nobody out in the field. The Bend was silent as the grave when he drifted by. And Mac Sweeney said, Oh sweet Jesus, boys! It's like I told you!

Crossing to Lost Man's first thing in the morning, we had rifles ready but we come too late. Smoke was rising from the shell ridge where the cabin was. Coming in there through the orster bars, I could feel something waiting for us on that shore. We was still a good ways off when Henry pointed.

Something had stranded on the bar, lifting a little on the current. "God, boys, what's that!" Mac Sweeney yelled.

"That's him," I said.

Wally's hair was lifting and his eyes was sunken back, made him look blind, and he hadn't been there very long cause his sockets wasn't loaded up with mud snails. Still had his boots on, slippery as grease from the salt water. A boot was what Walter grabbed ahold of, first time we tried him, and he slipped away. When I jumped over the side and took him up under the arms, the shadow of a shark moved off the shelf into the channel.

Hauling the body out onto the sand, I seen a dark stain spreading on my pants. It were not a shark bite leaking but a hole blowed through his chest, took his heart right with it. "Ah shit!" Gene said, and begun coughing. Walter looked peculiar for a dark-skinned feller, not pale so much as kind of a bad gray. Henry Short's light face looked a little green.

199

Me, I don't know how I looked, but it wasn't good. I was breathing through my mouth just to keep my grits down.

"Back-shot," Henry said, and us three brothers starting hollering and cursing – "Back-shooting bastard!" – to keep from puking or bursting into tears. Henry just shook his head a little, but he quit even that when he seen Gene watching.

Near the burned-out cabin we found a crate where Tucker had been setting, and his gill net and needle, and dried blood on the mesh and in the sand. There was no sign of Tucker's boat, no trace of Bet. We come on a circle in the sand and a bag of marbles, and a big sand castle by the water, like a boy had been there, but there was no sign of a boy neither. Must of been the tomboy in young Bet, passing the time. We hoped she'd run away and hid, but no voice answered our calls, only the crying of big orster birds out on the bar.

We rolled Wally Tucker in a piece of canvas and hoisted him into the boat. Nobody wanted to find Bet but we went looking, rowing east into First Lost Man's Bay and all around the back side of the key. We crisscrossed the island back and forth, we worked the riverbanks and the long strand of Lost Man's Beach, all the way south to Rodgers River.

"Sonsabitches!" Gene burst out, real close to blubbering.

We called and called. A hoot owl answered, way back in the trees. Dusk come from the mangroves and dark caught us at Wood Key.

Sarah came down to the boat and stared. All she seen was boots and canvas. She said, "Why did you bring him back?" I said, "We didn't want to leave him all alone." She whispered then, "Bet's alone too." One of the few times in this life I seen my Sarah cry.

Next morning Mac Sweeney took off for Key West. He was headed there anyway for a good drunk and wanted to be the first with the bad news. Sarah said we should take

200

Wally back and bury him close to his new house, and so Wally was still with us in the boat when Henry Short and us three brothers went next morning.

Crossing the flats, I seen a keel track in the marl. My heart give a skip and I hollered out, cause it never come to me before that I knew Watson's boat track when I seen it. Must of watched his big old skiff cross a flat somewhere back up into the bays and made a point to notice what his boat track looked like.

"Mist' Watson," Henry said.

Henry Short recognized that track the same time I did. Come to think of it, most men in the Islands would probably know that keel mark when they seen it. Noticing small signs is a good habit when you take your living from wild land. Maybe we all had the same instinct, to know where that man was, to know his markings.

I could feel Bet near, and pretty quick I seen her, though I couldn't rightly say what I was seeing. When you know a piece of country good, what nags you first is something in the view that don't belong, but sometimes it takes a blink or two to pick it out.

During the night poor Bet had surfaced in a kind of little backwater behind the point where a thing floating downriver might fetch up. Face down in the river, silted up, ain't no way at all to find a pert young woman big with child who laughed and waved the last time you ever seen her. I pulled Bet in toward the boat, using an oar, and she rolled over very slow, spun loose again. What I took for river silt was small black mud snails, giving off a faint dull glinty light. Them snails was moving as they fed, they was pretty close to finished with Bet's face. Weren't no blue eyes to reproach us, thanks to Jesus, and no red lips neither. Without no lips, them white buck teeth made that pretty little thing look like a pony.

Gene had ahold of her long skirt, and he hauled up on it and grabbed an ankle stead of taking the time to get a proper hold under the arms. Gene is always in a rush,

201

that's the life itch in him. Not wanting no scrap with him that day, I took the other ankle, but when we hauled on her, her head went under and her skirt hitched high on the oarlock coming in, and we seen the white thighs and hair and sex of her, and swollen belly. The indecent way we done it made me mad, and when I yanked that flimsy skirt back down her legs, it tore halfway off her hips cause it was rotted.

Being Gene, he has to holler out "Show some respect!' Much too rough, he stripped that canvas right off Wally's carcass, rolled that dead man out into the bilges, and flung it across to me so's I could cover her. "Make her decent!' he yells, giving the orders as usual.

Bet Tucker had a bullet through her head. There was no way to make that poor soul decent, never again. But what was most indecent came from Gene's hurry, so he scowls at Henry. "Don't want no niggers looking up her skirts, ain't that right, Henry?"

Henry Short don't show no more expression than poor gray Tucker laying in the bilges, so Gene hollers louder.

"That right, boy?"

"We heard you, Gene," says Walter. "No niggers allowed."

Now and again Walter is poked into the open, and even though Gene shuts his mouth, Walter don't let it go. "We heard you, Gene," says Walter. "No damn niggers." The bodies have him very bad upset, long with the rest of us.

Though he is older, Walter is the underdog, so I hoot at Eugene to back Walter up. Naturally Gene glares at Henry, not his brothers. Henry Short don't meet that glare but he don't cast his eyes down neither. He looks straight over Gene's shoulder like he's trying to read the weather in the summer distance, and his squint looks kind of like a wince.

Gene goes red, he snarls at Walter, "You want to call yourself a nigger, go ahead!"

Gene wants to grow up to be a cracker, so he thinks like his friends in Chokoloskee Bay. That's why they like him.

202

When me and Walter hoot at him, he says, "Dead people laying here and you make jokes? Show some respect!"

We went ashore and hunted around till we come up with Wally Tucker's shovel. There was high ground behind the bank, and we dug two graves in the sea grape above tide line, lashed together two crosses and stuck 'em in the sand. We buried Bet Tucker, mud, blood, unborn babe, and all. Gene was fixing to throw the sand down on her face, though he was looking pretty shaky, but Walter stopped him, took off his old shirt, spread it across her.

"That smelly shirt don't do no good," Gene muttered, and Walter said, "Just you shut up. Just shovel."

I went to the boat, took a deep breath, and grabbed her husband under the arms, got him hoisted up a little, leaking. Walter and Henry took his ankles. In the sun, he was warm on the outside, but under that warmth this fair-haired boy was cold, stiff, smelly meat, like some sun-crusted old porpoise on the tide line.

A dead man totes a whole lot heavier than a live one, don't ask me why. When I hoisted the head end so he'd clear the gunwales, his cold hair flopped forward over his face, and he seemed to sigh. When his belt caught, I had to grab a breath to wrench him free, and near gagged on a stink so sweet and heavy that I ain't cleared it from my nose hairs to this day.

We laid him in the ground face up, one arm beneath him – couldn't unravel him, he'd went too stiff. His eyes was bruised-looking, gone gray, but they still stared at the sky. When I closed his lids, they sagged back open like he didn't trust us. I felt ashamed of humankind, myself included. "I'm sorry we come late" – them words twisted right out of me, and tears behind 'em, but Gene didn't hear me, and he didn't see. He leans on the shovel and spits the dead-man's taste across the sand.

Before I puked, I grabbed that shovel and covered Tucker as fast as I could swing, covered that swollen-up face that was straining toward high heaven, crying for mercy. Never stopped to take off my own shirt – I wouldn't copy Walter out of pride. I closed both of them gray sockets with one shovelful, and with another filled that thirsty mouth. But throwing hot sand into his mouth shook me so bad that I let out a groan, and the next load hit Gene in the gut, to stop him smirking. Gene knew better than to say one word.

After that, I swore with every shovelful. Don't know what terrible things I hollered, I just hollered. I buried men since then, I buried children, but them poor Tuckers was the worst job in my life.

When the graves was banked, I looked around, getting my breath. It was so quiet on that little island, under that white sky, that I could hear the beat of my own heart. If I think about that morning beach, and it's been fifty years, I remember that silence and I smell him still, now ain't that something? Smelling a dead man after fifty years?

Being the oldest, Walter stood up straight, jammed the shovel blade into the sand, and growled a prayer: Almighty God, here's two more meek inheriting the earth. Something like that. Me and Henry said Amen, but Gene just hee-hawed and slapped Walter's back.

I took deep breaths, trying to figure out what should be done. I felt like heading straight for Chatham Bend to put a bullet through the crazy brain of that red bastard. Anyone else would of buried them bodies, at least got rid of 'em someplace, run 'em out into the Gulf and dumped 'em over – had the common humanity, I mean, to clean up his own mess, though he must of knowed there was no hiding from the Lord.

One time not long before he died, the Frenchman warned me about Watson. "Is truly *charmant*, I am as-tonish! I like vair much, I cannot help." He nodded, pointing at my eyes, "*Also* I hate Watson, you understand? John Leon! I warning it to you! This man is not vermins ordinaire, he is

204

other thing, he is . . . !" Chevelier struggled for the word, and failed. "Crazy?" I said. At that, he wagged his finger hard, tapped his temple, waved both hands, like a speared frog. "No, not foo! He is – *accurs-ed?*"

We never got cured of Chevelier's idea that Watson could not help himself, that he was cursed. That was the excuse we give ourselves for liking him. My Sarah, who had real good sense, thought the Frenchman must be right, and so did some of 'em in Chokoloskee. But now I ain't sure what we meant by "cursed," unless God cursed him. If God did that, then who was we to blame, God or Ed Watson?

Chokoloskee never known the Tuckers – not to eat and joke with, the way we done, not to bury – and in a few years the whole story got changed. Henry Short, he knew the truth of it, but he had sense enough to keep his mouth shut, even when a rumor come up from Key West about some young boy who had been visiting with Wally Tucker, and it was recalled how the Atwells thought they seen him. Smallwood and them put out that story how Watson killed "Tucker and nephew," not wanting to believe such a good neighbor would put a bullet through the head of a young woman. It took them Hamiltons, people said, to make up such a frightful story. And by the end of it, my brother Gene, who had seen right up Bet Tucker's skirt, came to agree with 'em.

We don't know a thing about no boy. But Watson – or somebody – killed Bet Tucker, and the four of us buried her that direful day.

Two deputies showed up a few days later, said the Key West sheriff had been advised by a Mac Sweeney that foul murders had been done at Lost Man's River. This Sweeney declined to name no suspects, but Sheriff Knight had reason to suspect Mr E. J. Watson. "Told us to deputize you mulatta boys here at Wood Key," one feller said.

Pap never give 'em a flat no, just started in to teasing.

Pap never teased lest he was angry. Spoke in a big muddy groan, more like a cow, moaning and mumbling and taking on how his only begotten sons was too young to die just cause these deputies was looking to get their ears shot off, and anyways, Mister Watson was their friend and generous neighbor, and how could Hamiltons turn around and go against him?

Walter had went out the door as soon as the law come in, that was his answer. How 'bout you, boy? Two dollars just for guiding us, they said, and I said, Nosir, I sure won't. I felt sick angry at Ed Watson, and wondered what Pap might have said if he'd seen and smelled and handled that cold flesh, but I told the deputies I didn't want no part of it.

Our mam was snorting loudly in disgust – she was disgusted most all of the time, on general principles. Pap said, Maybe you fellers can deputize that big white woman that's setting over there fixing them snap beans. She's tough as a nut, can shoot a knot out of wet rope, and won't settle for no ifs, ands, or buts.

Mam banged down her pot and went inside.

The deputies was scared of Mister Watson, and their nerves was short, so what they done, they advised Richard Hamilton that this was a pure case of cold-blooded murder and no time for no damn mulatta jokes. And I said, that's twice. Better take care who you go calling mulattas.

Pap hushed me. He said then, Don't you men get us wrong. This family don't hold with cold-blooded murder, nor warm-blooded neither, cause unlike some of your more common Christians, us Romans don't hold with murder of no size nor shape, nor race, color, nor creed. And some people was bloody murdered, they had *that* part right, but he hadn't seen no proof against Ed Watson.

Gene had come in just in time to catch our daddy playing possum. Hell, Pap, he yelled, we seen his *keel* track! Ain't that proof? And Daddy said, Might been proof, but like I say, I never seen it.

He was finished now, and his face closed down, but Gene did not take warning, he was too busy showing off for them two men. He stepped forward and got deputized, proud as a turkey, he even threw 'em a salute. Once he was deputy, he got to jeering, said, "Looks like Pap and his precious John Leon is scared to death of ol' Ed Watson."

Pap grabbed my wrist before I went for my own brother. You said a mouthful that time, Gene, Pap says, and now he's talking in his normal voice, only dead cold. You might got something there, Gene, who's to know?

Time Gene left to guide them deputies up Chatham River, he had already begun to sweat. Looked back over his shoulder, hoping his father would forbid his son to go. But Pap took no notice, he just set there in the sun, whittling him a new net needle out of red mangrove. He was finished with Gene, who had went against his father. Rest of his life, he was civil to him, but he never spoke to him again like his own son. That's the way our daddy was. Never got angry, but when he dropped something, he was finished with it, like he'd took a crap. Life was too short to waste time looking back, is what he said.

When the boat was out of sight, Pap said, "Maybe Eugene was cut out to be a sheriff's deputy, what do *you* think?" And late in life, a sheriff's deputy is exactly when Gene Hamilton become.

When the deputies dropped Gene off on the way back south, they wasn't going to let on what they seen. Gene was raring to tell but he was told, You ain't go no authority to comment. However, once Liza got to flirting 'em along, it come out quick as a squirt out of a goose.

The had found the Watson Place empty, cleaned right out. On the table was poor Wally's crumped-up message, the big letters printed onto it with pencil. Ed Watson never burned the evidence, and the deputies never bothered to collect it, cause they couldn't read. It was Gene had sense enough to bring it home. When he pulled it out, them deputies told us kind of cross that in a court of law handwrit notes weren't hardly worth the paper they was printed on.

Miss Sarah Johnson took one look, then sung out kind of sharp, This here note might mean nothing to deputies, but it is proof to anyone can read that Wally Tucker was the fool who got Bet murdered! Through her tears, she read out loud:

MISTER WATSON
I WON'T GET OFF OF LOST MAN'S KEY TILL AFTER
HARVEST COME HELL OR HIGH WATER

Hell showed up quicker than poor Wally Tucker had expected, and high water, too.

References to E. J. Watson's career in the Ten Thousand Islands appear at least as early as Florida Enchantments, published in New York in 1908. This account (referred to previously) describes the turn-of-the-century adventures in the South Florida wildernesses of a wealthy northerner, Mr Anthony Dimock, and his son Julian, who served as his photographer.

At least three figures in the Watson history are associated with the Dimocks. Bill House and George W. Storter Jr. (later Justice of the Peace) served him as guides, and Walter Langford apparently received the author at Langford's Deep Lake citrus plantation in the Big Cypress. Because Mr Watson was still very much alive, his name is changed in this lively account from E. J. Watson to J. E. Wilson, but there is no question of the real identity of that "genial" man referred to here as "the most picturesque character on the west coast of Florida." The otherwise ironical author seems in awe of "J. E. Wilson" and fascinated by the legends already beginning to surround him – the first but by no means the last writer to come under our subject's powerful spell.

While making no specific mention of the Santini episode, the Dimocks confirm Mr Watson's reputation as the barroom terror of Key West. (In this regard, see also "The Bad Man of the Islands," in Pioneer Florida, by the noted cattleman and former mayor of Tampa, Mr D. B. McKay – specifically a lively account of an episode in the Knight & Wall hardware store in Tampa when Mr Watson, arriving drunk, overheard a conversation about a dancing school, whereupon he "drew a large pistol and fired a shot in the floor near [his] feet and ordered, 'Well, let us see how nice you can dance!' " No one was hurt, and the miscreant was taken off to jail.)

The Dimock book refers to Brewer's failed arrest attempt and another such attempt by a Key West deputy who was disarmed and put to work in Watson's canefield. (Just when this oft-attested-to event occurred I have been unable to determine, due to the disappearance of old sheriff's records from Key West.) According to Dimock, this former deputy became his captor's admirer and friend, and on a later occasion introduced him in a Key West saloon as "Mr J. E. Wilson of the Ten Thousand Islands" who was preparing to shoot out the lights, whereupon the clientele ran out the door. Whether or not this story is true, it seems safe to assume that Mr Watson was chronically uproarious at Key West.

The Dimock book supports the local contention (and my own) that E. J. Watson was but one of many malefactors in this wild region:

Conditions in south Florida are primitive. Much of it has changed little since its recesses enabled the Seminoles to prolong a resistance to the United States Government that never was fully overcome. Three counties, Lee of the Big Cypress Swamp, Dade of the Everglades and Lake Okeechobee, and Monroe of the Ten Thousand Islands, contain the most that is left in this country of uncharted territory and wilderness available for exploration. . . .

Throughout these islands society is as loosely organized as it is sparsely distributed. One of the principal men of the coast told me that court justice was too expensive and uncertain for that country, and that people were expected to settle their own quarrels, a homicidal custom that has cost me four guides during the years of my own explorations. . . .

The mazes of the Ten Thousand Islands have proved a sanctuary for the pursued since before the Civil War. At that time they harbored deserters from the Confederate service, some of whom continue their residence *within its boundaries in apparent ignorance that the need therefor has passed. . . . Often, in the cypress or mangrove swamps which border the Everglades, you will meet men who turn their faces away, or if they look toward you, laugh as you ask their names. . . . These outcasts trap otters, shoot alligators and plume birds, selling skins, hides and plumes to dealers who go to them secretly, or through Indians who often help and never betray them. . . . Sometimes these outlaws kill one another, usually over a bird rookery which two or more of them claim. I passed the camp of two of them beside which hung a dozen otter skins and a few days later learned that both of them had been killed, probably in a quarrel, but possibly by some third outlaw, tempted by their wealth of skins. . . .*

The Dimocks describe what seem to have been the plantations of the Atwell family on Rodgers River, "all abandoned, all for sale, and all without purchasers. On them are splendid royal and date palms, palmettoes and tamarinds, but occupants have found skull-and-crossbones notices upon these trees, which latterly they have obeyed, influenced thereto by seven mysterious deaths which have occurred in the vicinity. The story of the murders, and the names of those who doubtless committed them, are upon the lips of even the children on the coast, but positive proof is lacking." Despite the judicious use of the plural pronoun in that final sentence, there is no question in the context that the suspected murderer is Wilson/Watson. (Ted Smallwood's memoirs also mention that Watson was accused in the death of seven men, including Quinn Bass and "Tucker and his nephew," but at least two of Smallwood's unlucky seven appear to have perished after the Dimock account was published.)

211

BILL HOUSE

I had the names of his plume buyers from the Frenchman,
and done my best to keep up the good work. For a time,
before the birds give out, my neighbors was collecting for
me, cause people was dirt poor in Chokoloskee, all but
Smallwood. Trap male redbirds, sell 'em to Cuban cigar
kings in Key West – them Cubans had 'em cooped in little
cages, liked to hear 'em sing. That was before the two bad
hurricanes around the end of Watson's time blew that
whole cigar business clear north to Tampa. (Many's the
Tampa Nugget I have smoked since them days.)

The Injuns was taking some egrets, trading 'em in with
their otter pelts for gunpowder and whiskey. The rookeries
over by Lake Okeechobee, they was shot out in four years,
and by the turn of the century the west coast birds was
giving out, from Tampa all the way south to Cape Sable.
If you recall that plumes would bring exactly twice their
weight in gold, you can figure out why men fought over
rookeries, and shot to kill. The Roberts boys went partners
with the Bradleys, and those fellers was still doing pretty
good around Flamingo, but most places birds had grew so
scarce that us regular hunters set guards around what few
poor rookeries was left. Them Audubons was agitating harder'n ever, and in 1901, the year that Watson disappeared,
plume hunting was forbid by Florida law. Yessir, our own
state of Florida passed laws against our native way of living!

All that ever done was put the price up. Them laws was
passed to quiet down them Yankee bird-lovers, but nobody
give a good goddam about enforcement. Only man paid
them laws any mind was young Guy Bradley, who got to

be first warden in the state of Florida and took his job too serious for his own good.

Guy Bradley was shot in 1905, not long after Ed Watson had showed up again, and when that bad news come in from Flamingo, Ed Watson got the blame for it, as usual. When another warden got axed to death in 1908, near Punta Gorda, that one was laid on Watson too, but every man at Punta Gorda knew who done it. No one ever got arrested, far as I know. I ain't saying that's good, I got my doubts, but in these parts any judge knows better than to mess with an old clan that is only taking what is theirs by God-given right. Wiped out a third warden along about that time, in Carolina.

Before Pap crippled himself with his ax, and I went home again to help him out, I went to work for a Yankee sportsman, Mr Dimock. Had his son along with him snapping pictures, that boy spent most of every day with his head in a black bag. A. W. Dimock was a pretty old feller by that time, but like most sports, he would shoot anything in sight, not only deer and birds but gators, crocs, and manatees. We even took sawfish out of House's Bay, where my family had our cane farm north of Watson's place. We'd cut the saws off, sell 'em for souvenirs, that's what the old gentleman wanted. Mr Dimock made out as how he had a good market up North, so we'd hack the saws off them big fish, leave the rest to rot. Lost his shirt, not that he needed money. Trying to sell saws was his excuse for all that killing, made him feel better about his life some way, but the only good it done was save some turtle nets, which sawfish used to mess up something terrible.

We harpooned sawfish from Chatham River all the way south to Cape Sable, and in that time I told Mr Dimock a fair amount about Ed Watson. Seemed like Watson was about all us local people talked about in them days. Mr Dimock put them tales into his book. Never read it myself, didn't know how, but I was told about it pretty good. Called him J. E. Wilson cause E. J. Watson was still going strong and might have took him into court for heartburn, but there weren't no doubt at all who he was talking about. Told the barber story on Ed Brewer, too.

Well, Dimock's book hinted pretty plain that this J. E. Wilson had killed seven in these parts. Damn if I know who them seven could of been, less they was stray nigras that we never knowed about. And if us natives never knowed about 'em, how did that old Yankee find it out? For quite a spell after Atwells went away from Rodgers River, and them Tuckers was found killed at Lost Man's Key, there weren't but hardly seven people *down* there, not if you left out them two big clans of Hamiltons. Their men was hard. If Watson killed any Hamiltons, them families never said too much about it.

Ed Watson were not by any means the only feller in our section who had took a life. There was murdering aplenty back in them days, but the law never bothered with it hardly cept to say good riddance. Sheriffs never did find out who was living back into the Glades, too damn hard to keep track of men who traveled very light and kept on moving. Some of these men were real old fellers, very wary, never let you near, just slipped like otters through them rivers where they could always scoot away into the Glades. One old feller come from England, Ted Smallwood called him the Remittance Man. Ted would have a check for him every six months there at the post office and he'd fix himself up with six months' worth of shine. Wanted to get away from it all, looked like to me.

Mr Dimock wrote up his adventures in a famous book called *Florida Enchantments*. That Yankee must of got delirious, too many skeeter bites or something, to be enchanted by these godforsaken swamps. Well, we was partial to 'em, too, never knowed why. He sent me the book, and I got my intended, young Miss Nettie Howell, to read it out to me. There was a picture of a sawfish guide in there, kind of murky but it might been me.

After I quit Mr Dimock, the feller who took my place

got pulled overboard by a sawfish, split his guts out, died before he'd figured out his own mistake. Outsider. Man from the east coast, y'know. Wasn't familiar with the way we done things in the Islands.

Nine years after Mr Watson's death, an article in the Home and Farm, *published in Louisville, extolling the wonderful sport fishing out of Chokoloskee, was still warning its readers to avoid a very dangerous islander named Watson. The charge of multiple murders in the swamps (and at Key West) would be repeated many times, with varying degrees of exaggeration and pure fantasy. But in every case, as the Dimocks acknowledged, positive proof was lacking, and this is true in regard not only to Mr Watson's guilt but to the numbers of killings that actually occurred.*

In a day when Negroes were discounted, it is scarcely surprising that not one of the names of his alleged black victims has been recorded. On the other hand, some supposed white victims are also nameless, leading one to suspect that their numbers are exaggerated. Indeed, the only ones identified by his neighbors during his sojourn in the Ten Thousand Islands were old Jean Chevelier and the two Tuckers, and the first seems problematical, at best. Local people assert that Mr Watson murdered "the old Frenchman," but when questioned closely, none of them seemed to believe it, least of all the Hamilton clan, which was close to Chevelier as well as Watson.

In their native courtesy and hospitality, one's informants imagine that the most sensational interpretation of the Watson legend is the one that the visitor wishes to hear, and one may suppose that this was true in the Dimocks' day as well. Not that the Dimocks were naïve; they had traveled widely in south Florida over many years, they knew the country and its people as well as might be expected of Yankees and outsiders, and they took an ironical view of all they saw. Nonetheless, the Watson legend may be counted among their Florida enchantments.

The most lurid view of Mr Watson is the one often

perpetuated by the islanders themselves, for as Dickens remarked after his visit to this country, "These Americans do love a scoundrel." Over long decades in lonely remote islands, where notable citizens have been few, Mr Watson's venerable contemporaries and their descendants have arrived at an "ornery" sort of reverence for E. J. Watson, who has transcended his original role as a notorious cold-blooded killer to become a colorful folk hero, the west coast counterpart of the bank robber and killer John Ashley, whose gang terrorized eastern Florida after World War I.

Mr Watson is considerably more intriguing than John Ashley, who was, in the end, a very ordinary sort of outlaw. By all accounts, Edgar Watson was a good husband and a loving father, an expert and dedicated farmer, successful businessman, and generous neighbor. Such virtues – not usually associated with notorious killers of the common type, who tend to be stunted and uninteresting in their social relations as well as in outlook and mentality – command our attention and explain why Mr Watson is so fascinating, not only to the Dimocks and later writers but increasingly – dare I admit this? – to the undersigned. As a professional historian, I had thought myself beyond such subjectivity, yet the enigma of our subject's character grows rather than lessens with each new fact unearthed, however much the vulgar legend is deflated. How else to explain that, seven decades after his death, Ed Watson remains the most celebrated citizen the southwest coast of Florida ever produced?

Of the "seven mysterious murders" cited by the Dimocks, we are left with the suspicious deaths of "Tucker and his nephew," as these victims are usually described by local people. The precise identities of the Tuckers remain vague, together with the circumstances. According to the Hamilton family, who were the Tuckers' neighbors and friends, they were Walter Tucker and his wife Elizabeth, known as Wally and Bet. Despite friendship with Watson, the Hamiltons assume that he killed these young newcomers from Key West, which he himself appears to have confirmed by his hasty departure from the region.

Thus only two out of these seven unsolved killings may safely be laid at Mr Watson's door, and probably this is a fair ratio of truth to legend when considering his lifelong career. The highest figure I have come upon is fifty-seven – Mr Watson's own figure, it is said, as recorded in a notebook allegedly once seen by his son Lucius, who later described it to my informant, Mr Buddy Roberts of Homestead. (Mr Roberts's uncle Gene was a friend of Mr Watson, and the whole family was involved in the Guy Bradley case.) There are many good reasons for doubting this story, among them Lucius Watson's well-known reluctance to discuss his father. Yet Sarah Hamilton recalled, quite separately, not only that Mr Watson kept a journal but that it was entitled "Footnotes to My Life." And Buddy Roberts mentions a detail that could only have been known by someone close to the family, to wit, that Lucius's father had a tiny foot, and wore a size seven shoe.

There is a widespread local rumor that Mr Watson forced one of his sons to assist him in the Tucker killings, ordering him to pursue and kill the Tucker "nephew," who fled down the beach. If such an episode took place, the victim must have been Bet Tucker and the accomplice was Rob Watson, since in 1901 young Eddie and Lucius were living with the family in Fort Myers.

Shortly after the Tucker deaths, it is related, Rob Watson fled in his father's schooner to Key West, where he sold the ship in order to finance his ongoing flight and final disappearance. Mr Watson pursued him to Key West and, failing to find him, assaulted one Collins, who seems to have abetted young Rob's flight. Shortly thereafter, Mr Watson himself departed southwest Florida, not to return for several years. A letter of unknown provenance written to the Smallwoods in 1904, mentioning that "friend

218

Watson" has been in touch with the Lee County surveyor, Joseph Shands, is the first indication known to me of his return into the region.

FRANK B. TIPPINS

I heard tell of E. J. Watson long before his family came to
live here. I was born in Arcadia and was back there on a
cattle drive at the time of the De Soto County range wars
in the early nineties. One day a local gunslinger was killed
in a saloon brawl by a stranger. Quinn Bass was a local boy
from the large cattle clan on the Kissimmee River, and the
hired guns Quinn rode with led a crowd of rowdies and
Bass relatives to storm the new jailhouse and lynch "the
stranger" – more in the spirit of hell-raising than justice,
since even his partners never denied that ol' Quinn asked
for what it turned out he had coming. The mob was slowed
by the new bricks and brave demeanor of De Soto County
sheriff Ollie H. Dishong, who smiled and waved from the
second story as if he was up there running for reelection.
But he wasn't calm inside, he told me, because as that
moonless night went on, the crowd grew so unruly that
Sheriff Ollie came to doubt he could save his prisoner to
go to trial. However, he reckoned that, no matter what
befell this Watson, no great injustice would be done, and
rather than see his brand new jail torn up, he unlocked
the cell and told the prisoner he might as well get going
"while the going's good."

The prisoner looked out the window at the crowd, then
went back into his cell and lay down on his bunk. Sheriff
said, What is the matter, and the stranger said kind of
ironical he didn't think the going looked so good. Not
enough evidence to hold you, Sheriff Ollie explained, and
this way, you got you a fighting chance. Lock that door,
his prisoner said. I'll sleep better behind bars.

But later the stranger sent some money to treat the crowd at a saloon some distance up the street, and toward daybreak, with the mob distracted, the sheriff rode him to the edge of town, told him to go to hell and stay there. The stranger grinned into the sheriff's face. Said, What makes you think we ain't arrived already?

Remembering those words, Sheriff Ollie shook his head. "That damn Jack Watson was the most friendliest sonofagun I ever met," he told me.

"You mean *Ed* Watson, don't you?" I said.

"Ed Watson?" Sheriff Dishong shook his head again. "Must be gettin old. Did I say Jack?"

That story got me kind of interested in being a lawman, but I had a career or two before that time, had some education. I was fifteen years of age when I took work as a printer's devil for the new Fort Myers *Press*, which in a town of about three hundred people was glad to come up with any news at all. That was 1884, when a typical headline story was the Debating and Literary Society's first meeting to decide the question "Are Women Intelligent Enough to Vote?" (Stamping their feet, the panel voted in the affirmative, at least in regard to the fair sex of Fort Myers.) In the same year I set in type the first advertisement for Roan's general store, offering top prices for deerskins, gator hides, and bird plumes. It was also the year of the first visit to "our fair city" of America's "electrical wizard," Thomas Alva Edison, who bought Sam Summerlin's place on Riverside Avenue – that's MacGregor now – and would one day make Fort Myers his winter home. And it was the year Jim Cole showed up in town. In those days, even Jim Cole was a "first."

The following year, the *Press* covered the big celebration at the river – balloons, fireworks, and oyster roast – when Grover Cleveland became the first Democratic president in a quarter century. That put an end to Reconstruction, those terrible dark years when nigras got treated better than the white people.

After four years as a printer's devil, I was sick of indoor life. I took a job with the Hendrys as a "cow hunter," rounding up the long-horned cattle scattered through the Cypress. Sometimes I rode all the way east to the Everglades, long silent days under the broad sky in the hard fierce light of the Glades country, lost in the creak of my old worn-out saddle and my horse blowing and hot wind whispering in the pines. For long years afterwards I missed the stillness of the Big Cypress, the slow time of those horseback days, the hunting and fishing for the cow camp, the slow cooking fires, the simple sun-warmed tools of iron, wood, and leather, the resin scent of the pine ridges, the stomp of hoof and bawl of cattle, the wild things glimpsed, wild creatures, the echoing silence pierced far and near by the sharp cry of a woodpecker or the dry sizzle of a rattler, and always the soft blowing of my woods pony, a small short-bodied roan. Race could find the short way home from Hell, "could turn on a dime and give back nine cents change," as the old hands said. Had me a good cow dog, Trace, for turning cattle, and was a fair hand with the braided buckskin whip that served us cow hunters as lariat.

Each time our cattle pens were moved, an Indian family would move in behind and plant new gardens in that fertile, sod-broke ground, sweet potatoes the first year, then corn and peanuts. Because they were forever watching, they came in almost overnight. I used to wonder what Indians thought of the Disston Company's rusting dredge far out to the east toward Okeechobee, that looming shape on the sparkling horizon of what the Seminoles called Grass River, Pa-hay-okee, and the hellish noise and smoke and smell of it, all gone now, and not one damned thing accomplished, only the unholy ruin of the beautiful Calusa Hatchee. The old silence had returned, but the white man's machine still rose above that river of white sacred sand that had filled with mud and would never come clear again. This was the dredge Ed Watson aimed to use at Lost Man's River.

In the nineties, I became friendly with Walt Langford, who was a cow hunter for his father's partners. Young Walt was a hard rider, too, with the sharpest eye south of the river for a stray cow hidden in the scrub. But Walt always wanted to be liked too much, he aimed to show he was not just a rich cattleman's son but a regular feller, so he led in the boozing and the brawling, the whooping, galloping, and gunfire, that kept nice people shuttered up on Saturday afternoons. Fort Myers was never so uproarious as Arcadia, we never had real cattle wars or hired guns. All the same, this Saturday pandemonium reminded the upset citizens that our new Lee County capital was still a cow town, on the wrong side of that slow broad river, falling farther and farther behind the country's progress.

Many a long day I spent alone out in the Cypress, but the lonely day was Saturday, when the other riders, already half-drunk, yipped and slapped off through the trees to spend their week's pay in the saloons of Fort Myers.

On Sundays I helped serve the flock at the Indian mission at Immokalee, riding twenty miles or more to attend the service. The Indians could not follow the sermon, but they came anyway to watch the white people. They sat in circles on the floor. Pretty soon, I quit my job for full-time work at the Indian mission. I was still there in 1897 when I first heard how this E. J. Watson, a leading planter in the Islands, was supposed to be the killer of Quinn Bass, and the lovely young girl at Doc Langford's house was this outlaw's child. Carrie, going on thirteen, was a strong, willowy young lady with big dark eyes, black hair to her waist, and a high bosom. When I first saw that vivacious young creature skipping rope in front of Miss Flossie's notions store, I knew that she and I were some way fated. When the time came, I would ask her daddy for her hand

223

in marriage, and shake his desperado's hand at the same time.

Cattlemen had run this town before it was a town at all, starting way back with Old Jake Summerlin at Punta Rassa. Old Jake was ruthless, people said, but at least he had cow dung on his boots. These new cattlemen, Jim Cole especially, worked mostly with paper, brokering stock they had never seen, let alone smelled. In recent years, with Doc Langford and the Hendrys, who bought out the Summerlins at Punta Rassa, Cole made a fortune provisioning the Rough Riders. One July day of 1899, according to the *Press*, these patriot-profiteers shipped three thousand head from Punta Rassa to their Key West slaughterhouse for butchering and delivery to Cuba.

Meanwhile, Jim Cole made a second fortune on Cuban rum, smuggled in as a return cargo on his cattle schooners, and naturally the cattlemen led the fight against liquor prohibition that the Women's Christian Temperance Union was supporting. The "drys" won in 1898, thanks to the accidental shooting death of a drunk cowboy. The saloon of Taff O. Langford was shut down, and two years passed before the "wets" could put Taff back in business. But the cattlemen still lived by their own rules, and Sheriff Tom Langford drank bootlegged rum at the wedding party in July when Walt Langford took the hand of Miss Carrie Watson.

Though I opened my livery stable that same year, I had some ideas about running for sheriff in the 1900 elections. I was shoeing a horse when this Jim Cole, who had got wind of my ambition, came in and offered me his help, having already figured what I hadn't understood, that I was pretty sure to win without him. Folks was real restless under the rule of cattle kings who ignored all protests against cattle in the streets, and the lard-assed incumbent,

Sheriff Langford, had lost most of his support for covering up for the cowboys in that shooting.

Walt Langford and some other riders had caught an old black man outside Doc Winkler's house and told him he must dance for them or have his toes shot off. People next door had closed their shutters but they heard it. And this old nigra close to eighty, white-haired, crippled up, bent over, cried out, No, boss, Ah cain't dance, Ah is too old! And they said, Well, you better dance! and started shooting at the earth around his feet.

Doc Winkler came running with his rifle. He hollered, Now you boys clear out of here, let that old man alone! And he ordered the nigra to go behind the house. But the cowboys kept right on shooting into the ground behind him, so Doc Winkler fired a shot over their heads, and just at that moment a horse reared, and the bullet caught a cowboy through the head and killed him.

At Jim Cole's request, Sheriff Langford called the episode an accident. Walt Langford and his friends were not arrested, and there was no inquest; Doc Winkler was left alone to chew the guilt. But the flying bullets and senseless death brought new resentment of the cattlemen, also a new temperance campaign to make Lee County dry, and the Langford family took Cole's advice to marry off young Walter, get him simmered down.

Of the town's eligible young women, the only one that Walter had an eye on was a pretty Hendry whose parents forbade her to receive "that young hellion" in the house. This caused stiff feelings in both families, and led eventually, from what I heard, to the bust-up of the Langford & Hendry store.

Well, my friend Walt couldn't help but notice – since she lived right in his house – the beautiful girl from the Ten Thousand Islands. Her mother was a lady by Fort Myers standards, a former schoolteacher and a religious person, cultured and well liked, whose husband would buy her a house on Anderson Avenue so that their three children might attend the Fort Myers school. But a recent book being passed around the town claimed that one Watson had killed the famous outlaw queen, Belle Starr, and it appeared that this bad man was none other than the husband of the refined and delicate Mrs Jane Watson. The lucky few who had met Mister Watson had been thrilled to find that this "dangerous" man was handsome and presentable, a devout churchgoer when in Fort Myers, a prospering planter and shrewd businessman of good credit among the merchants, and altogether more genteel than the frontier gentry who gossiped about his reputation.

Out of the blue, the Watsons announced the engagement of their beloved daughter to Walt Langford. It was all so sudden that some people figured this young hussy had accommodated Walter and was already in a family way. Well, naturally, she wasn't any such a thing! I spoke up loudly every time I heard loose talk about a shotgun wedding, I was so fierce about her purity that folks began to look at me in a queer way. Probably wondered if Frank B. Tippins was the father, which he wished he was!

Knowing Walt Langford, I guess that marriage was inevitable. No doubt Mister Watson's shady past made Carrie Watson all the more romantic to this good-hearted, rambunctious young man. But Carrie was not yet thirteen, and no one quite knew how agreement had been reached whereby such a young girl would be married the following year. From what we heard, it was Jim Cole who persuaded both families of the advantages of such a union. He had even met privately with E. J. Watson in a salon at the Hendry House, though what those two discussed was only rumor.

Walt and Carrie were married in July of 1898, in the great new day for the Fort Myers cattlemen that began when the Spanish War got under way. I went to the wedding and mourned for my lost bride, with her big wondering eyes and soft full mouth – a different creature altogether from the horse-haired thin-mouthed cracker women I was used to. When the minister asked if anybody present knew why Carrie and Walter should not be united in holy matrimony, a wound widened in my heart – *Because I love her!*

Love, love, love – well, who knows anything about it? Not me, not me. I never got over her, I do know that much. I wouldn't have gone to that wedding at all except to see what Carrie's father looked like, and I never saw him. The noted planter, Mr E. J. Watson, failed to appear.

CARRIE WATSON

May 10, 1898 Frank Tippins thinks he loves the girl who is engaged to his friend Walter!

Mr Tippins is nice-looking, I'll confess, tall and lanky, in his early thirties, black handlebar mustache down at the tips that gives him a thoughtful air, or rueful, maybe. Around his horses he looks quite at home in the boots and battered hat from his days as a cow hunter in the Big Cypress – that's where he and Walter became friends. My new admirer has told me more than once, I fear, how that poor old hat had sheltered him from the sun and rain and served as a water vessel for bathing. He might still bathe in it, for all I know!

Frank is thinking he might run for sheriff. His black and bag-kneed Sunday suit, a once-white shirt, bowtie and waistcoat, with the broad hat and boots, give him the look of "Wyatt Earp of the Wild West," a book much admired by the modest reading circle of our town. Like his Western colleagues, he seems calm, courteous, and soft-spoken, easy with firearms and horses, if not females, and a religious man with only his Maker to fear.

From Mr Jim Cole's point of view, says Walter, Frank Tippins would make us a good sheriff mainly because, as a onetime cowhand for the Hendrys, he was sure to sympathize with cattleman problems in regard to rustling, disorderly conduct by the cow-hands, undue enforcement of cattle-roaming ordinances, and the like. That's what Mr Cole, who acts like he discovered Frank, promised the cattlemen. And the cattlemen like Frank because he is so amiable with our rare Yankee visitors, making a virtue of the flies and cow dung and dirt streets that all the rest of us afflicted citizens perceive as our city's greatest liability. (To Walter, that highest honor falls to our disgraceful lack of even so much as a road north, far less a railroad, that might permit our isolated town to follow the rest of the nation into the Twentieth Century.)

Walter imitates Frank Tippins very well: "You bet! This is the leading cow town in the second largest cattle state in the whole U.S. And A.! The only state that got us beat is Texas. Second largest! I was a cowhand once myself!"

Mr Tippins says that when he arrived here from De Soto County, in the early eighties, Fort Myers had no newspaper, its school was poor, its churches were irregularly attended. Visiting ships were mostly small tramp schooners in the coastal trade, beating upriver from Punta Rassa. The last Florida wolves still howled in the pinelands to the east, and panthers killed stock at the edge of town.

"Be grateful, Mr Tippins," Mama told him. "Your city seems splendid, I do declare, after life in the Ten Thousand Islands, not to speak of the Indian Territory – !" She shook her head. "Or even Fort White, where Mister Watson found me!" She stopped right there, having quickly sensed Mr Tippin's peculiar craving to know anything we might reveal about dear Papa. "Fort Myers is wonderful!" she finished, already exhausted.

As a young man Frank worked at the *Press*, and learned something of local history and good grammar, though he affects a rough, bluff style of speech. When Mama and I first came to town, it was the ex-cowhand at the livery stable who informed us that Spanish Franciscans in the north part of the state had the first cattle ranches in the country. The first real cowboy-and-Indian fight occurred in Florida in 1647, he said, when Spanish *vaqueros* ran a herd through the Indian plantings.

Doubtless Mr Tippins guesses that learning is the way to show a former schoolteacher how serious he is, how deserving of her handsome daughter, even if that young

229

flibberty-jibbet is already engaged! And he speaks carefully, wishing to expose his attainments in a modest fashion that might captivate the Watson ladies' hearts.

And of course, Mama is mildly interested in what he has to tell her of Fort Myers history, and so he brought her an account of our small "Eden" that appeared in the New Orleans *Times-Democrat* after its Everglades expedition of 1882, which had Captain Francis Hendry as its guide. Mama observed graciously that the Calusa Hatchee, with its banks of large wild trees set off by the bountiful coconuts and guavas, by the flowering species – planted, Frank says, before the Indian Wars were ended and the Civil War begun – must surely be the most beautiful river in all Florida. (Fact is, the river water is unhealthy, and both dysentery and malaria – "chillin and shakin," for which the approved remedy is Blue Mass pills and turpentine balls – are epidemic.)

"Yes, ma'am, this was a cattle town right from the start" – news we both found less astounding than our own sudden interest in the ways of cattle. Until this century, he said, there was no farming, nothing but cattle and a little citrus and some fishing on the coast. Immokalee was an Indian settlement, but pretty soon it became a cow town, too. "Immokalee, that means 'my home.'"

He paused to see if he had rustled up some interest in his Indian lore, then hurried on. "Indians are mostly gone," he said. "Hendrys and Langfords ran cattle in that area when there was no bridge over the creeks; pony carried your gear, and you piled your gun and grub and bedroll on your head and waded.

"Old Fort Thompson was a cow town, too. Captain Hendry had a ranch, got a county separated off from Lee, called it Hendry County, then renamed the town for his daughters, Laura and Belle. Fort Thompson is La Belle, Florida, today."

"Laura and Belle! You don't say so!"

"Yes, ma'am. Course cowboys are pretty much the same

wherever you find 'em. Called us cow hunters around these parts because we had to hunt so many mavericks – some of them older riders called 'em hairy dicks, cause they wouldn't stick with all the others – "

"*Heretics*," Mama corrected him quickly, a rose-petal flush on her pale cheeks, and Mr Tippins glared down at his boot tops as if he had half a mind to chop his feet off.

"Yes ma'am! Your hairy ticks or whatever you'd want to call 'em, they'd lay low in the woods and hammocks, that's why we were known as cow hunters. Sometimes they called us cracker cowboys because we cracked long hickory-handled whips to run the herd. Besides his whip, every man carried rifle and pistol to take care of any two-legged or four-legged varmints we might have to deal with. A good cow hunter can snap the head clean off a rattler and cut the fat out of a steak – you can hear that whip pop two-three miles away. We rode what we call woods ponies, which is a tough small short-eared Spanish breed. Had us our cow dogs to run the herds, and at branding time we threw the steers by hand. Otherwise we weren't so much different from cowpokes you might come across in Texas or Montana."

I watched him, eyes wide, biting my lip in fond amusement. He knew I was teasing him but could not stop talking, like a show-off boy running downhill who gets himself going much too fast. But my heart went out to him all the same. His way of expressing some of the things that Walter never appreciated was almost beautiful, even when he couldn't find the words.

"Between the wolf howl and the panthers screaming, and the bull gators chugging in the spring, the nights were pretty noisy in the back country, and weekends were always noisy in Fort Myers. The boys would ride in on Saturday to gamble and get drunk, shoot up the town, just like cowboys were supposed to do, but we didn't have any houses of ill fame like the east coast, or at least none I was able to find out about."

I had to giggle at Mama's little *hymph*! and Mr Tippins glared down at his boots again, convinced he had fatally offended the prim Watson ladies. But kind Mama cried, "I pray you, please continue, Mr Tippins!"

"Well, the churches were pretty strong here, which means good strong women," Mr Tippins said, to recapture some lost moral ground. "Maybe that's why some of the boys went so darn wild! Oh, this was a wild cow town, sure enough! One time the cowboys rode their horses right into a restaurant, shot up every bowl. Course the fact that the new owner was a Yankee might have had something to do with it. That restaurant closed down then and there, for good, and later the owner took work as a yard hand, and him a *white* man – never saw *that* before!"

"Were *you* one of those cowboys, Mr Tippins?" I said, knowing he wasn't. And when he shook his head, I said, "But your friend Walter was, isn't that true?"

"I don't rightly know, Miss Carrie," Frank Tippins said.

"Well, you're certainly quite a talker, Mr Tippins!" tactful Mama declared, at which I tittered and had to flee the room. Of course I stopped to listen at the door.

Our would-be sheriff was explaining, more and more desperate, how our town had made small progress since his youth, when he had drifted down here from Arcadia.

Mr Tippins informed Mama that Arcadia was his birthplace. "Tater Hill Bluff, we called it then."

"Tater Hill Bluff! you don't say so!"

"Yes, ma'am!"

Fort Myers was still a cow town, that was the trouble. "Course the Hendrys and Langfords – I mean, these days, ma'am the cattlemen are making a hog-killing off the Spanish War, same as Summerlin made in the War Between the States."

"Dr Langford was a wonderful man," Mama warned when he drew breath so he wouldn't come out with any criticism of her benefactor. "When I arrived so ill from Chatham River, Dr Langford made me promise I would never return to those islands under any circumstances. He offered kind care and hospitality to a perfect stranger – "

"And the perfect stranger's daughter!" I said, popping back in with Delamene's tea and cookies from the kitchen. "You *are* perfect, dear Mama!"

" – until Mister Watson could prepare this house. When poor Dr Langford became ill he was scarcely a year older than my husband! He certainly took me by surprise when he beat me to the grave!" Knowing how much that remark would delight Papa, she did her best to keep a straight face, but her funny little smile, self-mocking, twitched one corner of her mouth. "You could have knocked me over with a feather," she added, to amuse herself, closing her eyes so as not to see me giggle.

"Mama!" I murmured. "How silly you are!" And we burst out laughing merrily, having made Frank Tippins too uncomfortable to join in.

"What was your maiden name, ma'am?" he asked Mama, going red again over this loose talk of maidens. Maybe he knew that in another life he would have fallen hopelessly in love with my sweet mama, not just me.

"Jane Susan Dyal. From Deland," said Mama. Jane Susan Dyal from Deland spread her fingers on her shawl, smiling prettily in pantomime of her lost girlhood. "As a young woman I was known as Mandy, but there is no one left who calls me that." She smiled again, faintly annoyed by her own bittersweet flirting with the past.

"Except Daddy," I reminded her.

"Except Mister Watson."

When Frank Tippins said, "I reckon a visit to Deland would do you good," she shook her head. "No, I think not. I'd already escaped Deland when Mister Watson found me teaching in Fort White's new school."

"That was before Mister Watson got in trouble?" His innocent expression didn't fool us, and he knew it.

"That was before he went away to Arkansas."

After a cool pause that she let serve as a rebuke Mama

233

looked up over her knitting. "Carrie's father is very generous, Mr Tippins. He is not a small man. He takes good care of his family, helps his neighbors, pays his bills. How many of our civic leaders can say the same?" She resumed her work. "I don't think this color suits me, what do you think, Mr Tippins?" She held up a swatch of the blue wool shawl. "I shall give it to Carrie."

FRANK B. TIPPINS

One evening in 1901, Little Jim Martin, former sheriff of Manatee County, came to my office to report that Mister Watson had went on a rampage, killed some people down at Lost Man's River. I knew Jim Martin for a man that did not care to back up, but all the same he had moved his family out of their new house on Possum Key took 'em all the way north to Fakahatchee. I told Jim that Lost Man's River being Monroe County, I had no jurisdiction unless the Monroe sheriff gave it to me. Next morning, in came the young man from the telegraph with a request from Sheriff Frank Knight at Key West that I detain a certain E. J. Watson.

Most mornings, I went unarmed in Fort Myers, but that day in late 1901, I had a revolver holster strapped under my coat. Usually I tipped my hat politely, saying "Howdy" to everybody who came by, but today I wore a squint to warn the citizenry that their sheriff was on serious business and would squander no public time shooting the breeze.

In order to locate Mister Watson it made more sense to go directly to house, but since Miss Carrie's beloved mother was on her deathbed, I decided halfway to Anderson Avenue that I would not trouble that sad family. Instead I headed for Walter's office to see what kind of information he could give me. If Walt Langford took advantage of my questions to warn Mister Watson, that was not the responsibility of the sheriff's office, and anyway, I had no warrant for an arrest.

If I did cross paths with Mister Watson, what would I do? Was I scared or just alert and leery? Both, I guess. I

235

hoped I wasn't headed for Walt's office just to be careful, but if E. J. Watson was hiding in his wife's house, feeling skittish, whoever went down to the telegraph office to send a message to Key West might not be me.

Remembering Carrie's wide eyes at her wedding, and also my envy of my old partner – brooding how a bad drinker like Walt might fail to treat such a young girl with the reverence Frank Tippins could provide her, and how Walt never deserved her in the first place – all this made me shift my wad and spit my old pang of regret into the dust beside the First Street boardwalk, making old Mrs Summerlin hop sideways, pretending I was aiming at her shoe. *Good morning, ma'am!* Carrie had been married three whole years and she still skipped rope sometimes down at Miss Flossie's and it interested me a lot more than it should have that there were no children.

To console myself – "to pick the scab," said that damned Cole, who saw right through me – I continued visiting her mother after Carrie's marriage, when Mrs Watson and the boys moved to Anderson Avenue. Walter and Carrie were still stuck at home with the Widow Langford, but having no children, Carrie escaped much of the day. My visits gave me an opportunity to observe her for exciting little signs of discontent, and perhaps to hear stray news of Mister Watson. At that time, I had seen him only once, a broad-backed figure in well-cut suit and broad black hat, walking down First Street to the dock one early morning.

Mrs Watson, who knew why I was so attentive, threw cold water, relating how, when the blushing newlyweds returned from their New Orleans honeymoon, Walter's mother had shown them to separate rooms, saying, "I declare, I can't get *used* to the idea of those two children in one bed!" Mrs Watson watched me flush, then soothed me with a quick warm smile.

"Why, heck, ma'am, talk about the *West!*" I said, trying to change the subject. "We had *buffaloes* here in Florida, as far south and east as Columbia County, right up until

236

the early eighteenth century!" But I recalled even as I spoke who'd told me that Columbia County lore – it was Walt Langford, who had got it straight from Mister Watson. I went red as a berry, while the Watson ladies feigned astonishment. In a duet, they cried out, *"Buffaloes? In Florida?"*

I tipped my small chair over backwards in my haste to rise, looking off somewhere so as not to see them smiling. Stung by those smiles all the way to the front door, I called back in desperation, "Why heck, ma'am, it was right here in Fort Myers that Chief Billy Bowlegs surrendered up his warriors and took ship for Wewoka, Oklahoma!"

Like all of the town's small emporiums, Langford & Hendry down on First Street was a scrawny old frame building, slapped up loose, unpainted, on a weedy dirt street with wood sidewalks, ramshackle storefronts, and a cow town's blacksmith sheds, livery stables, and saloons.

Outside the side door which led to the upstairs offices I saw Billie Conapatchie, a Mikasuki Creek raised up and educated by the Hendry family. He wore a long calico shirt with bright red and yellow ribbons, and also a red neckerchief and bowler hat instead of the traditional bright turban. Somehow he had stuffed his shirt into hand-me-down white man's britches, which stopped well short of his scarred ankles and his scuffed brown feet.

Squatting on favorite lookout points all over town, this man spied on city life, attending church services, public meetings, and theatricals without exception, whether he understood the words or not. For learning some English at Fort Myers school back in '78, he came real close to being wiped out by his own people, and he was the only Indian seen in town for years thereafter. All the same, he sent his son, young Josie Billie, to the Seminole School established by the missionaries at Immokalee, where my niece Jane Jernigan, lately of Arcadia, had married the

Indian trader William Brown. In my cowboy years, visiting the Browns, I came to know the Billie family well.

"Tell Josie we'll go hunting soon's I get myself caught up," I said. He barely nodded. Billie Conapatchie might speak English but he had not lost his Indian indifference to our white men's hollow social ways.

Past Billie's ear, which pushed through his black hair like a wood fungus, I saw a thickset curly man coming straight for me down the muddy street, fixing me in place with a pointed finger. Jim Cole was a city man at heart, and hated silence. Crossing the street from one group to another, he'd shout jokes to get attention to himself, taking over the conversation before he arrived. "Nailing down the Injun vote, that what you're up to? You go on that way, we'll have to *give* it to 'em!" The sally was certain to be followed by a backslap and loud laugh, he raised that meaty hand of his as easy as a dog raises its leg. But I didn't crack a smile or stop my squinting, and when his hand faltered, I lifted my own hand toward my hat, which I didn't tip. Being offended for the Indian, I only said, "That so, Captain?" His hand retreated to adjust his trousers at the crotch.

"Which one's gonna get it first, Frank, Injuns or women?"

Under Billie Conapatchie's gaze, we white men smiled in mutual distaste, and you had to wonder what was passing through that Indian's head. Billie watched us kind of sideways, not as a spy but as a sentinel, like the lone crow. He hung around the city, learning what he could, so's to warn his people of any dangerous new course that the white man's itch might take.

Jim Cole jeered at Billie's silence. "How'd that go, Chief? Don't talk our ear off, Chief!" He let fly a short laugh like a belch and followed me into the building, heaving himself up the narrow stairs.

I was rapping on Walt Langford's door, ignoring the noisy clumping boots behind, when a shadow appeared behind the glass of the adjoining office. Before his door closed, old James Hendry lifted a finger to his lips to hush my greeting and spare himself an encounter with Jim Cole.

"Climbed a lot of fences," Hendry had observed two years before, in warning me that "Cole will own you" if I made the mistake of accepting his help in my campaign. "Can't say just why they run him out of Taylor County, but that feller arrived here with hot buckshot in his butt, I'll tell you that much."

Like other cattlemen, Jim Cole invested his war profits in a big new house on First Street, but unlike the Summerlins and Hendrys, and the Langfords, too, this man had no sense of land, no feel for cattle. As Jake Summerlin used to say, Cole sat a horse with as much style as a sack of horse shit. Despite his big coarse cowboy talk, Cole had rarely ridden that wild lonesome country between the Calusa River and Big Cypress, and had more calluses on his broad ass than anywhere else.

Arriving at Langford's door, he boomed, "Look who's settling right into his dad's seat, and his dad not cold yet!" and shouted that raucous laugh of his to the whole building. Never thought once about Walt's feelings, or whether he himself might be unwelcome.

But Langford grinned at his old family friend, showing him in. "*My* office once," Jim Cole declared, throwing himself back in the big chair and slapping his hands down on its leather arms, his rough boots smearing street mud on the floor. He sprawled back, gut out, getting his breath in a redolence of hard sweat and cigars.

"How's the child-wife, you damn cradle-robber? How come we ain't seen no kiddies yet?"

I ignored his wink, feeling ashamed for wondering the same thing, and also sorry that Walt felt obliged to snicker.

Walt was still ruddy from his years out in the pinelands, and ruddier still because his morning had apparently been blurred somewhat by drinking spirits. Plainly James Hendry gave him too little to do.

"Got some business with you, Walt," I said. But when Jim Cole said, "Spit it out, then," I stayed silent.

Langford said gently, "No use trying to keep nothing from Captain Jim. A man can't cut a fart here in Fort Myers without your say so, ain't that right, Jim?"

"*Isn't*," Cole said, mopping his neck. "Ain't Carrie told you about 'ain't? You *ain't* out hunting cows no more, young feller, you're a damn cattle king, same as your daddy. If I'm putting you up for county commissioner, you got to talk right, same as the rest of us cracker sonsabitches."

Like him or not, I had to admit there was something shrewd and humorous about Jim Cole, something dead honest in his lack of scruple. All the same, I found it hard to smile.

They were awaiting me. Through the window I could hear faint barking, and the rattle-clop of horse and wagon.

"Heard yesterday your father-in-law might be in town."

Langford moved behind his desk. "That so?" he said, and glanced at Cole, who had rolled his eyes towards the ceiling. Then he took a seat and waved me to a chair.

I took my hat off but remained standing, gazing out the high and narrow window at the store-front gallery across the street. There on election day a Tippins crowd had been scattered by gunfire and the whine of bullets from the general direction of the saloon owned by the incumbent's cousin, Taff O. Langford. I stayed where I was until a few regathered, then spoke the lines that won me the election: *They have the Winchesters, gentlemen. You have the votes.* "*Ol' T.W.*" was turned out of office the next day.

"Shit!" Cole said, and banged his chair legs to the floor. "God-dammit, Frank, don't stand there looming just cause you're so tall!" His smile looked pinned onto his jowls. "You got a grudge against this Langford family, Sheriff?" The eyes looked hard in his soft face, just the opposite of Langford. Cole had a long curlicue mouth – kind of a

whore's mouth, I decided – and his nostrils, cocked a little
high, looked like pink and hairy holes, snuffling and yearning for ripe odors. "You ain't hardly run off with ol' T.W.'s
job and now you're dogging this man's father-in-law, who
ain't even in your jurisdiction! And here Walt's daddy ain't
been dead a year, and li'l Carrie's mother dying right before
our eyes! That's what Walt here has to think about every
morning, noon, and night, and you ain't got no more decency than that? Sweet Jesus, boy – !"

"Easy, now." Walter was holding both hands high.
"Frank and I been friends for a long time. It's okay – "

"No, it *ain't* okay!" shouted Captain Jim, cutting him off
with a show of anger as if afraid Walter might concede
something, or reveal it.

What Cole was angry about, or angriest about, was the
Lee County sheriff's refusal, three months earlier, to back
up his alibi when a federal revenue cutter seized the *Lily
White* at Punta Rassa. On her regular run, the *Lily White*
had delivered cattle to the Key West slaughterhouse, and
rather than make the return run with her holds empty, she
had met a Cuban ship in the Marquesas to take on a cargo
of contraband rum on which no duty had been paid. The
schooner was held at Key West for five weeks until Jim
Cole, still claiming innocence, still gathering testimonials
to his civic virtue, had paid the federal government a heavy
fine, not because he lost his court appeal – it hadn't been
heard at the time that he withdrew it – but because the
loss of income from the confiscated ship was far more
painful to this feller than any loss of honest reputation.
He'd even shouted at the U.S. attorney, "Don't you people
realize there's a *war* going on?" His lawyer had to remind
him that the war was over.

To keep his job, the skipper of the *Lily White* had sup-
ported Cole's version of events, but no one who knew
Cole could believe that his ship had taken on illegal cargo
without the knowledge of her owner. You had to wonder
at the greed that drove rich businessmen to twist the law

of the land they claimed to be so proud of, steal from the government by overcharging for their "patriotic" services, and do their best to cheat it of its taxes – not to make a living, either, but to heap up money.

"No, it *ain't* okay!" Jim Cole was yelling, so loud that people stopped out there on First Street.

I turn back to Langford. "There's been trouble, Walt . . ."

"I know it," Langford says.

"You know it. He's in town, then?"

"No, he ain't."

Langford glances at Jim Cole, who is still glaring at me. "No, he *isn't*," Langford corrects himself, looking quickly away because he sees we won't smile with him. "He already passed through on his way north. Wanted to visit with Carrie's mother one last time, and he told Mrs Watson there'd been trouble. She told Carrie." Walt Langford raises his hands high as if I'd said, This is a stick-up. "I never saw him. I don't know what he told her, and I don't know where he's headed, so don't ask me."

"Why, dammit, Walt, he's got no *right* to ask you!" Cole explodes. "Ain't got no goddam jurisdiction! That's Monroe County down there, Tippins! In Lee County, the man is clean, and aims to keep it that way!"

Because he kills across the county line, he's clean? But mainly I ignore Jim Cole, holding Langford's eye. "Monroe sheriff sent a telegraph, wants him for questioning. If he's still in town, I'd have to notify Key West."

Cole snorts with a contemptuous wave of his thick paw, but Langford's nod thanks me for the warning.

"Who was it?" Langford says.

"Young man named Tucker and his wife, some say a boy. Monroe sheriff can't get the whole story. They were squatting on Watson's claim, wouldn't get off."

"Niggers, you said?" Jim Cole sits up. "Wouldn't get off?"

This time it is Langford who ignores him. "And Carrie's father is the usual suspect, right?"

"No known witnesses, no evidence, no proof. And not much doubt." I tug my hat on.

Langford accompanies me onto the landing. "No *law*, you mean."

"Maybe he thought the Island men might make up their own law. That's why he left, I guess." I start downstairs.

"Don't pester Carrie with it, all right, Frank? He ain't in town no more. You have my word."

I tip my hat. Knowing I won't have to confront Ed Watson brings mixed feelings. A chance has gone that might not come again.

Walt Langford smiles. "Now that don't mean I'll let you know if he comes back!" he says.

Jim Cole booms out, "If he comes back, I'm nominating that sonofagun for sheriff!"

I manage a grin, to be polite, when Langford guffaws too loudly and too long. "Ol' Jim," Walt sighs, and pumps out another laugh, as if unable to get over such a humorous person.

"Ol' Jim," I repeat quietly, to help Walt out.

BILL HOUSE

Early in the century, the produce business for Key West begun to die. Ted Smallwood had two hundred and fifty alligator pear trees, reached all the way across Chokoloskee Island, used to ship barrels of them things to Punta Gorda, sent 'em north by railroad, got five cents apiece. Storters still grew cane at Half Way Creek, Will Wiggins, too, but nobody lived there anymore. Lopezes was on Lopez River, D. D. House had his home on Chokoloskee but his cane farm on an old bird rookery north of Chatham River we call House Hammock. Ed Watson was farming both sides of the river now at Chatham Bend, and he done better than us all. C. G. McKinney still farmed some up Turner River, and Charlie T. Boggess at Sandfly Key – these were small produce gardens – but Chokoloskee farmers give up one by one. Too much rain or not enough, too much salt water to leach out after a storm. That black soil on the shell mounds had no minerals to speak of, just tuckered out in a few years, same as the women. There was more livelihood in bird plumes, gator hides, and pelts of coon and otter. Then the wild things give out, too. Good thing the clam factory got started, cause there wasn't much left to us but ricking buttonwood, a little fishing.

Watson had been gone for years and nobody was farming Chatham End, although good ground high enough to settle was running out in all them northern islands. Our House clan came and went from Big House Hammock, but most of all that Watson country emptied out, all the way south to Lost Man's and beyond.

Used to be three plantations on Rodgers River, had beautiful royal palms, date palms, too, and tamarinds – quitclaims to all of 'em was up for sale and had no buyers. After all the hard labor and sweat and suffering them Atwells put in, near to thirty years of it, them houses was just rotting on them mounds, all sad and gray, boilers rusted and cisterns crusted over with green slime and rot from them poor animals that fell in trying to get their water. And the fields growed under with thorn jungle, and the dark river taking everything away, back to the wilderness, like nobody but the old Calusas ever been there. Later on, when the Storter boys and Henry Short went up in there looking for mullet, they seen signs posted on the bank at them old places, and what was on them signs was skulls and crossbones, kind of crude painted, white on black. No law against putting up signs, I guess, might been somebody's idea of a joke, ain't saying who.

People came and then they went. They never stayed long once the silence got 'em.

For some years after 1901, there was only two strong families around Lost Man's. Richard Hamilton and his boys lived on Hog Key, Wood Key, north of Lost Man's River, that was one clan; and Old Man James Hamilton and his sons Frank, Lewis, and Jesse was on Lost Man's Beach, south of the river mouth, that was the other. Henry Thompson was married in with the James Hamiltons there at South Lost Man's. He was Watson's friend, and the Richard Hamiltons got friendly with Watson, too, took pains to keep it that way.

Henry Thompson done some farming and some fishing, too, helped Old Man James and his youngest, Jesse, build a pretty fair shell road back in there to that old Calusa mound we called Royal Palm Hammock. Big grove of royal palms on there then, and grubbing out them palms paid for the work. Hamiltons claimed they aimed to farm, cause wherever royal palms raise above the mangrove, there is pretty sure to be a good high mound, with good black soil,

245

but I don't believe that was the only reason. Seemed kind of funny that big mound were so far back in from the water, like them old time Injuns was trying to hide it. Old Chevelier had got everybody thinking about buried treasure, what with Bill Collier's finds up there at Marco, and Old Juan Gomez's tales out on Panther Key. I do know Henry Short got a bad case of it. Henry's dream was to strike treasure and get away somewhere, though I'm damned if I know where a nigra could escape to, back in them days.

Headed down around Shark River, we used to see them beautiful royal palms along there back of Lost Man's Beach. That shell ridge must been five miles long, probably still is. All them fine trees along that coast are gone today, don't see a one. Nobody will miss 'em that never seen 'em there, I reckon.

One of them cattle kings, Jim Cole, claimed them palms was wasted where they was so he had us dead-broke Island men dig the last one out to prettify the city streets. Put 'em on postcards, bring in tourists from the north. Tropical paradise, y'know. Course the most of 'em died – nobody watered 'em – so they might's well lived along right where they was.

This was when Cole and Langford brung the railroad in, and the tourists started coming in their thousands, Godamighty! Too bad Jim Cole didn't order up some gumbo-limbos, cause them trees is scraggily, thin-skinned, always red and peeling. Us local folks call that the tourist tree.

It was along about this time that C. G. McKinney made the mistake of not keeping his post office money where he could put his hands on it. This was somewhere around 1906. They seldom inspected, but the day they did, the money was somewhere else. Wasn't lost, just in use, you know, he didn't have it handy, and by law he had to have it handy there and then. So Smallwood loaned McKinney the money to get him out of trouble, and before you know

246

it, Ted was postmaster instead, and not only that but biggest trader, owned most all of Chokoloskee Island, left the rest of us in the dust. For the next thirty-five years and more, Smallwoods was the main family on that island.

This was the year Mister Watson brought his new wife back to Chokoloskee Bay. First thing he done was pay a call on Storters, open a new account, and he done the same across the Bay at Smallwoods. Probably figured that so long as he stayed friends with the traders, he would be all right.

MAMIE SMALLWOOD

I recall the day in 1906 when Mister Watson came back to
Chokoloskee – everybody does, I guess, because he showed
up in the first motor launch we ever saw. Folks heard it
coming, pop-pop-popping down the Pass from Sandfly Key
– for years us young folks called that boat the *May-Pop*,
that's how cranky she was. Men and women both left their
tomato patch and hustled along after the children, who
went flying and hollering down to the landing. At Chokoloskee we were way behind the times, though not all of us
knew it, and pretty desperate for a look at something new.

Even a quarter mile away, out in the channel, the figure
at the helm looked too familiar, the strong bulk of him,
and the broad hat. When he saw the crowd, he tipped that
hat and bowed a little, and the sun fired that dark red hair
– color of dead blood, Grandma Ida used to say, only she
never thunk that up till some years later, when the ones
who never knew him called him Bloody Watson. Ida Borders House of South Carolina – well, we'll miss her. But
it was that little bow he made that told us straight off who
it was, and my heart jumped like a mullet, and it weren't
the only one. A hush and stillness fell on Chokoloskee, like
our poor little community had caught its breath, like we
was waiting for a storm to break from high dark thunder-
heads over the Glades in summer, just before the first cold
wind and rain.

"Speak of the Devil," says Grandma Ida, primping up
her hair, though no one had spoke of Him lately as I knew
of. Grandma knew she was looking straight at Satan, and
no mistake. *That man has dared to come back here among*

us! All around the shore they was raising fingertips up to their mouths, rolling their eyes, O Lord-a-mercy – now why do some fool women *do* that, you suppose? – and staring walleyed at each other like a flock of haunts. Then all together they dared look again, and all together gave a grisly moan of woe. Wouldn't surprise me if I gave a moan myself. It was like in Revelations, regular Doomsday. I didn't see no one rend their clothes nor tear their hair, but a couple of God-fearing bodies hurried their offsprings up the hill, squawking and scattering like hens, not cause they really thought Mister Watson might attack 'em but to show them other biddies how Mrs So-and-So wouldn't let her angels have no truck with no Methodist murderer.

Course them two hens turned right around when they heard that eager squabble from the other women, picked up their skirts and come tripping down the hill again. Might been scared of Mister Watson, but they was more scared yet of missing out on something.

When Mister Watson tipped his hat and bowed, who should stand up right beside him but a young woman with a babe in arms! Next thing we knew, he was handing her out onto our landing! After that, it was a barnyard around here, pushing and squeaking and flapping off home to find a poor bonnet or a pair of shoes for such a high society occasion.

Say what you like about Mister Watson, he looked and acted like our idea of a hero. Stood there shining in the sun in a white linen suit and a light Panama hat, not one of them rough straws we plait down here. And her on his arm in a wheat-brown linen dress and button boots, and sweet baby girl in brown frock and sunbonnet and big pink bow – you never seen a more upstanding couple!

For a few moments that fine little family stood facing the crowd like they were posing on a holiday. I see that picture each time I recall how he stood alone in that very selfsame spot on a dark October evening four years later, with that young woman turning slow to stare at me in my

249

own house, and his little girl squeaking her heart out in the corner like a poor caught rabbit, in that wild crashing of men and their steel weapons.

Since that bad business down at Lost Man's River there'd been plenty of talk that if Ed Watson ever showed his face round here again, the men would right away form up a posse to turn him over to the Monroe sheriff, maybe string him up if he gave 'em any back talk. But Mister Watson stayed away from Chokoloskee when he came through in 1904, he stopped off quick at Chatham Bend and was gone quicker. Returned later that same year, stayed a bit longer, burned off his plantation, which had mostly gone back to scrub palmetto. Never heard that he'd been there till after he was gone, but meantime folks got used to the idea that he might come again.

Whether that was his plan or it wasn't, you had to admire Mister Watson's nerve. He took all the steam out of the men, who told each other he would never stay, told each other he was fixing things up so he could sell the place on Chatham Bend, told each other everything that they could think of. And all this time he was tending to his business, seeing the Lee County surveyor about getting title to his land, bringing his own carpenter from Columbia County to build him a front porch, giving the house a new coat of white paint. Not whitewash, mind, but real oil paint. Only house with a coat of paint was ever seen down in the rivers. but that carpenter perished down at Watson's, and bad rumors naturally started to fly, and next thing we knew he was gone again. This was the year poor Guy Bradley was killed, and some pinned that one on him too, once he departed.

When he didn't show up for a year, and it looked like we'd seen the last of him for certain, the men concluded he had killed that carpenter along with the Frenchman and the Tuckers, and the lynch talk started up again. Some of these fellers got just plain ferocious.

Well, here he was, walked right into their clutches, but I never heard no mention of a posse. Most of them fools were jostling when E. J. Watson came ashore, that's how bad they wanted to step up and shake his hand. Nobody wanted to hang back when it came to showing how much they thought of Mister Watson, they wouldn't hear a hard word said against him. Told their wives later, Well, them Tuckers was just conchs, y'know, goldurn Key Westers. They might have had it coming, who's to know?

Yep, they joked and carried on with Mister Watson *that* day, he weren't nothing but our long-lost Island neighbor. Charlie T. Boggess asked what kind of motor Mister Watson had in that there boat, and he said, 'Why, that's a Palmer one-cylinder, Charlie T., and she's a beauty! – and all the rest of 'em nudging and winking nodding like a row of turkey gobblers, as if anyone but Charlie T. would have known it was a Palmer soon's they heard it coming up the Pass. Charlie and Ethel Boggess is our old dear friends, they was married back in '97, same year we was, and my Ted always held a good opinion of him, but Charlie T. was a pure fool around Ed Watson, and he wasn't near as bad as some them others.

Eugene Hamilton was here that day, who helped bury them poor Tuckers down at Lost Man's, and was all for lynching Mister Watson some years back. A young Daniels told him at that time, Ain't no damn difference if the man is guilty, boy, it ain't your place to go talking big about lynching *no* damn white man. And Eugene said, You saying *I* ain't white? and they had one heck of a fight right here behind the store, Gene Hamilton like to killed his own darn cousin. But this day he stood gawking with the rest.

The only one who took no part in all the hubbub was my brother Bill, and I was proud of him. Bill House was curious, no doubt about it, he puzzled over Mister Watson his whole life, but Bill had talked to Henry Short, who had helped the Hamiltons with that burial. Though Henry Short would never accuse nobody, Bill concluded that Mr

E. J. Watson was a cold-hearted killer, and never seen nothing else to change his mind. Bill had no kind of education, he took over for Dad when Dad went too hard for his age and crippled himself with his ax, down at House Hammock. Taking care of our House clan the way he done, Bill was always too busy to improve himself, but he had more sense than the whole bunch when it came to people.

Mister Watson must have felt Bill's eye cause he turned around in the middle of a sentence, eyed Bill a little bit too long, then said real quiet, "Well, hello there, Bill." And Bill said, calm and easy, "Mister Watson," and took off his hat to the young woman, and shook hands all around. Bill had growed up broad-shouldered and blond, broiled beef-red by the sun, steady as a tree.

"Glad to see you again," Mister Watson said, like he was testing him. But Bill wouldn't go that far with him, and didn't, though he had House manners and purely hated all his life to seem unfriendly. Oh, he *looked* amiable enough, but he just nodded without speaking and put his hat back on by way of answer.

Mister Watson sized him up a minute before nodding back. But Bill House was a man he wanted on his side, and Bill was the first one on the island that her husband introduced to "Mrs Watson."

I see her today as she was then, a handsome taffy-haired young woman of about my age, holding a pretty baby girl with the same auburn hair and sleepy smile as her bad daddy. And Mister Watson said, Now you boys watch your language, hear? Because this young lady is a preacher's daughter. That was just a joke, of course. Wasn't a man in Chokoloskee would dare to curse in front of all them women.

Ida Borders House was plumb determined not to take it like he meant it – nearly knocked herself out cold, that's how hard she sniffed. Mama dearly liked to make a point with that big sniff of hers, didn't care too much whether or not her point was called for. So she said aloud, "Well, praise to goodness, ain't no need to instruct First Florida Baptists about *blasphemies!*" But she was glaring someplace else by the time she finished. It was very hard to meet Mister Watson's eye.

I watched the young wife's face, see how much she knew. She caught me looking, and she cast her eyes down, and I seen that she knew plenty but not all of it. Then she looked up again and smiled, as if she'd spotted me as her new friend, or as her enemy. I went forward to welcome her, and the women followed.

For all the grinning and good fellowship, everybody there was bone-uneasy about what happened to them Tuckers down at Lost Man's – or *seemed* like it happened, as Ted says, cause there wasn't any proof, and nobody left alive to tell the tale. Knowing that, Mister Watson stood there quiet and easy, very patient, hands folded behind his back, nodding and smiling, more tickled to be home than the Prodigal Son. Never raised his voice nor cackled loud the way them others done, just acted sheepish about being gone so long. Just toed the ground with them nice boots of his, waiting for these folks to look him over and be done with it.

But all the while he smiled and nodded, he was looking the men over one by one, and very few besides Bill House met him head on. Then he winked at his wife and that wink give us a start, as if he'd seen from the quick shift in their faces which men had talked of lynching him and which had not, and which he aimed to settle up with later. The men knew this, too, and one by one fell still.

A bad silence was broke by Mister Watson, who declared he'd be proud to have a look at our new store. I sent Ted ahead to sweep out one them Danielses, won't say which, who was out colder'n a pickled pig's foot on my counter. Mister Watson led the way, and being as the store was in our house, he took his hat off as he climbed the steps and crossed the porch, probably the first save Old Man Richard Hamilton who ever come into our store without his hat on.

But that day, pushing in behind him, about half the men took off their old hats too.

Mister Watson, looking all around, was brimming over with congratulations to Ted Smallwood and "Miss Mamie," said no place of business had us beat this side of Tampa, though everybody knew that Storter's, right across the Bay, was twice the size. He shook his head like he couldn't believe his eyes, reminding Ted of them good old days when they first met, at Half Way Creek back in the nineties, and how far both of 'em had come in life since then. Because he always did feel shy and modest about doing better than his neighbors, Ted changed the subject. "Ain't hardly nobody no more at Half Way Creek, Ed Storters bought it all."

Now Ted wasn't yet twenty in his Half Way Creek days, while Mister Watson was already in his early thirties. It's true he built up a plantation in the Islands beyond any that was seen down there before nor since – every crop that feller raised just turned to gold – but I don't believe he done as good as Ted. By 1906 Ted Smallwood was postmaster and trader and biggest landowner on Chokoloskee, and never robbed nor killed to get there, neither. Course C. G. McKinney and William Wiggins kept their little stores across the island, but we was the main trading post on Chokoloskee from the day we opened, and we are still in leadership today.

Ted Smallwood worked hard for everything he had – getting him to *stop* work was the problem! If a man had money in his hand, Ted would come down in his nightshirt just to wait on him, even on Sundays. But this man Watson never lacked for money, not since the first day that he showed up here. The Good Lord only knows where that money came from and how much innocent blood might of been spilled.

That year we had us a young preacher that the skeeters hadn't yet run off the island, and this man of God came hurrying down to meet the newcomer, tell him how welcome he sure was to worship with us on a Sunday, when the Good Lord hung His hat in Chokoloskee. Mister Watson told the preacher that Chatham Bend was a long way from the house of God, but he certainly intended to continue his lifelong custom of reading aloud from the Bible on the Lord's Day whether his people needed it or not.

When everybody laughed, C. G. McKinney frowned. He pulled his long beard and he coughed, as sharp and sudden as a dog, to show folks he could take a joke but didn't like no jokes about the Bible. Besides, C. G. McKinney was our local humorist and never was one to encourage jokes from other people. This was the year we took over his post office, and without none of our mail to read, he was writing up our local news for the county paper, and if any jokes was to be cracked, it was our newshawk that was going to crack 'em or know the reason why. So what he done, he told the story of poor Reverend Gatewood, first man of God back in '88 over at Everglade. Reverend Gatewood come to the Bay on the old *Ploughboy*, and his first sacred duty on arrival was to preach last words over the body of a man killed in a dispute with the boat captain during the voyage. Captain Joe Williams was a woman man who was always in trouble with some husband or other, and the feller he put an end to was well liked, so Captain Joe had to lay low for some years after.

This Captain Williams was the selfsame feller who bought the honey farm from William Wiggins's brother at Wiggins Pass. Folks used to say that Captain Joe give some of his honey to Mary Hamilton at Fakahatchee when that old mulatta man of hers weren't looking, give her a boy with honey-colored hair.

I'm sure that Mister Watson knew the Gatewood story, but he had the manners to pretend he never heard it. Said he sure hoped good ol' Captain Joe had paid for all his sins, cause what was needed in the Islands was some law and order. Hearing that, Isaac Yeomans had a whooping fit till his eyes watered, and even Mister Watson had to laugh a little, though his laugh was quiet. Our men liked to tell each other that Ed Watson always spoke more quite the more he got riled up, but most of 'em had no idea what they was talking about.

After the Santini business, when word come out about Belle Starr, a story got going how our Mister Watson had throwed in with those Jameses and Youngers who rode with Quantrill in the border wars and become outlaws. Our men could talk of nothing else for weeks. You would have thought them cold-blooded desperaders was the greatest Americans since Lighthorse Harry Lee. And some way, just for knowing outlaws and getting the blame for killing that outlaw queen, Ed Watson became some kind of a hero, too. If he'd showed up with a jug of moonshine and a bugle yelling *Come on, boys, are you Americans or ain't you? Jump in them boats, we're headed for them Philopeens, see if we can't finish off them Spaniards*, why, half the fool men on the island would have marched off after him like the Rough Riders charging up ol' San Juan Hill, flags flying, tears in their eyes, without once asking where in heck they might be going, or what was right or wrong in the eyes of God.

"God works in mysterious ways," Mister Watson told us. "We must pray for the violent as well as for the victims." That prayer sure startled our poor preacher, who was small in the head, with tired ears, looked less like our shepherd than a sheep. He said in a kind of little bleat, "Amen."

Next thing we knew, Mister Watson was looking fierce, pounding his palm. Everyone fell still like they was in church and the preacher commencing to hand down the Word. "If the Ten Thousand Islands have a future," he declared, "and I, for one, aim to see to it that they do, then those who place themselves above the law have no place in a decent law-abiding community!"

Everyone stared and he stared right back with a great frown like Jehovah. "A-*men!*" he shouted, at which Isaac

256

give a whoop which he cut off short, as if Mister Watson
had shot off his Adam's apple. Excepting Isaac, my Ted
was about the only one who dared to laugh, and even Ted
held off a minute, and his chuckle never had much heart
to it. Then Charlie T. laughed, imitating Ted, and Isaac
whooped again and slapped his thigh, and some women
started in to hissing about sacrilege – they was *thrilled*! –
and some just tittered, tee-hee-hee, you know.

"Good thing you ain't smiling, girl," Grandma Ida said,
with one of her big sniffs, to make sure this Mr E. J.
Watson heard her good. No, I wasn't smiling, I was vexed,
cause this bold man was treating us like a bunch of ninnies.
Mister Watson seen I seen this, and his gaze held me,
them chestnut brows and blue eyes of soft stone. Mamie
Smallwood and her brothers were not liable to forget about
those Tuckers and he knew it, he knew what he was up
against with our House family. And so he gave me that
quick wink, the kind of wink made all our hopes and strug-
gles in this world seem kind of silly, due to our sinful
foolishness and greed. I bit my lip so as not to giggle, I
pretended I never even seen it, because *nothing mattered*,
according to that wink. It didn't *matter* that our mortal
days were bloodsoaked, cruel, and empty, with nothing at
the end but disease and darkness.

Mister Watson sighed and said how homesick he had got
for fresh palm heart and oyster-flavored pork at Chatham
Bend, and how fine it felt to be back home in the Islands.

All the while young Mrs Watson smiled politely, though
she never left off murmuring to her baby. She had nice
manners by our local standard, but she was tuckered out,
looked a bit peaked. As the poor thing had a babe in arms
and another on the way, Ted whispered it was only fitting
to put 'em up in our house of the night. I didn't want to
but I had to. Besides Laura Wiggins, nobody else had a
spare room to put 'em in, on account of we had planned
our house for children. Also – I might's well admit it – I

didn't want just anybody claiming Mister Watson, who was Ted's friend before he ever knew most of these others.

Aunt Lovie Lopez – Penelope Daniels she was, married Gregorio – Aunt Lovie was jealous, and she could not hide it. She said, What? You aiming to take a desperader in your house with two helpless little children? She meant Thelma and Marguerite, cause Robert and the youngers wasn't born yet. Ain't you afraid? Aunt Lovie said.

I was afraid, all right, but my man weren't, and that was good enough for me, I said. Wouldn't be near to good enough for me, Aunt Lovie said, and they don't come no meaner'n my husband.

Gregorio Lopez, he come with the bark on, he was *rough*. Course you had to be mean if you was a Spaniard, back in them grand patriotic days. From Injun times, Spaniards wasn't popular in Florida, nor Cubans neither, and that is about the only thing ain't going to change.

That evening Mister Watson gave us all the news of Columbia County, where the Smallwoods came from. Columbia always were a bond between them. Mrs Watson told me all about the fine new farmhouse he had built up near Fort White, how he got that land producing again after years of ruin, and how he aimed to do the same at Chatham Bend. She confided she was native born there in Columbia, said she knew about the blame was laid on Mister Watson in his youth due to his hellfire temper, as she called it. If she knew his evil reputation here, she did not let on. She was out to redeem him, it was plain to see, she had made that her holy mission in this life, she was real wide-eyed and serious about it.

Kate Edna Bethea, she was. He called her Kate, but that name was not for him. All the rest of us that came to love her called her Edna.

"He's got him a feud going in Columbia," Ted whispered when he came to bed that night.

"That why he got so homesick for these parts?"

258

Ted reached across and put his hand over my mouth, because Watsons was just the other side of a slat wall. I was irked that Ted was so impressed by Mister Watson, so proud about having a killer for a friend, though he wouldn't admit that in a month of Sundays.

Saying nothing, I just lay there in the dark, hearing the south wind toss the palms, the hard little waves lick at the landing. I had this intrusion in my heart, as if something bad was growing through the wall from the other room. Ted was restless as a deaf old dog, puffing and twitching. I'd be darned if I would show my curiosity, knowing he was waiting for that across the dark. Finally he muttered, "Family trouble. Couple bad actors name of Tolen. Watson come back down here to cool off."

"Cooled them off, too? Or are they still alive?"

"Still alive, I figure."

There was something eager in my man's voice I didn't want to hear. I picked it up every time he told them stories of the mayhem he had seen up around Arcadia or over to the east coast, Lemon City. Being a peaceable good man who hated fighting, he was kind of bewitched by men of violence, of which we had plenty down around south Florida back in frontier days. Most of our Chokoloskee men were gentle, though you'd never know it, with their old torn clothes, dusty bare feet, and beards. For all their men's talk, they were little boys awed by bad actors, same way Ted was.

"*Why* did he tell you about it?" I whispered back after a while.

"I reckon he wants his friends to know he is trying to avoid trouble, and if trouble comes, how he acted in self-defense."

"Are we his friends?"

When Ted just sighed and started to roll over, I kept after him. "That man Bass that Daddy knew up in Arcadia – didn't our 'friend' call that self-defense, too? If our friend

259

is such a peaceable feller, how come these people all attack him?"

"His wife believes in him, you seen that for yourself, and she was up there with him in Columbia. She knows his past. A preacher's daughter! If she believes in him, we got no reason not to."

I knew right then that Mister Watson had Ted Smallwood in his pocket. Ted weren't in the mood for no more questions, but we had Little Thelma and our Baby Marguerite under the same roof with a murderer, so I was determined I would see this through. I said, "Maybe them Tolens are in his way, like them poor Tuckers. And maybe one day the Smallwood family will be in his way too."

And my husband said, "It just ain't fair to talk that way. We know he cut Santini, but that's all we *know*. He never got convicted of a crime, far as I know of. There ain't no proof he ever killed a single soul!"

"How come he dusted out of here so fast after them Tuckers? And dusted out again, two years ago, when that carpenter just happened to die, too?"

"That feller's heart quit! And of course Ed knew that the blame would be laid on E. J. Watson, and by gosh, it was! He was scared about a posse, you can't blame him! When Guy Bradley got gunned down, who was the first man they laid it on? And Guy was killed way down there by Flamingo!"

I said, "I don't believe he was scared about a posse! He's too hardened by his sins to be scared of *anything*! He does what he wants and then he laughs at us, dares us to stop him!"

Ted's hand covered my mouth again. He pointed at the wall.

I was suddenly as bad upset as I ever been in my whole life, as if I'd known some dark truth all along but only recognized it after I had said it. Ted took me in his arms in that warm comfy way of his, big strapping man, you know, fine head of hair and big black mustache, and big deep voice he has only to raise once to clear the drunks and drifters from the store. "Ed Watson's a very good farmer," he reminded me, starting in on the little speech that all the women got to hear that night in every shack on our scared little island. "He's a hard worker with a good head for business, and a generous neighbor, too, always ready to help – they ain't a family in the Islands won't say the same."

This time he heard himself, the echo. "All right," he said. "But maybe a new young wife and family will steady him down. Ed opened an account this evening, paid out two hundred dollars just for credit. So I got no choice but to give that man a chance, cause he's the only customer we have that ain't behind."

"Talk about a good head for business, it's your friendship he has paid for, in advance! He thinks if he's got the postmaster on his side, and the House clan, too, Chokoloskee won't give him any trouble. Except he hasn't got the House clan! He hasn't got Daddy nor my brother Bill, nor young Dan neither. They're all leery. All he's got is you."

"How about my wife?" Ted whispered. When I didn't answer, he rolled his back to me to show he didn't want to hear no sassy talk. Being such a big old ox, there's no mistaking his intentions when he rolls.

I lay there quite a while. I wanted to say, Well, where does his money come from? You told me yourself, if that man had not had money, he'd be on the chain gang yet today, for attempted murder of Dolphus Santini! But I knew Ted would only say that Mister Watson's money must of come from farming in Columbia, and tell me to hush up and go to sleep.

Ted's esteem of Mister Watson was sincere, of course, and Daddy House felt somewhat similar. Admired his accomplishment, enjoyed his jokes, liked his good manners. And because they liked him – you couldn't help but *like* the man, Bill liked him, too – they was tempted to give him the benefit of the doubt. After all, Ted said, he ain't the only one makes his own law as he wants it, and most of them ones that criticize him ain't anywheres near to E. J. Watson, not when it comes to good providers, solid citizens. Why, them plume hunters, them moonshiners back in the Glades are a sight more dangerous, they shoot at anyone who messes near their territory! Look what they done there to young Bradley!

It was Gene Roberts, up here visiting Will Wiggins, who told us how plume hunters from Key West murdered the young warden at Flamingo. And Ted reminded me for the tenth time how there was other deaths down in the rivers that no one ever heard about. Big plume hunters like the Roberts boys, they never liked no interference and they never will, but Gene Roberts was spitting mad about Guy Bradley. South Florida won't never make it into the new century, Gene said, if every man is so darn quick to settle his accounts up with his rifle!

Whispering all this, Ted sounded triumphant, even in the dark, like he'd pinned the tail on his old donkey once and for all. But when I asked if what Gene Roberts said about settling accounts didn't go to show my point about Ed Watson, Ted just flounced over with that sigh that said, There's no sense talking *no* sense to a woman.

The postmaster was nearest thing we had to U.S. government, so the people were waiting to see what my menfolk would do. Ted Smallwood and Daniel David House were leaders in our community, and my brother Bill was already looked to for good sense. Though they kept their distance, Houses were farming pretty close to Chatham River, and didn't want a feud with their nearest neighbor. If my husband and the House men made up their minds to give Ed Watson a fresh start, the rest of the Island men would go along. Boggesses, McKinneys, Wigginses, and a few Browns was already on his side, and that was close to half of the whole island.

I went along with Ted after a while. Mister Watson was

such a gentleman, you see, without being fancy in a way that made the men suspicious, and the women could not help but like his fine clothes and his compliments, and the nice fashions worn by his young Edna, and that dear little Ruth Ellen, and the new baby, little Addison, who came south with the Watsons in the spring of 1907. The former Mrs Watson, Jane – Ted says Jane was the second wife, he never knew the first one's name, only that she died up in Columbia – Jane Watson took sick and went back up to Fort Myers and died just a few years after she first came here, so we never knew her, but Bill said Jane was just as sweet as Edna only not so pretty.

Now that he's been simmered down by that young wife, most people was just as glad to have him back. He took some interest in our common lives, which we had thought was dull and dreary, and he kept things lively. All his great plans for the Islands made us imagine that progress must be on the way. We were not so backward as we thought if a man as mettlesome as this one came to live here.

It wasn't Mister Watson's manners won me over, though Lord knows his manners was scarce in this rough section. It was the way he carried himself, kept a little apart. What that man understood so well – he explained this to me – you had to keep a sharp eye on your life. One careless mistake and a life unraveled, Mister Watson said, and there weren't no way in hell – Forgive me, ma'am! – to mend it back.

I said, "How come a man with such nice manners gets in so much trouble?"

He looked at me just long enough to make me nervous. Very softly he said, "I don't go looking for trouble, ma'am. But when trouble comes to me, why, I take care of it."

Later I figured he might been teasing, but the way he said "take care of it" made my chest go hollow, set my heart to jumping like it wanted to escape.

From 1906, the Watsons traveled between Columbia

263

County and the Islands and would stay with us sometimes on their way through. Other times they stayed at Wigginses, across the island. Laura kept her little store and William farmed good cane at Half Way Creek. Now and again Watsons visited McKinneys, and Edna and young Alice, who would marry J. J. Brown, got to be friends. Mister Watson kept up his credit all around, or maybe he thought that storekeepers was more fit company for his kind of people than the fishermen an drifters who lived in the little shacks along the shore. He had his syrup business going strong again, and already he was making plans to throw in with his son-in-law and a Chicago man in their big new citrus plantation at Deep Lake. "You can't keep a good man down" – that's what he told us.

In early 1908 he went up north again, and we didn't see him until 1909, cause he went to jail. Young Walter Alderman that married Marie Lopez, Walter worked for Mister Watson in Columbia that year, came back ahead of him. Said there'd been trouble, said he'd run off to avoid testifying. Walter Alderman would say no more in case Mister Watson got turned loose and headed south. And sure enough, that man came back to us right after the New Year, early 1909, this time for good.

Based on the account of Dr Herlong, Mr Watson returned to Columbia County after the Tucker killings (which were never investigated, to judge from the fact that no attempt to arrest him was made during his final sojourn in the Ten Thousand Islands. Smallwood remarks that those killings "cost him plenty" but this remark is not explained unless what's meant was a fatal worsening of Watson's reputation). Fleeting visits excepted, he had been absent from Fort White for at least twelve years, and his mother and sister and the long-established Collins clan were there to shelter him, and he had money. For these reasons, and perhaps others, he was permitted to return.

According to Smallwood, Mr Watson acquired a ruined farm and brought it back into production, and meanwhile he married a preacher's daughter, whom he later brought to the Ten Thousand Islands. But Mr Watson was not in Columbia very long before he was in trouble once again.

Herlong says that Watson's best friends were Mike and Samuel Tolen; that the ill wife of the latter was close to Watson's new wife and was commonly said to have willed her a lot of silver and a piano; and that when Mrs Tolen died, her husband refused to comply with her will. Not long thereafter, both Sam Tolen and his horse were shot to death on a lonely road. (According to some accounts, his brother was also slain, though Herlong makes no mention of Mike Tolen's death.)

Watson, arrested, was in such imminent danger of a "necktie party" that the sheriff had to move him out, to Duval County. According to Herlong, Watson's lawyers obtained a change of venue to Madison County, where the aforementioned Jim Cole, an associate of Watson's son-in-law with powerful friends in Tallahassee, helped pick the jury. As for the state, it mustered just one witness – a black man – against Mister Watson, who was shortly acquitted. Captain Cole (so Herlong says) was heard to tell him, "Now you get back to the Ten Thousand Islands as fast as you can! And stay there!"

Apparently Dr Herlong lived his whole life in north Florida after following the Watsons south from Edgefield County, and the substance of his account of Edgar Watson's life in Columbia seems as objective and dependable a Ted Smallwood's reminiscence of the later years. But finally he succumbs to the Watson legend, asserting that Watson "inherited his savage nature from his father . . ." and concluding his account in the best dime-novel manner. "No one can say definitely what happened to change him from a decent young man, son of a good mother, to a heartless killer. I don't suppose it will ever be known how many human beings he murdered."

Even were all his victims known – I am increasingly convinced of this – the number would not be revised upward, as Dr Herlong implies, but sharply down. Also, I question whether or not he was a "heartless killer," a designation that suggests a psychopath. Let me repeat here that Mr Watson had admirable domestic virtues, almost never associated with the "heartless killer," far less with what it termed these days the "serial killer," who seems unable to sustain human relationships. A dangerous brawler, yes, especially when drunk, a hair-trigger temper, a seeming paranoia when threatened with exposure, and a life-long banishment to one frontier after another in a period when making one's own law was the custom in backcountry America – and even, one might well observe, a philosophical foundation of the national policy that condoned high-handed seizure of the Spanish colonies and other territories in the Caribbean and the Pacific. While not everyone behaved as Mr Watson did, this headlong frontier climate must surely have contributed to actions that seemed to him justified by the brutal hardships of his life.

266

Carrie Langford

Christmas, 1908 When Walter and Eddie and Captain
Cole came back from Papa's trial in Madison County, Jim
Cole was the only one who seemed to celebrate.

Innocent? he'd wink. O' course! We got him acquitted,
didn't we? And he'd guffaw even louder if I frowned, and
try to nudge me. He thinks I'm charmed by him, isn't that
astonishing? To be so thick-skinned and stuck on youself,
I mean? That old piney-woods rooter, Mama called him –
oh, Mama, I miss you so!

Papa will return to southwest Florida for good, so Eddie
says. I don't know how I feel about this, either. This evening I asked John Roach in front of Walter if there was any
way of finding a position for Papa at Deep Lake. And
Walter burst out, Absolutely not! (Just as John Roach was
saying tactfully, Well, your dad has a good business head,
no doubt about it!)

Walter *never* speaks to me so sharply, I got quite upset.
It's not as if my father were a *criminal*, I cried. He was
acquitted! Even the Madison newspaper spoke well of him!

All the same, Walter said, in that low, stubborn voice
that warns me he is digging in his heels – all the same, he
said again, if Jim Cole had not arranged some things, it
might have been a very different story.

Was he guilty, then? I asked him later. Is that what you
are trying to say in front of Yankee strangers?

John Roach is not a stranger, Walter said, offering to
take me in his arms. (I will not tolerate this when he has
been drinking.) Didn't we name our little boy for him? he
said.

The very mention of our poor dead little John drained all my spirit. I wept, and went to Walter, and he patted my shoulder, the brisk domestic pat-pat-pat that has no warmth in it, and precious little patience.

I don't claim to know about your daddy's guilt or innocence, he said into my hair. All I know is, you are cold with Captain Jim, considering what he done for your daddy.

Did, I said, picking the wrong moment to correct him. Walter gave me one of his flat looks and let me go. *Did*, he said.

December 30, 1908 For the first time in our married life, I cannot sway Walter. (If it were anything else, I might be glad!) He says, *I had to lie for him, perjure myself. We all did. That don't mean he's welcome in my house.* Though he doesn't say it in so many words, Walter believes Papa is a killer and always has been, he wants nothing more to do with him. And though I flew at Walter and said dreadful things, he would not relent. He went off to the bank feeling miserable, too.

Papa showed up on Tuesday with Edna and her two little ones. Fay and Beuna yelled *Grandpapa!* and rushed toward the front door but never reached it. I made them cry by sending them upstairs with their Uncle Eddie.

Eddie is living here until his lodgings at Taff Langford's boardinghouse are ready, and meanwhile Frank Tippins has found him a deputy clerk's job at the courthouse. Eddie testified for the defense at Madison, he told them how one Tolen man tried to ambush Papa at Fort White. But now he imitates Jim Cole's curled lip and Walter's words, says perjury was about as far as he aimed to go. He did not even come out to greet his papa, and Lucius wasn't home. Not knowing his daddy would arrive, he'd gone off bird hunting.

Through the curtains I watched my father at the door. He gave it a good rap, he had his chest out, but the rest of 'em hung back, out in the street. It was very plain their money was all gone because they brought no help at all, only a somber Negro man in dirty overalls. In a cart behind them from the railroad station was the sad heap of their worldly goods, down to boxes and bedsteads, reminding me of those poor "Sooners" we children felt so sorry for back in the Territory.

It looked like this time he was headed south for good.

Papa was unshaven and pasty-white from jail, and his Edna looked hollow-eyed, drained of her color, and the tear-streaked children were too worn out to whine. It's so hard to think of these forlorn small creatures as my brother and sister! Goodness! They are younger than their nieces! And they smelled like poor people!

I sent the servant to the door while I composed myself. She asked if she should show them in. I shook my head. Just bring some milk, I whispered, and a plate of cookies.

I went to the door after a moment, and we faced each other. There seemed to be some sort of mist between us. I was trying not to look at something wild and scary in my papa's gaze, something that horrifies me. Or was it only my imagination, after all this rumor? Oh, Papa, I said, taking his hands, I'm so relieved about that awful trial!

My voice sounded false and faraway. He saw right through me. Though he smiled, there was no spark in his eyes, he looked burned to ash. He just nodded, just a little, waiting to see if I would ask them in. Just wanted to wish you folks a Happy New Year, Papa said. And because he was trying to sound cheerful, I had to fight back tears. How shameful to make my own dear papa feel unwelcome in my house, just when he needed his family most, and was reaching out for help!

He made no attempt to hug me, which was most unusual. Poor Papa feared I might not hug him back, was that it? Then he said quickly they would not come in, thanks, they were just on their way to catch Captain Collier, who would carry them south on the *Eureka* to Pavilion Key and arrange for a clammer to take them home, up Chatham River.

Before he left, he asked about the children. Are those sweet things hiding from their bad old grandpa? I saw he was hurt that Fay and Beuna had not even called out, because they do love him and have fun with him and usually fly to the sound of his growly voice. Eddie must have hushed them, held them back.

The girl came with milk and cookies for Ruth Ellen and Addison. The silly thing was deathly scared of Papa, all the darkies are, though how they hear these things I do not know. She set the tray down too quickly on the steps between us, everything askew. Unable to bear it, I came forward and hugged those poor soiled little creatures and pecked my stepmother, who is younger than I am, and said good morning to the colored man.

Papa frowned when his field hand did not look at me or take his hat off, far less answer. Mama always taught us that what people call stupidity or sullenness in darkies is usually no more than common fear, but all the same I was astonished by his rudeness, and terrified, too, that Papa might assault him on the street. But Papa just touched him gently on the shoulder, and the man started violently, like a dog in nightmare, and took off his hat. Seeing the cookies, still unaware that I had said good morning, he murmured, Thank you.

That poor man wasn't rude, of course, he was just sunk in some dreadful melancholia. (Later I asked Walter if he thought Negroes become melancholy the same way we do, and Walter said that he supposed so, he just hadn't thought about it. Overhearing, Eddie burst out, That's ridiculous! Eddie gives these big opinions when he's feeling most uncertain of himself.)

Papa said, "This man got tried with me up north. He's not quite over his close call yet." Smiling, he drew his finger under his chin and popped his eyes out like a hanged man. Papa was angry, and his eyes had no relation to his smile. The whites seemed to swell under those blue pupils, and Edna gave a peep of fear and turned away.

I tried so hard for Papa's sake, tried to encourage the children to take a cookie. But he had seen my struggle, and he would not help. He pointed at the children's plate on the steps between us.

"They're not pets," he said.

"Of *course* they're not!" I snatched up the plate and offered it, bursting into tears.

"Good-bye, then, Daughter," Papa said. Those were the last words he ever spoke to me.

BILL HOUSE

Watson had went home again to Columbia County, where he took him to wed a Baptist preacher's daughter. I sure liked the little that I seen of her. My sister Mamie knew her good, said Edna Watson was a very fine young woman. Folks hoped she'd calm Ed down a little, although he was the calmest man to meet you ever saw. But Watson went back to his farm up north, this was long about 19 and 07, and got himself into a scrape with his own kin. They tried him for murder but some way he got clear of it, and come back south after nine months in prison. Said he was home again for good, and damn glad of it. Probably he told 'em the same thing in Columbia County back in 1901 when he showed up there again after fourteen years.

The men were scared of Watson now, including the ones who told him Welcome home! And Watson knowed people was leery of him though he pretended not to notice. No one messed with him. They kept on pretending everything would be all right so long as they stayed on the good side of ol' Ed, who never been nothing but friendly to his neighbors.

In the old days, Watson hid his past and was touchy about people telling tales, but he had learned how he could use all the attention come his way for knowing them famous outlaws in the Territories, he made the most of all them bad-man stories. Didn't encourage but never quite denied them. Knowing how few had the guts to ask him for the truth, he only smiled. Mostly he thought it was a pretty good joke, or that's what he told Henry Thompson. His reputation as a fast gun and willing to use it was what kept deputies off the Bend and helped him stake claims on abandoned mounds, which was pretty near all that was left down on the rivers.

One day at Everglade, Watson come in to Storter's for his mail, took some coffee and tobacco in trade for a crate of syrup. Watson was first to put up syrup in them screw-top gallon cans, six to a crate. I had some rum in me that day and was feeling cocky – grinning, you know, teasing him a little, the way Tant Jenkins done. I got along with Watson well enough. There was some other men around, and I guess I figured he'd hate to shoot us all, so I asked him how come such a good farmer was always getting into so much trouble.

Another day Ed might have grinned, you never knew how anything was going to strike him. But this day the eyes under that hat faded out to a pale smoky blue, like that dead blue scale on a snake's eye when it is shedding. He didn't speak for a long time, just looked me over, trying to see behind my question. Them eyes hunted out each man there in the store, one at a time, see if anyone else had something smart to say. You could of heard a little tree toad sip the air. Weren't a man in the place would of claimed acquaintance with Bill House, not if I'd went up to him, paid out ten dollars.

Storter's black hound was laying in the sunshaft in the door. That there was the lovinest dog, always picked the place she was most underfoot, just so you touched her. Damn if that bitch don't sidle out of the door, tail hunkered under, like she'd been caught making off with the church supper. When Watson's eyes come round to me again, my ol' tail was tucking under, too, that's how much I wished that ol' black hound had took me with her.

I knowed that day how a treed panther feels, snarling and spitting at them hounds, and the hunter coming, taking his sweet time, walking in across the clearing. That's when you yell and jump, do something stupid, just to end that tightness.

Watson held my eye for quite a while there, wouldn't let me go. He never blinked. I was blinking, all right, but I stayed right with him, that grin stuck on my teeth. I grinned right onto them blue eyes like a damn mule.

"When trouble comes hunting me, boy, I take care of it." And he looked all around again, just to make sure that no man there had missed that message.

My sister Mamie recollects how he said this to her, but it was me.

An interesting source of background material for Chokoloskee Bay is the writing of Mr C. G. McKinney in The American Eagle. Mr McKinney, storekeeper and pundit, contributed the Chokoloskee column (usually signed "Progress"), which he commenced in 1906, not long after Ted Smallwood took over as postmaster.

On June 3 of 1909, the week Count Zeppelin's airship was disabled by a tree – the week in which, in burgeoning Fort Myers, "electric lights have been placed along Riverside Avenue as far as Mr Edison's residence, and the rush of automobiles and the tooting of their melodious horns make the night hours lively" – McKinney reported that Chokoloskee "had a lot of drunken Indians with us this week . . . Mr D. D. House is on his farm, hoeing out his cane . . ."

The following week, as a national "Committee of 40" announced plans to raise five million dollars for "the uplift of the Negro," two Negroes were "strung up" at Arcadia. The lynchings evoked editorial cautions against crazing Negroes with cocaine to get more work out of them. At Fort Myers (where the price of eggs had risen to 25 cents a dozen) the "craze" was baseball. At Chokoloskee, Mr D. D. House, whose doings were ever prominent in his friend's column, was preparing to plant tomatoes, alligator pears (avocados), and corn. Louie Bradley and parents were visiting from Flamingo, Andrew Wiggins was moving to the Lost Man's region, and Mr Waller came in from McKinney's farm at Needhelp reporting forty rotting carcasses of deer skinned out by Indians for the buckskin trade.

In early July, "Mr House the cane man was up on Half Way Creek looking at Mr Wm. Wiggins and Dr Green's fine cane." William Wiggins was being visited by Gene Roberts and family from Flamingo, who were soon to acquire his son Andrew's house on Chokoloskee. Waller

275

was down again from Needhelp, where he was growing melons, beans, and corn, and Bill and young Dan House had gone off "prospecting" to British Honduras. Caxambas reported the return from "Sheviler Bay" of Mr J. E. Cannon, who was farming these days on Chevelier's old place at Possum Key.

In mid-August, Mr Waller was preparing for a "gator hunt," and the island's erstwhile preacher, Brother Slaymaker, "has invested in the bicycle business." McKinney also reported that "Mr E. J. Watson was with us this week."

In early September, Waller reported that Miss Hannah Smith, now in residence at Needhelp, was "ailing." McKinney, observed, "We had some drunken folk on the Island last week. We think it was drinking brackish water that caused their troubles." In his twenty-three years at Chokoloskee, he had never seen sandflies so bad or guavas so plentiful.

On September 23rd, it was reported that the House boys, gator hunting in Honduras, were doing fairly well, and that George Storter was "logging heavily" up Turner River. "Mr, E. J. Watson and family have been with us this week."

In early October, tomatoes were blooming. D. D. House, was bound for Key West with a cargo of cane, while Gene Roberts was going back and forth from Chokoloskee to his cane-fields at Flamingo. At Fort Myers, dispute over cattle in the streets was raging, and meanwhile Captain Cole had left for New York to buy a passengers-and-freight steamer for service between Punta Rassa and Key West. Weather on the coast was dark and ugly, despite little rain.

On October 12, the coast was struck by the "West Indian Hurricane," with winds up to 120 mph, which did such damage at Key West that the city was put under martial law to deter looters. Ninety-five vessels were driven out to sea, ashore, or sunk; nine cigar factories were utterly destroyed; the roof was removed from the First National Bank. Among those who lost their boats was Mr D. D. House, who had discharged his cargo, loaded up pro-

visions, and set out on his return before the storm drove him back into Key West, where he lost everything.

In late October, Mr Charley Johnson slaughtered his hogs and sold the meat at 15 cents a pound. Mr Waller had departed Needhelp and was "working for Mr E. J. Watson at Chatham River."

In November, the trading vessel Ruth loaded at Chokoloskee for her last trip of the season. "Chokoloskee will be dead then," McKinney wrote, "or at least deader than usual. We have no preacher, no Sunday school, no dancing, but we have noticed someone being around once in a while with some low bush lightning [moonshine]." Up at Needhelp, Miss H. M. Smith had "chills and fever. She is very brave to face all that wild woods and chills and fever alone."

In early December, Hannah Smith came to Chokoloskee to be treated by Mr McKinney. Mr Waller was expected back at Needhelp to help her finish up her business. Gene Roberts, Charlie McKinney (the columnist's son), Andrew Wiggins, and Jim Howell were hunting deer and turkey around Needhelp, and once again, the column lamented deer slaughter by Indians for the buckskin trade.

Hookworm was "rife" at Chatham Bend. Mr D. D. House was still shipping tomatoes from his Chokoloskee place but had returned now to House Hammock to commence syrup-making.

In late December, while the cattle in the Fort Myers streets ate Mr Edison's newly donated royal palms on Riverside Avenue, Charlie McKinney and Jim Howell killed ten gators in one night up Turner River, under the dark of the moon. The Indian Charlie Tommie, who came in to sell 15 otter pelts to George Storter for $9 each, reported that Miss Hannah Smith had suffered a fall and broke her rib at Needhelp, and that Mr Waller was there assisting her. Bill and Dan House, discouraged by Honduras, returned home in time for Christmas with a monkey and four parrots.

The Key West trading ship, carrying Christmas goods, had not arrived. "We learn from Mr E. J. Watson that he [the captain] was not in Key West last Monday at 9 a.m."

Cold weather at the end of December 1909 ruined the last of D. D. House's tomatoes. Ice was seen in an old boat. In early January, in his column in The American Eagle, *C. G. McKinney reported that the hunters were still taking coons and otters. (Ft. Myers reported that on a visit to Immokalee, Sheriff Frank B. Tippins shot a turkey.) The Chokoloskee school reopened, and not long thereafter a new preacher came. Hens were laying again despite lot of showers "unusual for this time of year." D. D. House, William Wiggins, and George Storter were producing fine syrup – Storter's cane mill was "running full blast" – but everyone was short of syrup tins; Mr Wiggins put up his syrup in white bottles.*

In February, Miss Smith at Needhelp dug her last crop of potatoes, which traveled to Chokoloskee in Charlie Tommie's dugout. Andrew Wiggins was raising potatoes and cane in Rodgers River. Bill House traveled to Key West to buy a boat.

Halley's Comet was glimpsed, it would return in May.

(Increase Mather of New England witnessed "the Star of Bethlehem" on its traverse of 1682, when Edmond Halley gave his name to it, and exhorted his flock not to persist in their sinning until "God sends his arrows from Heaven to smite them down into the grave." In 1910, in the huge consternation caused by the Great Comet, it was predicted that the earth's passage through its streaming tail might bring about the extinction of the human race by "cyanogen gas." Though unfamiliar with the perils of cyanogen gas, Chokoloskee residents had little doubt that the comet portended the arrival of Judgment Day upon the earth in the form of storms, floods, droughts, and plagues and other natural afflictions, among which not a few would be laid at the door of Mr Watson.)

"Mr E. J. Watson will finish syrup-making this week

[early March]. He reports having made nearly twenty thousand gallons."

Miss Hannah Smith had dug 2000 lbs. of "malangoes," killed her last hog, plans to leave Needhelp with her dog and two cats once she has harvested her cabbages, which she plans to ship to the Key West market on W. W. (Bill) House's new boat, the Rosina. *Bill House and Young Dan are now partners in the shipping trade, and are loading cargoes of cane, syrup, fruit and oysters.*

Charley Johnson and Walter Alderman have contracted "Honduras fever," and are talking about seeking their fortune in Honduras.

"Everyone approves the new preacher, Brother Jones, but the teacher, Mr Daughtry, has closed the school for want of pupils."

The Eagle *reports much excitement over the upcoming fight between the black champion Jack Johnson and Mr Jim Jeffries, the White Hope.*

"In April, the coast weather is still dry, and most of the island's fresh water is brought down from Needhelp. No fishing yet to speak of, but new icehouses are being built for the summer season."

McKinney noted that few actually danced at a dance given by Gregorio Lopez – they were either too old or too young, he comments, and there was "no booze." Charlie McKinney, Charley and Mack Johnson, and Jim Demere leave on a long gator hunt. Mr Shorty Weeks will be running the mail boat, Chokoloskee to Marco.

"Mr John A. Johnson and Mr Leroy Parks were on the Island today from Pavilion Key." (Johnson was one of seven husbands outlived by Pearl Watson's mother, Josephine Jenkins, and Leroy Parks was her son by another.)

"Captain W. W. House, his brother Dan, and their father are going to sail tomorrow for Ft. Myers with a cargo of ornamental plants for the homes of the upper ten."

"Miss Hannah Smith has left the Needhelp settlement and is now staying at Mr E. J. Watson's place at Chatham Bend."

BILL HOUSE

I remember the day, it was April 1910, when Watson hired
poor Miss Hannah Smith. Old Man Waller, worked at
Watson's, come in to the store with a woman three times
the common size, introduced her to his boss as a prime
female who could outwork three men ricking buttonwood
and show a horse a trick or two about spring plowing. By
that he meant *behind* a horse, not putting the traces to
Miss Hannah.

Well, Watson said he had a horse already, but Dolphus
was old and useless now, and the sorry help he had at
Chatham Bend – and he winked at Waller – couldn't pour
piss out of a boot with the instructions written on the heel.
That was the first time we heard that one, and us fellers
roared. There was some shine being passed around, and
we all decided we better have another. If Hannah Smith
would come on home with him, Watson was claiming, show
this old hog thief Waller how to work a ax, maybe he could
yoke her up alongside Dolphus when time come to plow.
Or maybe – he said this real serious, lifting his hat – him
and her could get yoked up together when poor ol' Green
had drunk hisself under the table.

Well, they laughed hard over that one, too, all but Old
Waller. I seen straight off Waller was sweet on Hannah,
cause she was handsome way a man is handsome – looked
like a man wearing a wig – while he was ugly, and lame,
too, all bones and patches. From the wear on him, he'd
had more rough in life than smooth, and had that habit.
Watson was tipping his hat to him – this was the bully that
come out when he was drinking – and Big Hannah looked

281

across at that old man of hers, see what he'd do. But Waller only belched and then looked vague, like *that* was a belch that needed some consideration.

Before she drifted down to Chatham Bend, this Hannah Smith from the Okefenokee Swamp in Georgia had been around the Bay a year or two. Had a sister, Sadie, was camped across the Glades northwest of Homestead, where they call Paradise today. Their folks got word to Sadie that Hannah was at Everglade, and asked would she kindly pay a call on her little sister, see if she was getting on in life all right.

Now Sadie Smith was well knowed as the Ox-Woman, and when she found out that Everglade was clean over to the other side of Florida, maybe two–three months around to there by land and sea, she bided her time until the dry season, then hitched up two young oxen and cut and burned and hacked her way across the Everglades by cart. First time *that* was ever done, might been the last. Went north along Shark River Slough and followed the Injun dugout trails west through the Big Cypress, dug out wheels and chopped whole forests down to get that cart through. She come out near the head of Turner River and come on down to Chokoloskee Bay. Just showed up one day in her black sunbonnet, smelled like a she-bear.

Up to that time Hannah Smith was the biggest female ever seen around these parts, she was knowed as Big Squaw to the Injuns. Well, Sadie went a whole hand bigger, six foot four, built like a cistern, with a smile that split her whole face like a water-melon. Said she was hunting Little Hannah, aimed to come up with her little sis or know the reason why. Well, there weren't one thing little about neither of 'em, and there was two more, bigger yet, back up there in the Okefenokee, that's what we was told by that there Ox-Woman. Said her sister Lydia was so big she would sit in a rocker on the porch, holding her husband in her arms, singing him lullabies. Married at sweet sixteen, Sadie said, but her husband got hung at Folkstone, Georgia, so she took work hauling limestone and cutting cross-ties for the railroad. Ran a barbershop in Waycross for a while before she went off to have a look at Florida, said she could handle a razor so good she could shave a beard three days under the skin. I'll go along with that one, too, cause that big woman, and Hannah, too, could work a ax good as any man I ever saw, made that ax sing. That was the old style of pioneer womenfolk, come down out of the Appalachian mountains. Don't make females like that no more, or we'd have one running the whole country.

Hannah had her a sweet voice to go with her feats of strength and winsome ways. In the evenings she would haul on her other dress and set out on McKinney's dock, singing "Barbry Allen" to the Injuns that was in to trade. Remembering the way she was out there, that big old heap of womanhood just a-singing so sweet under the moon over the mangroves, and them Injuns by their fires staring past her – that's their polite way of keeping an eye on a wild thing that might turn dangerous – that picture still gives me the shivers just to think about it. Course I was too young for her, and probably too small, one way and another, and besides I aimed to marry up with Nettie Howell.

Tant Jenkins, now, Tant was an expert in the hunting line, always claimed that common labor disagreed with him, and I told Tant if he was smarter'n what people said he was, he'd send away to the Okefenokee for one of them big lonesome sisters, do his chores for him, keep him in whiskey, and rock him to sleep when he come home at night drunk and disgusting. And Tant said, "Best keep talking, boy, I ain't heard nothing wrong about her yet!"

So them giant girls from the Okefenokee had a real reunion, and they drunk Tant and two Danielses to a stand-still, with a young Lopez thrown in. Sadie said them four fine boys sure made a body feel at home, long as they lasted. Only trouble was, she couldn't find land enough to farm here, said she needed ROOM! Next day she hitched her oxen up and trundled north, found a good big hammock in the cypress east of Immokalee, lived on there quite a while and died there, too, while she was at it. Might been from heartbreak over Little Hannah.

It was not so long after Sadie left that Hannah decided she would try her luck down Chatham River. She had got sick of farming all alone up there at Needhelp, and was pining away as you might say for her mangy old admirer, who had went down ahead to tend Watson's hogs, help cut the cane. Now he was back to fetch her and had Watson with him.

This man Waller, Watson was saying, might act like a God-fearing farmer but he'd never amount to nothing more than exactly what he looked and smelled like, and the first time a hog was missed at Chatham Bend, a well-knowed hog thief might come up missing, too.

Waller could laugh over coming up missing but he couldn't laugh none about Hannah, cause he was in love, and women in his life was very, very few and far between. Matter of fact, Big Hannah was the first, and he didn't care who knowed it. Said, Made my old mama a promise on her deathbed that her virgin boy would go to his grave as pure in the Lord as the first day she wiped his bottom. Them words, he said, made his old mama die happy. But Satan had sent this big Smith girl to Needhelp, and she is stronger'n what I am. Old Waller hollered, and next thing I knowed about it, boys, she had me down and was doing something dirty!

Meantime Big Hannah fetched her stuff, had all she owned save her ax and gun in a burlap sack she could swing across her shoulder with one hand. The day she went down to Chatham Bend was the last day on this earth I ever seen her.

That big bashful virgin and her ragtag old man – he wasn't much more than Watson's age, but looked like he'd come around the bend a second time – they lived with all their sinning in the Tuckers' little shack on a knob of ground not far downriver from the sheds and workshop. Hannah cut fuel for the syrup boiler, helped the young missus with the kitchen and the chores, then washed up good under the arms and lugged her hog thief home, put him to bed. Ed Watson claimed they yelped all night like a pair of foxes.

MAMIE SMALLWOOD

Mister Watson kept bad company but doted on his family, and anyone as ever seen him said the same. 1907, he took Edna home to Columbia County for the birth of little Addison, and her Amy May was born at Key West in May of 1910. Mister Watson would not stand for having his young wife pawed over in her pregnancy by that barefoot old man down in the Islands, using his oyster knife for the delivery, more than likely. Ted didn't like it when I talked like that, claimed Mister Watson had nothing against that old mulatta, he just wanted the best there was for his young Edna. But Ted only said that cause them people was his customers and he didn't want 'em switching to McKinney's.

Excepting maybe for Gene Hamilton, who was ashamed about his family, Ted didn't like that bunch no better than I did. Didn't know their place, or never paid attention to it, one. Course you'd have to say that Old Man Richard knew his birthing business, because there's quite a few was shucked by him down in the Lost Man's section that growed up none the worse for wear.

Long before Amy May was born, Mister Watson had the Bend right back to where it was the best farm in the Islands, never mind his unpaid legal debts. The word was out that field hands were welcome on the Watson Place, no requirements of sex nor color, no hard questions. No real trouble down there neither, not to speak of, or we'd of heard about it from Miss Hannah, who kept in touch with her many friends at Chokoloskee. Mr Jim Howell, whose daughter Nettie was engaged to my brother Bill,

Jim Howell worked down there one harvest season, and Mister Watson made a fast worker out of a slow one. Jim Howell said he was "scared to death the whole durn time" but never got treated better in his life. Even folks who lived in dread of Mister Watson began to cheer up some and crack some jokes, cause it sure looked like that man had changed his ways.

First one give me a clue there might be trouble was Henry Thompson, who still ran Mister Watson's schooner now and then. Henry mostly stayed down there at Lost Man's, he wasn't on the Watson Place no more, but he had worked for that man since a boy and knew his ins and outs as good as anybody.

One day Henry was trading in Fort Myers when an old darkie come up and asked if her son was still hoeing cane down there for Mister Watson. Said the colored there on Safety Hill had no word from the missing man for close on to a year, and another field hand that she knew about had never turned up neither. Well, Henry seemed to recollect that Watson himself had run that darkie back up to Fort Myers when his time was up and he needed his pay. Mister Watson visited with Carrie and her children, then picked up another colored and came back.

"Funny we ain't seen him, then," the woman said.

"Probably took his saved-up pay and run off to Key West," Henry Thompson told her. "Might of heard about them nigger-lovers down that way." Didn't say that for a joke, cause Henry never was a one to joke much, and he never bothered his head about her nigger feelings.

Next, a pair of men showed up in a small sloop, said they was just out gallivanting from Key West. Mister Watson decided they wasn't no such thing, he got to brooding about how them two might be deputies out to make their mark at his expense, just waiting for their chance to lay him low. But the cane was ready so he put 'em to work, kept a close eye. Well, one day Henry brought the boat back from Port Tampa, and their little sloop was still tied to the dock but the men was gone. Mister Watson mentioned he had bought the sloop and run 'em up the coast as far as Marco, paid 'em off, give 'em the names of some likely folks in Shawnee, Oklahoma. Henry never thought a thing about it at the time, but another day, cleaning out that sloop, he came upon a picture of a woman and small kids, love letters, too, that was stuck in a dry cranny under the cabin roof. He wondered why those men would leave such things behind, and he put that stuff away in case they sent for it. They never did.

One day I took Henry to the side and asked what he was really saying with these stories. Was Mister Watson killing off his help instead of paying 'em? Because if Henry had no such suspicions, how come he was spreading these darn stories – well, not so much spreading 'em as letting 'em drop for the rest of us to sniff over.

Henry's eyes opened up real wide, first time in years I seen him pay attention. He backed up fast, got mean-mouthed on me, saying it just goes to show how rumors get their start, said he never believed no such thing about Mister Watson! Why, that man was like a father to him, always had been! Ask Tant Jenkins, Tant would say the same! But Tant would never say the same, cause Tant left Chatham Bend after the Tuckers and did not go back, and anyways, I knowed James Henry Thompson since a boy. Henry and I was always the same age, he couldn't fool me.

Henry Thompson was loyal to Mister Watson and he always would be, leastways until he grew old and needed drinking money. And drinking money was about all he got for that magazine interview about his dangerous youth with Bloody Watson. Maybe he started dropping hints to let off his own worries, cause there weren't no doubt at all Henry was troubled. And if *that* feller was troubled, so was I.

Another man knew Watson pretty good was Henry Short, and I knew Henry Short real well, he was our nigger. Called him Nigger Short, sometimes Black Henry, to keep him separate from Henry Thompson, Henry Smith. He was the same age as my brother Bill and raised right up by the House family, and he stayed close to us the first half of his life.

Back there before the century's turn, when Bill was working for the Frenchman, Black Henry used to visit Bill down in the Islands. Stayed with them mulatta people, and for a while he sailed Ed Watson's schooner. Well, one time he sank the *Gladiator* in a squall down off Cape Sable, got picked up by Dick Sawyer, who was headed north. Henry owned right up to Mister Watson, which is more than most of our men would have done. Gregorio Lopez always said, That nigger was too scared to think if he took a piece of news like that to E. J. Watson.

Mister Watson had to chase off Key West scavengers to save his boat, but never once did he raise his voice to Henry. He was very tolerant that time, Henry never forgot it. Course Henry Short was always saying how good he was treated by this white man and that one, he sure knew better than to speak out otherwise. But the way he carried on about Mister Watson, he was not just grateful, he was truly *thankful* the Lord had let him live to tell the tale. Cause he never forgot that day at Lost Man's when he went upriver with the Hamilton boys to find the Tuckers.

After Mister Watson disappeared, back in 1901, I asked Henry Short straight out if Watson done it. Black Henry never said one word, just kept on sorting avocados in the sun. Jim Crow days was well begun, and cruel punishment was being done to upstart niggers all around the country, and after the age of about twelve, this feller would never talk alone with any white woman. So I told him give me a hand packing tomatoes, led him over toward the produce shed where the men could see us talking but not hear us, and I whispered, Answer me! Did he do it or did he not?

Henry Short was looking straight ahead, and he turned his head away like he was talking to the skeeters, but I heard him murmur, "Mister Watson was sure good to me."

289

That was Henry's way of telling that in his opinion, E. J. Watson killed them Tuckers.

When Mister Watson come back here in 1909, he tried to get Henry to come work for him again, offered good pay, because Henry always was outstanding at whatever he would put his hand to, he could farm, fish, or run boats, mend net, set traps, go hunt a deer and not come back without one. Henry was working at House Hammock on and off, and he got my dad to advise Mister Watson that he could not spare him. That colored man was just plain spooked by Mister Watson.

Sometimes in that last long summer Henry Short went mullet fishing with the Storter boys and their nigger man Pat Roll, set gill nets down around the mouth of Chatham River. Most of them Storters lives at Naples now, long with my brothers Dan and Lloyd. Well, not so long ago Claude Storter told me that Henry never once went past the Watson Place without he had his rifle loaded in the bow. That might could be, but all the same, Black Henry thought the world of Mister Watson.

Mister Watson had a fugitive off of the chain gang hiding out down there, a desperado, killed a lawman in Key West; he also had a older man, Green Waller, supposed to been some kind of jailbird, too. The only law-abiding help was Hannah Smith, great big strong woman, farmed awhile on them Turner River mounds at Old Man McKinney's place, where he called Needhelp, not so far from where our family settled when the House clan first come down into this country. Hannah worked good as any man, and the men will tell you so, though they was mean about her. "The next size comes on wheels," Charlie Boggess said. Well, you know something? Her sister showed up at Everglade not long after Charlie said that, and she come on wheels! Sadie Smith went a size bigger than Hannah, and she drove an ox-cart!

Green Waller was at Needhelp for a spell, them two old

loners got along like rum and butter. Waller went down to Chatham River to tend Mister Watson's big prime hogs, and Hannah got sick and fidgety all by herself, fighting skeeters and panthers for a year with no man to help her haul her crops, and that old breed Charlie Tommie trying to take advantage. Long about April 1910, Old Waller went up there and fetched her back with him to Chatham Bend. We heard there was also a Injun squaw got kicked out by the tribe for laying with white men, and a black man who come south with Watson from Columbia. If that field hand ever had a name, I sure don't know about it.

In that dry dark year of 1910, the evil feeling that was growing in the Islands come out in the open and could not be put away. Even my Ted knew something bad was stewing. The one that brought the whole stew to a boil was a "John Smith" who come through Chokoloskee that same spring. He was a well-set-up young feller, middling handsome, with dark brown hair worn long, close to the shoulders, and close hard green eyes. His lower lids cut straight across, no curve to 'em, and his eyebrows grew too close together. Had a old-fashioned kind of black frock coat that he wore over torn farm clothes, looked halfway between a gambler and a preacher. As Tant remarked, you couldn't bet your life he would go to Heaven.

Ted was leery of this stranger right from the get-up-and-go. Said, Sure'n hell, that hombre has run off from *some*place, way a tomcat runs off to the woods, goes wild and mean – Ted took agin him soon's he come into the store. Kept tugging at my apron strings, with all his whispering. Young man that's lived according to God don't never have a face as hard as that one! That durn frock coat might be hiding a whole arsenal! I never paid Ted much attention, knowing how excited my man got when he smelled an outlaw.

We asked John Smith if he might be kin to Miss Hannah Smith down Chatham River, or to Henry Smiths, who was one of our ten families here on Chokoloskee. He said, real short, "They ain't no kin at all." He was looking for an E. J. Watson, and he wasn't bothered the least bit to hear that Mister Watson was away down in Key West, with his wife expecting. "I'll wait on him," that's all he said.

This man paid John Demere to run him down to Chatham River. After he'd gone, my husband said, "Ed might be tickled pink to see this hombre, but I doubt it. I believe this could be that feller from the north he's always talked about."

When Ed Watson returned from Key West with his wife and baby, they traveled by steamer to Fort Myers, then came back on the mail boat far as Chokoloskee before they went on home to Chatham River. Ted warned him on the way through that a stranger had come lately, and was waiting on him. Mister Watson turned real quick, to check behind him, then glared at Ted kind of impatient. Ted said, "I mean, waiting at Chatham Bend."

When Mister Watson got took by surprise, he kept his mouth shut, not like most people. Making that little bow, he asks me, Please Miss Mamie, could he impose on my hospitality again? Would we take in Edna and the children while he looks into the situation at Chatham Bend? As I enjoyed her company, I did not mind.

Before he left, he said, "This man look Injun?" and Ted said, "Dark straight hair. Might be a breed." Watson said, "Does he look like some kind of a defrocked preacher?" This time it was me who nodded, but Ted said crossly, "No, he don't look like no preacher." Ted Smallwood would not tolerate the least resemblance between that stranger and a man of God.

I didn't contradict my husband, but Mister Watson never missed much, and when he seen me nod, he had to smile. Said, If this John Smith was who he thought it was, he might *look* like a preacher but he wasn't.

When I asked, Is John Smith his real name? he said, "Today it is," and went on out.

Next day he came back for the family, and him and Edna had a quick cold quarrel up in our spare room before she came down all teary-eyed to pack the children. Whoever this stranger was, it was pretty plain that his coming was a dreadful blow to that young woman, and all the way down to the dock, she done her best to persuade her husband to let her stay behind. Going aboard his launch with her new baby on her arm, she waved back at me real sad, you know, shaking her head. I didn't pester her about the stranger, and Edna would never tell me nothing, then or later. She always said, "Mister Watson wouldn't like it," even after Mister Watson was stone dead.

A few months before the stranger came, Mister Watson's gun-slinging young foreman done some vandaling down there and then run off someplace. Mister Watson made this John Smith his new foreman because Old Waller drank too much, but next thing you know, the first feller was back, asking after "Mister Ed." On his way through, he told Charley Johnson he would get his job back or his name weren't Dutchy Melvin.

Ted said straight off, "There is going to be trouble." And I said, "Fine. Them two young devils might shoot each other dead, which is good riddance." But the one I resented most was Mister Watson, for bringing these hellions into our community.

Mister Watson always dealt fair with us, and he done a right smart amount of trade with Smallwood's store. One year syrup sales was slow, and Snow and Bryan up in Tampa paid him off in trade goods for several hundred gallons of his syrup, and we took those goods and sold 'em on commission. In Watson's years the store was in our house, long with the post office; wasn't until 1917 we rebuilt it down beside the water, and wasn't till 1925 that we had sense enough to put it up on pilings, way it is today. Nick of time, cause that Hurricane of '26 would of cleaned her out. That was a bad one, killed a lot of folks when Lake Okeechobee busted out its dykes, but it wasn't near so terrible as the Hurricane of 1910, not in the Islands.

Now that storm of October 1909 was plenty bad enough, tore away half of Key West, blew the cigar business all the way to Tampa. We plain wasn't ready for another one still worse in 1910. But there was that comet in the sky, April and May, *that* was bad sign, and the worst drought in years all that long summer, with our crops withering, poor fishing everyplace. Even Tant Jenkins had to go dig clams to make a living.

Through all that hot dry summer of 1910, Edna Watson and her children visited regular at Chokoloskee, she spent more time here than at Chatham Bend. Stayed with us, stayed with the Wigginses, stayed with Alice McKinney and with Marie Lopez, who married Walter Alderman under that dilly tree at Lopez River – first real wedding with a preacher we had around these parts in years and years. Walter Alderman had worked for Mister Watson up Columbia County, but he left there quick when Mister Watson got arrested, Marie said, so's he wouldn't have to testify in court. Forbid Marie to tell us anything about what happened, that's how scared he was that you-know-who might come at night and shut him up for good.

SAMMIE HAMILTON

Ed Watson were as nice a fella as you'd ever want to meet, and as good a farmer as has ever cleared a piece of ground; he could make anything grow. My uncle Henry Thompson had worked for Watson quite a good number of years, Tant Jenkins, too, and never had nothing bad to say about him.

Now my uncle Lewis Hamilton was married a little to Jennie Roe, who claimed that she got raped by Mister Watson. Nobody put too much stock in that one. Jennie Roe was a beautiful young woman, but she wasn't so particular. Her mother might been Josephine Parks, unless it was Henrietta Daniels – had to been one of them two sisters, what I heard. Them Caxambas families was all tangled up, and both half sisters had little girls by Mister Watson. Netta's Minnie was first, she was born the year Mrs Jane Watson come home from the Wild West. Minnie had her daddy's chestnut hair. Aunt Josie's straw-haired girl, she was born at Chatham Bend round the turn of the century, they called her Pearl. Minnie growed up sweet, got married in the year of the Great Hurricane, 19 and 10. He was a Key Wester named Jim Knowles, his daddy might been ol' Bob Knowles, cooked for Bill Collier on the *Eureka*. Minnie was still living at Key West, last thing I heard, and Pearl stayed up around Caxambas.

Tant was more hunter than fisherman, you know, and he weren't no farmer at all – never had a hair of farmer in him. He'd cook a little if he had to but it weren't much good. Even when he worked for Mister Watson, fish is all he ever done besides go hunting, maybe run the boat. But now the wild critters was too scarce even for Tant, and he'd took work digging clams for his half brother Jim Daniels, who was the clam crew boss on Pavilion Key. Tant was going partners with Henry Smith of Chokoloskee, who was kin to that same Daniels bunch, had the same black Injun hair as they did.

Last time Mister Watson was over to Pavilion, that was late summer, he weren't hardly on the shore before ol' Tant was hollering, Lookee who's coming! Be damn if it ain't that dreadful desperader! See that wild and crazy look in them damn eyes?

Everybody was looking for a place to hide, but Mister Watson, he just grinned. And seeing that, Tant got cranked up, started showing off – Well, I'm tellin' you now, Mr S. S. Jenkins don't aim to take no shit off this dang feller just because he s'posed to be Ed Watson!

Oh, Mister Watson dearly loved that bony feller, he'd take about anything off Tant where he'd of took his knife to someone else. He'd knowed Tant since Tant and Henry Thompson lived at Chatham Bend, they was kind of family, and he never did offer to fight him, not even once, even though Tank left him for good after the Tuckers. And since the Tuckers, Tant's teasing had an edge to it. Tant would just strut all around, tossing his head back, y'know, looking him up and down, sneer at him, spit near his boots. Hell, I ain't a-scared of you just on account you're packing so much hardware under that coat you cain't hardly WALK! And he'd go to dancing in and out around Mister Watson, fists up, snorting, little mustache bristling, saying, Step up here and take your punishment if you are man enough!

With Tant around, Mister Watson laughed till he wiped his eyes. Tant purely made him feel good, you could see it. But if Tant himself ever dared to laugh, even a little, Mister Watson's mouth closed tighter'n a clam, and Tant would roll his eyes back in his head like his last moment was at hand. And Mister Watson might clear his throat, maybe he'd take that watch out, maybe not. Then he would say something like, Ever hear about that feller who died laughing? And Tant would only shake his head and kick the ground. He'd never go back to teasing Watson that day, not even if you paid him fourteen dollars. Tant just *knew*.

Anyways, Mister Watson was well liked in our family, we never seen nothing the matter with him.

Down in the Islands back in them days, weren't too much of enough to go around, and families would help other folks get by. Sometimes we'd go up Chatham Bend to borrow something, and Mister Watson would give my dad, Frank Hamilton, a gallon of his fine syrup, one of them four-sided tin cans. Used to take us kids around the place, show us his horse that he named Dolphus Santini, show us his cows and his hogs. I'll never forget it. Nicest man I ever met in all my life. Had great *big* hogs, y'know, tamed to pet by hand, and a grizzled kind of old man name of Waller to take care of 'em. Had one pig, Betsey, that they'd trained up like a dog, she could do tricks.

Overseer down there then was Dutchy Melvin, a Key West desperader. Burned down a cigar factory or two on account them Cubans wouldn't pay him not to. Dutchy claimed he killed a lawman who tried to keep him from his work, and escaped the noose due to his youth and winning ways, but others said they caught him looting after that October storm of 1909. Whatever he done or didn't do, he got sent out on the chain gang and escaped. First place he thought to go hide out at was the Watson Place, because it was known around Key West that Mister Watson weren't particular about his help so long as a man weren't afraid of work.

Dutchy Melvin never went nowhere without his guns, wore 'em right out where everyone could see 'em, to avoid confusion. Dutchy said, I'll go to hell before I go back to that chain gang, and I ain't going neither place without I take a few of my feller men right along with me. Meant what he said, I do believe, cause the Florida chain gangs, they was hell on earth, no place at all for a well-brung-up young feller.

Dutchy Melvin was a common-sized man, maybe one hundred sixty pounds, kind of dark-complected. My daddy knew his people in Key West, nice people, too, but if you didn't know how much he hated Spaniards, you might of seen a hair of Spaniard in him. In one way young Dutchy was like Mister Watson, very soft-spoke, nice to meet, and everybody liked him, but he was a bad actor all the same. Even Watson, so they say, was kind of leery of him.

Dutchy Melvin was a real acrobat. One day there on the dock front of the Watson Place he took off his gun belts, give 'em to my brother Dexter Hamilton to hold for him, and did a front flip for us kids, not a somersault but a real front flip, he landed on his feet just like a cat. Only time I ever seen that feller with his guns off.

The first year Dutchy came, Mister Watson made him foreman, cause Dutchy's guns scared the help so bad they was glad to work as hard as they was told. They knew this feller hadn't one thing left to lose, and if he got the idea to blow their heads off, he might do it. But him and Mister Watson quarreled because Watson wouldn't pay him, not till they got the last cane in and boiled the syrup.

So that boy waited until Watson was away, and then he spoiled maybe a thousand gallons of good syrup, he threw salt in it. Lit out for New York City, some such place, sent back a sassy postcard. *Well now, Mister Watson, while you was roaring around pleasuring yourself down to Key West, I was passing the time taking some sweet out of your syrup..* Mister Watson was swearing mad and never cared who knowed it, but my aunt Gert's husband, Henry Thompson, he was running the schooner at that time and brought the mail, Henry Thompson told the family that Mister Watson read that card and laughed! This was a fortnight after Dutchy spoiled his syrup, and he had cooled off just a little, and he stood there on his dock and read that card he got from Dutchy Melvin and just laughed! Said, That young feller knew enough to get up to New York before he wrote me *that!*

Well, that crazy fool popped up again, summer of 1910, had jokes for everybody. He had swore he would not go back onto the chain gang, and had no other place to put his feet up, and anyway he was so cocky he thought Mister Watson probably still liked him. Probably true, but "like" don't mean "forgive" and never did.

By that time a stranger had showed up there, took Dutchy's place as foreman. When the census come around, spring of 1910, this stranger called himself John Smith, but it come out later that his rightful name was Leslie Cox.

I seen this Cox a time or two but never got acquainted. While he was here, he never left the Bend. He weren't around here long enough so folks can picture him. Had hair short on his head and down his neck, same length all over, looked like fur. It's like Uncle Henry Thompson used to say, I can't recollect just what Cox looked like, but I do recall I never liked his looks.

Cox was a wanted man, and wanted bad, but nobody knowed that at the time. Some way Cox was acquainted with Ed Watson, and come looking for him, fetched up on the Bend. Some said Cox was Watson's cousin, and some said he saved Watson's hide one time, out West, but later we heard he was a killer, he'd run off from the chain gang, same as Dutchy. Leslie Cox was quiet-spoken, too, from being on the run, spoke in a kind of low and raspy voice, had a bad mean mouth. Uncle Henry used to tell us all about it.

Dutchy Melvin wasn't mean, he always had a friendly word, but he didn't take to Cox, wouldn't take his orders. He was fixing to run that somber sonofabitch right off the property, that's what he told Mister Watson. Dutchy grinned when he said that but he meant it. Said he made his grandmother a solemn promise never to consort with common criminals, which was why he had felt honor-bound

299

to run off from the chain gang. Mister Watson thought that was pretty good about honor-bound and common criminals, and him and Dutchy had a good laugh over it, and then Mister Watson sat back a bit, the way he often done, watched that boy laughing. Uncle Henry Thompson who never did find out how to have fun, Uncle Henry noticed the way Mister Watson done that. But Dutchy was too tickled to notice. That was *his* mistake.

In them days Injuns wouldn't work for nobody, but Tant Jenkins, hunting in the Glades, come back that spring with a young squaw girl, left her off at Chatham Bend. Her family had turned their back on her for laying with Ed Brewer to settle up her bill for Brewer's moonshine, and if Tant hadn't of run across her, back up Lost Man's Slough, she might of died. Mister Watson took her in to help young Mrs Watson with the children, cause Hannah Smith had other business to attend to.

Nobody at Chatham Bend spoke Injun enough to tell that girl where she should sleep at, they figured Injuns probably slept out in the woods. Leslie Cox didn't hold with talk, just took her over to the shed and raped her, done that regular. Got her pregnant, too, is what we heard. And knowing her people would never take her back, knowing she had no place in this world she could ever go, the poor young critter got so lonesome and pathetic that she hung herself, unborn baby and all, down in the boat shed.

That was a story that never got out about the Watson Place until long after. The nigger told it but nobody believed it, cause by the time the men went down to Chatham Bend, her body was gone. But I was friendly with the Injuns when I lived on Possum Key in later years, and they all knowed about it. How they took care of it they would not say.

My granddaddy James Hamilton and my dad and uncles, they was pioneering at South Lost Man's when Mister Watson got the Atwell claim, which was Lost Man's Key and the farm patch at Little Creek, across the river. My other granddad, Captain Jim Daniels, was down there at that time. Him and his boy Frank, they seen the smoke of Tucker's sloop, burning away as she drifted out to westward in the Gulf, with the sunset like a halo all around her. Looked like she'd been set afire by that ball of light and just melted down into the sea.

Mister Watson got so scarce for a few years that we figured he was probably gone for good, so our bunch started in to farming Little Creek, which had growed over since the Tuckers' day but was handy to our place on Lost Man's Beach. Next thing we knew, Ed Watson had come back, friendly as ever, like he never even heard of Wally Tucker, and he made no trouble over Little Creek. For a start, he had enough to do bringing the Bend back to production and taking care of his north Florida farm. His young wife had him calmed down some, and anyway, he didn't need no fight with neighbors.

However, he had no money left and more work than he could handle, so he took any labor he could get. Chatham Bend got a bad name for escaped convicts and stray niggers, and pretty soon a rumor went around that people down there was just disappearing. Course there was no way to keep track of them runaways that worked that man's plantation, cause nobody knew who was down there in the first place, but more and more, people was saying that Mister Watson was scaring people off the islands, and killing his help when the time come to pay 'em, and who was to say that he would let it go at that? He was a man who had killed before, he had the habit of it, and they couldn't hang him twice if he tried again. Had a carpenter named Jim Dyches there with his wife and children that last summer, and them folks got so nervous at the Watson Place that one day they just left without Jim's pay, took off on the mail boat with Gene Gandees.

Even Uncle Henry Thompson didn't like the feeling in

that place, not by the end of it. Uncle Henry will tell you that himself, and he was a feller never failed to speak up for Mister Watson.

In May 1910, Mr McKinney reported that the weather remained dry and the fish few. The pear crop was poor and the horseflies bad, but there were no mosquitoes yet to speak of. At the end of the month, it was "dry, dry, dry: limes, grapefruit, guavas will all fail; fish still scarce."

"Jim Demere reports no luck on gator hunt."

"Hill House has shipped on the Rosina a cargo of wood, hogs, eggs, chickens, and pickled rabbits."

"Walter Alderman has moved into the Andrew Wiggins house vacated by Gene Roberts and will go fishing."

"The most of us have seen the comet but now we are expecting to get another look in the west soon."

In June, the Rivers and Harbors Act authorized the dredging of the Calusa Hatchee, whose white sandy bottom had been increasingly covered with silt due to the widening of the Okeechobee Canal. Under Governor Napoleon Broward (who would die that same year in October 1) widespread canal dredging had been resumed, and big sales campaigns had started up for the sale of Everglades land.

The Monroe County census taken in May listed Green Waller, 53, and Mrs Smith (cook), 40, at Chatham Bend, as well as Mr and Mrs Watson and their two young children – the third child was born later in this month. There was also Lucius Watson, age 20, a fisherman, and another white man, "John Smith, age 33."

Early June brings warm and cloudy weather, with mosquitoes. "I have been here twenty-four years and have never seen the fruit trees so near dead as now, near the first of June . . . don't know what the effect will be when the rain comes, if it ever does. . . . We see the comet in the west now, but not so brilliantly as in the east. . . ."

His brother Horace from Marco visits Walter Alderman. He will move onto the island in July (Horace Alderman

303

became notorious in later years for his exploits in the rum-running and Chinese-smuggling trades. He was hung at Fort Lauderdale in the mid-twenties for the murder of two Coast Guardsmen who had detained him.)

Mr George Storter, his two sons, and Henry Short have "fair luck" on a gator hunt and go again.

Game laws protecting alligators are passed in Lee County, since the dry season the gators dig out water holes used by the cattle.

"Mr C. T. Boggess and family have moved on the island to dwell among the righteous for a while."

At the end of June, the rainy season arrives at last, nearly two months late, with lots of Indians, mosquitoes, and "blind tiger" (moonshine).

Walter Alderman, Henry Smith, C. G. McKinney, Jim Howell, Willie Brown, D. D. House, Charlie Boggess all growing vegetables for the Key West market.

In early July (as Admiral Peary claims discovery of the North Pole) McKinney teases the preacher Brother Jones, who chronically defers his visits due to the torments visited upon him by the "swamp angels" (mosquitoes).

Henry Smith and Tant Jenkins go to dig clams at Pavilion Key until the fishing improves.

Charlie McKinney and Kathleen Demere are married at the schoolhouse on July 28 by Justice George Storter.

In early August, the Rosina, which now sails twice a month, leaves for Key West with Mr and Mrs John Henry Daniels.

"Green peas and beans are being harvested; fish are fat."

"Mr Walter Alderman has a (chronic) infected foot."

McKinney reports lots of rain, thunder, and lightning for late August, also "low bush lightning." The "truckers" (truck farmers) are setting out their crops. McKinney is getting in his pepper crop while fighting rabbits.

A baby girl is born on the island to Andrew Wiggins and his wife on August 20. She is the former Addie Howell.

His father, William Wiggins, has moved to Fort Myers, but his younger brother, Raleigh, is on Chokoloskee.

Bill House and Miss Nettie Howell are wed at the schoolhouse on the last Sunday of August "just as we have been expecting for two years." They have their honeymoon at Key West on the *Rosina*, and will live on the boat. Dan House now plans to acquire his own boat.

In early September, Miss Lillie Daniels, daughter of Jim Daniels, marries Capt. Jack Collier at Caxambas. "Lucius Watson was here [Caxambas] Sunday for the first time since April." (One may guess that he was visiting the Daniels-Jenkins clan, including his young half-sisters Pearl and Minnie.)

Henry Short has gone back fishing. The fishing is good but the hens are not laying.

School reopens. Gegorio Lopez and sons have gone to Honduras hunting alligators, while Lovie Lopez and the younger children move to Chokoloskee "for the school season."

BILL HOUSE

Somewhere around October 10, Mister Watson brought his family up to Chokoloskee. His wife and children, visited commonly at Chokoloskee after the baby's birth in May. She told my sister and Alice McKinney she could not tolerate Chatham Bend with Leslie Cox there. She would never let on what she knew about Cox, she only said that wherever that man was, trouble would follow.

Mister Watson had one of his outlaws with him. The men liked Dutchy Melvin, what they seen of him, they were leery but allowed as how he was full of fun. That October day at Chokoloskee, there was some tension between him and Watson, something to do with Cox. Dutchy got drunk and foul-mouthed, sneered at Mister Watson to his face, in front of everybody. Pretended he was fooling but he wasn't. Even dropped the "Mister," called him "E.J.," even "Ed." Said, Don't know what's eating on you, Ed, but how about let's you and me settle this fucking goddam thing right here and now.

Mister Watson explained calmly to that young feller that no man, not even E. J. Watson, could draw as fast out of his coat pocket as a feller drawing from a holster. You want me dead as bad as that, you better shoot me in the back, Mister Watson said. And Dutchy said, I heard back-shooting was *your* specialty. Mister Watson raised his eyes and cocked his head. After a little while he said, 'You're not careful enough for a feller who talks as smart as that. And Dutchy said, I'm getting more careful all the time. But under Mister Watson's gaze, his eyes shivered just a little, the men seen it.

When Mister Watson turned his back on him, there come a gasp, but Watson knew his man. Dutchy was no back-shooter and never would be. What was needed was another drink, Ed Watson said. They got some more booze from the Lopez boys and drank together, took the jug along for the trip to Chatham Bend. That's the last we ever seen of Dutchy Melvin.

Henry Daniels likes to tell about the day when Mister Watson come in to see Pearl and Minnie at Pavilion, maybe visit a spell with Josie Parks while he was at it. And Tant Jenkins yelled some teasing at him by way of saying hello, and Dutchy Melvin, hearing that, made the bad mistake of figuring, Well, if that fool Tant could do it, he could, too. So what he done, he teetered Mister Watson off the plank that led across the mud flats to the shore, done it to show them clam diggers and whatnot that Dutchy Melvin weren't afraid of E. J. Watson. Got Mister Watson's good boots wet in the salt water, and the pant legs of his city britches, too, and hooted just to see him slog ashore. Nobody else who seen it laughed at all.

Dutchy Melvin thought a heap of Mister Watson, he was like a barking pup jumping around, trying to play with a quiet dangerous dog. He was excited to see what that man would do, and looked kind of crestfallen, Henry said, when nothing happened.

Mister Watson never once looked back, he kept right on going. But Henry Daniels seen Mister Watson's face as he went by, said he knowed right then that Dutchy's days were numbered. Would of bet money on it, Henry Daniels said.

SAMMIE HAMILTON

If Mister Watson killed them Tuckers for that Lost Man's claim, there weren't nothing to keep him from coming farther south, kill a few Hamiltons. Grandpap James Hamilton figured Mister Watson might suspect we had some money saved, might demand them savings as due rent, on account he'd paid the Atwells for the claim at Little Creek but we was farming it. That goes to show how fear grew in the rivers. Fear was always in the air, like the scent of haze from far-off fires in the Glades. The more us young fry thought about it, the more certain we became that Mister Watson would come get us, sooner or later. I was having nightmares. Mister Watson would loom up in the window, just the outline of him, that big barrel chest and that broad hat, and the moon glinting on his gun and whiskers.

Our mama never put no stock in it, I know that now – He's been our generous neighbor, not a thief! – but even Mama used him as a bogeyman. *You don't jump in that bed quick, Mister Watson'll gitcha!* Toward the end she gave up, she seen how scared we was, and maybe she'd got a little nervous too.

Sure enough, Mister Watson came, maybe two–three days before the hurricane. We heard that motor popping from a long ways off, coming up across the Gulf wind, a sound like muffled rifle shots, but steady. He called that launch the *Brave* but us kids called her the *May-Pop*, on account she didn't always run too good. Later on Gene Hamilton had a launch just like her, but the *Brave* was the only motorboat down in the rivers before 1910, so we had no doubt about who was on his way.

When the motor stopped, kind of too sudden, we thought he'd beached her and was sneaking up along the shore. But soon he come drifting around the point on the flood tide, poling, y'know, the way the Injuns do it. He worked her over to our little dock, where he took his coat off and begun to tinker with his engine. My uncle Henry Daniels at Pavilion Key had fixed that engine earlier that season, and she had got the man all the way here. Not being so sure why she broke down smack at our place, we became uneasy.

My dad, Frank Hamilton, was back inland with Uncle Jesse Hamilton and Henry Thompson, grubbing out royal palms on the Johnson Mound, cause times was very hard and getting harder. Mama said, I hope our men have heard that motor. They heard it, all right, and they come quick as they could, but they weren't quick enough.

At that time, fall of 1910, we had just got word that the state of Florida had passed more laws against the plume trade, and gator and otter already so scarce down in the rivers that it didn't hardly pay to hunt no more. We couldn't compete in the fishing trade with them other Hamiltons, who had a rancho out there on Wood Key and a dock where the runboats could bring in ice and take their fish away. Our few vegetables didn't mean a thing no more in the Key West market, even when we could get 'em down there without spoiling. Wasn't nothing much left but grubbing our royal palms for Fort Myers streets or ricking buttonwood for charcoal. Got to cut ten cords a day, tote 'em and stack 'em, then cover the pile with grass and sand until it's airtight, all but a few holes at the bottom to fire it and a vent on top. You get you a crookback and maybe twenty bags of charcoal for all that heat and dirt and donkeywork, and twenty bags ain't going to buy a living.

Grandpap said, "Get up at daylight, work like mules till dusk, lay down stinking and half bit to death by skeeters, too damn tired to wash. Get up next morning daylight, do it all again, year in, year out. See any sense to it?"

Grandpap wasn't up to the cutting and stacking, not no more, not ten cords in a day. No old man is going to last long ricking buttonwood, and this one figured to die in the attempt. Down to Shark River, they cut mangrove for tanning, one of the Atwell boys was in on it, but that work was too heavy for Grandpap, too. It sure looked like we would have to leave all our hard work behind, say good-bye to Lost Man's, go to Pavilion Key, where Granddaddy Jim Daniels was foreman of the clam crews and Uncle Lewis Hamilton cooked on the dredge – either that or work in the Caxambas cannery longside the niggers. So Mister Watson was standing by to take over our claim on Lost Man's Beach, and Grandpap had it in for him on general principles, not on account Mister Watson done him wrong but on account he'd used up his old heart at Lost Man's, and it was too late in life to start again.

Our family always ambled out to welcome visitors at the landing, that was the custom among Island neighbors. But this day Grandpap stayed back in the cabin, sore as a damn beetle blister cause his arthuritis had flared up on him, he couldn't work. What with them life pains he was feeling, Grandpappy had his rifle cocked, and had drew a bead on Mister Watson's heart. He told his daughter-in-law before she went out to the dock, "You hear me, Blanche? That outlaw makes just one false move, I aim to shoot!" And he told her to keep her children clear of his line of fire. My mother was disgusted, y'know, told him he had frightened us kids for nothing. He hollered back that he knew what he knew about this Watson, and I guess he did.

Mister Watson seen straight off that he weren't welcome. He never got out of that boat, never tied up. The onshore wind held her snug against the dock, but with that chop she made a steady bump against the pilings. I ain't never forgot that hollow thumping, like a shit-quick's ghosty booming in the swamp.

"Good day, Mister Watson!" calls my mother. Her hands was dead white, that's how hard she clenched 'em, she was almost whimpering. But she was a long sight more upset about not offering him a bite to eat than she was about him killing us to get our money.

That man took off his hat but he did not answer. This was unusual, being his manners was so up-to-date. His clothes weren't soiled but they looked slept in, he was hollow-eyed and grizzle-chinned, and we smelled whiskey. But he never seemed bothered by the silence in that clearing, which any moment was going to explode. He studied all around awhile, just listening, trying to feel out what was in the air. He must of wondered where my dad was, and Henry Thompson, whose boat was tied up at our landing, and why Grandpap James Hamilton stayed back into the house, never called hello.

Mister Watson was careful not to stare, he covered that window out the corner of his eye. It's like when a bear ambles out of the brake much too close by. You load quick but you load real easy, and no extra motions. You don't startle him, and you don't look in a bear's eyes, cause a bear can't handle any kind of challenge, he might charge.

Mister Watson studied up on the whole clearing but he kept coming back to the cabin window. In them gray old weatherboards, that window looked black as a square hole, and crouched back there was Grandpap Hamilton, muttering and agitating with his trigger.

Poor Mama had the twitches, she was swaying back and forth like some old woman with St. Vitus dance. Ain't it strange? Mama was a plain embarrassment to me and Dexter even though we was fighting a hard fight not to piss our pants. Mister Watson stayed calm, smiled kind of quizzical, like he hoped some little bird might tell him why these Hamilton kids was acting so scared stupid and their mother crazy. Later we knew Mister Watson's calm was his way of getting set, like a cottonmouth gathering its coils.

311

Mama moved a step too quick between Mister Watson and the window. He paid no mind, like he never knowed she done it, but he knowed, all right, cause he kept his hands out wide so's to be seen by whoever might of drawed a bead on him. "And a good day to *you*, Miss Blanche," he says at last, with a warm smile for us children. "Henry around?" It had been so long before he spoke that his quiet voice made Dexter squeak.

Mama says, "Why, yes, he is! Frank, too! And Jesse!" Aiming to show how well we was protected, she done just the opposite. Anyway, she regretted it right off, cause hearing our men was near might make him stay.

To get his mind off it, I squawked, "How's Betsey?" My voice was changing and my brother hooted, but Mister Watson shook his head, real serious. Betsey, he said, had ate her shoats and he had a good mind to eat *her*. Might teach her not to try that trick again, he said. And he give my mother a wink, and she busted out giggling, mostly from nerves. As she said later, A man could joke about his sow did not have killing on his mind, and Grandpap snapped, A female says such a fool thing as that don't know the first thing about killers!

A few years later it came out on his deathbed that Grandpap himself knew a thing or two along that line, which was why we lived at Lost Man's River with no neighbors – unless you would count them other Hamiltons, who were not our kind of people, Aunt Gert said. Well, maybe they had a nigger in the woodpile, maybe not. I always liked 'em. So far as we heard, they never had no killer in the family, and they had more claim to their family name than we did.

That day, Mister Watson told us he was calling in on his way back from Key West, just wanted to know if Henry Thompson could make a run for him to Tampa, cause he had four thousand gallons of last winter's syrup set to ship. If there was anything we needed in Fort Myers, why please say so, because he would be heading north in the next few days.

My mother thanked him kindly, said we lacked for nothing, meaning there wasn't a sack of beans that we could pay for. When she just stood twisting her hands, never invited him to eat, Mister Watson acted like he never noticed. Said that he'd like nothing better than to visit with us for a little, but he had to be getting back to his wife and children, and soon as he got his boat cranked up, he'd be on his way.

Her small moan told how shamed poor Mama was, it was all she could do not to bawl her head off over menfolk foolishness. Wasn't Mister Watson kinfolks, in a manner of speaking, with daughters by Aunt Netta Daniels, and Aunt Josie? But she bit her lip hard and said something polite, still shifting and swaying, still trying to keep herself in Grandpap's line of fire, in case Mister Watson went for his handkerchief to blow his nose and the old feller hauled back on the trigger.

Mister Watson noticed her peculiar movements and he watched our eyes. He did not know who was hid back in the house, but he sure he knew somebody was there. At that range Frank Hamilton could drill him dead on the first shot without no trouble, and Grandpap, too, if he wasn't too worked up to put his mind to it.

The wind was out of the northeast, had held in that quarter for two days, with squalls and rain, and we was already wondering about a storm. Didn't have no radios in them days, we just had to go by signs we knew. Mister Watson looked at that dark sky and said be believed a hurricane was coming down on us.

That wind was gathering a little, sure enough, racketing the sea-grape and palmettas, yet all around, the world seemed deadly still. Later we learned there was a federal warning – this was around October the 13th – but where did Mister Watson hear about it? He knew, all right. Said

313

he'd already taken his own family up to Chokoloskee, and he'd be proud to take us up there, too.

Our mama said she sure was much obliged, but if her men got worried, Henry Thompson could take everyone to Chokoloskee on the *Gladiator*. Course that old schooner still belonged to Mister Watson, Uncle Henry only kept her between cargo trips. Mister Watson had to smile a little, and our poor mama went red as a berry.

"I'll be on my way, then," Mister Watson said.

He stooped half out of sight to crank his flywheel, and my mother, skirts spread like a broody hen, rushed forward to cover him. There was just no way for Grandpap Hamilton to get a shot off. Us kids was crowded around him, too, hoping for a motor ride up river. The *May-Pop* started fine, everyone smiled, there was nothing left to say. Mister Watson spread his hands out to the side before reaching up slowly for his hat and tipping it to my mother. He tipped it to the empty window, too.

"My respects to Mr James," he said. "And Frank and Jesse, and the Thompsons, too."

My mother busts out, "I'm so sorry, Mister Watson! Sorry you can't set awhile, I mean!"

He understood just what she meant, and made that kind of little bow, mostly with the head, that us kids was imitating for years afterward. Mama gave a quick, queer bow like a bird, and never curtseyed. She was so mortified by her own gawkishness that she wept all over again during the hurricane, her tears fell right along with the wind and water. In this terrible forsaken place, she mourned, she had lost the last of the nice etiquette she had learned at Caxambas School, and now she might perish in this storm before she could go home to a civilized life on Fakahatchee.

Mister Watson went away downriver without waving. The shape of him looked hunched and black against that narrow band of light out to the west where the weather was moving in on us off of the Gulf.

I never had nothing against E. J. Watson, but I believe

314

that hurricane is all that saved us. What we found out later was, the dreadful doings at the Watson Place had happened on October 10th, a Monday, just three or four days before he stopped by. Another thing: He told us he come up from Key West but he didn't. The men heard his motor from way off upriver. He come down the inland route along the creeks, then Lost Man's River to First Lost Man's Bay. Drifted the delta on account he didn't want nobody along that coast knowing where he come from or where he was going.

Pretty soon my dad showed up with my two uncles. Always see light like that before a hurricane, he humphed, when we told him about Mister Watson's warning. All the same, Mister Watson said it first, there weren't no talk of hurricane before his visit. Dad was running around all flustered up, tying our few worldly goods to the trees. Dad always done things inconvenient, as Mama complained the whole rest of her life. She couldn't find a pot while that storm hung fire, hung around over that Gulf and would not come in.

HOAD STORTER

October 1910, my brother Claudius and me and Henry
Short and our own nigra was fishing them bayous northwest
of the Chatham River mouth – on the chart it's Storter Bay
today – and selling our catch to the clam diggers on Pavilion
Key. Coming and going along Chatham River, we might
pass the Watson Place, and knowing that, Henry Short
took his rifle in the boat. Never went without it, and never
said what it was for. Nobody asked him questions, neither,
we was glad he had it. Weren't nothing but one them old
1873-model Winchester .38s with lever action, but that
colored man knew how to work it. He was a fine hunter
and a expert shot, I never seen him shy away or lose his
head. But one way and another, he just dreaded Mister
Watson, he was scared to death of him.

One evening we was selling mullet at Pavilion when who
should come in all in a uproar but Jim E. Cannon from
Marco and his boy Dana, who was farming vegetables on
Chevelier's old place on Possum Key. Folks suspected that
Jim Cannon was hunting the Gopher Key treasure that
Chevelier was supposed to have left buried. Some said it
was the Frenchman's own misered-up money, some said it
was Spanish gold that come into the hands of the Calusas
back in days of yore. Either way, this treasure was the
reason why Mister Watson went and killed Chevelier. By
now they was laying everything on Mister Watson, made
him responsible for every killing on southwest Florida. If
he'd still been in jail up in north Florida, wouldn't of made
one bit of difference. There was one I could tell you about
but better not, one that was planned and got away with

clean, in the knowing that Mister Watson would get blamed for it.

The Cannons was provisioning the clam crews, same way we done. Bananas and guavas was still thick on Possum Key in years the damn bears didn't clean 'em out, and there was two alligator pear trees, and key limes, all put in by the Frenchman. Over the years the garden was kept cleared and the cistern fresh – that's why Injuns always camped there when they come along inside the Islands, north through the salt creeks from Shark River. The house that belonged to Old Chevelier had disappeared after his death – not rightly knowing what become of it, people blamed Richard Hamilton – and someone burned Lige Carey's house down to the ground, probably cause he put a padlock on it. Another house built at the turn of the century by a feller name of Martin, who cleared off there after Tuckers was killed, that one went, too. Plume hunters and moonshiners used Possum Key after Jim Martin moved to Fakahatchee. Probably they got drunk, set things afire.

The Cannons hoed 'em out a real nice garden, but after Watson had come back for good, early 1909, they never cared to stay the night at Possum Key. I like to wake up in the morning, is how Jim explained it. Camped with the clam crews on Pavilion Key and went to and fro up Chatham River on the tides. Jim Cannon Bay is on your chart today.

Going upriver with the tide that morning, it was dark and squally, but the boy seen a pale thing swaying in that raining river, and he yells, Pap, I seen a foot sticking up, right over there! And Old Jim Cannon says, Foot? No, you ain't never! Must been a ol' snag or something! But Dana says, Nosir! I seen a foot! Well, Jim Cannon paid no mind, and they went upriver.

His boy knowed what he had seen, and coming back, he was on the lookout, and pretty soon he's hollering again. Know that eddy two hundred yards or so below the Watson Place, north side the river? You don't? That's where it was.

317

So Old Man Jim swung the boat in there, seen something unnatural sticking out, kind of white and puffy, and sure enough, a human foot is swaying and trembling in the current. The ebb was so strong curling around it that they had to tie up to it just to stay put. They seen it was a woman's foot, but there weren't nothing to be done, they could not come up with her. That female was heavy as a manatee, and fast to something way deep in the river, and they pretty near capsized trying to boat her.

Looks like she's hung up bad! Jim Cannon hollers. Jim had him the almighty creeps, and the boy was scared and getting scareder. He figure that giant gator that was seen sometimes in Chatham River must be hanging on to her, right down below their boat in that dark water. Staring at the ghosty face mooning around in the dark current, and the hair streaming like gray weed, so old and sad, that little feller bust down in tears. So Jim said to hell with it and let her loose, he come up with some kind of a prayer instead, said, Rest in peace. By the time he had the Amen finished, he had to shake his boy to get some sense back into him, cause Dana was having some kind of a fit, and had got seasick.

Jim said, We'll row back to the Bend and report this here calamity to Mister Watson. But the boy had more sense than the father, always did. He pipes up, No, Pap! I ain't going! Young Dana had heard the stories about Mister Watson, he was scared stiff, and soon as he got done being sick, he commenced to cry again.

So Jim told Dana to hush up so he could think, and he set there and give the situation some more thought. I thought long and I thought *hard* is what Jim told us. Even saying that, he frowned like anything. Said he had noted from the rough way she was gutted that the woman was not drowned but murdered, and whoever done such a foul deed had nothing to lose by getting rid of witnesses, maybe gutting 'em out and throwing them into the river right alongside her! The more Jim thought, the more frighted he became, and all of a sudden he decided they would go and ask the clam diggers' advice. So the Cannons took off to the clam bar, brought the news.

Early next day some men went up the river with Tant Jenkins, cause Tant was about the only one who wasn't deathly scared of Mister Watson. Tant and them got Hannah floated, hauled her out. Sure enough, that poor big woman, going on three hundred pounds, was gutted out same as you'd gut a bear. She was anchored off with an old flywheel, worm rock, pig iron, and who knows what. But Hannah Smith were a stubborn soul and always was. She had never took no for an answer all her life and didn't aim to start now she was dead. So she bloated up and dragged that pig iron back up off the bottom and use her foot to wigwag the first boat to come along.

Big Hannah had her hog-thief boyfriend still tied to her apron strings, as you might say. Somebody looked down and there he was, he was weighted, too. If things was left to poor old Green, they would probably stayed put on the bottom, but he never had no say about it, she raised him up right along with her.

Nobody wanted to look at 'em, let alone smell 'em – made their eyes water. They dug 'em a pit and buried the pair of 'em across the river and down a little way, thirty-some feet back of the bank on that point where Mister Watson had his other canefield. Maybe someone mumbled a few words and maybe not. Wasn't too many in our section had much practice.

Our colored boys was along to dig the hole, but them two knew much better than to touch her. Every man was boiling mad to see a good woman gutted out like a damn animal. Even Tant didn't make no jokes that day. Once she was covered, the men talked about going up to Watson's place, ask a few questions. But they never went, and he never come down from the house to see what they was up to in his cane patch.

Starting downriver, they come upon Dutchy Melvin in

the mangroves. He was swole up and rotted, too, but not so bad they couldn't see the gator bites. They threw a hitch on him and towed him back, laid him right in there alongside them others, practically poured him into Hannah's grave. Tant almost upchucked, and he weren't the only one.

All the way back to Pavilion Key, Tant never spoke, the only time Tant held his tongue in his whole life. Henry Daniels asked what he was thinking, and he said he was thinking about Mister Watson.

You can go down there yet today and see that lonely grave. Looks square and maybe sunk about a foot, with nothing growing, ain't that funny? As if you picked up a old tabletop stuck in the marl. There's three lost souls laying down there if tides ain't took 'em. You can open up that grave, have a look at Hell.

When we got back from burying Miss Hannah, in come this nigra from the Watson Place, dark husky feller in torn coveralls, pretty good appearance for a nigra. He had took a skiff and got away from Chatham Bend – a desperate act, cause he were a field hand and no boatman. He had wore the skin right off his hands, that's how hard he pulled on them old splintery oars. One minute he was moaning and blubbering so much you couldn't hardly make him out, next minute he was very quiet and his eyes was calm. Henry Smith gave him a cuff to make him talk straight, and finally he hollers out how three white folks was dreadful murdered on the Bend.

"We know that!" someone shouts. "Who done it?"

"Yassuh! Mist' Watson's fo'man!"

Tant asked if Mister Watson ordered them three murders. This man said yes. We heard him say it. Said Watson was at Chatham Bend when Cox killed Dutchy.

There come a ugly silence in that crowd, part dread of Watson, part disapprovement of a nigra who would try to get a white man into trouble. Looked like he'd figured out in that burr head of his that we'd go along with any blame he laid on Watson. Well, he might been right. Captain Thad Williams got rough with him then – Are you accusing Mister Watson? And the man stared bug-eyed at the crowd, you know, looked too scared to speak. I believe right to this day he were playing possum. Cap'n Thad advised him to be careful who he went accusing, cause Thad knew them men was all excited, might string him up before their supper if they took a mind to.

Tant Jenkins and his sister Josie, and Aunt Netta Roe who run the post box at the little store – all that whole Jenkins-Daniels bunch that used to live at Chatham Bend and was what you might call kissing kin to Mister Watson – they wanted to put a stop to that darn nigra then and there. And seeing the way the wind was blowing, the nigra switched his whole story, says Nosuh, he sho' mistook hisself! Mist' Watson was done gone to Chokoloskee, never knowed nothin about *nothin*!

When the nigra was told how that big woman's body had rose up out of Chatham River, he lets out a yell, Oh Lawdamercy! They slap him again, to keep him quiet, because everyone's trying to think what they should do and his nigra racket is getting on their nerves. But in a minute he finds his tongue again and yells about how Mist' Cox done told him he was done for if he didn't shoot into the bodies and lend a hand in the gutting and hauling, and if anyone asked, just blame this mess on Mister Watson.

That nigra had to be so terrified or crazy to tell them men something like that. He'd confessed he had took a part, confessed he'd shot into the body of that white woman and maybe worse. Maybe he was in on it from start to finish – that's the way them men started to talk, that's how upset they was. There come a kind of ugly groan out of that crowd, and one of them Weeks boys started slapping on that nigra, looking for a way to ease his nerves. You shot a white woman, *that* what you said, boy? Laid your black hands on her?

321

Going off half-cocked, is what they were. Good thing they wasn't no big limb out on that key or they would of took and strung him up right there.

But if he was guilty, why was he there? Why would he ever say a word? I couldn't believe that man had been so foolish. I caught his yeller eye again, and I shook my head, as if to say, Boy, you have *asked* for it! And again his gaze give me the feeling that nigra did just what he aimed to do – reckless, yessir, but he weren't no fool.

Papers reported that this here nigra was young and frightened, done nothing but moan and carry on like the Devil was after him. Well, maybe he looked young but he weren't, because I seen him, I seen the little gray along his temples. He acted scared, but back of all that nigra shouting was something cunning. It was only after he got Watson suspected that he switched his story, tried to save his life. Next time he looked up, I seen that quiet in him, and he knew I seen it, cause he cast his eyes down. He was more angry than scared is what I seen, and bitter, bitter, bitter.

Henry Short and Erskine Roll – we called him Pat – had eased out of the crowd, not wanting to pay for this feller's mistake. Claude and me walked along with 'em to our boat, case there was trouble, told 'em to go on across, sleep on Little Pavilion, come back pick us up first thing next morning.

By the time we got back to the clammers, the men was angered up and frustrated. They started in to drinking and concluded pretty quick that Watson's nigra would be much better off lynched, just to be on the safe side. Captain Thad was shouting at the crowd that his vessel was the only one could carry 'em safe home from Pavilion Key if a bad storm come down, which sure seemed likely in a day or two, from all the signs. Said any man tried to come aboard to harm that nigra would get left behind.

Captain Thad locked the nigra in his schooner cabin for

safe-keeping. Later on I went on board and told this black boy to calm down and make sense cause his life depended on it. He was still pretty bad shook up, or played that way, but what scared him most was Cox or Watson finding out what he had told.

Asked his name, he said Little Joe was what Mist' Watson usually called him. Seemed kind of funny, cause he wasn't little by no means. Said that name was as good as any, from which I knew he was a wanted man, most likely, same as all the rest of Watson's people. Said he had knowed Mist' Watson for a good number of years, both here, he said, and there, though he couldn't quite remember where "there" was. Just wouldn't talk straight, everything he said had two–three meanings to it. There was a lot else he knew about Cox and Watson. I could feel it boiling back in there behind his eyes, but all he would tell over and over was his story about the murders at the Bend.

Trouble started, he said, when the Injun hung herself cause Cox had got her in a family way. Figuring her people would kill her and the child, she done it first. I said to him, You had her too, I bet, and he said, Nosuh.

Mister Watson had went to Chokoloskee to see to his family, he took Dutchy with him. The other three was drinking pretty good, that restless weather all week before the storm had riled up everybody's nerves the way it will, and the nigra in the kitchen fixing supper heard everything they said about the Injun girl that Waller had found hanging in the boat shed. Hannah was upset and she told Cox. The least thing you could do is bury her. Cox said, That squaw ain't my business. Said if Hannah wanted her buried so damn bad, then go bury her herself or let the nigger do it.

"That's me," Little Joe said. Again I seen something in his eye I didn't care for.

"This ain't no joke," I warned.

"Nosuh, it ain't."

Hannah was never one to hold her fire, so she come

323

right out with something about Cox's manlihood he didn't care for, and he called her by some very ugly name. The nigra allowed as how he always liked Miss Hannah, always respected her real good – he said that twice, make sure we heard it – so he dast not repeat the dirty name Mist' Cox called her, but it was that foul word got her old man into it. Green Waller told Cox that was no way to talk to a lady, and Cox said, I ain't talking to no lady, unless you mean this fat lady out of the circus. And Waller said, White trash like you wouldn't know a lady if she come from church to help your mother off the whorehouse floor. And Hannah screeched at her old man to shut his drunken mouth, cause she knew loose talk about Cox's mother was a bad mistake. White trash has their honor, too, and loves their mothers good as anybody.

Cox said, That done it, and hauled out a pistol. Waller was scared but wouldn't quit, so he just cackled. He was crazy with love for that big woman, you know, and showing off for her, letting her know he weren't some drunken hog thief, the way Watson said. He pointed right at his own heart, said, Are you skunk enough to shoot a old man twice your age?

Maybe Old Green had Cox figured for another Dutchy Melvin, dangerous talker with his heart in the right place. Hannah Smith didn't make no such mistake. She's fighting to get up out of her chair, to get between them, she is hollering. Don't pay no attention to that drunk old idjit! Little Joe claimed he come in from the kitchen, said, Nemmine, Mist' Leslie, he just foolin. But Cox had more excuse already than his kind ever needs, and he drew down on Waller. Lined him up real careful, being so drunk, arm wobbling, you know – Sit still, you sonofabitch, is what he told him.

Waller's still cackling, but he seen the muzzle, and that cackle's starting to go high, more like a rooster. His hands are coming up real slow so as not to flare the man behind that pistol, cause it's high time to get serious, the fun is over.

Ever hear a gun go off in a small room? That nigra thought the roof fell in. They all set there a minute in the crash and echo, staring at Waller, and him looking back, kind of puzzled, trying to cackle like it all must be a joke but spitting up a lot of fizz and blood.

"Well, hell,' Old Man Green Waller whispered in the echo. He looked kind of sheepish. And them were his last words, though Hannah shook him. The nigra backing up into the kitchen was pretty sure he seen God's light die out in Waller's eyes.

And Hannah whispered, "Oh, dear Jesus, Green, won't you never learn? Oh Christamighty, Green."

Hannah barged out of her chair and waddled to the kitchen, from where there come a howl of purely woe. She screeched at Cox for a yeller-bellied dog, and Cox grabbed up his gun and took out after her, never thought to duck till the split second before he went through the kitchen door. That flinch saved his life, cause Hannah Smith damn near beheaded him. She split the pine frame with her big two-bladed ax, which she always kept behind the kitchen door. She took a bullet in the shoulder, dropped the ax, then headed for the stairs, hunting a weapon, cause she had no chance of escape across the yard.

When Cox picked himself up off the kitchen floor, he pointed his gun at Little Joe, dead furious the nigra had not warned him. Said, Don't you move, boy, I got business with you.

Miss Hannah were so cumbersome that Cox caught up with her at the first landing. He give her room, knowing how strong she was, he stood a step below while they got their breath. Sounded like they was snarling, Little Joe said. Hannah weren't the kind to beg for mercy, and knew she wouldn't get none if she did. So Little Joe claimed he tried again, he said, Mist' Leslie –, and Miss Hannah screeched, Get away while you got the chance, boy, cause he'll kill you!

At the first shot, the nigra run outside, he was past the cistern by the time the shooting ended. He hadn't took no side in the argument, he was just scared that Leslie Cox aimed to murder any witnesses, settle Watson's payroll once and for all. He heard a shout and then some kind of crash. Then Cox was hollering, telling him to get his black ass up the stairs, give him a hand with this here sea sow, that's what he called her.

Cox shot poorly, being drunk, and sure enough, she were bleeding like a sow by the time he finished her. She went close on to three hundred pound, so he couldn't work her carcass down that narrow stair, and he got sniggering so hard with nerves that he fell down the whole flight and hurt his shoulder, which was when he commenced to holler for the nigra.

By now Little Joe was hid back in the mangrove, wouldn't come out when the man hollered, so Cox yells out the window he won't hurt him, he just needs a hand, and if the nigra don't come out, why, he's going in there after him, shoot him in the belly, leave him right there for the gators or panthers or bears or snakes, whichever was hungriest and got to him the first. Had big crocs up them southern rivers, too, least back in them days, but maybe Cox never knew that or forgot to mention it.

The nigra is so scared that his brain quits on him, I guess, cause after a while, he decides he will come out. Watson's skiff is tied up in the mangroves down below the house, but he can't reach that skiff without crossing the clearing. He knows Cox needs him, for a while, at least, and playing along is his one chance to reach that skiff – that's what he told us, and I don't believe a nigra would know how to make that up. So he waits a little for Cox to simmer down, and then he comes out, asking for mercy when Cox raises up the gun. But Cox just marches him into the house, hands him a gun, makes him shoot into both bodies. Says, Now you're in it right along with me.

Only a nigra would know, I reckon, why he never put his bullet into Cox instead. Probably Cox had him covered the whole time, and anyway, shooting a white man just ain't a thing your average nigra thinks to do, leastways back then. And if he shook that day holding a pistol like he shook at Pavilion Key, he wouldn't have hit a lean feller like Cox on the first ten tries.

So then Cox tells him he's successory to the crime, and will hang for murder if he ever breathes one word about it.

Well, they drug poor Hannah down the stairs and out into the yard, got blood on everything. We'll have to gut her out, Cox said, so she don't gas up. They weighted her with pig iron, done the same for Waller, and rolled 'em both into the river, but they don't do nothing with that Injun girl that's hanging in the shed. Cox went right on acting like she wasn't there.

Cox tells the nigra to go mop that blood that's nastying up the house, "get everything tidied up real nice for Miss Edna." Cox is in a high state of excitement, but he has to laugh when he says this, he's putting down a lot of shine. Before Little Joe can find a mop, Cox waves his gun and pushes Waller's glass at him. Don't let's go wasting that good likker, boy! Tells him they're in this thing together so might's well be friendly, tells him to set down and drink with him, try out some of his nigger conversation. Seems like these two knowed each other someplace, but the nigra wouldn't say how come, least not to me.

Not that they talk. They sit there drunk and getting drunker, Cox's gun square on the table. Little Joe's not only scared to be setting at a table with a white man, he's scared that Cox will blow his head off any minute. He is feeling dizzy. Maybe Cox has forgot about the skiff, maybe he aims to take care of his black sidekick soon's he gets his breath. His one chance is that Leslie Cox don't want to be alone with his dead, knowing he is abound for Hell already. So them two set there getting drunk and looking at flies on the walls while they think over the day's work. Finally Cox informs the nigra that Mister Watson wants Dutchy Melvin dead. Once that is taken care of, Les Cox says, everything is going to be just dandy.

Pretty soon the nigra slips back to the woods and don't come out again till two days later. Cox is wandering around the yard, yelling and cursing. This was October the 13th, a few days before the hurricane. Cox has had no sleep, and his nerves are shaky. He swears he won't hurt Little Joe if Little Joe will tell Mister Watson how Les Cox were not at fault, tell him how them two drunken old fools went after Les for no damned reason – look at that there ax mark on the door! – how they give him no choice but to shoot in self-defense. And if Mister Watson was to ask why they sunk them bodies, why, heck, they done that so nobody wouldn't come snooping around to bother Mister Watson with no stupid questions.

Little Joe was surprised to see Les Cox so skittish. He doubted Mister Watson would believe that story, but he decided he had to go along with it. But when he come out, Cox locked him in the shed, said he wanted him where he could find him in a hurry.

That same evening, that was Thursday, he hears Mister Watson's motor, *pop-pop-pop*, coming upriver. Cox comes running, turns him loose, warning he'd better do right by their story.

Cox took Waller's shotgun and went over to the boat shed, next to the bunk room where Dutchy slept. He waited there inside the door with that young squaw turning slow in the dusty light behind him, and Hannah and Waller lifting in the river current right where Dutchy and Watson come in at the dock.

Weren't much of a life, but Dutchy Melvin got cut down in the prime of it. Cox shot him dead through the slat on the door, resting the barrel on the door hinge. Young

Dutchy, that had been so cocky, took a charge of buckshot square in the face, died on that path kicking like a chicken with the head cut off. He never had no chance to draw his guns.

So Mister Watson don't say nothing, just turns the body over with his boot, takes them two Colts, and gets back in the boat. Cox hollers, Where the hell you going now? and Watson says, Nowhere at all. I haven't been here in the first place.

Little Joe was going back to his first story, and he knew I knew it, but before I could say so, he said, Nosuh. *Nosuh!* I mistook my self! Mist' Ed Watson dropped Mist Dutchy on the dock and headed off downriver, never knowed a thing about it, never seen them other bodies neither!

I asked him where Watson was headed, and he didn't know. I asked him why Watson never come on back when he heard the shooting, and he said, "Might be Mist' Watson thought Mist' Leslie was shootin for our supper, back to Watson Prairie."

Fed up with his lying, I hollered at him. How come Cox didn't kill you? Don't that mean you was mixed up in it yourself? He said Mist' Leslie might been spooked by all them bodies and needed somebody to talk to. Might been Mist' Leslie figured niggers didn't count, cause no nigger would dare to tell no stories on no white man. Might been Mist' Leslie had enough killing to do him for a while. All the same, he rowed for his life before Mist' Leslie changed his mind, cause all them dead folks could just as well been him.

All this made some crazy kind of sense, but I weren't satisfied.

I couldn't figure why he took his story to Pavilion Key, and why he hinted he knew Cox for a long time, like they was partners. Why did he own up he shot into them bodies, and laid his black hands on that woman when he helped to gut her and throw her in the river? And why did he cause trouble for himself by trying to get Watson suspected? If

329

he'd said nothing about Watson, just let on that Leslie Cox killed them three people, there weren't one person would have doubted him, not for a minute.

As it was, nobody trusted him, not even me. The way I figure it, any nigra whose mouth done so much damage must be too panicky to make up lies – either that or too damn ornery and stubborn and plain furious not to tell the truth.

Watching him work his story back and forth this way, I realized that this feller just played at being panicky. He changed his story cause he didn't want to die, but first he took his risk and told the truth. Probably knew he was a goner anyway, so he wanted justice done, no matter what.

The day that colored man showed up was October the 14th. Them people must been killed about the tenth. For some days the weather had been restless, with bad squalls and rains. Come out in the paper a week later that the Weather Bureau had issued storm warnings on the thirteenth and changed that to a hurricane south of Cuba the next day. But on the fifteenth, just when the storm seemed all set to come down on us, the Weather Bureau predicted it would sheer off toward the west, through the Yucatan Passage.

Well, us poor fellers in the Islands didn't have no radio, we didn't know the first thing about it. All we knew, we was troubled by the wind, we didn't like the looks of that hard sky. Feeling so sure a storm was coming down, we naturally took what happened at the Watson Place as evil sign, like that light that tore across God's Heaven every night back in the spring. So silent it was, and faraway, like a lonesome thing in the deeps of the black ocean.

Old Beezle Bub, Aunt Josie said, had took the upper hand. She wanted to see the nigra punished to trying to lay it all on Mister Watson, said she'd take care of it herself if a few of them no-good ex-husbands of hers would lend a hand. But then Thad advised he'd take no lynchers on his boat, the men decided they'd see justice done in court. Josie called 'em yeller cowards. She swore she'd never set foot on Thad's boat if it was her last day on this earth, and neither would her new baby boy that she never did deny was Mister Watson's. Well, she'd had some drink, and we let her rant and rave.

By Saturday, all but Josie Jenkins was ready to return to Marco with Captain Thad, go to church, hear Brother Jones on Sunday, see if *that* done any good. Josie sent off her little Pearl with her latest husband, Albert, went down with her baby on her arm to see 'em off. She swore that she and her little boy would see it through. Asked poor Tant if her own brother would stand by her, and he gives us all a comical look, but said he would.

So Captain Thad set sail from Pavilion Key on the sixteenth of October. Fine clear weather with light winds, but a strange purple cast to that blue sky. Us Storters was in our own small sloop, and kept right up with 'em. Hit a squall off Rabbit Key Pass on Sunday afternoon but got Henry Short to Chokoloskee by that evening. Mrs Watson and family was staying with Walter Aldermans, I heard, but I never seen them. Before we went on home to Everglade, Claude seen Mister Watson at Smallwood's store and told him almost all of the whole story.

MONROE COUNTY ISLAND SCENE
OF MURDERS

WHITE MAN AND NEGRO GET IN
BLOODY WORK LAST WEEK

WHITE MAN STILL AT LARGE

Estero, October 20, 1910 A horrible triple murder is reported to have been perpetrated below Chokoloskee, at the place of E. J. Watson of Chatham River. We have very few of the particulars, but we learn that a negro has confessed that he was forced by threats on his life to assist a man named Cox, who shot and killed three persons, two men and a woman, who were working for Watson, and sunk their bodies in the river. The woman's body was discovered floating by a passerby who pushed it under the mangrove to hide it while he went for assistance. Upon returning the body was found to have disappeared, but a trail showed where it had been dragged inland. On following the trail, Cox and the negro were found near the body. The confession of the negro implicates Watson as having engaged Cox to do the deed.

MAMIE SMALLWOOD

When Mister Watson come up here to see his family – this was early October – he told us all signs pointed to a hurricane, though that storm never struck in for another fortnight. "Something is coming down on us," is what he said. Them were his very words to us, gives me chills to think about it even today.

I don't know how that man knew about the hurricane but he sure did. You ask me, this was his inkling of his own dark fate.

Mister Watson brought his children here because Chokoloskee was the highest ground south of Caxambas. He trusted his strong house to stay put, but with Baby Amy only five months old, he didn't want to take no chances on a flooded cistern and unsanitary water. Later he claimed to Sheriff Tippins that he brought his family here on account of Leslie Cox was out to kill them, but he never said nothing about that to us.

Young Dutchy was with him when he brought his family, and Dutchy went back with him to Chatham Bend, and a few days later Mister Watson returned all by himself. That was October the 16th, a Sunday.

Late Sunday young Claude Storter came up from down coast with the news of dreadful killings at the Bend. Said Watson's nigra got away, out to the clam shacks on Pavilion Key, and the nigra claimed that Mister Watson ordered the three killings. Mister Watson's backdoor family was living on that key, and when Josie Parks – Jenkins, she was – challenged his story, the nigra switched and laid it all on Leslie Cox.

Hearing Claude's story, there was talk among our men of arresting Mister Watson, holding him here for Sheriff Tippins. Well, right about then, speak of the Devil, Mister Watson come into the store! Took his usual seat with his back into the corner, and told us he thought the hurricane was on its way.

When no one could look him in the eye, Mister Watson gazed all around the room, and then he eased onto his feet, straightened his coat. Maybe his back hairs didn't rise and his throat growl, the way Charlie T. Boggess has described it, but he smelled trouble. He picked Claude Storter right out of the crowd. He said, "Something the matter, Claude?" And knowing his temper, and knowing what he wore under that coat, Claude bravely advised him as soft as he knew how about the dreadful murders at the Bend. The only part he decided to leave out was the name of the man the nigra accused first.

Mister Watson had sat back kind of slow, but now he jumped right up again, startling a lot of 'em back out onto the porch. By God, he swore, someone would pay for this! Someone would hang! He was off to Fort Myers to fetch the sheriff before "that murdering sonofabitch – if you'll forgive me, Miss Mamie! – could make his getaway!" Well, it was E. J. Watson made the getaway, right from under the men's noses. His determination to seek justice seemed so darn sincere that it let all the steam out of their plans, or so they was telling one another for years afterwards.

Seems like yours truly, Mamie Ulala, was the only one suspected that his outrage was put on to fool us. You never saw an upset man with eyes so calm. Runs upstairs, hugs his sweet wife and children, comes down again with his big shotgun, he's well armed and out the door before anybody thinks to stop him. They was falling all over themselves to clear his way.

Our men were not cowards – well, not most of 'em – but Mister Watson took 'em by surprise. My brothers were young men who enjoyed a scrap and most folks would count a few others pretty fearless, but them men was confused and angry, and they had no leader. They knew Ted was a friend of Mister Watson, Willie Brown and William Wiggins, too. Gregorio Lopez was gone down to Honduras, D. D. House and Bill was on House Hammock, and C. G. McKinney, who lived across the island, claimed he never heard a thing about it.

HOAD STORTER

Sometime that week before the storm, Mister Watson was seen by the Frank Hamiltons at South Lost Man's, claimed he went there hunting Henry Thompson. He was gone another day or two before he come back to Chokoloskee. That was Sunday evening, the sixteenth. When we come in from Pavilion Key and Claude told him the news, all he could say was, Where in hell they got that damn fool nigger?

Captain Thad had took the nigra up the coast, aimed to hand him over to Sheriff Frank B. Tippins. When Mister Watson learned the nigra was in custody, on his way north, he said he was off to fetch the sheriff, then go to Chatham Bend, straighten things out. We reckoned he chose Sheriff Tippins because his son-in-law was a big shot in Fort Myers, so Tippins would have a better attitude than the Monroe County sheriff in Key West. And maybe he thought he'd catch up with the nigra at Marco, get to him before the sheriff did.

Next day early, in a southeast wind, Mister Watson crossed over to Everglade in his launch, paid down good money to my dad and Claude to carry him as far as Marco that same morning. Uncle George Storter would take care of the *Brave*, Mister Watson being one of his best customers. I don't know why he didn't take the *Brave* – no fuel, I guess. Also the barometer was falling fast, so it made more sense to go in a bigger boat.

R. B. Storter never cared to go in that black weather, but being as how they was old friends, he did. My mother got pretty bad upset that Dad was leaving right into a storm, she was scared for him and scared for Claude and scared for the home ones left behind in the rising waters, because Everglade weren't nothing more than mud banks on a tide creek back in them days. To make it worse, she was afraid that Watson might up and do away with 'em, cause the awful tale about the killings was all over the Bay, and she knew him for a desperate man that would try anything. But Mister Watson were a hard feller to say no to, it was always easier to go along.

There was northeast winds gusting to fifty by the time they came out Fakahatchee Pass. The *Bertie Lee* was banging hard and shipping water, and near to Caxambas, it wasn't a hard blow no more, it was plain some kind of storm was on the way. That wind had gone southeast to south, then around to the southwest, and building steady. From Marco Island all the way north to Punta Rassa, a small boat could mostly stay inside the barrier islands, but my dad didn't like the way them clouds were churning down that sky, ugly purple and yellow, like the firmament itself was torn and battered. He was more and more worried all the time about the family, and finally he told Mister Watson they could not take him to Fort Myers but was going to leave him at Caxambas and head on back. He'd have to walk from there to the Marco settlement, at the north end of that island, where somebody might carry him to the mainland.

Mister Watson looked 'em over for a minute there, went all wooden in the face the way he did sometimes. Had his hands in his coat, and Claude was scared he would haul out his revolver, order our dad to keep on going. Maybe he'd shoot 'em, dump 'em overboard, take the boat himself. But I guess he figured he had trouble enough without killing the brother of the justice of the peace, and his nephew thrown in. Cussed 'em out pretty darn good, but when he seen that wasn't going to change nothing, he give it up. Anyway, he always liked my dad. When they set him on the dock there at the clam factory, he wished them a safe voyage home, and waved good-bye, and strode off toward the north, his slicker flying.

The *Bertie Lee* never made it back to Everglade, she had to put in at Fakahatchee, where Dad and Claude took shelter with Jim Martin. That night the schooner dragged her anchor, drifted up into the mangroves. Claude and Dad never got a wink, that's how frantic they was about the family, and next morning Dad borrowed a skiff and rowed the last eight miles to Everglade. Found out how Uncle George had come over to our house, took everybody aboard the big old lighter that Storters used to carry cane across from Half Way Creek. Herded half the settlement onto one lighter, that's how few was living there back then! Men pushed and poled upriver far as she would go, but Storter River – that's what us old-timers called it – rose ten or twelve feet before midnight till that barge tore loose and carried farther up into the trees. Tide turned before dawn, and barrels, boxes, cows, and all Creation drifted by, and the next thing you know, along come the new schoolhouse! Us kids had a high old time waving it good-bye! But all that while, we was worried sick about Dad and Claude. Never knowed if they was drowned or what, till our dad showed up the day after the storm, asked how we was.

That storm in 1910 lasted thirty hours, seemed like the world was coming to an end. Barometer at Sand Key Light, down by Key West, registered 28.40, the lowest ever recorded in the U.S.A. The Great Hurricane of 1910 was a dreadful, dreadful hurricane, worst in memory along this coast before nor since.

Folks was quick to connect that terrible hurricane with that sky fire that showed up in the springtime of that year and set the sky ablaze night after night. The Great Comet was first seen due east from Sand Key, April 22nd, twenty-five to thirty degrees above the horizon, with the scorpion tail of it curling right over us like an almighty question mark in Heaven.

Brother Jones was ranting on about a great war between Good and Evil, and how that comet was a messenger of Armageddon. The Good Lord aimed to wipe out the whole world, punish us poor sinners for good and all, leave just a few pure in heart to get the world cranked up again. By the time that man of God was done with us, the pure-in-hearts was the only ones breathing easy. But pure-in-hearts was never plentiful around the Bay, and once the sinners went to Hell, it might of got pretty lonesome around here, crying in the wilderness and all like that.

So when this angry storm come down right after word come of them bloody murders, it was seen as the first blast of Judgment Day. In the ruin and silence on the land, no one could doubt that Satan had reared His ugly head amongst the sinful folk of the Ten Thousand Islands. All these signs from Heaven and earth could only be God's wrath at E. J. Watson, and maybe the Lord God Almighty had still worse up His sleeve, for all we knew.

MAMIE SMALLWOOD

That Sunday night in the old store, our menfolks got real busy spreading blame. No sooner was Mister Watson safely on his way than some started hollering how he should be taken prisoner, and others hollered, Why, hell no! Ed was right here on Chokoloskee! There ain't no possibility he done them crimes! Other ones said it must been Cox that made that nigra put the blame on Watson, and "anyways you could never trust a nigger." Well, now, some said – and could be I was one – even if Cox had put a gun up to his head, no nigra would be fool enough to lie about a well-esteemed man like Mister Watson.

Ted heard me say that and he didn't like it, but I just set my jaw and wouldn't look at him. In my belief I said the truth: Ed Watson's nigra must of had a reason.

By that time Mister Watson was long gone, headed for Everglade. He knew from hard experience, he'd told us, how quick a gang of flustered men can turn into a mob that has to *do* something, and somehow he sweet-talked R. B. Storter into running him north as far as Marco even though the hurricane was on its way. Had to pay Bembery pretty good, I shouldn't wonder, them Storters never give you much for nothing. That's what Storters say about us Smallwoods, too.

The storm came in next morning and built up all day. Our house was the old Santini house, come with the property Ted bought, 1899. Santinis built her well above the drift line of the hurricane of '73, and that were good enough in '96, and again in 19 and 09, but it weren't near good enough for that hurricane of 1910, which come roaring in

340

around us like a dragon. Rain and sea was all mixed up together, the trees all around lost in the swirl until we couldn't see 'em anymore. Gray thick waves heavy as stones pounded our shore as if our island was way out on the open Gulf, and the island grew smaller, smaller, smaller, as the water rose. Seemed like our little bit of land had been uprooted and had gone adrift, far out to sea.

According to C. G. McKinney, who passed in these parts for somewhat educated, nine tenths of Chokoloskee Island and ten tenths of Everglade was underwater. Had to abandon our poor home and then the schoolhouse, which was ten foot above sea level. Edna Watson was up there with the Aldermans, he carried Addison, she had little Amy and was leading her Ruth Ellen by the hand.

Storm water rose up to its highest maybe four o'clock that morning, left a line on the wall ten inches higher than the schoolhouse floor. The men begun to make a raft out of the schoolhouse, and the bang of hammers was all that could be heard over that wind. Meanwhile we hurried all the kids to the top of Injun Hill.

Poor Edna was close to hysterics. Having been raised far inland from the sea, she never believed such a fearful storm was possible. She promised her kids they would all stay in the schoolhouse and face together whatever dangers was to come. That way they would not get rained on, Edna told 'em. Finally we persuaded the poor thing that she better come uphill long with the rest of us.

By the end of it, all ten families on the island was perched out like wet birds in the black weather. It was late October, don't forget, our teeth were chattering in the cold rain. All night we were staring at that rising water, until finally the Good Lord heard our prayers, and the thundering eased a little and that coast got a breath, and we seen that the seas weren't climbing any more but sucking themselves back down into the torrents, leaving behind dark dripping silence, mud, and ruin.

At daybreak, this was the eighteenth, there was no real

341

dawn at all, it stayed half-dark. The water still swirled around our house, and what goods from the store weren't gone into the Bay were washed way back up into the woods. I lost my whole new set of china, and seeing that, I just shook my head and laughed and cried. Grandma House was hollering, How can you laugh, girl, with all your livelihood lost in the mud? The former pert Miss Ida Borders of South Carolina was pretty disappointed in the Lord, seemed like to me. And I said, Well, Mama, I am thankful we are all alive and in one piece and lived to tell about it. This ol' mud looks pretty good to me.

Only one hurt was Charlie T. Boggess, who threw out his ankle bad, tending the boats. Jumped off a boat where the dock was underwater, and the dock weren't there no more. Fetched Old Man McKinney over here to yank him straight again and bind him up, and after that Ted lugged him on his back all the way across the hill to his own house, told him to stay there and not cause any more trouble. That's why Charlie T. still limped so bad, and why he was bringing up the rear when the posse came down to our landing here a few days later. He made it, though, he never was a feller to miss out on nothing.

SAMMIE HAMILTON

Sunday had some sun and a light wind, but by ten that evening, the sixteenth, the barometer commenced to fall too fast, with wind from the northeast, thirty, forty, fifty miles, and climbing. At dawn high tide come right up to the cabin, the seas was washing all across the ridge back of Lost Man's Beach. By noon that day the wind, still building, shifted over to southeast, then south, and that afternoon of October 17th, when she blew hardest, she blew steady out of the southwest, all the way across the Gulf from the Yucatan Channel.

I was only a little feller then, seven years of age, but I never forgot how the sky fell, that black and awful sky rushing off the Gulf and looming over us, the whole earth turning black at noon. Seas come in off the horizon, crashing on the coast, couldn't hear one wave break no more, it was all thunder. And the rain slashing straight across in sheets, and that groaning wind twisting the trees when the gusts struck us. When the thatch tore off of our poor cabin, what few worldly goods we had was snatched away. By nightfall, we knew we was the last ones in the world, with the whole universe caving in on us poor lost souls.

The cabin begun to shift a little after dark, though when high water come it was past midnight. We abandoned our old home for the skiff, let the wash carry us well up in the black mangroves, lashed the boat tight, and prayed to the Lord Almighty for deliverance. All huddled up, white-faced as possums on a limb, hour after hour, and worried sick the whole damn time about Aunt Gert's family. Well, them Thompsons rode the storm out in a skiff tied up into the mangroves, same as us. Shine Thompson – that's my cousin Leslie – Shine was just a little feller then, and Aunt Gert set a washtub over Shine to keep him dry. The hurricane washed Uncle Henry's sloop so far back in the swamps we never got her out. Might be there yet.

By daybreak, the worst of it was past, the wind was down, but all the banks of Lost Man's River was broken snags and thick gray marl, like a coat of death on every living thing. We could see ripped trees swirling past with wild things clinging, staring back as they was carried out to sea. Lost Man's Key was awash in a tide so high that the river looked a mile across, and the sea and the river were jumbled up together, thick chop and wind roil of a dead lead-gray, like all life color had been bled away.

I asked our mama was this Judgment Day that was spoke of so much in her Holy Bible? Was we in Purgatory or in Hell? And she said, No, honey, best I can make out, we are still on earth. And Grandpap James says, That is Hell enough for me. And Frank Hamilton, my daddy, told us, This here is like the Flood of Noah's time, come around again as warning from the Lord. And we knew he was thinking about Mister Watson.

Over that long night, Grandpap James Hamilton fell quiet, wouldn't talk at all, and after the wind died out a little, he looked all around that silence like he just woke up. Everything poor Grandpap put together in a lifetime was twisted down to trash or washed away, but he didn't act jagged and mean no more, he looked round-eyed as a little child. Finally he started in to murmuring, never stopped again. He was speaking in tongues, that's what my daddy told us, but I believe it was mostly his old memories of days gone by.

Come Wednesday, Henry Thompson took a row skiff up the rivers to the Watson Place, and was kind of surprised no one answered him when he sung out. Said that big house looked like she drifted in and stranded, cause everything around her was smashed flat, boat sheds, bunkhouse, little cabin, most of the trees, too. Uncle Henry come to the conclusion that Mister Watson had taken the whole bunch away before the storm. His schooner had rode it out all right, because somebody had lashed her tight to them big poincianas by the house, and they was about the only trees left standing.

Henry Thompson figured Mister Watson would not mind if he brought the *Gladiator* south and took us Hamiltons aboard for Chokoloskee. Andrew Wiggins had walked Lost Man's Beach from the mouth of Rodgers River, him and his wife and homeless baby, they was with us, too.

We arrived on Chokoloskee the 21st of October, 1910, and that was when we first had word about the murders. The news give Henry Thompson a bad start. Now that he thought about it, he recollected evil in the air, said the silence on the Bend was something terrible, said the reason Cox never sung out was because he had a bead on Henry from up under the eaves. Way we imagined it, Cox's mouth was set the way a snake's mouth sets, kind of a smile, while that shiny black forked tongue slithers in and out.

Fortnight later when my dad told Grandpap that the Chokoloskee men had killed Ed Watson, the old man shook his head. He did not believe it. Said, "You just tell that bloody-headed devil he is welcome to my Lost Man's claim if he can find it."

Most of Richard Hamilton's gang moved to Lost Man's River after the Hurricane of 1910 swept 'em off Wood Key. People would perch from time to time on our old territory, but them Choctaws or whatever the hell they called theirselves, they was about the only ones that never left. I'm talking about good steady folks was trying to make a life down in the Islands, not moonshiners nor renegades that came and went.

My grandmother Sallie Daniels and old Mary Hamilton was Weeks sisters from Merco Island, so Walter and Gene and Leon and the girls was Mama's cousins. But the two families wasn't close because we was not so proud about 'em, they was another bunch of dogs entirely. Some of 'em was pretty dark, though the dark ones had good features and the girls was comely. Mama and her sister-in-law, Aunt Gertrude Thompson, decided we weren't no kin whatsoever. How they figured that one out they never said.

I guess I wasn't proud about our cousins, but they never bothered me, we got on good. Like I say, I never was ashamed about 'em, ceptin maybe the one who acted shamed about himself. No, me and Dexter never had no trouble with them boys. They was all nice fellers and fine fishermen, they just wanted to be left alone, but folks didn't like their standoffish attitudes, wouldn't let 'em be.

Way I heard it, one time Old Man Richard Hamilton was telling Henry Short from Chokoloskee how he was Choctaw Injun out of Oklahoma. And Henry told him, You ain't Choctaw, you're chock full o' nigger, just like me! Henry Short was a good nigger, and I reckon he still is if he ain't died or something.

In the spirit of its epigraph ("No Stormy Weather Enters Here, Tis Joyous Spring Throughout the Year") the Fort Myers Press ran the headline THE STORM CAME BUT WE ARE HERE. It conceded the devastation caused by the Great Hurricane of October 17, reporting, however, that "All Are Optimistic" and that "No Fear for the Future" could be detected.

Fort Myers, October 20, 1910 *In Key West, the storm disabled the anemometers at the weather observation office, along with seven hundred feet of new concrete dock being installed by the War Department, and finished off the three-story concrete cigar factory of the Havana-American Company, severely damaged in the hurricane the year before. Winds reached their greatest velocity on Monday afternoon of the 17th, with gusts up to 110 miles per hour. The rainfall, however, could not be measured, the gauge having been carried out to sea.*

The recent storm occupies the thoughts of everyone . . . one's sympathies are with the small householders, who in many instances have spent their savings in erecting a little home, often built in the cheapest style, which was ill-fitted to withstand the violence of the storm, and is either shattered or so injured as to require considerable outlay in repairs before becoming habitable. The colored population has in these ways encountered heavy losses. . . .

Estero, October 20, 1910 *One peculiarity of the wind was that it would blow steadily for a minute or more with increasing violence, bending the trees before it, then there would come a hard puff that appeared to have a circular motion, twisting and whipping the trees until it seemed they must be torn to pieces or lifted out of the ground. About midnight the wind began to shift from northeast toward the south, until by Tuesday morning it had veered around to almost the opposite direction, that is, from the southwest ... then abated. ...*

Chokoloskee, October 21, 1910 *We are all in a fearful condition here. Some are destitute of a house, or clothing, only what they happened to have on when the gale struck on the night of the 17th.*

Mr J. M. Howell lost his home, and quite a number of people lost their homes down the coast and at Fakahatchee. All our crops are gone. Water rose about eight feet, filling a lot of cisterns with salt water. Some of the folks ran out and climbed trees; some fled to the highest mounds and had a bad, damp rest. Fishermen lost all nets and some boats.

One poor woman on Pavilion Key climbed a tree with her baby and was compelled to let it go adrift from her arms. She had the luck to save herself and buried her baby after the water went down.

We are all in a bad fix; provisions nearly all ruined in the stores.

Notwithstanding water ran eight feet on some cattle pastures, some of the cattle lived it out. I have seen some dead rabbits, and a big lot of fine chickens got drowned. ...

Mr C. T. Boggess sprained his ankle or at least it slipped out of joint. His little power fish boat was driven up in the bushes a good ways and is nearly a wreck.

Great quantities of dead mullet and other fish are on the shores, and some today are not dead, but cannot swim, possibly from muddy water getting into their gills.

The Everglade schoolhouse went off of its foundation and went up the river.

Mr Wm. Brown, on Turner's River, lost his crop, and

348

his cistern – the best and largest in the country – was filled with salt water. All the Everglade cisterns were ruined with salt water.

A lot of our folk here fled to the schoolhouse. The water ran up over the floor ten inches and they took off the door and the blackboards and made a raft of them, tied with a rope, on which to flee to other parts if the house left its foundation. Nearly three fourths of Chokoloskee Island was underwater. We began to realize what those high mounds were built for.

All of our own folk are very busy hunting up their lost household goods and stores of grub, boats, nets, etc. Some of us are planting again. I find a few of my peppers sprouting out and growing and some tomatoes and cabbage that the water was six feet deep over are growing. Okra could not stand the racket at all, but I have some seven-top turnips that are growing and they were under three feet or more. . . .

SAMMIE HAMILTON

The day Mister Watson come to Lost Man's was a Friday, three days before the hurricane and four days after Cox went wild at Chatham Bend. Where was he all them days in between? Mister Watson told us he come up from Key West, but later we learned he was at Chokoloskee, him and Dutchy. Did he come to us after he dropped off Dutchy? What was he doing so far south? Where was he headed? Did he want us to back up his Key West story so he had an alibi? And where was Cox? Was that bloody-handed sonofabitch hid in the cuddy of that launch while he was talking to us?

I believe he knew about the killings, I believe he was setting up an alibi he never needed. Being such a thorough man, he must of knowed he was in bad trouble whether he ordered them three deaths or not. Maybe he figured if he took our savings, he could head out for Key West or Port Tampa, find a ship out of the country. Tampa, more likely – they would be looking for him at Key West. If so, something changed his thinking, cause he showed up again in Chokoloskee one jump ahead of the bad news from Pavilion Key, and he talked his way out like he had so many times before. Swore he was going for the sheriff, swore he would bring Cox in, then got away from there while the getting was good.

By the time the hurricane struck in, Leslie Cox was all alone on Chatham Bend, if you don't count that dead squaw in the boat shed or them three bodies in the pit across the river. You had to wonder what was going through his mind, if he was dead drunk or just wild-eyed and jittery, like

Watson's horse, whinnying away out in the shed. That storm must have looked to him like the wrath of God come to strike him off the earth.

We was down there in the rivers and we seen it, and I'm telling you now, it filled our hearts with dread. That howling sky and gales and roaring river in that Hurricane of 1910 was enough to scare the marrow out of anybody, let alone a direful sinner that has slaughtered three poor souls and gutted out their carcasses like they was hogs and rolled the bodies off the bank into the river. If Leslie Cox had a human spark left in him, he spent that night upon his knees just a-howling for the Lord's forgiveness. Whether or not he got it no one knows.

Few days later, Mister Watson come back through alone, and went hunting for Cox down Chatham River. So many times I have pictured him walking around that place of his, shouting and listening, feeling them old ghosts. Maybe Cox hailed him from the mangrove, maybe they talked. All we know is, there was no sign of life when Henry Thompson went up there after the storm. Course Uncle Henry never knew there was three dead buried by the river, never imagined Leslie Cox might been watching through some crack or broken pane. When he realized *that*, he got the shakes. Took a snort every little while to stiffen up his nerves, and never lost that habit all his life.

Yessir, we had a time of it that day! Hurricane of 1910, October 17th of 1910. That storm was the worst to strike this coast until Hurricane Donna come along fifty years later. Every house at Flamingo washed away. Louie Bradley and the Roberts boys, all the docks and houses down there, even that old copra warehouse on Cape Sable. As for us islanders, most was living in board cabins, and some had lean-to camps, y'know, moving from garden to garden, way the Injuns done. Excepting Ed Watson's big strong house at Chatham Bend, there weren't one roof in that whole stretch of Islands. Course Chokoloskee is four miles inland, with high ground, but Jim Howell's Chokoloskee house, that was lost, too.

Hurricane caught twenty-two clammers out on Plover Key, took all their skiffs but three. Rowed back to Caxambas, but they were in poor shape by the time they got there. Brought the news that Josie Jenkins lost her baby boy to drowning while she hung on where her brother Tant had her hoisted up a tree. Got tore right out of her poor arms when the waves broke all across Pavilion Key. She found him when the seas went down, where his little arms stuck up out of the sand. Later we heard he was a Watson, and far as I know, Aunt Josie never denied it. Some folks made too much of it that Mister Watson's little feller was the only human soul lost in that storm.

Us Hamiltons come out all right, the Lord be praised, but that hurricane blowed what fight was left out of our family. When that storm got done with us, we didn't have no home nor garden, we had to take what help we could at Chokoloskee.

After all them years, the time had come to say good-bye to Lost Man's River. Grandpappy James was old and poorly, and times was plenty hard enough without having to wonder where Cox might of got to. We took Grandpap to Chokoloskee and from there to Fakahatchee but he never came back from the woesome ruin of that hurricane of 1910, and died soon after. Before he passed, he told his sons that his name was James Hopkins and not Hamilton. Said he come from a rich Baltimore family but acted rashly in his youth, had to kill some dastard in a duel, something like that, had to change his name and travel to other parts to seek his fortune. So his sons went down to Everglade to discuss this matter with Justice Storter, and George Storter said, You boys come into this world with the name of Hamilton, so you might's well go out of it that same way.

FRANK B. TIPPINS

"You boys know Sheriff Tippins," Collier says.

At Marco Island, most of the men are gathered at Bill Collier's Mercantile Store. The small limestone building stands apart from his Marco Hotel, with its twenty small guest rooms, parlor, dining room, and bathroom. Constructed from burnt oyster shell the year before, the store has a hurricane crack three inches across from roof to ground and is still draining eighteen inches of high water. The bare ground around both buildings, littered with brown fronds, is set about with salt-killed planted palms.

Worn by wind and liquor to a nervous edge, the men talk fitfully. Two days before, on the eve of the hurricane, Captain Thad Williams had delivered the black suspect at Fort Myers. I returned with Captain Thad to Marco, where the Cannons and Dick Sawyer and Jim Daniels had confirmed Thad's story that in his first testimony at Pavilion Key, the black suspect had implicated E. J. Watson.

Turns out Watson had come through here on Monday, and crossed to the mainland before the storm struck in. He had probably arrived at Fort Myers this very morning. Said he was looking for the sheriff, Bill said, and might be hunting up that nigra, too, while he was at it.

"You ask me, that nigger told the truth when he claimed that crazy Watson was behind it."

"Nigra changed his story," I tell this man. The Monroe sheriff has been notified to come get him, and I wonder if I shouldn't start on back, in case Watson finds a way to get him first.

Teet Weeks snuffles his tin cup, wipes his stubbled chin

with the back of his hand, gets my boots in focus. "Them fucking cattle kings and bankers gone to cover up for him again, ain't that right, Sheriff? Likely got you in their pocket, too – "

Bill Collier sets down the spring line he is braiding and hoists Teet off the floor and sets him down again facing the other way. Weeks spins and draws his fist back for a comic roundhouse punch, knowing that some kinsman will catch his arm before he gets himself in too much trouble. When no one bothers, he feigns imbalance, which carries him back to a safe distance, bobbing and weaving by himself in a small circle. That's how Teeter Weeks, a drunkard at fifteen, had got his name. Taking the laughter as approval, Teet winks and prances, spits on his hands. "Damn you, Bill Collier, you looking for a fight? You found your man!"

Captain Bill Collier is a broad-backed man, calm and slow to anger. His father founded Marco settlement way back in 1870. Today the son is storekeeper and postmaster, trader and ship's master, he is shipbuilder and keeper of the inn. He has a copra plantation of five thousand palms and a citrus grove on the mainland at Henderson Creek with fifteen hundred orange trees. He designed and owns the floating dredge that works the clam flats at Pavilion Key.

It was Bill Collier who discovered the strange Calusa masks off the Caxambas trail while getting out muck for his tomatoes, Bill Collier who lost two sons when his schooner *Speedwell* sank off the Marquesas. He has done a lot and seen much more. Ignoring Teet Weeks, he picks up his rope and resumes braiding.

I ask if anyone knows Watson's foreman.

"Your prisoner seen him last, on Chatham Bend. Nobody knows where he might of got to now."

What I *should* do, I think, is deputize some men, keep right on going, south to Chatham River, jurisdiction or no jurisdiction, because whoever was responsible for those three killings was not likely to wait there for the sheriff.

". . . and no goddam *law!*" Teet cries. "Ought to take and put a bullet through them kind of crazy sonsabitches fore they get loose from their damn cradle, be fucking well done with it – "

"That where you're headed, Sheriff? Chatham River?"

"Cross the Monroe line?"

The men grin when I play dumb and say, "That's not Lee County? Guess I lost my map," but they keep pressing.

"John Smith. You found out who he is?"

"I believe the nigra knows, but he's not telling."

"Had that black boy here tonight, I guess he'd tell us."

"That could be."

The restless men half listen as Dick Sawyer describes how he once saved Watson's life.

One day he'd seen the *Gladiator* at Key West, and getting no answer when he hallooed, he went aboard. Ol' Ed was down with typhoid fever, couldn't move or talk. Dick Sawyer went up the street, brought Dr Feroni back down to the boat, and the doctor cured him. "Ed give me not one word of thanks for saving his damn life," Dick Sawyer says. "And that is funny, cause Ed's manners was so excellent."

"Yes, sir," Jim Daniels says, disgusted. He is worried about his sister Josie on Pavilion Key. "Very well knowed to settle his accounts, keep on the right side of the store-keepers, but he still owes my oldest boy eighty dollars for motor repair. Watson as much as told my Henry he could go to hell, but he says it real polite, cause his manners is so excellent. A very mannerly man, specially when he has you where he wants you. And he has most everybody where he wants 'em, that right, Dick?"

"Had a couple your sisters, Jim, right where he wanted 'em, as you might say – "

Jim Daniels, in his fifties, hard-armed, dark-haired, with a trace of silver, cuts off Dick Sawyer just by sitting up straight.

"I was down at Lost Man's, 1901, nearby my daughter Blanche's people – that's her brother-in-law, Lewis Hamilton, cooks on the clam dredge? Well, one evening I seen a little boat burning down against the sun, way out there on the Gulf horizon. Went out there to see if we could help, found what was left of Tucker's little sloop, no trace of nobody. Nice mannerly job." He looks grimly at Sawyer. "Before that it was mostly rumors. Wasn't till after Tuckers died that folks got scared of him. If he hadn't of took off for the north, he could of had about any mound he wanted cepting Richard Hamiltons'."

"Old Man Richard's bunch, they's kin to your wife, ain't that right, Jim?"

Jim Daniels says, "Not so's you'd notice, Dick."

"Now Netta and Josie – "

"You speaking about my sisters, Albert?"

"I'm speaking about their little girls, over Caxambas. Ain't them kids Watson's?" The speaker is a morose man whose wife, Josephine, had presented him only this year with a chestnut-haired baby boy. Josie Parks – she used the name of the original ex-husband – had refused to abandon Pavilion Key before the storm, and her latest spouse, who had left without her, had been drinking for two days to drown his worry. "Thought that was common knowledge," he adds carefully, seeing Jim's expression.

"Best ask Mister Watson about common knowledge, Albert. Might could tell you some more common knowledge that you ought to know."

In the hooting, Josie Parks's drunk husband raps his cup down hard, as if set to fight, but Captain Collier, waving his long arms, has no trouble at all deflecting his attention.

"Talking about common knowledge, Albert," Collier says. "One time on his way back from Fort Myers, Mister Watson got as far as here but needed a boat to take him down to Chatham River. Hiram Newell setting over there, he worked for Watson, but Hiram had his boat up on the ways, so them two went on over to Sawyer's, that right,

Dick? And Hiram told Dick through the door that Mister Watson was outside, said he wanted to know if Dick would take him home. And Dick thought Hiram was playing fun on him, and hollers out, 'To hell with you and your goddam Mister Watson!' Then he come to the door, and when he seen who was standing right outside, he said just as nice as rice, 'Why hello there, Mister Watson! How the hell *you* been?' Remember, Dick?"

"I took that sonbitch home, yes*sir*!" Dick Sawyer says. "Too damn scared not to!"

Josie's husband yells at Sawyer, "You *always* been his friend, ain't that right, Dick? Friend of Walt Smith, too. How do you like them two fine fellers now?" Dick Sawyer, as every man there knew, had been aboard Smith's sponge boat a few years earlier when Smith had killed the game warden, Guy Bradley.

"I worked with Walt Smith, that is right," Dick Sawyer says, "and I left Key West right after that and come up here. Cause I ain't Smith's friend after what he done, and I ain't no friend to Watson, neither, not no more!" Sawyer, frowning, pounds his fist, but he has to give this up. "Ol' Ed told me that himself," he says, and laughs.

"This here time," Dick says, "me and Tom Braman was having some drink in Eddie's Bar there in Key West, and Ed Watson banged in there roaring drunk and set up shots for everybody. And two black women came in and ordered rum, because Key West being a Navy town, it allowed niggers to act that way ever since the War Between the States. So Watson turned at the sound of nigger voices, and one of them females, she lifted a glass to him, she was drunk, too. There was a bad silence for a minute while he thought that over. He did not toast back. Everyone felt a whole lot easier when Ed got up off his stool without a word and left the place. *Ain't nobody never going to see Ed Watson take a drink with niggers!* – I hollered that out to make sure them women knew what was what.

"Turned out two niggers was waiting for their women

357

right outside. One of 'em said how-do to Watson, so Ed took out his knife and went right after him. There come a shriek and Ed's friends ran out, thinking to keep him out of trouble. They yelled, No, no, don't do that, Ed! Better listen to us, cause we're your friends! And Watson rolled up onto his feet as the crowd backed off. He was panting, you know, squinting. When he yanked out a neckerchief to wipe his knife, every man flinched, thought he was going for his pistol. But all he said was, very calm and quiet, *I don't have no friends*. Not sorrowful about it, more kind of confused, you know, like he was trying to remember something."

"Watson said that?" Jim Daniels looks surprised.

"*I don't have no friends* – that's what he said! You ask Tom Braman!" Dick Sawyer looks all around the place, triumphant. "Then Ed put his black hat back on and went down to the wharf to where his schooner was. On the way, he run into a deputy, and he says, Depitty, best get your ass on up to Eddie's Bar before they kill someone. Course by that time, he had one them niggers killed already, and the other one figuring he might as well be dead. By the time a posse got back down to the wharf, his boat was gone, and nobody went north eighty miles to Chatham River after E. J. Watson, not on account of no dead nigger."

"Way I heard that one, Dick, you wasn't even there! Heard it right from Braman and you wasn't there!"

"I wasn't there, Jim? Where was I at, then?"

"Way I heard that one, wasn't no niggers messed up in it at all. Ed Watson had some mixed-breed feller on the floor and was hauling out that goddam bowie knife, said, Maybe I'll fillet this one here in case he's a damn Spaniard, cause I never got to go to San Juan Hill.

"The Roberts boys, Gene, Melch, and Jim, was over from Flamingo, tried to talk him out of it. Gene Roberts was always Watson's friend, and he'd tell you that today. And Gene said, Come on now, Ed, you're looking for some trouble, and you don't need no more. You better listen here to us, cause we're your friends. And Watson looked around at all them men, then blinked as if he was coming up out of a dream. He wiped his knife off on the Spaniard's hair and snapped it shut, let that half-dead bleeding feller crawl away like he'd never noticed him in the first place. Got up and put his knife away and dusted himself off. Then he looked all them men over once again, and said real quiet, Boys, I ain't *got* no friends."

"*Haven't* got no friends, more like it,' Sawyer says. "Ed don't say *ain't*."

Hiram Newell, who had served as Watson's schooner captain, clears his throat. "Well, I ain't ashamed to say ain't, Dick, and I ain't ashamed to be in friendship with Ed Watson. If Tant was here tonight, he'd say the same. Ed Watson got him a big heart – "

"Jesus!" Jim Daniels snorts, and stamps the floor. "Got him a big heart, all right, to go with them good manners. Too bad them Tuckers ain't here this evening, tell us *their* opinion! Jesus Sweet Christ!"

"Where *is* Tant, anyway?"

"Pavilion Key, unless he been washed off." Daniels scowls again at Josie's husband. "Had to stay on there, tend to his baby sister."

"Your sister, too, ain't she? Half sister anyway."

"Big family," Jim Daniels says.

"The reason Ed and me ain't friends no more," Dick Sawyer says, taking advantage of a silence, "he got in trouble some way in Wakulla Springs and was headed back to Chatham Bend. Come through here, asked me to take him home. No moon that night and no stars neither, I didn't want to go. But I seen that stare he gets sometimes, and knew not to say no. We weren't hardly clear of Marco when he went below to sleep it off. Pretty quick he stuck his head out of the cuddy and looked around him at the night. He shook his head, says, Can't see much, from the look of it. And I said, Can't see is right! Can't hardly *navigate*! I was thinking he would tell me to turn back.

359

And he said, Partner, if you run this boat aground, I guess I'll kill you.

"That was the first time I was not so sure Ed Watson was my friend. Might been one of them little jokes he makes when he is drinking, but I couldn't count on it. So what I done, I headed way off shore, let the flood tide rise a little before I tried them flats off Chatham River.

"Well, we never once scratched bottom. Landed Ed safe on his dock, and he yawned and stretched and told me then, You come on in and drink with me, have a bite of supper. So I said, I'd be proud to do that, Ed. Be with you in a minute. But when he went on up to the house, I just slipped my lines and drifted off downriver. He come out of his house and looked, but he never called. Just stood there in the moonlight up against that big white house and watched me out of sight around the Bend."

Since my chance of finding Cox is small, I had to locate E. J. Watson. That's what I'm thinking when the door bangs open in the wind, bangs closed again with a man backed up against it, as the Marco men heave back, groaning like cattle. Hand hid in his baggy coat's right pocket, the man is watching nobody but me. Picked me out through the window, and picked out his own vantage point, as well. He knows that every man in this small settlement would be here in Collier's store, leaving the women to huddle where they could.

"Mister Watson."

Bill Collier's greeting warns the room. Collier gives me a blank gaze of comical astonishment, but Watson hasn't missed the shift I make to free my holster, so I elevate my knee real slow with both hands clasped on it, resting my boot carefully on a keg of nails.

Watson acknowledges the signal with a small nod of his chin and draws his hand out of his pocket. He stays where he is against the door, to cover his back and the whole room at the same time. He looks windblown and sleepless, waterlogged, his ruddy sunburned face packed with dark blood, his breathing hoarse. Also, he appears alert, even exhilarated, not the least likely to make a move that would put him at our mercy. Being endangered, he is very dangerous.

"Mister Watson." E. J. Watson nods. He grins. He has been drinking. But Watson could come in here dead drunk and buck naked and still have us buffaloed, that's how surprised we are. Where did he come from, how did he get here? Worn stubbled faces are turning toward me to see what the sheriff will do. What I am trying to do is to think clearly.

Teet makes a half move toward the door. When Watson turns, Teet freezes like a dog on point, and his tin cup clatters to the floor. A voice whines "Jesus!"

Watson removes his hat and sets it on a peg. Keeping his hands loose at his sides, he spreads his feet a little. He is wearing a soiled white shirt missing the collar, and a frayed Sunday frock coat over rough pants. On his face the friendliness subsides like a wash of tide sucked down into the sand.

"I didn't do it, boys. Let's get that straight."

The room is silent. Sawyer says, "Ed? Ain't no one *says* you done it, Ed."

Watson nods sourly, as if Sawyer's plea only confirmed his poor opinion of the man. Watson says, "What brings *you* out in such weather, Sheriff?"

I tip my hat. I could try an arrest with all these Marco men behind me, but if I do, Watson will resist, and somebody will get hurt, most likely me.

"Heard you was looking for me, Mister Watson."

"That depends. Maybe we better discuss it, Sheriff, see who's looking for who."

I get up slowly, taking a deep breath to calm myself. Here is the meeting that I'd always wanted, and my stomach rumbles as my guts go loose, and my voice is reedy, saying, "You fellers stay here."

361

"Nobody's going no place," says Bill Collier, braiding line.

When Watson holds the door open, I don't want to turn my back. However, I walk straight on out. The door bangs behind me, cutting off the light.

In the wind and darkness his gun barrel prods me and he takes my gun.

"Someone set you on shore someplace? You walked here?"

"Know Caxambas? South end of the island!" He prods me toward the dock.

Black ragged clouds race across the moon, which casts dim light on the white sand. Already we have left the glow from the store lantern. With the open hole of the gun barrel behind me, my back feels naked.

At the dock where the *Falcon* is tied up, I turn my head, keeping my hands out to the side. I cannot make out the face under the hat, only the barrel-chested silhouette and the small feet.

"After you, Frank," E. J. Watson says politely.

At the schooner's mess table, we are face to face, by lantern light. Watson leans back into the corner of the bulkhead where he cannot be seen from outside the cabin window. I say, "You'd be safer in jail." I am not calm yet.

"Ever hear Ted Smallwood's story about Lemon City? The mob goes right into the jail to get this feller, shoots the nigger jailer, too, while they are at it."

"They won't lynch you in Fort Myers."

"No? How about a legal lynching like that stranger got, a couple of years ago, for self-defense against some local meanmouth who picked a fight with him? That feller was as good as lynched, my Carrie tells me, not because he deserved to die but because that's what the local people howled for. And nobody had to dirty their hands excepting you." He puts his watch back, then waves his hand to quiet me, as if reminded by the hard night wind that the world

362

is closing in on him too fast. "I know, I know, the law's the law, it was your duty."

"You knew that feller?"

"Nobody knew him. That's why he was hung."

After six months in jail, that prisoner still wore his hat, as if certain he would go free at any moment. I invited him out of his cell to eat a dignified last supper on my desk. He took his hat off. The drifter – Edwards was his name – was almost bald under his hat, skin white and raw. He looked up grizzle-chinned from his tin plate when he was finished. "Sheriff," he said, "I never picked that scrape, it was him or me. And if it was me, that feller would be free today, you know that just as good as I do." He wiped his mouth. "You got a planter down here name of Watson, escaped the noose up where I come from on account of his daughter married the bank president, that's what I hear. But I'm a stranger with no money, so I'll pay with my life tomorrow morning."

The man stepped over to the sink and scraped his plate. "Justice," he said.

"No need to wash up," I said.

Stolid, the man washed the plate. "What kind of justice you call that?" he insisted.

Unable to answer, I shrugged as if to say, The law's the law. He said it to me, bitterly, "The law's the law." Then he said, "I've had enough of people, you know that? Enough of you and especially of me. First time in my whole damn life I ever thought I had enough of anything." He set down his dried plate carefully, with its knife and fork, then put his hat back on. "Thanks for the feed," he said. He walked back into his cell and shut the door.

The man lay on the bench knees way up high and to the wall, awaiting daylight still and mute as if waiting to be born. Seeing the sad round holes in the cracked boot soles, I was surprised by a wave of sorrow that this drifter's road was coming to an end. I longed to go in there, touch his shoulder, but could see there was nothing of comfort to be said, so I locked him in.

"Don't stare," he said in a muffled voice. "It ain't polite."

At daylight the preacher came, fearing his duty, and the man refused him. "Brother, your God and J. P. Edwards has parted company for good." He wet his pants before the public hanging in the yard. Who knows if God watched over him or not.

Watson has been ranting, his words hang in the air. *So don't try telling me they won't hang Ed Watson high, first chance they get, because you don't know any such thing!*

In the echo, he hauls a small flask from his pocket. "Island Pride?"

The white lightning surprises me. I shiver like a horse. "Whoo, boy," I say, eyes watering.

"Ed Watson's syrup turned a little hard, that what you're thinking?"

I nod, in a warm flush, trying not to smile. "I saw an article in August, out of Kansas City, says Ed Watson was hung in Arkansas back in the nineties. Any truth to that?"

"Get downwind of me these days and you'll sure think so. They don't give us wanted men much time to dab under the arms." He refills my cup. "I'm not the wanted man you want," he says.

"Where do I find him?"

"Deputize me. We'll go get him."

"He's still there?"

"No way to get off. My launch is at Chokoloskee, and the nigger took the skiff, and this John Smith is dead scared of the water. Don't know enough to run that schooner by himself, even if she's still afloat after the storm. And he won't have the first idea of the bad trouble he is in, so I can come right up on him, he won't suspect me."

"He won't suspect you."

"He doesn't know that anything went wrong."

"Something went wrong, then."

Watson's eyes go flat, to measure me. The pause before he answers is one breath too long.

"If you were this man Smith, and you found out that the one witness to your crimes got away to Pavilion Key and told a story, I reckon you might conclude something went wrong." Grimly he considers me. "Am I a suspect, then? I wasn't there."

"Your nigger says you were behind it."

Under the black hat, the eyes go oddly pale as if the blue was fading back into the white. A wolf or a treed cat would show more agitation than this man is showing, an ear twitch, a shifting in the eyes, a little curl along the gums. What I see instead is the stiff muzzle, the bald unblinking eyes, of a turned bear, a transfixed visage like a block of hairy wood – like an ancient spirit mask of the Calusas, drained of all expression. I feel faint. "That was his first story." My voice sounds far away but oddly calm. "When he was warned he'd have to face you with that charge, he took it back, blamed the killings on your foreman."

The life returns to Watson's face, the blue eyes soften. "John Smith," he murmurs.

"How come you don't use Cox's name?"

Watson refuses to show surprise. "Because *he* don't, I imagine."

"What was Cox's motive, Mister Watson?"

"Cox don't need a motive. Not to kill."

"You knew that, but you kept him there with your wife and children?"

"Needs a motive to work, maybe, but not to kill." When I don't smile, he says, "The family mostly stayed in Choko-loskee. Also, I owed Les a favor."

"You owed Les a favor," I repeated. "Want to tell me about that?"

"Nosir I don't!" Watson drinks and gasps and frowns hard at his flask, to clear his flash of anger. "Looks like some dumb sonofabitch distilled my syrup."

"Why did you come hunting me if you won't talk straight?"

His eyes go flat again, and I say in a more careful tone, "You warned me twice not to try any arrest. That's resisting arrest. So is pointing a gun at the Lee County sheriff. You want my help, you better stop breaking the law." I am talking much too much, and cannot stop. "Next time I get the drop on you, I'll take you in."

"You threatening Carrie Langford's dad?" Watson nods a little. "No sense us two quarreling, Frank." Then he says tiredly, "You get the drop on me, you'd better shoot, cause you're not taking me in." He shakes his head. "No threat intended, Sheriff, I am just informing you."

"Let's start again. Who's Leslie Cox?"

"*Shit!*" Watson snarls, as if I am just wasting his good time. He bangs his palm down on the mess table. "I went to Fort Myers in a damn hurricane to report a dreadful crime, tell my side of the story, before someone gets a rope around my neck! You think I don't know my reputation? If I was guilty, would I go chasing the sheriff?"

"Lee County sheriff. The murders took place in Monroe." I pause. "You're gambling you'll get better treatment in Fort Myers." I pause again. "You think maybe your daughter's friends will help you."

"Am I wrong?" Watson sticks the flask out. I shake my head. "Why don't I run? Is that it? Well, I thought about it. Could have kept right on going when I hit Fort Myers, took the railroad to New York." He drinks. "Well, I got sick of running. I decided to stand up to my own life."

We sit silent for a time, listening to the schooner creak against the pilings, the dying wind still wandering the rigging. Over by the store, metal is banging, in the star wind sucked down from the north in the storm's wake.

"Look. I want someone to hear my side, that's all. Just hear my side. Then you make up your own mind, all right?" He cocks his head, squinting at me over his glass. "I never told Cox to kill those people. You ask about Cox's motive

366

– how about mine? I have the best plantation in the Islands, the best house. Every kitchen from Tampa to Key West uses my syrup. I have grown children and two grand-daughters you've seen yourself, there in Fort Myers. I have a young wife and three pretty little kids. I have a good strong land claim pending, and a plan to develop this whole coast! And I have the goodwill of the governor's office. Why would I invite more trouble? And for *what*? Hell, I knew Broward at Key West way back in the days he was running guns to Cuba on the *Three Brothers*."

The ship lifts and bangs.

"Governor Broward died. Two weeks ago."

Watson shrugs. "You know John Roach? Bought Deep Lake with my son-in-law for growing citrus? Those two are counting on a new cross-Florida road to get their produce out, but the way the politicians work, that could take years. They're growing citrus, all right, but it's rotting." Watson leans forward. "Henry Ford came to Fort Myers a few years ago to visit Edison, and those boys met him. I said to Roach, How about you lay twelve miles of small-gauge rail from Deep Lake down to Everglade, use a Ford motor on a freight car, take that citrus out by sea, Key West or Tampa?"

Watson sits back, expansive, blue eyes bright. "John Roach was tickled pink. Those men have as much as told me that if I can stay out of trouble a few years, I'll take over at Deep Lake as manager, because Deep Lake has problems and I have ideas. Even Cole admits Ed Watson has a head for business. And now that Broward got those canals started, it's going to be just one big farm out there, right across the state. That's *progress*! And I am to be in on it!"

I keep my face closed, not knowing what to say.

"A man who can prosper on forty acres of hard shell mound way down there to hell and gone in the damn mangrove – what do you think that man could do with three hundred acres of black loam at Deep Lake?" Watson drinks again. "*That* was the question Roach asked Langford!" He clears his throat, then speaks more quietly. "Think I don't want Carrie proud instead of always nervous and ashamed?"

I feel tired of Watson, why is that? And tired of Frank Tippins, come to think of it. With Watson's references to Carrie, a kind of dog-eared sadness has come over me, I feel indifferent. My two boys bring more headaches than pleasure, much like the former Fannie Yates of Georgia, their dear mother.

"If I was the killer some folks say, do you think my own people, who know me best, would still be loyal? Does that make sense? The only man against me is Jim Cole, and Cole himself is the biggest crook in your damned county. Backs temperance laws to raise his bootleg liquor prices, uses the law to break the law, that's what it is!"

"That is a serious accusation – "

"And that's bullshit! You can't catch him, or you *won't* catch him is more like it. You are in his debt, the same as I am, but you don't like that big-mouth bastard either. Buys and sells but don't produce a thing. Bought the Royal Palm Hotel, had it sold again within the year. Bought the first home automobile, too, that damn red Reo he ran up and down the streets last year, scaring the horses. He's sold her off already, got a Cadillac."

"Weren't for Cole, you might been strung up two years back, from what I hear."

Watson has a fit of coughing. "Rigged the Madison County jury, that what you heard? Well, he did his part. Spared the Langfords a scandal, and he'll get himself well paid, you wait and see." He nods drunkenly. "You'll have to pay him, too, one of these days." He cocks his head. "Deep Lake? County road-gang labor fees?" He shrugs. "Don't know what I'm talking about, Sheriff?"

Sending county road-gang labor to Deep Lake to help Walt Langford – that was Jim Cole's sneaky suggestion, but the original idea, Cole told me once, came from this man here.

"Your idea, right?" I shrug.

"Look," he says, "I have great plans, I'm not waiting for Deep Lake. Know what these plans for Everglades drainage mean? Progress up and down this coast! That's going to happen in our lifetime!"

At the stubborn hope in him my spirit sinks.

"Not in Ed Watson's lifetime – that what you're thinking?"

The wind carries sand from the bare yard against the window.

"Why would I *want* those people dead? Hell, they were friends of mine! Miss Hannah? Green? Some days I even liked young Dutchy!" His voice is rising. "Think I don't know the rumors going around? *Sure*, I'm in debt! Those lawyers ruined me. But a few pay days saved – *that's* not going to help!"

I wait.

"Look, I'm a *businessman*! I keep my credit up! Ask Ted Smallwood, ask C. G. McKinney. I've had no trouble since I came back to the Islands! My wife warned me I shouldn't let Cox stay, but I owed him something, that's what it was, a man has to repay an obligation. 'Honor is the highest good' – ever heard that? Plato said that. Never read Plato?" When I shake my head, Watson shakes his, too. "Well, I paid Cox back that obligation, and he'll pay me this one. If you deputize me."

"Deputize a man pointing a gun at me?"

Watson opens his hand, lets my cartridge roll across the table, then returns my revolver, barrel first. "Take it," he says. When I take the barrel, which is pointed at my chest, he grips it, holding my eye before releasing it. "Don't load up," he says.

Putting the gun away, I lay both hands flat on the table in sign that our talk is over, but he raises his hand abruptly when I start to rise.

369

"All I want – "

"If Cox is taken alive, then it's your word against his, and due to your past reputation, his word might get you hung even if you're innocent. So either you kill him or you make sure he escapes." I'm feeling out of breath. "You want to go down there and kill Cox, because killing Cox would destroy a witness, maybe tend to show Ed Watson's heart is on the side of justice. And you want the sheriff alongside of you, to make it legal."

Watson nods. "That what you think?" Slowly he takes up his own gun and looks it over. "Man that cold-blooded, now, no telling – "

"I don't know what I think." Seeing his face, I am so scared I have to piss, I don't want to hear the end of Watson's sentence. Where's Bill Collier? All those men? Why don't they come?

Later I wonder why I got so scared, and why, so suddenly, my chest has eased and I grow calm enough to say, "You're a suspect, Mister Watson. I can't throw in with you, and I wouldn't do it if I could." I take a breath. "As far as Lee County is concerned, you are under arrest." When Watson says nothing, inspecting the gun, I rise carefully to my feet. "You have a clean record in Lee County – "

"Oh, shut up!" He lurches to his feet, waving me at pistol point into the night. He totters and stumbles, heaving around to close the cabin door, turning his back to me. He doesn't hurry, that is his contempt. He knows I won't jump him from behind, and shout for help. He knows I won't try an arrest, though whether out of fear or pity, he will never know, and I won't either.

To his back, I say, "I'm heading to Fort Myers, meet the Monroe sheriff. If you kill Cox or take him off the place before we get to Chatham Bend, you will be prosecuted to the full extent of the law."

Watson considers me, but already his mind is someplace else. With me in Fort Myers, he will have three days head start.

"Just you trot over to that store," he says, "and don't look back."

Crossing the sand to Collier's store, I duck out of the light. Under the eaves, in a stew of bad emotions, I piss my tension and relief into the dark, nagged hard by the night wind, the heavy wash of seas in the night channel. When I get my breath, I fish out my cartridges, reload my gun.

BILL HOUSE

Ed Watson's house at Chatham Bend was strong constructed, probably the only building south of Chokoloskee that come through that hurricane of 1910 all in one piece. It sits on a mound as high above the water as any place down in them rivers, probably as safe a place as you could find. So you have to ask why, a few days before the hurricane, Watson took his family up to Chokoloskee, taking Dutchy with him, then went on back to Chatham Bend, unless he had an idea what might happen down there and wanted his people out of the way. Could be he wanted Dutchy out of the way, too, let "John Smith" do his dirty work in peace. By now it was known on Chokoloskee that John Smith's rightful name was Leslie Cox.

Watson said he moved his family back to Chokoloskee because if their cistern flooded out in hurricane, they wouldn't have no clean water for the baby. He told Ted Smallwood that him and Dutchy was going back for the people still at Chatham Bend – Cox, old Waller, Hannah Smith, the nigra, and a Injun girl we never knowed about till later. Errand of mercy, that's what Ed Watson called.

When he come back, he come alone, the day before the storm. Said he'd dropped Dutchy at the landing, told him get everything tied down for storm, get everybody set to go. After that, he said, he went on down to South Lost Man's, stopped in there to see if Henry Thompson and his people was all right. On the way back north, he swung in to the dock and hailed the house, but the place was dead silent, he couldn't raise a soul. Something didn't feel right to him, but he figured his people had already been picked

372

up by passing fishermen. He came on up to Chokoloskee and was there late Sunday when Claude Storter come in with the news from Pavilion Key. But when Hamiltons showed up after the storm, they said he showed up at Lost Man's on a Friday, and he never got to Chokoloskee until Sunday morning. Where in the hell did he go in between? And what was Cox up to all them ten damn days between the murders and October 21st, when Watson went down hunting him into the rivers?

Could be Cox was laying for Dutchy when he got dropped off, that's what Watson said – and that's about the *only* thing he said that fitted with his nigra's story. What we don't know is whether Watson was behind it. I think he was, and my dad thought so, too. I think he knowed about them bodies in the river when he went down to Lost Man's to see Hamiltons, or be seen by 'em.

When Claude Storter brought word back to the Bay about cold-blooded murders at the Bend, Watson got terrible excited and upset, and some of 'em, like Ted, that wanted to believe in Watson seen his upset as a proof he was not guilty. Well, he *was* upset, that was sincere, cause he'd just found out how the nigra took the story to Pavilion Key, he'd just found out how Hannah Smith had rose out of the river, pointing her big toe right at his door! His partner had made a mess of it is what he just found out, and he shook his fist and swore to Christ that Leslie Cox would be brought to justice or his name was not Edgar J. Watson. Never saw a man so sincere in all your life.

Sure enough, all people could talk about was Watson's foreman. And seeing how dead scared they was of that murdering stranger, Watson decided he would change his story. Before he left, he allowed as how that Dade County pine in his strong house would stand up to any kind of storm, and his cistern, too. Confided to Ted how he'd brought his wife and children to Chokoloskee not on account of no old hurricane but because this murderer was out to kill him and his whole damn family. Why he had aimed to rescue such a feller when he went back to he Bend on his errand of mercy he forgot to say. And all his time he called Cox "Smith," like he was still concealing his identity, which made me suspicious at that time and does today.

Watson departed quick as he could, caught the high tide and crossed over to Everglade that evening. Stayed with his good friend R.B. Storter and persuaded Bembery and his boy Claude to take him north. From Caxambas, he walked across to Marco, and someone took him on to Wiggins Pass, where Naples is today. He borrowed a horse, took the sand track through the woods to Bonita Springs – called Surveyor's Creek or Survey back in them days. That's where he was on Monday night when the full force of the hurricane struck in, ninety miles and better, blew trees down right through daybreak Tuesday, blew down my father-in-law's house, blew down our old packing shed up Turner River. Come morning, with the wind still rough, Watson went up inside the coast to Punta Rassa. Caught a boat upriver to Fort Myers, found Frank Tippins gone, caught up with him next day at Marco. It was the day after that – this was a Thursday – that he come through Chokoloskee, bound for the Bend.

By now our people was dead scared of Watson, knowing it might been him ordered the murders. The way we tell it in our family, some men collected and my dad told Watson that he'd better wait there for the sheriff. So Watson declared he had waited long enough, cause Cox was going to escape unless these fellers stood aside and let him go. We noticed he weren't calling him John Smith no more. Declared he didn't need no help from no lily-livered lawman to take care of a skunk like Leslie Cox, that it was his bounden duty to them poor friends and neighbors that perished on his property to go down there before Cox could sneak away and straighten out that blood-splattered sonofabitch and once and for all.

To prove how sincere he was, Watson said he would

leave his wife and children hostage in his neighbors' care: 'The Devil take E. J. Watson, boys, if he don't return in two days' time with Cox's head!' He made that promise to kill Cox right out plain in front of everybody.

People were more scared of Cox than they was of Watson, and he made the most of it. A murdering family man was one thing, but they didn't want no murdering stranger on the loose. They told one another that if Ed did not kill Cox, Cox would kill Ed, and either way they had seen the last of both of 'em.

Well, by God, his neighbors cheered him, and they cheered again when he bought some buckshot loads at Smallwood's store for that old double-barrel. My dad and them never realized till he bought them shells that his damn shotgun were not loaded while he was persuading them to let him go. Dad still wanted to arrest him, but none of them others had the stomach for it. If I had been there to back my father like I ought to been – that's what Dad told me – we would of put a stop to him right there.

Well, I said, somebody would been put a stop to, that's for damn sure, and it might been you!

Oh, D. D. House was hopping mad. Said them damn fool men he was ashamed to call his neighbors had been "bamboozled" by Ed Watson, or maybe "hornswoggled" is what he said. Rest of his life, my dad blamed me for staying at House Hammock to clean up after the storm, the way he told me to.

So that first gang formed up to arrest Ed Watson watched him wave his hat at them as he went free. Only one feller waved back, and that was my brother-in-law, Ted Smallwood.

Truth was, our men were just ordinary fellers that didn't care to come up against no desperader, they was grateful to be buffaloed out of a showdown if Watson would just go and keep on going. So Watson talked his way into the clear again, just like he done so many time before. That feller was a borned politician, probably could of got hisself elected president.

Soon as the man was out of sight, they started in about how they would have grabbed him but for this and that. Very sheepish and disgruntled bunch of men, my daddy told me, like he himself wasn't never nowhere near it. Already they were muttering about how sick they was of fooling with Ed Watson, and how they aimed to take care of that there outlaw the very next time he made him a false move.

Pretty quick some started saying. Maybe Watson went down there to help Cox make his getaway. When two days went by and he never come back, the story spread that he'd carried Cox around to the Key West railroad, which laid rail down the east coast that year as far south as Long Key. And that was fine, so long as Watson dusted out at the same time. Nobody said that right out loud, only the women, but that's what everybody hoped, that's how fearful Chokoloskee was of both them outlaws. It wasn't justice they was after but a good night's sleep.

MAMIE SMALLWOOD

Grandma House declared how meet and fit that Mister Watson should vanish in great storm, like the demon she herself had always said he was. And we thought we seen the last of him when he went north the day before the hurricane, cause he surely had his chance there to go free. But Mister Watson wasn't done with us, not by a long shot. Came back through from Fort Myers on the twenty-first, brought his launch across from Everglade, saw to his family. He was so red-eyed with hard travel, day and night, that he laid down on our counter while he talked, keeping a sharp eye on the door. He told us Sheriff Tippins got as far as Marco, then turned tail and head back up to Fort Myers, awaiting reinforcements from Monroe County. The sheriff would not deputize Mister Watson, so Mister Watson deputized himself. He was on his way to Chatham Bend to "apprehend that scoundrel" while the apprehending was good.

Mister Watson had stopped off at the store to pick up some shells for that old double-barrel, but shells was paper-wrapped in them days, and all we had was swollened storm-swept shells. I said, These ain't the shells you want when you go *man*hunting! Because I wanted him to kill this Cox, shoot him down same as a panther or a wolf. Everyone did. And he give me his little wink and said, Well, now, Miss Mamie, if these shells are the best you've got, they will do me fine.

The House family was back on Chokoloskee, also Lovie Lopez and her boys, and Tant Jenkins, Henry Smith, from Pavilion Key. A lot of folks from Lost Man's straggled in

377

after the hurricane – Thompsons, James Hamiltons, young Andrew Wiggins. None of them families ever went back south, the storm left 'em nothing to go back to.

Daddy House and Charley Johnson, a few others, came down to where our landing used to be. They had a plan to arrest Ed Watson, though they never let on about that plan till he was gone. Mister Watson had his double-barrel out where they could see it, he had come too far to tolerate no interference, and nobody wanted to stand in his way, cause he looked half-crazy with exhaustion. His eyes were dull and teeth gone yellow, and that lively chestnut hair of his all dank and dead.

He said, "I will be back," as if to challenge anyone might try to stop him, and Daddy House, who had some dander, said, "If you are aiming to come back, you better bring Cox with you." Mister Watson said, "Is that a warning, Mr House?" And D. D. House said, "You could take it that way, Mister Watson.'

Mister Watson didn't like that, not one bit. He said, "Dead or alive?" and D. D. House said, "Dead is good enough."

Mister Watson pushed off in his boat. He said, "If I don't bring him, I will bring his head," and cranked the motor.

He went away without a word, pot-pot-potting down the Bay toward Rabbit Key Pass. For the second time that week we told each other that if that feller had one bit of sense, we'd seen the last of him. But Mister Watson, as Ted said, never did learn where to draw the line, he weren't that kind. Maybe we were finished with him, but he weren't finished with us, not with his family here.

Mister Watson weren't hardly out of sight when his poor wife felt a shift toward her on our island. Folks closed her off, wouldn't look her in the eye. They walked around her, moved out of her way. It got so bad she wouldn't let her kids out of her sight, for fear that one of 'em might come up missing.

The silence that followed that poor body all around our

ruined island weren't nothing but pure fear and hate – fear of her husband and his murdering henchman, and hate toward this fool north-country girl who must of known what kind of bloody man fathered her children – that's what the women muttered – and more fear yet because her being in our midst with his fire-headed little demons might be enough to draw that devil back. And the people who was coldest of them all, she told me later, was the ones invited her into the house where she was staying.

BILL HOUSE

Our house was just east of Smallwood's store. We were still patching up after the storm when we heard that *pop-pop-pop* down to south'ard. Pap sighed and stood up straight and listened. Then he put his ax down, very careful – "Boys, that's him."

Pap and me and Dan and Lloyd picked up our rifles and went on down to Smallwood's landing, Henry Short a little piece behind. Long ago Pap give Henry his old gun, but I was surprised that he brought it along. Nobody told him he should come, and nobody told him he should go away. Never said a word to nobody, just set himself off in the trees. I never did learn what was in his head, we never talked about it even once, but Henry Short were not a careless man. He knew his place and always did, and I guess he figured his place was there with us.

My father-in-law, Jim Howell, and Andrew Wiggins, who married Jim's daughter Addie – they were with us. Close to twenty, give or take a few, was in the crowd, most all the men on Chokoloskee Island. Some carried guns so's they wouldn't be thought less of by their neighbors, but even the few present who meant business were dead scared. The sheriff hadn't showed up, so our idea was, we would try to arrest him by ourselves, hope for the best. Others, I ain't saying who, was declaring for the past three days that if Watson showed up again before the sheriff did, they was for shooting him straight off, no questions asked, that's how bad they wanted the suspense over and done with. Better to finish him once and for all, they said, cause with all his son-in-law's powerful friends, and nothing against him but a nigger's word, he was certain to wriggle loose again same way he done so many times before.

Them fellers claimed to be worried sick about miscarriage of justice. But I believe they was worried a lot more than ol' Ed Watson, left alive, would come settle up his business quick with anyone he thought had turned against him. That was a feller kept his accounts straight, like Ted said. Eye for an eye, that were Watson's motto, if he had one.

Pap said, "He won't murder twenty men." And that bunch never would of bushwacked him, not with D. D. House dead set against it, and his three sons, too. But later on, the story was put out how the House clan wanted that man killed no matter what, because Emperor Watson with his 150-gallon boilers, all his up-to-date equipment, was aiming to take over our cane syrup business at House Hammock, drive us out.

Ted Smallwood came out from beneath his house but would not join the posse. Said this trouble hadn't one damn thing to do with him. Said Ed Watson was his best customer, all paid up and fair and square, and he had nothing against Watson, never did. Said he had nothing against us other fellers, neither. Said anyway he was down with his malaria, though I noticed he felt strong enough to crawl in under his house after them drowned leghorns.

Ted said too damn much altogether. The more he talked, the harder it was to tell what the heck he wanted.

Later people got the idea, mostly from Mamie, that her husband was the only one kept out of it. He wasn't. Some came unarmed because they passed for Watson's friends, and that includes the men from Lost Man's River, but they came anyway, and never said a word. I believe they were as anxious as the rest to see this finished.

The hurricane had took away Ted's dock, so Old Man Watson run the *Brave* up on the beach. It was near dusk. He must of seen that body of armed men when he was still

381

a hundred yards offshore, he must of known this was going to be a showdown he might not survive. Why did he keep coming, then? – that's what plagues me. He never hesitated, he never shied, just cut the motor and let her stern wave ride her in, west of the boat way.

Coming ashore hard and quick as that, he took the whole bunch by surprise. Mister Watson's eyes were opened up real wide and kind of comical, like he never noticed all them neighbors until now. He waved and smiled, looking pleased to see such a fine welcome, never mind all the shifting eyes and scowls and shooting irons. He looked eager for us to let him in on our big joke, let him know what we all had in mind.

Some will tell you today he never left his boat, but it ain't true. Hadn't hardly waved when he jumped ashore, and was already set when he hit the ground, his shotgun down along his leg on the left-hand side. He must have known the risk of that bold move, he could of got himself shot to pieces out of pure buck fever. But he knew his neighbors, knew the most of 'em lacked his experience at pointing loaded guns at men, never mind the will to pull the trigger. There we was standing in a herd feeling more and more stupid, like all the grown men on Chokoloskee had come out here of an evening to have 'em a miskeeter shoot or something.

That innocent grin, that twinkle, took the last fight out of the men that wasn't scared half sick to death already. They seen that shotgun down along his leg and knew how fast we could be looking down them two black holes.

"Well!" he said, with a big smile around. "And where are Mrs Watson and the children?" This was his way of reminding us he was a family man and neighbor. Ed Watson knew from start to finish just what he was doing, he had bluffed us twice in the last fortnight and had no doubt he would bluff us this time, too. But just to make sure, he slid his pistol hand not so casual into his pocket, and there come a kind of shiver from the crowd.

Daniel David House was closest man to Watson. I was alongside Pap on his right hand, young Dan and Lloyd were on his left, and all the rest were kind of bunched on that left side.

When Watson jumped ashore with his old shotgun, Henry Short must of crossed behind the crowd, because very quick he was right there beside me. Couldn't see around me, so he waded out a little. He was near up to his knees in water, and he had his Winchester down along his leg on the right side. I thought, That nigra's getting set to rust up Dad's old rifle in salt water. But Henry Short made no mistakes like that, he always was a man who paid attention, and his rifle was kept cleaned and oiled, as good as new. With his elbow hitched for a quick swing, his bead must of been a foot above the surface.

Ed Watson, he saw Henry, too. He raised his eyebrows, drew his head back on his neck as if asking that nigra to explain himself. Henry had worked for him one time, and those two got on pretty good, but Watson didn't care to see him with no rifle. The anger flickered all over his face, quick as heat lightning.

Slowly Henry lifted his left hand, took his straw hat off, put it on again. "Evenin, Mist' Ed" is what he murmured, but I don't think nobody heard it cepting me. And Watson gave a kind of little nod, said something quiet that I didn't catch because skeeters was getting to Pap bad, and Pap was slapping. Us other men was getting bad bit, too, and didn't even notice, that's how stiff we was.

Pap was always in a hurry, never liked to wait. Pap said, "Well now, Mister Watson. Where is Cox?"

Watson said, Boys, here was the story, and he sure was sorry. Said he'd shot Cox through the head when Cox came down to the boat, but damned if he didn't roll right off the dock. Dragged for two days, high tide and low, and never come up with the body, not in that terrible high water pouring down out of the Glades after the hurricane. Nosir, boys, the best he could come up with was his hat. And he grinned a hard grin and dragged a old felt hat out of his coat.

Holding out that old hat with the hole in it, as if that proved something – that was an insult, and Watson knew that was an insult. He poked a finger through the bullet hole and beckoned, like he was trying to distract small kids or idiots. He was rubbing our nose in that fool hat, defying us to do something about it.

Maybe it was Lloyd House whispered, "Cox didn't ever *wear* no hat. I *seen* him."

Mister Watson waited us out, looking polite. Looked like he enjoyed the little wind and water wash along the landing that was rasping our nerves worser than a skeeter whine. Probably figured time was on his side. He was still offering that hat, and meanwhile he looked from face to face, watching 'em flinch when he brought his hand out of his coat to slap a skeeter. Didn't slap it exactly, just reached up slow and pinched it, then looked at the blood between his thumb and finger and opened his eyes wide with that look of his that was almost comical but not quite.

Nothing was said. Somebody broke wind, nobody laughed. The slapping was well started now, it was getting to that fiercest time of evening. Probably them swamp angels plagued me, too, but I was too tense to pay 'em any mind. On that dark evening, the only man who appeared easy – only man "look like he leev in his own skeen," as the old Frenchman used to say – was E. J. Watson.

Afterwards, when my heart eased, I heard that breeze that racketed the battered palms, and the *Brave's* wake still coming in and coming in across the bay, still curling and whispering along the shore – all them soft sounds of wind and water that nag me every year, first time I see that old October twilight.

Finally my pap shook his head and said to me, not loud, not soft, "Hell, that's not good enough." Watson heard that, cause Pap meant it to be heard.

"Mr House? Your questioning my honor?"

"That hat's not good enough, is all."

"Good enough for what?" Ed Watson said. His voice was calm, too, and very, very cold.

Seeing Watson so cocksure as that, Isaac Yeomans coughs and spits, maybe more loud and disgusted than we might have wanted. Isaac pointed at the hat. He growled, "That hole were never made by that there shotgun."

Watson looked at him a minute. He said, "Well, Isaac, are you calling me a liar?" And Isaac, glancing at the rest of us for some support, said, "I am asking you a question." And Watson nodded, very, very calm. Not that it's anybody's business, he remarked, but it so happened he had put away the shotgun to make sure Cox would let him come in close enough to talk, after which he done the job with his revolver.

So Pap informed him they were sorry but they would have to send some men back to the Bend, see if Cox might of come up and washed ashore. Mister Watson would surely understand why they'd have to hold him till they came up with that body or till the sheriff got there, either one. Said, no hard feelings, but it might be a good idea if Watson was to hand over his shooting irons.

At that, there come a little gasp and shuffle. I didn't have to look across my shoulder to know which ones was getting set to scatter.

Watson said, kind of slow and growly, Nosir, I can't understand any such a thing. Another thing he couldn't figure – and he hitched his gun – was why his neighbors was acting so suspicious. When those murders was done, wasn't he right here with his friends on Chokoloskee? And he smiled a sad and disappointed smile, shaking his head.

Pap pushed right ahead, that was his nature. "We are warning you to lay that gun down, Mister Watson."

Ed Watson gazed over our heads, inland toward the store. His Lost Man's friends were watching from the steps, none said a word. He must of seen they were keeping a good distance, out of shotgun range. Perhaps he saw his wife start down the rise and perhaps not, for his shoulders sagged a little, and again he shook his head.

For just one moment there he looked uncertain, like a dreaming man who has woke in a strange place. I felt bad about him then, or sad – that once I seen him look unsure was the one time I felt sorrowful about Ed Watson. Well, that sad feeling passed quick, I'll tell you that much. There come a eye shift, and he didn't look confused no more, he had that ears-back look, hard and sly and mean. He looked like a man who would take your life away from you and not think twice about it.

Nosir, he could not figure out, he said, why his good friends and neighbors were treating him this way when they knew he'd took no part whatever in them crimes. They knew Les Cox was the guilty man, and Cox was dead.

"Till we make sure of that, you are under arrest," I told him, just so Pap would know he was backed up.

Watson winced. He sucked his teeth and spat, and ground the spit into the ground, hard, with his boot.

"No, I am not under arrest," he said, shifting sideways a little, shifting that gun a little, "because you people don't have no fucking warrant." And he stared up the line and down again, jerking his chin when he came to Henry Short.

Hearing the anger, so sudden and so cold, the line of men went kind of wobbly, and some of 'em, we won't say who, commenced nodding and frowning in a hurry, like there sure was something to what Mister Watson said, like it might be best to run on home and think this through. There come a whispering behind me – *I mean to say, boys, if there ain't no warrant, well, to hell with it, maybe we'd best go home, mind our own business.*

But D. D. House had his dander up, the same as Watson, he had set like glue. People talked later about how our pap took such a fearsome hate for life in his old age, and how a angered-up old feller had nothing much to lose starting a fight that might get younger fellers killed, his boys included. Well, it weren't like that, it weren't that at all.

Daniel David House had to finish what he started, boys or no boys, he didn't really know no other way.

So Pap said, "Mister Watson, lay that gun down." That was meant as a last warning to Ed Watson, but it was also a warning to his boys to start in shooting at the first false move.

Up until now, Watson had played for time, maybe figuring this crowd would lose its nerve. Or he might of suspected that we aimed to kill him whether he gave his weapons up or not. He had to make a very quick decision. Truth was, if he'd surrendered up his guns, only one of his neighbors had the temperament it would of took to shoot him, and that feller was away, down to Honduras.

Knowing how quick Watson was, there is no doubt in my mind he had calculated chances even before Pap asked him for his shooting irons – hell, even before his boat had struck the shore. Probably figured if he made it into court, he'd beat the charge, because only a nigra had him implicated in the murders, and the nigra had backed off his story in front of witnesses. There was no good evidence against Ed Watson, not one bit.

Being so smart, he would also figure that we knew that, and knowing it, might take him out and lynch him, to make sure. After so many close calls in other places – in Oklahoma and Arcadia and Columbia County – he might conclude that his luck had just run out. Those stiff faces must of told him that this time he could not talk his way into the clear, but being so angry, it never occurred to him to give up. He must of seen these men were scared, which made 'em dangerous, but because we were bunched up and stiff, he had the jump on us.

When Pap stepped forward, Watson raised up that big hand, like some kind of old-time prophet in the Bible, and Pap halted.

Later we realized he had stopped us at what was the best range for a double-barrel if you wanted to kill and cripple more than two. Maybe that was not his plan, but that's the way we figured it out afterwards. To back that up, he carried a revolver in his coat, and maybe two. Two charges of buckshot right together would knock down the leaders and scatter the rest, and he might keep 'em ducking with his revolver while he pushed his boat back off the beach, shot his way out of there. At that range, with a panicked crowd, he might have got away with it, because when that anger took him, he moved fast and to the point, before we could take in what was happening – before we got it through our heads that a neighbor we had known near twenty years would shoot into the flock of us, like we was turkeys.

Some tell tourists yet today how they seen a sudden blush on Watson's face and a hard shine of crazy anger in those eyes. There wasn't enough time nor light to see no such a thing. The ones that say they seen that was so scared they couldn't see straight, or more'n likely wasn't there at all. But I'll swear to my death I heard his teeth grit when he swung that shotgun to his hip and snapped both barrels right into our faces.

I thought we was done for, I was curdling up inside myself, trying not to screech when that charge hit me, and I know Pap thought that he was done for, too.

Watson had peeled them wet shells once too often, cause they didn't hold. Hardly a thump in that wet powder, and buckshot came rolling right out the barrels. Pap was facing both them barrels at the time, and he said he seen the muzzles jump, that's how hard Ed Watson yanked on his dead triggers.

Watson was going for his revolver by the time I swung my rifle up and squeezed the trigger.

P-dang – that fateful sound still comes back yet, the first lean crack of rifle fire. Two together. Maybe the first shot was mine, maybe it wasn't. After that the evening broke apart, it was purely uproar.

Watson's legs shuffled him forward a few steps, leaning like a man on deck in a hard storm. But even while he walked, he was falling forward, falling against that roar and wind and fire, painful slow at first, like a felled tree. His coat and shirt jumped, buffeted by lead, the whack of a man's life being knocked out of him. His gun stock splintered, his revolver spun away. I seen his mouth yank, saw red jump out of where his left eye burst, and still he fell.

I reckon Mister Watson died before his shotgun hit the ground, but his legs drove that dead man on, pitching him forward. I believe he was killed by the first bullet but he kept on coming. We all seen it, there ain't one won't say the same. And seeing him come after 'em that way, most of them men yelled and crowded back and kept on backing, even after he was down, flat on his face.

Ethel Boggess used to claim she was right under that big fig down there when Watson fell, and she swore he came eighteen or twenty feet before he struck the ground. With all that lead in him, he would not go down, that's how headstrong that man was even in death – that was the Devil in him, is what my mother said for long years after. Said only a demon could scare folks bad as that after he was dead.

Then the line surged back around us, near to knocked me down. They were still shooting! They were a damn mob now for sure, men hollering and cussing, and young boys running up and down yapping like dogs, and bullets flying. It's a miracle some poor soul wasn't killed.

I never seen a man struck down so hard. He lay face down on the bloody ground, the broad back with no breath to swell it, not a twitch, only stray threads on the holes tore through his coat, the night wind lifting them dark red curls on his creased neck.

Them threads and curls was all that ever stirred. Mister Watson never gave a gargle. I never saw a man so dead in all my life.

HOAD STORTER

In Everglade, the cisterns was four–five feet below the ground, two–three above, and the water generally stayed cool and clear, but after the storm our cisterns was all flooded out with brine and mud, and no fresh water. What we had was a hard drought, more'n a month. Heavens was wrung dry, gray as old rags.

On October 24, late afternoon, my brother Georgie and young Nelson Noble rowed over to Chokoloskee for some drinking water. They was just rounding the point west of Smallwood's store when they heard a bang and racketing of guns, broke out like fire-crackers. It was dark enough by then to see the muzzle fire, which carried on for ten seconds or better. Then silence fell across the island like a blow, and out of that silence – they both tell it – rose the chanting a chuck-will's-widow, so loud and clear they had to wonder if that night bird had been singing all along, and never even slowed to hear the shooting.

Smallwood's dock was washed away, and the *Brave* was run up on the shore, and Mister Watson laying there like he'd fell from Heaven. Cepting two–three sniffing dogs, nobody wanted to go anywheres near him. Our boys stood with their water jugs but kept their distance.

Some of the men there was upset, and some was angry, and some of 'em seemed kind of shocked, wouldn't talk to nobody at all. Other ones could not stop talking – not listening, you know, just talking, the way crazy people like to do – and these ones were swearing how that man there tried to murder the whole crowd, how he kept on coming after he was shot to death three or four times over. And

all this while, over the voices, that night bird never let up
– over and over and over, *wip, wip-WEE-too!*

Georgie and Nelson never got home till close to bedtime.
George told us all he seen and heard, and still we pestered
him with questions, not rightly knowing yet just how we
felt. Mister Watson was well liked in our family, came
for dinner every Tuesday noon and never arrived without
something to offer, even if it was only jokes or news. "I
ain't going to speak agin Ed Watson," our dad said. "We
was in friendship, and he helped me where he could and
never harmed me." All the same, Dad seemed relieved,
he couldn't hide it.

Watson claimed he had killed Cox, and Old Man D. D.
House told Watson they would have to go to Chatham
Bend, see for themselves, and said he'd better turn over
his gun. Watson said Nosir, he sure wouldn't, being as how
that bunch was there to lynch him. He swung his shotgun
up, pointed it at Old Man House, and pulled the trigger,
but it never fired – that's the story was told by them that
done the talking. But something was wrong about the story
no matter how often Georgie told it, and to this day we
never figured what it was.

Dad said, "Well, now, if that shotgun never fired, how
come they're so sure he pulled the trigger?"

"Seen his gun yank when he hauled on it," Georgie
explained.

"They tell you that, boy? Or is that what you imagine?"
We were all upset.

"You sound like you doubt your son's word," my mother
said.

"It ain't his word I doubt," he said. "But I doubt *some-thing.*"

Some men come out with it in later years, said folks had
enough of Mister Watson, said the execution had been
planned, though not all knew it. Others claimed that was
the first *they* heard about it, said if they'd of known, they

391

wouldn't of took part. So the Bay people was already split up over Ed Watson.

Dad said, "Only thing that ain't in doubt, they killed him."

Harry McGill, who later married my sister Maggie Eva, he was among them men who fired. So was Charley Johnson. Old Man Dan House, Bill House, young Dan and Lloyd – them four never denied that they took part. I don't know who else for sure, cause too many of 'em changed their stories, but I heard it was men from almost all ten Chokoloskee families, along with a few fishermen on the way through. Isaac Yeomans, Andrew Wiggins, Saint Demere, Henry Smith – all them fellers might been in on it. They was at least twenty there with guns.

Nelson Noble's daughter Edith, married Sammie Hamilton, she always said her dad was in on it, but he sure wasn't. He was coming around the point with my young brother, like I said. They seen the finish. And others that said they was just there to arrest him, not to shoot him, said they never fired – well, they *did*.

A lot of people still ask me about Mister Watson. I don't like to speak about him much. I like to talk about him as a gentleman, because that's the way Storters remember him. I didn't know what was inside of him, I just knew him for a jolly friendly man.

Until all this killing started, Ed Watson was all right, wasn't nobody down on him. My dad always said Ed Watson'd give you his last dollar with his left hand, slit your throat with his right. You hear a lot of people saying that today. I can't recall if anybody said it while Mister Watson was alive, but he already had a reputation at the time I knew him.

Folks just got tired of him, I guess.

BILL HOUSE

My Nettie has read me from a famous Florida book where
the man who fired the first shot at Watson was Luke Short,
a white fisherman. That is dead wrong but about as right
as all the rest. Same writer claimed that the leader of the
posse, C. G. McKinney, got wounded when Watson fired.
Well, Old Man McKinney wasn't leader of the posse, he
wasn't even there, and the only man got wounded on that
day was E. J. Watson.

All them stories in the books and magazines, they never
mention who was on that posse, and that is because nobody
would tell 'em. When strangers came around asking nosy
questions, nobody would talk to 'em at all. Me, I don't
know for a fact who pulled the trigger and who didn't, but
from the look of him when they got done, very few hung
back.

If Watson's gun had not misfired, my daddy would been
deader'n a doornail. Knowing that, he turned his back on
all that racket and just walked away. Some way he had
busted a gallus and was holding up his trousers with an
arm across his belly, walked soft and slow like he had a
gut ache or was carrying new ducklings. I never forgot that
way he walked, I never before seen my pap as an old man.

We followed him, though us boys wanted to stay, being
so bad twisted up over the end of it. Dan was in tears, he
was so mad, and didn't even know what he was mad at.
The men who shot and the men who stood aside, they felt
relief and they felt sick, too, because all of 'em had enjoyed
Ed Watson and didn't have nothing personal against him
– the most of us had known his generosity, one way and

another. We tried to spit it up, over and over. But D. D. House never spoke of it again, and it went bad in him, turned him stiff and sour and old within the year.

When the crowd drifted back into the dark, and the dogs forgot why they was barking, Charlie T. Boggess hobbled down there with a lantern, helped Ted turn him turtle, drag a canvas over him. Smallwood tried to fold the arms across the chest, but ever so slow them arms opened up wide, like the two claws on a crab. Or that's how Charlie Boggess told about it, cause Charlie T., he made up for his short size with his tall stories. He was spooked by them slow-opening arms much worse than by that bloody eye, is what he would tell to visitors in later years, when everyone had forgot the truth, Charlie T. included.

Ted tried to close the blue eye that was left, but he come too late, the dead lid peeled right back off the gory eyeball. So they hunted around amongst the hurricane scraps spread through the bushes, found a boy's flag from the Fourth of July to lay across his face. Might been a sacrilege up North, who is to say. In the South it wasn't fifty years yet since the War Between the States, and D. D. House, who had rode off for a soldier, he never did get used to the Stars and Stripes.

Leaving a body out all night on the cold ground was bothersome. Didn't feel no guilt or nothing, just couldn't sleep with Watson laying down there by the water, so I went and paid my respects under the moon. Ted and Charlie aimed to drag him under cover but they didn't, and I went down with the same plan, didn't touch him neither. There was no place for him, he wasn't even welcome where he was. Dogs or boys had snapped away the tarp and tore that flag off him. I tucked him in again as you might say, then took my hat off and said, Mister Ed, I stand by what was done, but I want to say it sure weren't nothing personal.

One-eyed Ed Watson stared up at the stars, arms wide in welcome. Looked kind of strange with his black hat off, you didn't often catch him out without it. Hadn't been no rain at all, not since the hurricane, and the beard and mouth was caked with dust and blood, like a bear that's snuffled out a gator nest. In the lantern shine, that one bald eye was glaring through the black snakes of dry blood down his forehead. One of them little cowboy boots was shot away, and the other stripped off for a souvenir, and his small feet looked like gray-white dough, with yellow toenails. That broad tooled cowhide belt from the Wild West was missing, and that good black hat from Fort Smith, Arkansas.

Already kids was acting out how Bloody Watson fell, you could hear the yelling *pow-pow-pow-pow* all over the island. Got too excited altogether, it took 'em a good week to calm down – course this was natural, Watson being the first violent death they ever seen. Charlie and Ethel's boy Dinks Boggess, down the street, I believe that Dinks was one them little fellers prowled around that body, and he might could recall which one of 'em got Watson's revolver. More likely Dinks won't talk at all, cause Dinks don't like invaders. Willie Brown's boy Billy, he was there, too, but he's another one don't take too good to questions.

That night it was agreed without no argument that there wouldn't be no burial on Chokoloskee, cause even dead, that man still scared the island. It was voted we would take him out to Rabbit Key. By the time we went to scrape him up, at sunrise, he'd lost his good eye to a crow or gull, or a poked stick.

In the hard daylight you could see how E. J. Watson was pretty well shot to pieces, mostly buckshot but plenty of bullets, too. Them nice clothes was black-caked with blood – Bloody Watson! – a stiff blind carcass in the dirt, shirt ripped, hairy belly-button, black pellets deep under the skin and all them mean red holes like bites, and the flies buzzing. The mouth in them sunburnt dusty whiskers was the worst of it. His front teeth all busted out, lip tore and stretched like he was snarling, but a little twist to his expression like a smile. Seeing that, the men scared themselves all over again, telling how Mister Watson grinned as he kept coming at the crowd through the hail of fire.

Looking around, I seen no sign of Edna Watson. My sister was making sure she didn't see him. "Give us a hand," I told the men, but only Tant stepped forward, who had took no part. Tant was tearful, might of had some drink. He took the ankles. Hoisting him, he give the opinion that dead men are heavy cause their bodies yearn for rest deep in the ground. Well, Tant, I said, he's full of lead, besides.

"It ain't no joking matter, Bill," Tant says, because Tant loved him.

"No, it sure ain't," I said.

A angry moan come from the burial party when we swung that bloody carcass to the gunwale. Wouldn't help hoist him over, lay him in the cockpit, wouldn't even touch him – as if touching him might be bad luck – though I reckon it was more some kind of horror. Some then announced they would not travel with him in the boat, you'd of thought one slow black drop of Watson's blood might could start a plague. We had to hear all this superstitious horseshit while we was still struggling to get him in.

Then the boat rolled and Mister Watson got away from us, slid off the gunwale, flopped into the mud. Now *that* was the real horror, and it made me mad. I hollered out, To hell with it, let's get this done with! I was in outrage and did not know why, but there ain't no doubt I was too rough, and some would bring that up against me long years later as a way to show how Houses had it in for E. J. Watson. I grabbed some line, bound up his arms and run a hitch around his ankles, yanked it up hard like he was some kind of dead gator, then run a bridle off the stern cleats of his boat. Then I cranked his engine and dragged the body off that shore like some old log. That rolled him back over on his belly, and he come along backwards and face down, and the kids darting right into the shallows, kicking and flailing him. I seen Jimmy Thompson, Raleigh Wiggins, Billy Brown, one–two others. It might been Raleigh who was wearing Watson's hat.

"Get away!" My own voice sounded cracked, half kind of crazy. Where in hell were their parents, who claimed to be Watson's friends? How come they let their kids behave like bad-trained dogs? Night before, not one of them so-called friends of his had tried to warn him, wave him off, nor even advise him to put down his gun. Were they that scared to go up against their neighbors? I don't think so, not them Lost Man's fellers. They was always pretty ornery, went their own way.

My opinion, even his friends knew that his time had come, and his reckless behavior makes one wonder if Ed knew it too, though there ain't a soul I know of who agrees with me. Smallwood knew, too, for all his protest. But I will say this for Ted, he didn't watch it. The rest stood in a line there by the store and watched us kill him.

On the way to Rabbit Key, the body caught up on an orster bar, got tore up worse. Them little feet come twisting up out of the water as he rolled. The grisly head was thumping on the bottom, I could feel the thrumming when I took in on the bridle – damn! It turned my guts. Finally we got him in the channel, and he towed all right the whole rest of the way. But that was a very long slow trip, cause a boat motor in them days had more pop than power, and that dead weight down there dragged like a sea anchor. By the time we got to Rabbit Key, the clothes was tore off him and what was left of his face, too. Didn't hardly look like a man, he looked like something from the ocean deep thrown up by storm. He was scraped so raw you could not say what kind of sea monster this might of been.

Same rope was used to haul the body from the shallows to the pit, trussed like a chicken. Them men were still so

397

fevered that they buried him face down. "Give that bloody devil a good look at Hell" is what one said. They dragged two slabs of coral rock right in on top of him, one across the upper legs and the other across the back, to make sure this thing – cause a thing is all he was, with legs and arms bound tight and no damn face on him – make sure this thing would not rise at dusk and come hunting the ones that turned against him. Before throwing the sand back in on top, one of them brave fellers who boasted how he'd emptied his gun into the body – I won't mention his name, him being kin – he rigged a noose around the neck, hitched it up tight, then run the bitter end across to that big old twisty mangrove that stood alone out on the point, the only tree left standing by the storm.

These same brave fellers was the most confused about the killing of their neighbor E. J. Watson, cause he never fit their notion of a bad man – shifty-looking, dirty, don't you know, pocked skin and scars, maybe an ear gone, or one eye. Watson didn't look that way at all. Oh yes, you'd hear 'em talk about "them crazy Watson eyes," and it was true, those soft blue eyes could set real hard, they kind of fixed you. Mostly they was a mild pale blue, as Nettie said, that went good with his ruddy skin and chestnut hair. He was strong and handsome and his clothes was clean, altogether a fine-looking man. Maybe they hated him and feared him, the way they say today, but they esteemed him, too.

His boldness, facing 'em down that way, disturbed 'em bad, but that temper got the better of him, that was the end of him. And now he was all shot to pieces, it was real pathetic. He wasn't "Mister Watson" anymore, and they could take out on this meat lump with no face the anger and despising he had made so hard for 'em while he was still alive – while he was still "made in God's image," like the rest of us.

Wouldn't be surprised it was me started it, the rough way I dragged him off the landing, but I didn't want no part of mutilation. I was relieved that he was dead, but I missed him, too. I run into many a man in life was a lot less likable than E. J. Watson, I'll tell you that much.

Over by the shore, ol' Tant was telling how Mister Watson treated him so good all them long years. When we seen them fellers lead that rope out of the grave, Tant only shrugged, he just stayed out of it, but I went back over to see what was what, and got too hot about it. I told that feller to take that noose off his damn neck right now cause he were as dead as the law allows already.

Man said, Well, ol' Bill thinks hanging is too good for this fine feller, that right, Bill? And another said, Now, Bill, don't you go getting lathered, we just rigged a rope so's them cattle kings can find him, case they send down for the body.

Around the *neck*? I said.

But them others backed the first one, cause they was feeling ugly, they was spoiling for a fight, same way I was. I was so disgusted I just washed my hands of it.

That's how that story started up about crackers who shot Watson to pieces, then hung his neck to a lone tree and piled on coral slabs so big that it took a couple chain-gang niggers to lift them off when his Fort Myers kin sent down for Mister Watson a few days later.

Sheriff Tippins was down from Marco with the Monroe County law when we got back to Smallwood's, long about noon. Bill Collier brought these lawmen on the *Falcon*.

The men told the law how nobody killed Watson, they fired all at the same time in self-defense. "Did he fire at you first?" says Tippins, and the men scratched their heads and looked around to see if anybody could remember. Isaac Yeomans didn't care much for that question. "Nosir," he growled.

"He tried," I said.

Tippins looked me over, that's his habit. Then he mimicked me, kind of ironical, you know – "*He tried.*" And

399

then him and his Monroe County sidekick exchanged a look that was supposed to mean something, except it didn't, cause they didn't know nothing.

Right from the start, Frank Tippins seemed as tangled up about this death as we was, couldn't set still for a minute, he was fuming. Only difference was, he had somebody to take it out on. "Your name's House," he said, like the name had me incriminated right from the start. "You was the ringleader, they tell me."

"We didn't have no ringleader. No leader, neither."

He looks me over again, so does his Monroe sidekick, who's got a cowboy hat on too.

"How come you're so fired up? You ashamed of something?"

"Nosir, I ain't. I ain't got a thing to be ashamed about."

Tippins was trying to make us mad so we'd bust out with something. Mister Watson's death was homicide, he said, and "those responsible" had to go to Fort Myers for a hearing, and any man who did not come of his own free will would go in handcuffs.

Charley Johnson asked the postmaster to come along to testify to our God-fearing characters, Ted being the closest thing we had to a upstanding citizen. Bill Collier said he'd be glad to take Mrs Watson and her family at no extra charge.

After Watson's death, Ted Smallwood had to hold his wife in Chokoloskee. Mamie was scared and she was horrified, she didn't want to live in such a place no more, she wanted to leave the Ten Thousand Islands for good. She knew Ed Watson for what he was and never said no different, but she hated the way them men licked his boots, then turned and shot him down, is the way she said it. My sister took it hard.

Them men weren't bootlickers, not by no means. We were just ordinary peaceful fellers, never knew how to handle this wild hombre till we had him laying face down in the dirt. If ever a man brought it on himself, it was Ed

Watson, but somehow we was getting blamed for doing what the ones who blamed us wanted.

I never cosied up to Ed like some, and I never had no regrets, that day or later. We done what we had to do, and I stand by it. But I will admit I am still ashamed of how the crowd kept shooting after he was dead, as if trying to wipe the memory of him off of their conscience. Some of them men shot and shot until their guns was empty, wasn't one live shell that left that place that day. There was a young boy run in afterwards, shot his .22 into the body. His older brother was standing right there with us and never stopped him.

The boys agreed we would leave Henry Short out of it, we didn't want to cause Henry no trouble, because word had come down from Deep Lake that around Frank Tippins, things went hard with niggers. Never did find out what happened to Watson's colored man who come to Pavilion Key and was handed over to the sheriff at Fort Myers. Can't recall his name if they they ever give him one. They say he was sent to Key West, but there ain't many as believes he ever got to go to his own trial.

One thing I ain't never going to forget. After all that noise, there come this echoing silence, like the Lord was about to send down word from Heaven. There was only the fool chant of a scared bird. Then we heard Edna Watson's high clear voice, *Oh my God, they are killing Mister Watson!* By that time, of course, he was in Hell already.

Mamie stood guard where Watson's little family had sunk down before the store all in a heap. My sister wore a look of last perdition, bored right through me. I knew from my Nettie that our Island ladies had shunned Edna Watson for some days, and I seen at once that the poor woman was plain terrified that this night crowd of armed men that had tasted blood might put to death the victim's wife and little children. I hate to say it, but knowing how feverish some of 'em got, she had good reason.

The ones who was most dangerous in that crowd was the same ones as had looked the other way for years and years, same ones who said Ed Watson never killed a soul down there cept maybe a nigger or two that had it coming. These very same fellers was the ones that eased their nerves by pumping every last bullet that they had into his carcass, the very same ones was so angry he had scared 'em that they had to scare Mrs Watson just as bad, scare her so bad that she grabbed her kids and crawled under the store on hands and knees before Mamie could stop her. They was the ones liked to dirty joke about how lucky Old Man Watson was to mount this firm young filly, and jeered and hooted at the fine sight of her hips in her nice petticoats when her store-bought dress got hung up on a slat as she crawled down in the filth to get away. If E. J. Watson could of seen how that crowd terrified his poor young wife and children, he'd of stood right up in his life's blood, come straight back from Hell to kill us all.

I felt terrible, and sick. I went to my knees and I called in there to Mrs Watson, It's all right ma'am, ain't nothing to be scared of! Poor woman must have thought I was a crazy man, to say something like that with my gun still warm and her husband, too, still warm and bleeding, and boys and dogs running around, gone wild.

Well, I weren't one bit better than the others. No, that young woman had got deep under my skin, though she never knew it, and she stirred my desire then and there, may God forgive me. And here I was just newly wed to Nettie Howell! I was so ashamed that I hollered at the others, shoved them away, like we'd caught some lady in the bushes by mistake.

The swamp angels was something terrible that evening, but that poor little family crouched back in the dark with them putrefied chickens for damned near an hour and never made so much as a whimper, that's how frighted they was. They lay there just as still as newborn rabbits. Mamie done her best to soothe 'em, murmuring down

402

through the storm-raised boards in the house floor, same sweet way as a young girl she talked a scairdy cat out of a tree. When finally she got the poor things calmed, and coaxed 'em out of there, them Watsons stunk so bad of rotten chickens that the people where they was staying wouldn't take 'em back. Said they wasn't fit to set foot in a decent house with that stench of Hell on 'em, and here it was dark, and three scared hungry little kids whimpering for their daddy and no place to turn to, and their mama's poor mind starting to unravel, what with all her terror.

The stink of that pathetical little family was only the excuse for what them people was aiming to do anyway. They didn't want to be anywheres near no Watsons, not with Leslie Cox still on the loose. Man sent his wife out to tell Edna Watson they couldn't put up with 'em no more. Never even let 'em in, they pushed their stuff at 'em through the cracked door.

The ones that drove that desperate family from their house, the husband was supposed to been a friend to Watson, and the wives was close – well, this man and his brother, who was visiting from Marco, they was in that crowd. He was one of 'em claimed later on he never pulled the trigger, which means he was along with us for the wrong reason. Don't matter if he pulled the trigger or he didn't.

I don't need to name no names. The men who scared Watson's little family and those folks who drove 'em out, they know who they are right to this day.

So Mamie took Edna and her children into that tore-up house of hers, and that family never did forget her kindness. Mamie had redneck ideas when it come to certain people, but she had grit and a big heart, no doubt about it. Lots of Chokoloskee folks are the same way – you hate some of that stubborn ignorance, that prejudice against everyone except their own, but you got to admire 'em all the same. They are good, tough, honest, and God-fearing

403

people, got a lot of fiber to 'em. They have 'em a hard life, and they don't complain.

The lawmen went down to Watson's on the *Falcon*, picked up Mister Watson's horse and four thousand gallons of his syrup to be taken up and sold off at Fort Myers. Four thousand gallons! By Jesus, if I had sweated out the hot hard hours that man must of worked that hot hard ground, raking the shell off forty acres every year to grow good cane, I'd be heartbroke to leave it all behind. All the point of his whole life was in that cane patch he had made with his bare hands in the meanest kind of snake-crawling scrub jungle.

Oh, that was a fine plantation, I can see it yet, the boathouse, sheds, that dock, that strong white house! Chatham Bend was what he had to show at the end of his hard road. He was not a youthful man no more, he was sick of running, and maybe that is when his life caught up with him.

After a while, some of them folks that had took a liking to Ed Watson and didn't feel right about the way he died, they got to saying all the trouble come from rumor and misunderstanding, that the killings down there never started until Cox come, so it must been Cox who give E. J. Watson his bad name. For some years afterward, people was nervous that Cox was still around down in the rivers, cause that was a hombre that would shoot a man just to see him wiggle.

Unless them Injuns got to him first, Mister Watson rescued Cox or killed him. Otherwise he'd be there still, because Chatham Bend is on an island in them rivers and Cox couldn't swim too good, the nigger said, and anyway he was scared of them big gators that follow the overflow down from the Glades after a hurricane, tracking fish and turtle all along the edge of brackish water. There was no one to come by and take Cox off, lest it was Watson, cause that terrible storm just cleaned the Islands out.

Some years after, one of the Daniels boys claimed he seen Cox in Key West. He said Cox spotted him, ducked away quick. We figured Cox might of shipped out on a freighter. That was the first word of him in a long time, and the last one, too.

I never met one person yet who believed Watson killed Cox. To believe that you would have to believe that hombre set there on the Bend day after day, thinking his thoughts, until Mister Watson come back home and blowed his head off. But if you *don't* believe it, then you have to explain how in hell Cox got away, and where he went to, and where he is living at today.

Anyway, they dug up E. J. Watson, reburied him beside Mrs Jane Watson in the old Fort Myers cemetery. I keep meaning to get up there, have a look, but I never do. I always heard them older children built a statue to Ed Watson by the cemetery gate, but maybe they didn't. Anyway, he's still up there, I imagine, resting in peace as good as any of 'em.

THE END OF A MOST DEPLORABLE TRAGEDY
HAS COME DOWN NEAR CHOKOLOSKEE

Fort Myers, October 30, 1910 *On October 23, a week ago, the lawmen investigating the dreadful happenings at Chatham River sailed for Chokoloskee, where they arrived on October 25. By happenstance, a group of citizens of that island was just returning from Rabbit Key, where they said they had buried Mr E. J. Watson, owner of the plantation where the murders occurred.*

Sheriff Tippins was informed that after their meeting on October 19 at Marco, Mr Watson had stopped over at Chokoloskee to advise Mrs Watson that he was on his way to Chatham Bend. The people there were in a very high state of agitation, especially about the killing of the woman, Miss Hannah Smith, of Georgia, with whom many in the community had been friendly. Due to his past reputation, it was generally suspected that Mr Watson must be implicated, but nobody attempted to detain him. However, the men said, Mr Watson was to produce Leslie Cox dead or alive or accept the consequences, and he thereupon stated that he intended to return with Cox's head.

When Mr Watson reappeared in Chokoloskee on the evening of October 24, he produced a hat pierced by a bullet hole, said to have been worn by Cox. He claimed he had killed Cox – here was the proof. Declaring that this hat was insufficient, a posse of citizens demanded that he return with them to Chatham Bend and produce the body. He refused, stating that Cox's body had fallen into the river, and that only the hat had surfaced. When this story was challenged, Mr Watson appeared to become incensed that his neighbors were questioning his word, and one exchange led to another. The witnesses furthermore stated

406

*that when ordered to put down his gun, Mr Watson
attempted to fire into the crowd, and the posse killed him.*

*Thus ends one of the darkest tragedies ever recorded in
the history of this State. Leslie Cox – if indeed he is alive,
as most believe – is still at large down in the Islands. Even
if the Negro's account of the murders can be accepted, the
real truth of what happened that day, and why it happened, may never be known.*

MAMIE SMALLWOOD

I don't care to speak about what happened. Three House boys and their father had a part in it, maybe they will say why and maybe not. Ted took no part. He was one of the few could hold their head high in the long years after, cause he didn't have no cause to feel ashamed. Course the House boys never felt shame neither, which might been why we had hard feelings in our family.

The twenty-fifth, Sheriff Frank Tippins finally showed up with the Monroe sheriff, Clement Jaycox, brought down by Cap'n Collier on the *Falcon*. This was a week after the hurricane, and Chokoloskee was still cleaning up. The men told the sheriff he had come too late, so they was obliged to take the law in their own hands. Others blamed the death of Mister Watson on his late arrival.

Some men went with the law into the rivers on a hunt for Cox. Never found hide nor hair of him, of course. They took aboard a large cargo of Mister Watson's syrup, and they come on back.

Sheriff Tippins issued a summons to the men who took part in the death of E. J. Watson. He had that authority cause in 1910 Chokoloskee was still Lee County, and Chokoloskee is where E. J. Watson died. The men wanted the postmaster to go with 'em to Fort Myers and vouch for their upstanding characters, which he did. By that time there was a few complaining that the only one didn't have to go was the one who killed him – didn't count, I guess.

I asked my brother Bill about it, he just shook his head. Well, Bill, I says, what in the name of goodness does that darn old headshake tell me, yes or no? And Bill said,

Mamie, there is no way to explain. It ain't a matter of a yes or no, so just forget about it.

We done our best to forget about that killing, but no one forgot that hurricane, not around here. Everything got all tore up, salt-soaked, and rotting, everything mildewed, trees down everywhere, and everlasting mud. It seemed like our world was covered in muck and would not come clean again. Mullet cast up by that storm was a foot deep on the beach. Poor Ted raked out most of our drowned chickens the first week, but putrefaction rose up through those loose boards a month or more before he could get the store put back together and take the time to crawl back under there, bury the last of 'em.

Poor Edna was very grateful we had took her in but the smell of corruption was something terrible. Mama called it the stink of Satan's sulphur coming up from Hell. Might of had a stuffed-up nose or something. Anyway, she upset Edna, who got that chicken stink confused with everything, said she feared that stench would fill her nostrils till her dying day.

Chokoloskee, October 27, 1910 *We are still having trouble here. On the 24th Mr E. J. Watson came up from his place in his launch, and came to the shore and had some words with some of the folks. There was a little misunderstanding, and Mr Watson pulled his gun and tried to fire on some of our neighbors. His gun failed to fire, and he lost the deal, and was shot and instantly killed. His body was taken out to Rabbit Keys and buried on the 25th. I don't know of any other grave out there. A lot of men went down to Mr Watson's place on the next day to hunt one Leslie Cox that Mr Watson said he had killed when he was there, but they did not find him.*

Fort Myers, October 27, 1910 *Thomas A. Edison, the famous electrician telegraphed on Tuesday to know the depth of the water on the Caloosahatchee. . . .*

Mrs Watson and children arrive from down coast today. . . .

HOAD STORTER

Later years, Old Man Willie Brown would tell how he tried to stop them men that day, tried to see Justice Storter about what to do, get a warrant for Mister Watson's arrest. But Willie's boat was still at Smallwood's landing after the shooting, right there alongside of the *Brave*, so I don't know if he recollects things right or not.

My uncle George Washington Storter Junior was justice of the peace for the Chokoloskee Bay county, closest thing to law we had in them days. But Uncle George was in Fort Myers, summoned to jury duty, him and C. G. McKinney both. They was the two most solid citizens on Chokoloskee Bay, I guess, along with Smallwood. They was there in the courthouse when Sheriff Tippins brought them men from Chokoloskee for a hearing and ended up deputizing 'em instead. Appointed deputies to arrest a man that was already stone-cold dead by their own hand, stretched out in the bloody sand on Rabbit Key.

Before he deputized 'em, Sheriff Tippins took some depositions on the death, and the court clerk who wrote all of it down was Eddie Watson. After their mother died, back in 1901, Eddie and Lucius had lived awhile with their sister, Mrs Langford, but pretty soon Young Ed went to live with his daddy in north Florida, never came back again until 1909. Walter Langford and Tippins was good friends – Tippins named his second son Walter Tippins – and Tippins seen to it that Eddie Watson got a job down at the court when he come back.

Well, Uncle George never got over seeing Eddie Watson on that day. Uncle George's own children done their schooling at Fort Myers, and he knew them older Watson children pretty good and liked 'em fine. That day in court, Uncle George told us, young Eddie Watson looked like he'd been bent by lightning. Never cracked during the hearing, but he never got unbended neither. Done his duty in life as a husband and provider, he was a ardent churchgoer, always up in a front pew where it was hard to miss him. He run a nice insurance business, slapped a back or two, and told some jokes. But there was something stiffened up in Eddie Watson, like a tree dead at the heart, like if he fell down he might split in two.

James Hamiltons and Henry Thompson and their families left Lost Man's River for good, and so did almost everybody else. Their houses were all swept away and their gardens spoiled by four foot of salt water. They had to make a fresh start somewheres else, cause that storm left nothing they could work with. So there was a lot of Islanders in Chokoloskee by the time Mister Watson come back from the Bend.

Folks hung on in the Islands after bad hurricanes in 1873 and '94 and 1909, but that hurricane of 1910 cleaned 'em right out. In my opinion, Watson and Cox was a big part of it. Them dark mangrove walls closing out the world, with the empty Everglades to eastward where the sun rose, and that empty Gulf out to the west where the sun set, the silence and miskeeters and the loneliness, the heavy gray of land and sea during the rains, the knowing that all you hoed and built, so much hard work and discouragement for years and years, could be washed away by storm in a single night – put that together with the fear that any stranger glimpsed around some point of river might be the man who called himself John Smith, come to take your life. All that dread had wore 'em out, never mind the blood in them black rivers.

FRANK B. TIPPINS

When those men told how E. J. Watson died, I kept my boots spread and my arms folded on my chest. I didn't show them sympathy or comment, only grunted, so pretty quick the talk diminished into mutters.

Something was missing in the story, and I said so. Sheriff Jaycox took the hint and whistled and sucked his teeth in official skepticism. Questioning their word made them draw together and fall still, like quail. Their faces closed. They had told their story, and the sheriffs could take it or the sheriffs could leave it, because no man there was going to change a word.

Well, boys, the law's the law, Jaycox informed them, and they had took that law in their own hands where it don't belong. Never mind if Mister Watson had it coming or he didn't, there was murder done here on the shores of Monroe County, Sheriff Jaycox said. Begging your pardon, Sheriff, I said, this here is Lee County, ever since 19 and 02, when they checked the survey. Mister Ed Watson was massacred in Lee County, Florida, and the Lee County sheriff could not just walk away, forget about it. Besides, the deceased had folks back in Fort Myers, and fine upstanding folks at that.

"Well, we ain't so particular which county," Charlie Boggess said. "What we been looking for is law. Ain't none showed up." Charlie T. Boggess was Ted Smallwood's sidekick and some way kin to my own clan up around Arcadia, and so felt entitled to speak his mind. But when I took a pad out of my pocket, Charlie T. thought better of his attitude, explaining that while he himself, having been

413

crippled in the storm, had took no part, he could not find
it in his heart to blame his neighbors for what they had to
perpetrate in self-defense.

"That so?" I said.

"That's the way I look at it," Charlie T. concluded mod-
estly, and everybody nodded, all but Smallwood, who
harumphed and put his hands behind his back, as if encour-
aging us lawmen to get cracking and lay down some law.

All well and good, I told them, moving cautiously, but
still and all I had to take those men responsible back to
Fort Myers, procure some depositions in the case for a
grand jury hearing. That put a scare in them, and certain
men wanted the postmaster to come along to explain their
situation, even though he disapproved of what they did.

Smallwood had an awful mess to clean up at his store,
but after he had thought a minute he agreed to go. "All
right, Bill?" he asked his brother-in-law.

"Up to you," said W. W. House, who was short-spoken
that day with almost everybody.

At Chatham Bend we found no sign of Leslie Cox, nor the
dead squaw – that's where all the trouble started, went the
story. The men decided her own people "must of cut her
down and took her home," but how did the Indians know
that she was dead? Had the nigra lied about Cox and that
squaw, and if so, why? And if he lied about the Indian,
what else did he lie about?

We took aboard four thousand gallons of syrup for safe-
keeping. Mister Watson's old horse wore no halter and ran
wild around the thirty-acre canefield, the men wasted half
an afternoon trying to catch him. For all I know, that wild-
eyed thing is running down there yet.

At Chokoloskee, on the way back north, we took the
witnesses aboard. Mr D. D. House was the only one who
had a suitcase. He stood apart, hands on his hips, close to
the boiling point. Bill House announced in no uncertain
terms that it wasn't right to drag his dad off like a criminal

414

when he had been known for honesty throughout his life. If his father could be left behind, and his young brothers, too, he would speak up "good enough for all of 'em." Young Dan and Lloyd were all slicked up, with shoes on, set to go, but D. D. House turned and marched them home, never said good-bye, never looked back, never said one word.

The widow and her children were all packed and ready. There hadn't been a drop of rain, and a dark place by the shore where the body laid upset her when she came down to the landing. Seeing the men on the *Falcon*'s deck, she grabbed her children, started in to trembling, then fled back to the house. One man yelled after her, You can claim the body if you find the rope! Bill House told him to shut up. Rope? I said. Some men looked down. I went over to the store.

Mrs Watson had come all apart, and her kids were crying. She told me she forgave those men but she was afraid to travel with them on the *Falcon*. Mrs Smallwood advised me she would take good care of Mrs Watson and the children and put them on the mail boat in a few days' time. She was furious. She came back with me to the boat and hollered, Which one stole his watch? Nobody answered. They were angry too.

On the voyage to Fort Myers on the *Falcon*, more than one explained away his own role in the killing while the rest were out of earshot. Pled self-defense – they all did that – having agreed on this tall tale about how the famous desperado E. J. Watson had endangered the lives of twenty or more armed men. They also agreed that every man there had fired at exactly the same instant, making it impossible to identify his killer. "You'll have to hang the whole damn crowd!" Isaac Yeomans cackled. Some men were positive that they had missed, and there was one who claimed he missed on purpose. Bill House was about the only man who did not deny or defend or even comment.

While they talked, I thought about the week before, when the man now dead had sat across from me at this same mess table. We didn't make friends, not exactly, but we got friendly in some way, we laughed a little. I couldn't get Watson's voice out of my mind. Maybe, in saying he killed Cox, he told the truth.

With each hour I grew more impatient with the Chokoloskee men. No matter how often I heard 'em out, I remained dissatisfied with the whole story, yet I had faith in their sincerity. These Chokoloskee pioneers were good and honest settlers who had sent away for a teacher for their schoolhouse and held prayer meetings whenever they could catch the circuit preacher. They were fishermen and farmers, they had wives and children, and for fifteen years and more they had suffered rain, heat, and mosquitoes in these endless islands, trying to take root. None of them had the smell of liars. Yet when twenty men slay one, someone's to blame. I only hoped that the whole truth and nothing but the truth would emerge under oath at the court hearing.

Bill Collier sailed out Rabbit Key Pass so I could see just where the grave was. Rabbit Key was four miles west of Chokoloskee, on the Gulf, and the Monroe County line went right across it. One man sang out, "We was careful to plant him on the Monroe side!" and another yelled, "We run that devil clean out of Lee County!" but nobody laughed, so these two shut up quick.

What was left of Rabbit Key was a stripped sand spit, with one lonesome big old mangrove twisted hard by wind. Old Man Gandees said, The boys run a rope right to that tree. You follow that rope and dig down deep, you'll find his carcass. He shrugged when I asked him, Why the rope? and the others gazed away in different directions.

Isaac Yeomans explained that with bound limbs, the body towed better, but hearing that, Ted Smallwood whistled loud – That ain't the only reason! The men were

416

scared Ed Watson would rise up, come back to life, and walk on water back to Chokoloskee, Smallwood said, disgusted.

When I asked why they had towed him in the first place, instead of wrapping him in a piece of canvas and laying him in the boat's stern, Ted Smallwood said that treating Ed Watson like something dirty made 'em feel like they was right to kill him. Treating him like filth, they could feel cleaner, maybe.

Bill House didn't care much for Ted's theory, but he kept his mouth shut till he'd thought it over. Then he said, Ted? How come you claim to know how we were feeling, when you don't hardly know how you felt yourself? And Smallwood said, We ain't going to settle this one, Bill. Not this year.

Ted Smallwood took his hat off as the *Falcon* passed the grave, but the others glared out from beneath tattered straw brims and never spoke. They sat dead quiet, looking out to sea.

The *Falcon* sailed north past Indian Key and Fakahatchee Pass. What little talk there was concerned the strange dry weather. There hadn't been one drop of rain since the hurricane, and no sun either, a man had to row near to the head of Turner River to find good fresh water.

Off Panther Key, Bill Collier pointed out the place where Hiram Newell and Dick Sawyer's boy had come up with old Juan Gomez's body back in 1900. That got the men talking again, and pretty soon somebody mentioned that the James Hamiltons and Henry Thompson had a plan to move in alongside J. H. Daniels on Fakahatchee, which lay a few miles up that pass. Those folks had seen all they cared to see of Lost Man's River.

The Gulf grew rough where the tide changed, going against the wind. Off Cape Romaine, Isaac Yeomans became seasick, and the men laughed and called him a dang farmer. Smallwood told how years ago, crossing the

417

Gulf Stream over to Bimini with Isaac and his older brother seasick in the cabin, he remarked to the Bahama pilot, "Pretty rough out, is it not?" And the nigger tells him, "Nosuh, Cap'm, boss, dis yere smood Gulf."

Jim Yeomans had been on the run from killing a man at Fakahatchee over unpaid debts. Isaac sat up to explain how the man's widow came around early next morning, just when Jim was getting set to leave. She repaid the money, and Jim said, "Ain't it a shame you didn't do that yesterday."

Isaac Yeomans blew his nose and spat and laughed. He yelled, Dis yere smood Gulf! and puked again. When he came up, wiping his mouth, he nodded in my direction. "Later on Jim was living on a boat at Clearwater. He walks past the drugstore minding his own business, and damn if the new sheriff don't step out and arrest him."

"Tippins, I believe his name was," Bill House said.

"Something like that, Bill," I said.

"Took Jim to court," Isaac Yeomans said. "And Jim's wife testifies that Jim *told* her how he aimed to put a stop to this damn feller that wouldn't pay Jim what he owed, and how Jim didn't have no choice but to keep his word. Open-and-shut case, says the new sheriff, but the case weren't quite so shut as what he thought, cause being Jim's wife, her word weren't worth the piece of paper it was wrote on. Had to let Jim go for lack of evidence, is what it was."

"Jim went back home, I always heard," I said, mild as could be, and Isaac turned and looked back south and east into the mist toward Fakahatchee.

"Might be killing a few over there today," he said.

"Wouldn't be surprised," I said.

Yeomans spat. "Remember them two Texas fellers, Ted, at Lemon City? Said they'd come gunning for Ed Watson but got shot by Sam Lewis before they got it done?" Isaac said that Lemon City folks had dreaded Lewis the same way people on this coast were scared of Cox.

"Every time Sam Lewis pulled the trigger there was one

418

man less," Ted Smallwood said, like he'd said it more times than he cared to remember. Isaac complained, "I was just coming up to that part!" and Ted said, "Well, come up, then." But when Isaac told about a boy at Lemon City who itched to put some bullets into Lewis, the men commenced to grow uneasy.

I said quick and hard, to startle them, "I heard there were boys like that around Watson's body." Nobody said a word. The brooding men looked out to sea again. Then someone said, Might been one them boys got his damn watch. Isaac finished his story quickly and said to Ted, "Ain't that how *you* remember it?" And Ted said, "Close enough, I guess."

'Anyways," said Isaac, cross, "them two Texans from Dallas was friends of Belle Starr, and they aimed to find the yeller-bellied skunk that bushwhacked her." And Ted said, "Well, that was only rumor, Isaac, and them two was in no shape to confirm it." And Isaac said, "Yessir, them Texas gunslingers was hunting E. J. Watson! Ted Highsmith told that to Ed Brewer. Ted Highsmith, he allowed as much to anybody as would listen!"

"*Ed* Highsmith," the postmaster said.

Isaac Yeomans was ready to fight, but Bill House told him to simmer down or he would throw his little carcass in the water.

This was only the second time Bill House had spoken, he had kept himself apart, in heavy humor. I told him he was merely going to give an affidavit, and he said he disliked being taken to court when to his way of thinking no crime had been committed. Hadn't he explained to me that they'd all fired together, in self-defense? Was the sheriff questioning their word?

"Did the victim injure anybody first?"

At that hard question, the others looked around as if trying to recall if anyone was hurt. Bill House said, "No. But he sure tried." Angrily he turned his back, knowing I was trying to poke up trouble. He'd already told me that he'd liked Ed Watson – "a man couldn't help but like Ed Watson" – but had no doubts and no regrets about what happened. People living where there was no law was obliged to make their own, Bill House concluded, and he'd looked straight at me when he said it.

The *Falcon* put in for water at Caxambas – Arawak Indian for "wells," Bill Collier said. The men from Chokoloskee looked surprised. Old Man Henry Smith said he had lived along this coast most of his life, before some of the men aboard of here was even born. hardly, and never knowed Caxambas meant a goddam thing.

Like Everglade and Chokoloskee, the small settlement at Caxambas looked like a place blown in from someplace else. The hurricane had ripped the roof off E. S. Burnham's clam factory and smashed Jim Barfield's store, and kids were diving for his canned goods in the channel. All the families had huddled for the night up at the Barfield Heights Hotel, which sat there on an Indian mound a few yards above high water.

Josie Jenkins, who'd been brought home from Pavilion, had been drinking somewhat with her son Leroy Parks, and she dragged her little Pearl down to the dock to tongue-lash "the men who massacred Pearl's daddy." Pearl Watson was about ten at that time, and kept her scared red eyes turned to the side. She had taffy hair, a pretty face, a long, brown, skinny frame – too skinny and young, seemed like to me, to be wondering what was ever going to become of her.

"Shame on you!" her ma was shrieking. "Shame on you! Took the whole trashy pack of you to bring him down!"

The small wild woman wore her long hair loose, which wasn't considered decent back in those days, and she tossed that black mop and cursed the men in no uncertain terms, till I warned her about causing a disturbance. Well, Sheriff, she said, a lady has prescribed herself a little spirits for a broken heart, is that a crime? But in the end she became

420

dignified, and let her daughter take her hand, lead her away.

It was known by now how Josie Jenkins rode out that hurricane on Pavilion Key, how her brother Tant pushed her up into the mangroves with her five-month baby boy, and how that child was stripped away when a series of big seas washed over, and found again by some dark miracle after the seas went down. Josie hollered that her boy was taken by the hand of God and the Chokoloskee men said that was sure right, because the boy was the accursed infant of that bloody-handed sinner who had brought God's punishment down upon them in the first place, that's why his life was the only one lost on the Islands. "The living proof" – that's what Charley Johnson called the perished boy.

When I brought the men into the courthouse, young Eddie Watson, the deputy court clerk, stood up behind the desk. I'd hired him when he came back from north Florida because Walt Langford asked that favor, and Eddie promised I'd have no cause to regret it, and I never did, or not until that day.

The damned young fool, all red in the face and dropping papers, claimed he'd come in to finish up some work on his day off.

I decided not to introduce him, but one of the men knew him by sight, and the rest learned in a hurry who he was. Bill House whispered, Well, for Christ's sake, Sheriff, how about giving *that* young feller a day off! I didn't like Bill's tone one bit, and gave him a hard look, which was returned, but he was right. I took Eddie Watson to one side and told him to go home, take the day off, I'd find someone else to record the deposition. Eddie said, no, he wasn't going to flinch from them damn lynchers. As deputy court clerk, he got paid to do a job, and he aimed to do it, he declared, hoisting his chin as I struggled to control my aggravation.

Young Eddie resided at the boardinghouse of our erstwhile saloon keeper, Taff O. Langford. Whatever he knew about his daddy's trial in north Florida two years earlier he kept entirely to himself, so what his heart's opinion of it was, I could not say, but since returning to Fort Myers, he had missed no chance to announce he was *not* and never had been E. J. Watson Junior. Said he was his own man, Mr E. E. Watson.

Eddie fetched his pad and sat himself in the clerk's chair, stiff as a stick. In his rufous looks, he took after his daddy, he had the same kind of husky mulishness, but he lacked the fiery color and bold eyes.

The men seemed more uneasy than young Eddie. Some tried to look outraged when they testified, to justify themselves, others looked peaked and sad, as if to hint that their experience had hurt them worse than it hurt E. J. Watson. A couple tried to smile at Eddie, who ignored them. That boy set it all down in his notebook as if reporting a church supper for the *Press*. When the men were finished, he whacked his notes hard with his pencil and slapped his book shut, to show just what he thought – *Never mind all this lying and false witness, you men lynched him!*

Bill House nodded at Eddie before he began his deposition, friendly but not anxious to make friends. He didn't smile. As Eddie took down Bill's account of how he and the rest shot Eddie's dad to pieces, it was easy to see that House felt worse and worse. But this was Chokoloskee's version of the Death of Watson, and the affidavit of William Warlick House spoke for them all. The others added only a few details. Ted Smallwood came last and testified he had not witnessed the shooting but "I sure heard it." Said, "Far as it went," he had no reason to doubt what House had said.

That was that. I got Smallwood and a couple of others to sign their names, and the rest of 'em took plenty of time drawing their Xs, to make certain it weren't mistaken for someone else's. I told them they could go back home and wait for the grand jury to decide if and when they were going to be indicted.

"You decide if we are criminals," House said. "That what you mean?"

"Sheriff don't get to decide that," I notified him. "Least not in court."

Walter Langford and Jim Cole arrived in time to hear me say "grand jury," and Cole started hollering before I finished. How could a grand jury convict when the only eyewitnesses were the defendants? According to the American Constitution, these here men could not be compelled to incriminate themselves. Why, it made no goddam fucking *sense*, he yelled, to summon a grand jury–!

Walt Langford raised both palms to slow Cole down. The president of the Florida First National had the jowls of a real banker these days, not a trace of those honest cowboy bones showed through the lard. Had him a stiff collar and cravat to go with his new million-dollar smile, which was served up with everything he said. His nails were pink and his honey hair was slicked tight as a duck's wing, ol' Walt smelled like a barbershop and no mistake. But lotion couldn't cover up the reek of whiskey. Walt was a drinker, I knew that, always was and always would be, though he did his best to drink on his own time.

Walt spoke in a hushed-up voice "on behalf of the victim's family," glancing at Cole every few seconds to be sure he was making the right speech. He told us "the most merciful solution" was to "forget the whole tragedy" as soon as possible rather than "waste our public money dragging these men through the courts when there was no way justice could be done." So anxious was he to spit up his speech that he ignored the victim's son, never mind the feelings of my suspects.

Isaac Yeomans hollered out, "Justice *was* done, you dumb bastard, and I'm proud we done it!" The men were already upset by Eddie Watson's presence, and Langford gave them an excuse to get mad. Bill House banged his

423

hand flat on the table, then rose up, saying, "*His* death weren't no tragedy! The tragedy was them deaths at Chatham Bend!"

Walt went red in a split second. "Oh Lordy, I'm trying to *help* you people!"

"Go on home, then," Isaac Yeomans said.

After the hubbub died a little, I advised the banker and his friend that murder was murder and could not be ignored by law. Orderly steps had to be taken to establish responsibility for the shooting – inquest and grand jury hearing, indictment, circuit court. Right about then, Cole took me by the elbow in that way he had and coaxed me aside as if the pair of us was up to something sneaky. He was wheezing, and as was customary, his breath stank of onions.

"Why not drop it? Just forget it?" Jim Cole said.

"Lee County can't 'just forget' about a murder."

"It ain't murder if you deputized that posse, Frank."

"Little late to form a posse, Mr Cole."

"Is it? State's attorney owes me a favor, and he won't ask questions about dates. You got my word."

"Your word," I said, feeling worn out again. "How about justice?"

"How about it, Frank?" Cole snorted out a sort of laugh, slapping my biceps with the back of his thick hand to remind me I owed him a favor, too – to remind me yet again that ten years ago, young Frank B. Tippins "came into this sheriff's office barefoot," as Cole said.

I came in barefoot, but I came in honest, too. I never asked for Jim Cole's backing. Young Frank Tippins learned the hard way that the cowmen and their cronies ran this town any damn old way they wanted. To get my job done, I had to work around the cattle kings, learning the art of give-and-take, and I reckon I took a little finally, cut some corners. My worst mistake was renting buck niggers off the county road gangs for cheap labor at Deep Lake. Cole fixed it with Langford to pay me nine dollars per week per head,

424

plus fees for Indians to hunt them through the hammocks when they ran away.

Paying chain-gang convicts for their labor was against the law. My idea was to settle when they'd served their time, but very few came pestering me about their money, they just disappeared. The fund was illegal anyway, so I'd borrowed off it some to pay my bills.

Jim Cole would wink each time he brought the money. "Don't want to catch you giving one red cent to them bad niggers, Frank. Don't want our sheriff to do nothing that ain't legal!" And he'd slap my arm with the backs of his fingers in that same loose way he did it now, to remind me how deep he had me in his dirty pocket, along with the sticky coins and stale tobacco crumbs.

Well, I went back into the courtroom and I swore in every man except House and Smallwood. Nothing was done, then or later, to establish responsibility, since deputizing the shooters made the shooting legal. Langford and Cole were overjoyed to get the case dismissed without a trial – last thing these well-fixed fellers wanted was a scandal – and young Eddie seemed to see it the same way. As for the new deputies, they went home feeling a whole lot better about what was done on October 24th in the line of duty.

The only discontented ones were me and House. He drew off by himself, he fumed, he punched the wall. Then he came forward. In front of the rest, he denounced the tricky way they had ducked criminal charges, when in his estimation no crime had been committed in the first place. He said he'd sooner go to Hell than be deputized in this dishonest way, said he'd damn well go to trial by himself if that was the only way he could get vindicated.

Bill House stayed behind when the others left. At the court clerk's desk where I stood sorting Eddie's documents, he said in an accusing way, "What's going to happen to that nigger, Sheriff?"

"Key West," I said, not looking up, to show him I was

busy. When he waited there, expecting more, I said, "Justice." Finally, I cocked an eye at him and said, "That nigger's gonna see some justice, Bill." I managed a wry smile, making a joke of this, but I wasn't in a mood to smile, and he wasn't, either. I held his eye, to warn him, and he stared right back. "Same justice you gave Watson, Bill," I said, "according to your Chokoloskee story."

For a florid feller, House went a dangerous color. When I said, "No hard feelings," and held out my hand, he shook his head, turned toward the door, and kept on going, following the rest out into the sun, down toward the wharf.

Cox had closed the book on Dutchy Melvin, who was the man most wanted in Key West. As for Green Waller, if that was his real name, he was on the books here in Fort Myers as a hog thief, twice convicted back in the late nineties. After that nobody knew what had become of him. Got sick of running and drifted south to the Ten Thousand Islands, I imagine. Ed Watson had plenty of hogs to keep Green happy, and Big Hannah was down there later on to warm his bones.

In the opinion of my new-sworn posse, Cox might still be down there in the Islands, and nobody could say when or where he might show up. They had decided Cox was crazy, Cox would kill again. If E. J. Watson had saved his life by setting him ashore someplace, Cox might stop at nothing to avenge him, might sneak back in and kill some posse members in the night.

At least they had known Watson to talk crops with, at least their women had passed the time of day with his wife and children. For better or worse Ed Watson was their neighbor. Cox was a stranger, known to no one, and strangers were capable of almost anything.

Afterwards, trying to piece it all together, I came up with more questions than good answers. I knew one thing. My witness fooled the men at Pavilion Key by acting the part of a dumb, scared coon after doing his best to implicate Ed Watson. No matter how much I cuffed him in the jailhouse, that smart, hard nigger stuck like wet rice to the second story that he gave Thad Williams, who had messed things up by challenging the first one. *Nosuh, nosuh, Mist' Ed ain' nevuh knowed one thing about it! Ah jes 'cused him cause Mist' Leslie tole me do it!*

Thad admitted he had always liked "Ol' E.J.," and so had his nephew Dickie Moore and all that family. They wanted to believe in Ol' E.J.'s innocence, and they weren't the only ones. But if Watson was innocent, why did the nigger make up that first story, which could only get him in more trouble? Was he really so scared of Cox he couldn't think straight?

In my belief, he told the truth the first time, and he went over to Pavilion Key to tell it. If Jim Cannon and his boy had not passed by on the day that woman rose out of the river, the sharks and gators would have beat us humans to the evidence, and if that nigger hadn't told the truth at Pavilion Key, no man would have ever known what fate befell those three lost souls, never mind the squaw. There would only be more rumors about Watson.

I signed the prisoner over to Sheriff Jaycox for transport to Key West. On the dock Jaycox summed up his understanding of the situation with the prisoner standing right in front of him.

"White woman. Foul-murdered, mutilated and left for nude," Clem Jaycox said.

"That is sure right."

"No jury ain't going to stand for that, what do you think, Frank? Don't hardly seem fair to ask the citizens of Monroe County to waste their money on no trial, when we know the verdict 'fore it starts."

"No, it sure don't."

Jaycox straightened his hat and waited. I didn't like this much. His prisoner wouldn't sit down on the cargo where

I pointed, just stood up straight, hands tied behind, observing us.

"What you looking at, nigger boy?" Jaycox said, real soft and low, hiking his belt.

"The prisoner is now in Monroe custody," I said, "so you got to do what Monroe thinks is right." Clem Jaycox winked at me to show he understood, which he probably didn't. "It's surely been my pleasure working with Lee County, Frank." And he winked again.

I was still trying to stare down that nigger, but never once did he lower his eyes. He knew he had nothing more to lose, I guess.

I said, "Your last chance, boy. Did Mister Watson order those three deaths or didn't he?"

But he never even blinked, nor moved his head. A very, very dangerous type of nigger. Wasn't surprised when a rumor came back from Key West how he fell overboard and drowned trying to make a getaway.

When Carrie Langford visited the courthouse to ask after the remains, the posse was already gone – a mercy. I was full of admiration for her courage. Upon learning from Eddie that their father's "gruesome carcass" – those were Eddie's words – had been towed four miles to a sand spit on the Gulf and dumped in a crude pit without a box, Carrie busted out in tears about "those dreadful men" and the lonesome fate of her poor papa. I had my chance to take her in my arms, the first time ever. Told her I'd be happy to arrange with Captain Collier to have the remains brought to Fort Myers for a decent burial, as she wished.

"The remains," she said.

I told her the sheriff would go, too, to make sure everything was decent, and next day I decided to take the coroner along. Jim Cole wanted to know why, since neither the family nor the state desired an autopsy, nobody wanted that autopsy except for me. Anyway, as Doc Henderson pointed out, it could have been done more efficiently "at home." There was plenty of rotted dead men in Doc's line of work, and the fair sex, too, without having to hear shovels scrape the bones. That body would have to be boxed, I said, no sense doing it twice, so bring a coffin. He finally admitted he was scared to see Ed Watson glaring up at him out of the sand. "It's okay, he's face down," is what I told him.

Lucius Watson favored his late mother, very gentle, graceful in his ways. He often hummed some little tune to let people know that he was there, that's how hard it was to hear him coming. This quiet of Ed Watson's younger boy was already unsettling to certain people, and so was his determination, which was not what you expected from the look of him.

I told Lucius. You're not going, son, and that is that. But Lucius followed me to Ireland's Dock, came up behind as silent as my shadow. That tall slim boy – he was going on twenty-one – could do handsprings in the courtroom and you wouldn't hardly know that he was there, while his brother Eddie could peek in the window and you'd feel his weight all over the damn building.

Lucius said softly, "I am going, Sheriff. I aim to make sure he's treated with respect."

The day before, he had protested the family decision not to prosecute his father's killers, which his brother and his sister had approved. Lucius thought those men from Chokoloskee should be prosecuted. He said he'd lived at Chatham Bend for the past two years and seen no evidence whatever for their stories, whereas the evidence of his father's murder had never been challenged even by the perpetrators.

"Well, now, it is not that simple, son–"

"Murder is murder. You could have charged them with or without his family's cooperation."

Though Lucius was furious, he never made it personal, in fact, he never raised his voice. And he had an argument,

429

no getting around it. Bill House and the others might have told me nothing but the truth, but it wasn't the whole truth, and I knew it. Lucius admitted he had no experience with death and didn't really know how he might react. "You're not going," I said, as he stepped aboard the boat. "One day you'll thank me."

Mister Watson lay face down beneath two crossways slabs of coral rock that the hurricane broke loose and heaved ashore. His wrists and ankles were lashed tight to discourage locomotion, and the gray flesh of his mortal coil had swollen so that it almost hid the twine. Dick Sawyer threw a hitch onto these bindings, and the body, like a side of beef, was hoisted by my niggers from the hole and set on a canvas tarpaulin brought by the coroner. The terrible sight and stench of Mister Watson scared a yell out of the diggers, who tried to back away.

Doc, a trim and silver man, said "Ready?" His voice was muffled by the gauze over his nose. When he rolled the body over, Lucius turned and peered away to sea over his handkerchief.

The late E. J. Watson was crusted with blood-black sand and blind, with bullet-smashed teeth, nose and lower lip half shot away, black-and-blue face and neck and arms and dead-white farmer's body turning a bad gray-purple around the bullet holes and buck-shot rashes, and sand fleas hopping all over the whole mess.

I shuddered hard but only once, the hard shiver of a horse, or a wet dog. Lucius was coughing, and went off to be sick. He was back quickly. He knelt and cut his father's bonds, looking surprised that the unbound limbs didn't spring free.

Lucius said vaguely, "Are you sure it's him?"

Doc whipped around on Lucius, clutching his small knives, as if his handiwork had been insulted, and I told Lucius, Go back to the boat.

"Looks like something washed in from the sea," Lucius

was whispering, very pale, and I came up close behind in case he fainted.

"Not to me he don't," said Doc, whose hands jittered when he got upset. "What he looks like to me is the goriest case of homicide I ever come across in my career!"

Lucius stood up, swaying, going white again, starting to tremble, and I said sharply, "You seen what you came to see? Then walk away from it, and don't look back." But he didn't hear me, and began to shake. I slapped him hard across the face three times, shouting at him with each slap, *Forget it*! Then I took him by the shoulders, turned him away, and led him to the boat. "You set right here until it's finished."

Doc cut the last rags off the body. Small knives flashed. The autopsy was done in the hard sun and sea air, with little Gulf waves rolling up on the white sand and the green water shimmering on the boat's white paint of the hull, and gulls crying in the smoky light of the last hot day in that long shadowy October. An hour passed with only the small slitting sounds, low gasps for breath. Doc never bothered about buckshot. Thirty-three slugs, one by one, clunked into the coffee can.

Lucius was back. He cleared his throat and said in a soft voice, "You've cut him up enough, wouldn't you say so?"

Doc's ears turned red, and his hands stopped, but he did not look up. "Probably a few more in there yet," he said.

'You'll never know," Dick Sawyer said, and winked at Lucius, trying to curry favor. "Not if you want to leave him in one piece. Like ol' Ed here used to say, it's a lucky man who gets to his grave all in one piece."

I advised Doc that Lee County was now satisfied that the proximate cause of death had been determined. Sawyer laughed but the coroner reproved me with a doleful bark like a dog sicking up its bone. What lay before them on that sand, he mourned, was not a laughing matter. In a manner of speaking, you might say – Doc paused to rig a sort of loincloth, make the body decent – I think of this here thing as my own patient.

"Get the box," I told the diggers. Doc used his heel to wipe off his thin knives as the rest of us backed off a ways to get a breath.

The diggers hoisted up the carcass and set it in a strong pine box. They laid rags across their hands before they touched him, and no amount of shouting stopped their moans and prayers and yelps and nigger racket. Well, you couldn't blame 'em. Between the wounds and knife cuts, this hard-swollen red-gray-and-blue carcass looked more like some skinned animal than the dangerous man I had drunk with on the *Falcon*.

Sawyer said, "I been reading where they fill 'em full of lead out West, but I never thought I'd see that in south Florida."

"You talk too much," I said.

Lucius knelt before he fell. He touched his father's forehead with his finger. He said, "The Lord have mercy on you, Papa." He laid the lid and took the nails and hammer from Dick Sawyer and did his best to nail that stench in tight.

As Dick Sawyer would declare for years thereafter, Well, we moved him, that's God's truth. But any man goes ashore on Rabbit Key can get him a whiff of that ol' devil yet today!

CARRIE LANGFORD

October 25, 1910 It's over now. I am exhausted, as if I had fled before this day for twenty years, breathless and despairing, filled with dread.

Dear Lord, I knew this day of woe must come, and now it's here. My heart is torn by a sharp pain, this awful *ache* of loss and sorrow, never to be assuaged here on this earth. *His daughter could have done something and failed to do it. Instead she turned her own father away.*

The agony is real, but is it grief?

Oh Mama, if only you might slip through that door to hug me, tell me what to think, because there is no one near me who can understand. In this life, Our Lord seems very far away, and so I open up my heart to you, knowing that you are nearer God, in prayer that you will hear me and forgive me, heal me, because you know that I loved Papa, too.

I'm *glad*, Mama. I grieve but I am glad. I repent but I am glad.

I'm glad, I'm glad! May God forgive me.

October 27, 1910 "It's over, Carrie" – that's all Walter will say to comfort me.

It's for the best, says Eddie (who sounds as pompous, copying Walter, as Walter sounds when he copies Mr Cole). I can't imagine what goes through Eddie's head. I love him dearly, and I grieve to see him so congested, but I long to kick him. As a boy he was so open to life, so filled with curiosity, but when he came back from north Florida, something had thickened. He seems curious about absolutely nothing. He talks too much, he drones, he blusters. He is conceited about his clerk's job at the courthouse though everyone knows it was arranged for him by Sheriff Tippins. He wears that public smile like a cheap necktie.

When I asked Eddie how he could commit to paper the lies told at the courthouse by those awful men, he said wearily, How are we to know which are the lies? And anyway, they are not *awful* men. They are merely men.

He is so worldly-wise I want to smack him. A job's a job and someone's got to do it – that's the kind of wearisome dull thing he says these days, shrugging philosophically. He's affecting a pipe, which doesn't suit him, only encourages him to weigh his words, which have no weight, so far as I can tell.

When Papa's name comes up, Eddie goes deaf, and he's been that way since he came back from Papa's trial. He has hardly spoken to Papa in two years. I asked him – *begged* him – Papa was innocent, wasn't he? Wasn't he, Eddie? And finally Eddie grumped, That's what the jury said. He refused to speak about it anymore.

Because of this unmentionable hurt we share, we are estranged. That's not poor Papa's fault, of course.

Eddie was living with Papa at Fort White when all that trouble happened back up north, but he won't talk to anyone about it, he calls it "a closed chapter" in his life. He won't discuss it even with poor Lucius, who seems less bitter about Papa's killers than about Papa's so-called friends at Chokoloskee, all those men who failed to intervene.

Even so, Lucius went to Eddie for the list of names of those men at the courthouse, and when Eddie refused him – he had *that* much sense! – they had an ugly argument in public! What can folks think of our poor ruined family! Eddie said he was concerned about his younger brother's safety, and besides it would be unethical for the deputy court clerk to reveal the names of witnesses. Lucius shouted that the deputy court clerk didn't care about his father, and wasn't "concerned" about one d——— thing except his stupid little title, which wasn't nearly as important as he thought it was!

To lose his head and shout that way is so unlike poor Lucius, who is taking Papa's death harder than anyone. Lucius spent most of his time at Chatham Bend after Papa's return, two years ago, and was friendly with those poor wretches who were killed. He stayed for weeks last summer with his friend Dick Moore, hunted and caught fish for the table, worked in the fields and on the boats, went on an excursion with his father to Key West – he refuses to believe that the jolly generous father he thought he knew was the evil murderer that people say. Lucius intends to go up to Fort White and learn the truth in that part of the country, and after that he will go back to the Islands, ask some questions. Lucius has already talked to someone who witnessed just what happened, he is making a list of the men and boys involved.

Winking at Walter, Eddie warned "dear baby brother" to "leave bad enough alone." In that bored voice of his, the phrase seemed disrespectful to our father, and Lucius jumped up and demanded that Eddie take that back or step outside!

Leave *well* enough alone is all I meant, said Eddie, winking again at Walter, who rattled his paper unhappily, pretending not to see. And Lucius said, What's well enough for you may not be well enough for me.

I saw our Eddie clench his fists, outraged by this impertinence. Eddie favors Papa, he is huskier than Lucius, who is lean and taller. But Eddie got himself under control, and shrugged, as if nothing his young brother might do could be taken seriously.

Walter walked Lucius out of doors and came back with worry in his eyes. "It's only his way of thrashing out his grief. He won't *hurt* anybody." When I snapped impatiently, "Can you imagine Lucius *hurting* anybody?"

435

he said nothing. He sat down, picked at his paper, drove me crazy.

"Well, for pity's sake, what is it, Walter?"

"He better not go back down there hunting no names."

"Stop him, then. I don't *want* him to go back!"

Walter doesn't care to interfere in Watson family matters, never has and never will. He hid behind his paper. "That boy is just as stubborn as his daddy," his voice said. "There ain't *nobody* going to stop him."

"Isn't," I said.

"Isn't *nobody* going to stop him" Walter said before I snatched his paper from his hands. "If I know Lucius," he said gently, taking the paper back, "he'll be asking them hard questions the whole rest of his life."

October 30, 1910 How changed is poor young Widow Watson from his girlish Kate brought here by Papa just four years ago! Miss Kate Edna Bethea, as I still think of her, lacked utterly our mama's elegance and education, but I saw at once her merry spirit and high bust and drayhorse haunches, her rosy prattle about farmyard animals back in Fort White – this young thing suited our vigorous papa better than Mama's indoor virtues ever had.

Oh, she was his young mare, all right! I don't care to think about it! And Papa walked and spoke like a young man again, he fairly strutted. He had stopped drinking – well, almost – and he was full of great plans for the Islands, full of *life*!

The whole dreadful business is "a closed chapter in my life," Edna Watson says. Did she get that phrase from Eddie, or did he get it from her, or is it simply a popular expression at Fort White?

Stepmother Edna is three years my junior. I paid a call on her at the hotel. She has a glazed look, a dull morbid manner. She tried her best to be polite, but she can scarcely bring herself to talk about it. Isn't it peculiar? The aging daughter wept and sniffled, the young wife never shed a tear, just sat there tight and stunned and scared, breaking her biscuit without eating it, not tasting her tea. Edna won't go to her people in Fort White but to her sister in west Flordia, where no one knows her. She wants to get clean away, she says, so she can *think*. What she wishes to think about I cannot imagine.

Edna's clothes are nice (Papa saw to that) but she was wearing them all wrong, and of course they looked like she had slept in them, which perhaps she had. I urged my darlings to play with their little "aunt" Ruth Ellen, but Papa's kids are desperate creatures these days. Addison pulls and tears at Edna – When is Daddy coming? Where is Daddy? Baby Amy's big eyes stare all around even when she's nursing, hardly five months in this life and already alarmed!

But Edna scarcely notices, she cannot hear them, just herds her brood gently as if tending them in dream. In normal times she is surely a doting mother, since she is so easy with them even today, when the poor thing has no idea what will become of her. What little Papa did not owe is all tied up in house and boats and livestock, farm equipment. Walter explained to her that Papa's huge legal expenses of two years ago put him deep in debt, but she scarcely listened, didn't seem to care. Nor did she find words to thank him when he promised to send her whatever was left over once the debts were paid. I believe that Walter has advanced the money for their journey, and she has given him power of attorney to sell the last of Papa's syrup. She would have given it to anyone who asked.

When I told her we would remove Papa from that lost lonely grave out on the Gulf and give him a decent burial here in Fort Myers, she said quite simply, Beside Mrs Watson? She didn't say that with resentment of Mama but to be polite – she might just as well have said, How nice! After five years, three children, and her shocking widowhood, she does not yet regard herself as Papa's wife!

Like Walter and Eddie, Edna believes that the less said

about Papa the better. The important thing is to protect our children from malicious tongues. That will be easier for her than us. Our life is here, we cannot flee, as she can, to west Florida, leaving everything behind, even the corpse! She is convinced that she and the children are not safe from their former neighbors, and so she will not even wait to see her husband buried properly. For that I cannot quite forgive her.

That's not true, Mama. I forgive her with all my heart. To think what this poor body has been through! Her stunned manner betrays how terrified she was, how desperate she is to put that dark accursed coast behind her!

We took her to the train in the new Ford – their first auto ride! She sat huddled in the coach, clutching her infants, her few scraps, longing for the train to blow its whistle and take her away. I noticed – my dear girls noticed it, too! – that she glanced over her shoulder every moment, as if that Chokoloskee mob might still catch up with her!

Then she was passing from our lives, a lorn face at the window. I said I was sure we would meet again one day. She looked away, then murmured aloud, just blurted it right out, No, I don't think so. She meant no harm, but by expressing no regrets, she hurt my feelings. Am I still so silly? Yet I wanted so to hug her, or hug someone, almost anyone. I mean, she *is* my stepmother, after all.

"Say good-bye for me," she whispered, in tears for the first time, as if the tears had been yanked out of her by the first yank of the train that would carry her off on its bright rails to a new life.

"Good-bye?" I sniffled, too moved by my own tears to realize her mind had wandered back to the reburial.

I walked along the track with her a little way, my fingertips on her windowsill, seeking her touch. She was aware of my hand there, but not until the final moment did she lay her fingers shyly upon mine.

"Good-bye to Mister Watson," Edna said.

November 3, 1910 There was a norther on the day we buried Papa. A cold hard light glanced from the river to the last leaves on the magnolias. Our little group gathered beneath the banyan, then followed the casket in by the main gate. The cemetery had sunk under the thorn since Mama and Walter's dad were buried there ten years ago, but now it's being fenced and cleared, "out of respect for our dead" – do we own our dead? How grateful they must feel, to be claimed this way! Our mama is surely smiling in her grave to hear such nonsense, her little skull, I mean. Oh, *don't*! I mean, I'm trying to think – did Mama ever laugh out loud, in joy of life?

We buried Papa beside Mama. It's a comfort to think that Papa is reunited with dear Mama, though somewhat the worse for wear, as he might say. I said so to Eddie, and Eddie said, No, they are *not* united. Mama's in Heaven, and that man is in Hell.

The darkie laborers stopped to watch, doffing their hats. Perhaps the ones who went down south and dug him up have passed the word about who was to be reburied, for the diggers knew all about the body in that casket. They did! I'm not being oversensitive. They *knew* something!

Frank Tippins came, he stood behind me, I heard him order them roughly back to work. The sheriff's voice seemed very loud in the old cemetery.

Goodness knows, our dreary little party needed any support that it could muster, and it was kind of Frank Tippins to appear, out of loyalty to Walter, I suppose. I wish he hadn't. In his black suit, he stood over Papa's casket looking fierce, as if delivering up his prisoner to the Lord. When I thanked him for coming, he exclaimed, "Mister Watson had my respect, ma'am, no matter what!" He was very embarrassed, as if he'd said something crude and tactless, and turned on those poor darkies once again. He looked confused. Frank's mustache, overlong and droopy, gives him a doggish look. He imagines he has always been in love with me.

439

After Papa's trial, when I understood that he had got off through political influence, I tried some political influence of my own. I went to see the sheriff about that poor man at the jail, condemned to hang. Papa and Walter agreed for once. If that prisoner had any influence, they said, he would be free, since he had slain the other man in self-defense. When I suggested this to Frank, he looked disturbed, and nodded a little while as if persuaded. I was thrilled! I'd saved a life, and maybe that deed might help as penance for any life our Papa might have harmed.

Instead Frank said, "Miss Carrie, you are twisting the arm of justice."

I got spitting mad. "Is hanging 'justice'? In a plain case of self-defense? My father says it's nothing but a lynching!"

And the sheriff said, "The prisoner was found guilty by a jury and condemned to death. Maybe it's not right but it sure is justice. Justice under the law."

At Papa's graveside I whispered to Frank Tippins, "Was justice done here, too?" He knew what I meant at once and got real agitated. He said, "No, ma'am! No due process! This was murder!"

Having spoken too loudly, he stood there gulping like a turkey, getting red. Then he came out with it: "Yes, ma'am." He whispered, "This was murder, yes, Miss Carrie. But I reckon maybe this was justice, too."

Only three men came up from the Islands. Stiff and shy, they stood apart in ancient suits and overstarched white shirts buttoned to the collar, without ties. I did not speak to them until Lucius shook hands and introduced them – Captain R. B. Storter, Gene Roberts, Willie Brown. Where, I thought, was his friend Postmaster Smallwood? Where was Henry Thompson and Tant Jenkins, who knew us as children in the Islands?

Nearby was a small common woman – pretty, I suppose – with bright dark eyes and long black hair not put up as it should have been in one her age. She had a child with

440

her, a ten-year-old or thereabouts, eyes leached out by weeping, rather plain. It was their real grief, not their poor clothes, that distinguished them. When the child caught me peeping, she tried a little smile, then looked away.

Lucius greeted them a bit familiarly, I thought. When I asked him who they were, he blushed and said, That's Tant's sister from Caxambas and her daughter, Pearl.

I said, The one who used to be housekeeper for Papa? Lost her baby in the hurricane? And Lucius nodded. Is that the one that he called Netta? No, Lucius said, this is Aunt Netta's half sister. I kept after him, feeling mean: Was this one close to Papa, too, like your "Aunt Netta"? Why is she sniffling so hard? She enjoy funerals?

He looked at me, not sure yet what I knew. Guess she took it to heart, he said, with that shy bent smile, wrinkled at one corner, that always reminded me of our dear Mama.

Frank Tippins was frowning hard at Lucius, shaking his head. People had commenced to notice, and Lucius moved away. My father was no saint, I murmured, to let Frank off the hook. No, ma'am, he wasn't. That child is my half sister, I insisted, putting him back on it. Yes, ma'am, she is, the sheriff said.

The gash of raw earth looked desolate, unwelcoming. I was glad of this cold norther because even in the wind, the odor of that box was something terrible. It was shocking, truly. Surely these would-be mourners must abhor the rotting human whose awful face was glowering at this pine lid from the inside. I felt sick – and sick with shame at my own shame – that my own flesh and blood could smell so dreadful. The infernal stench of Satan, said these Baptist faces, risen from Hell! The men looked stuffed, that's how hard they were holding their breaths, and the women coughed, resorting to their hankies. *Everyone* must be tussling with poor Papa, doing their utmost to pretend nothing was wrong.

Oh, dear Lord, have them hurry my remains into the

ground before anyone can even think about the worms, the odor, the dank gray hair and fingernails that grow like fungus, so they say, from our poor dead flesh in the grave. Have them remember "the real me," a fresh-smelling young foolish and romantic girl, Miss Carrie Watson!

Walter put his arm around my shoulders, drawing attention to my distress by his loving kindness.

Lucius ground his teeth, he could not stand still. He was absolutely furious, with God, I guess. He wandered away from our stricken party to stand beside Papa's little woman and the thin little half sister that I didn't even know I had until today! As for Eddie, the poor fellow was so upset by the stink of his father's corruption that he stood stiff as a wood Indian, as if he might topple right into the grave.

The only man who dragged out his big kerchief and held it to his nose, the only one who hawked and spit, was ol' Jim Cole, who drove up late in his new Cadillac, you would have thought Mr Edison himself was getting buried. I was very, very sorry that he came, and did not greet him. Even Walter turned away from him with a curt nod. He had no business here among the mourners. Captain Jim Cole hated Papa because Papa had contempt for him and didn't hide it.

Am I being unfair to "Captain Jim"? I am, and I don't care. He was only there not to miss out on something scandalous that he could jeer and chortle over later.

Dear gentle Mama could not abide what the *Press* calls "this fine upstanding citizen." Once Mama said, Your father has his violent spells, he is accursed, and I fear for his immortal soul, but he is also kind and generous, and he is manly, and he does not stint. This greedy, cruel man, with all his getting, does violence to the spirit, and I would understand the Good Lord better if I knew which man He would raise up on Judgment Day.

When Papa came north through Fort Myers not long before she died, poor Mama guessed that he was on the run. He

442

said good-bye to her and went away for the last time, cursing the fate that prevented him from taking care of her. Mama told me she had asked him where poor Rob was, and he said, If God knows, He has said nothing to me. Telling this, she looked bewildered, as if wondering at the last minute if she had known her husband after all.

Mama lay with her hands flat on the coverlet, those fine hands with their long sensitive fingers that had the same waxen hue in death as in her life. She was mustering up strength, I think. While I went downstairs to make her tea, she scratched a note.

There is a wound in your poor father I could never heal, and may the Lord who gave him life have mercy and forgive him at the last, and give him rest. Because Papa, too, is made in our Lord's image. He is a man, a human being, whose violence is only the dark part of him, there is also a life-giving side that flourishes in the full light. That side is loving, merry, full of courage, and that is the side that you must cherish, knowing he loves you children very dearly.

The family had agreed there would be no eulogy, but I had kept that pitiful scrawled scrap, and I read it aloud at Papa's graveside. It got tear-spotted some more as I read along, but my tears were like lost raindrops in the sun, I could not grieve. Poor Lucius wept without change of expression, his tears rolled down quiet as dew. I hoped that letter would redeem some of Eddie's anger and permit his grief, but I couldn't tell how Mama's words affected him. He acted as if unaware of my beseeching, he pretended he was hardly there at all.

Our Papa and Mama lie just near the Langford plot, with its two little stones: *John Roach Langford, 1906–1906. Infant Langford, 1907.* Two little stones. So much for Mother Carrie.

Whichever bunch they put me in, I'll be near Papa. The Langfords arranged for a small stone, without an epitaph.

EDGAR J. WATSON
November 11, 1855–October 24, 1910

My Fay asked in her sweet clear voice what the *J* stood for, and the "mourners" looked a little startled. All these years he was known as E. J. Watson, and it took a child to ask about that *J*! Mama once told me that his given name was E. A. Watson. When and why he changed to *J* she did not know. Our Granny Ellen in Fort White can no longer tell us, since she died before her son, early this year – God's final mercy! As for Aunt Minnie Collins, who was said to be so beautiful, she was "indisposed," her family wrote, and could not come.

Papa's woman from Caxambas had already turned to go when she heard Fay's question. In a whiskey voice, more like a croak, she called out "Jack." When Lucius kindly hurried her along, she tottered backwards, still seeking my eye. When I turned to her, she called out "E. Jack Watson!"

As we left the cemetery Walter's Aunt Poke asked aloud why Eddie didn't use his middle name. Couldn't he call himself Elijah, like his grandfather? Her idea was that a change of name might spare the poor boy (as she called him) difficulties in the future – *that is, if he means to stay here in Fort Myers*, Aunt Poke said.

We had all thought about Eddie's name, poor Eddie most of all, but no one but Aunt Poke had said a word. Eddie knew Aunt Poke was speaking "for the family." So did I. We thought she was suggesting that he move away. He went red but managed to control himself and not burst out with anything unseemly.

But Lucius said in a flat voice, "To change his name could only mean Eddie had something he should be ashamed of." And he gave that old lady a hard look that challenged her to say just what she meant right then and there. One hand flew towards her throat but she made no sound. It was only later that she said to Walter, That younger boy has something of his daddy in him, don't you think?

I was very proud of both my brothers, and grief came quietly, at last, at last.

Zhang Xianliang

Getting Used to Dying

'The Chinese Kundera' *New York Review of Books*

After his release from the prisons of China's Gulag, a writer travels to the West to lecture, to write and to visit relatives and lovers. Having known only the harsh and bitter realities of captivity, his life becomes distorted and surreal against the terrifying and vivid memories of labour camp executions, corpse sheds and near-starvation.

Zhang Xianliang is a remarkable and unique voice in China today and this autobiographical novel speaks movingly of the plight of the country's intellectuals. Unsentimental, erotic, full of surprising humour and courage, *Getting Used to Dying* is an honest and graceful portrait of a man striving to lead a normal life against all the odds. It is an unforgettable testimony to the human spirit.

'Intensely acute account . . . unforgetting and unforgettable.'
Sunday Times

'With his strong sense of irony and of the abnormality behind the familiar, Zhang has produced a powerful image of the paralysing pressures imposed on intellectuals by China's politicised society.'
Independent

'Zhang Xianliang shares with Primo Levi the gentle lucidity that is the hallmark of *If This is a Man*.'   *Literary Review*

'Light-hearted, humorous and erotic.'   *New Statesman and Society*

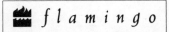